CHRISTINE ROI

BURIED IN EMBERS

A BLACK FATES NOVEL

This is a work of fiction. Names, characters, places, and incidents either are the product of the author's imagination or are used fictitiously. Any resemblance to actual persons, living or dead, events, or locales is entirely coincidental.

Copyright © 2026 by Christine Roi.

All rights reserved. This book may not be used, input, uploaded, transmitted, or otherwise provided to any artificial intelligence (AI) system, machine learning model, or similar automated tool, including for training, analysis, or content generation purposes. No portion of this book may be reproduced in any form without written permission from the publisher or author, except as permitted by U.S. copyright law. For more information, email *authorchristineroi@gmail.com*.

Cover by Dana Islay

www.christineroi.com

Contents

Dedication	1
Trigger Warnings	2
Author's Note	4
Two Years Ago	5
1. Casey	10
2. Clayton	16
3. Casey	23
4. Clayton	29
5. Casey	36
6. Clayton	41
7. Casey	48
8. Casey	53
9. Clayton	57
10. Casey	65
11. Clayton	72
12. Casey	76
13. Casey	82

14. Clayton	86
15. Casey	92
16. Casey	100
17. Clayton	106
18. Casey	110
19. Clayton	115
20. Clayton	120
21. Casey	124
22. Clayton	131
23. Casey	135
24. Casey	140
25. Clayton	144
26. Casey	150
27. Clayton	157
28. Clayton	164
29. Casey	170
30. Clayton	177
31. Casey	181
32. Casey	186
33. Clayton	192
34. Casey	197
35. Casey	203
36. Clayton	210

37.	Casey	216
38.	Clayton	222
39.	Casey	228
40.	Clayton	235
41.	Casey	241
42.	Clayton	248
43.	Casey	254
44.	Casey	259
45.	Clayton	265
46.	Clayton	268
47.	Casey	273
48.	Clayton	281
49.	Casey	286
50.	Clayton	295
51.	Casey	302
52.	Clayton	309
53.	Casey	313
54.	Casey	317
55.	Clayton	322
56.	Clayton	329
57.	Casey	333
58.	Clayton	338
59.	Casey	346

60.	Clayton	351
61.	Casey	356
62.	Casey	360
63.	Clayton	364
64.	Clayton	368
65.	Casey	372
Epilogue		377

Dedication

*For the girls who want to reclaim what was not freely given.
And for Joanne, who lived happily ever after.*

Trigger Warnings

This book deals with recovery from sexual assault, including allusions to repeated occurrences. As always, my priority is your mental health. Other triggers include:

- References to Child Abuse

- References to SA

- References to Human Trafficking

- Gun Violence

- Drowning

- Burning Alive

- Edgeing

- Orgasm denial

- **Trauma, PTSD, and C-PTSD**

- **Casual alcohol use**

Author's Note

This book touches on serious traumatic events involving violence of a sexual nature. Without going into too much detail, I will only say that there is a little bit of me in Casey. Just as I'm sure there is in everyone who has experienced sexual assault. Because of this, I want to assure you, my reader, that this is a subject I have approached with as much seriousness as possible. While romance novels have been a wonderful contributor to my healing journey, I know that they are also not a substitute for professional guidance.

If you have experienced assault, know my heart is with you. Please proceed with caution. Or not at all, if that better suits you. Your wellness is of paramount importance to me.

With love,
Christine Roi.

Two Years Ago
Clayton

Casey Arawn pushed her luscious, waist-length red hair over her shoulder. It was deep red against the flame of all the candles I'd lit. I moved closer to thread an arm around those shoulders, the ends of its silky waves tangling in my fingers. After months of texting. Talking. Flirting. She was here. At my place. On my sofa.

In my arms.

The daughter of the most dangerous mob boss in Los Angeles met me at her lowest point only a short while ago. A memory that may never leave either of us, but we certainly weren't thinking about it now. Right now, we were staring into each other's eyes, silently daring each other to make a move. My record player was warbling out some Hozier, a record I'd picked up just for her because it was quickly becoming clear that I'd do just about anything for this woman. She moved a little closer to me. Close enough for our noses to touch. Her breath warmed my lips as she sighed, long black lashes fanning across rosy cheeks as her brown eyes blinked slowly.

"You were a Navy SEAL before you were a mercenary, right?" Casey asked, voice husky and low.

The perfectly pink manicured tip of her index finger scraped over my forearm in a tantalizingly light caress. Little hairs on my arm stood on end in its wake.

"Yeah," I laughed, not expecting that to be on her mind.

"You've been to war zones, then?"

"Something like that," I smirked, moving my hand more deeply into the red waves splashing across the back of my sofa until it was cradling her head. She returned my smile, wry humor twisting those perfect lips as her nose crinkled.

"Then you should sack up and kiss me."

Another laugh burst from me, the hand I'd let fall to my lap snaking to her waist as the one in her hair gripped the silky tangles to angle her perfect mouth to mine. My thumb brushed her linen-covered ribs as I gave one last pep talk to myself. That red pout had been tempting me for hours. It was time to dive in. Take the leap.

Just fucking kiss her.

A sound of surprise hummed against my lips as I brought them to hers. Kissing Casey felt like nothing else. Nothing in the world, and I'd seen a whole lot of this world, could match the way her soft lips moved against mine. The way they parted for me. Sucked at my lower lip before her tongue licked at the upper. Electric currents ran through my nerves at the sweet friction of her. The velvet slide of her tongue against mine. Especially when she started making those sweet little noises.

One movement turned into another until I was pinning her to the sofa, one hand hooked beneath her knee as the other moved to support her head. The jeans I had on felt too thick and too thin. Dense enough to protect her from what thickened behind my zipper. Thin enough that my skin ached to feel more of her.

"Fuck," I huffed between kisses.

Heaven. She tasted like heaven. Heaven and the wine we'd been drinking after we'd gotten back from watching the sunset. Grapefruit and nectarines. The little floral dress she wore had been torturing me all evening. Its skirt barely covered the shapely thighs I'd let myself touch as we rode my motorcycle up the highway. Her skin was soft and warm, just as it was now, despite the cool evening air. Its cream and pale pink flower pattern was parting to show more of that bronzed, freckled flesh.

Casey arched into me, another soft moan on her lips that sent a jolt straight down my spine. So fucking responsive. I drank down her kisses, her smoky amber scent heating my blood. Those muscular legs squeezed around me as her hips lifted to meet mine. She was so soft like this. So warm. This gorgeous, perfect creature was grinding against my cock. Seeking pleasure from me. Pleasure that I was more than willing to provide. I couldn't help the anticipatory growl that escaped me.

I stopped myself for a second. Just a second. Wanting, needing, to enjoy the sight of this masterpiece below me before carrying her into my bedroom to worship her properly. Pupils blown wide with lust. Painted red lips swollen from my kisses. Except that wasn't exactly what I saw. Casey smiled up at me, but there was something else in her eyes. Panic. I'd seen that same look on the faces of my fellow soldiers before storming a stronghold. Even though she seemed to be stuffing it down, attempting to look willing, I could see that she wasn't. The look she'd been giving me only a moment ago, that look that said she wanted this too, that was gone.

Alright, so I hadn't been thinking about what happened to her, but she clearly was. We hadn't talked about it. I wasn't going to pressure her to say anything. Except now, it was all I could think about. This beautiful face drenched in fear as she sprinted through a hail of gunfire for her freedom away from the confines of that trafficking outpost in the middle of the Mojave Desert. It was like someone threw a bucket of ice water over me. I sat up, trying to keep the concern I felt from my voice as I said, "We don't have to do this, Casey."

She stiffened. Blinked. All of the softness disappeared from her features as she rocketed upright. Hands swiftly righted the dress that had shifted over her to reveal sumptuous lilac lace-covered mounds in the last few minutes. Then they went to work smoothing her hair. Her cheeks were rosy before, but they turned a deep pink now. She wouldn't look at me. Mood destroyed. Spell broken.

"I can't believe this."

"I just don't want to push you to do something you're not ready to do," I explained as I tried to place my hand on her leg, to undo the distance I'd apparently created.

Manicured hands shoved me away as Casey shot up from the sofa. The mood we'd been drowning in dried up in the heat of whatever this was. I didn't have time to think, to figure out just how exactly I'd fucked this up before her small feet rushed for the door. Shit. Stuffing those feet back into the tall brown boots she'd discarded as we had come in, Casey braced a hand on the wall. I didn't miss the way her free hand darted up to her eyes to wipe away tears because it made me want to crawl into a hole and die there.

"I'm getting an Uber."

"Casey, wait!"

The brown suede jacket that I'd taken off her upon entering my place was now being shoved over her arms again as she stomped down the hallway toward the elevator. She flicked her thick red hair out from the collar. I had to stop her. Had to do something because, goddamn, what had I done? Even if it was uncomfortable, and fuck me, it was completely uncomfortable. My hand circled her wrist, trying to stop her from getting on the elevator as it pinged to announce its arrival.

"Casey, please. I'm sorry. I didn't mean to—"

The slap was hard and brutal. For a small woman, she was strong. Blinking away the shock of her strike, I took in her face. The hurt in it. My stinging cheek didn't hurt nearly as bad as seeing her lip wobble. Another tear trailed down over the apple of her cheek as she sniffed. So beautiful, even when she was angry. It was that sight that stopped me in my tracks, letting her slip through my fingers. The freight elevator door swept closed as she warbled her command.

"Stay the fuck away from me, Clayton Wrigley."

ONE

CASEY

"Thank you for sharing that, Ashley. Alright, folks. That's our time for today. I hope to see everyone here next week."

Another meeting. Another hour gone by without my saying a word. Chairs squeaked on the yellowing linoleum of the recreation room as people stood from the circle to leave. I tucked my chair away and wondered how long it would be before I'd have the courage to speak as so many of these attendees did. Eighteen months in and I still hadn't opened my stupid mouth beyond polite introductions. They shared their stories openly. All our experiences were different, but they held a common thread. Brave people shared how they were feeling. It made me feel less alone. I wanted to be able to do that for them. They were so much stronger.

Lisa watched me pick up my purse and leave. *I'll never push you to share*, she'd told me when I first started showing up about eighteen months ago. And she hadn't. The problem is that with every passing day I sat here listening to everyone pour their guts out, I felt more and more guilty. As if my trauma would somehow not be enough to justify my silence. It wasn't big enough. I was afraid that the day I chose to open my mouth and tell the truth, tell everyone what happened, they would wonder what took me so long, and I'd feel like an even bigger coward than I already had. It wasn't a rational way of thinking about it. I knew that. But in my experience, fear wasn't a rational emotion.

Even if it was fear that kept me alive.

The prospect of being alone in a room with my thoughts and someone else felt suffocating. I'd made several appointments with several different specialists, only to blow them off at the last minute. I couldn't explain it, so instead, I stuffed it down. Everything that happened. Everything I thought or felt about what happened. Until I felt completely disconnected from myself. Like when you have an out-of-body experience during surgery or something. Dead and alive at the same time. I convinced myself that it was better than feeling what those men did.

Better to feel nothing.

Before these meetings, I went to work and came home to my father's house. Bathed in that numbness. Then life crept in around the edges of it. Little things made me feel connected to myself again. The sun on my face. Yoga in the morning. Doing things with Ainsley, a sister I'd accepted in much the same way Killian had accepted me. It all felt like warmth leaking into frostbitten fingers. I'd never imagined I'd have a little sister. A little sister who had endured an experience that wasn't far from my own. Being abducted. Held with others.

It helped me to be present for her. It helped me to finally set foot in the survivors of sexual assault support group meetings for the first time. Coming to it on my own was more helpful to me when I showed up at the community center. As if seeing the value in it reflected the value I'd started to feel within myself. On Tuesdays and Thursdays, I met with Lisa and the other survivors. Different people on both days, but they all got familiar with my face. I tried to engage. To listen and be there for them. That was enough at first. Soon, that numbness stopped feeling like a permanent fixture and started to feel more like an overcoat. Something I could slip into and let things roll off my back when the world felt like it was too much.

Today was an overcoat day.

My skin. It clawed at me from the inside, like each inch of it felt like plastic wrap stretched over my body. It had felt like that as I made my way from my father's house over to the center for this meeting. Overstimulated. That's the word. Listening to the survivors of assault talk about the things they were going through unwound some of that tension. The rest. It lingered. Even as I drove to the bar.

Soft fiddling flitted through the air like a butterfly on a summer breeze. I loved early mornings here. Sunlight caught the steam billowing up from the cup as I poured coffee for myself in one of the many bulky ceramic mugs, readying for a quiet day shift at the Chancer.

Fine, I didn't exactly need to work at my father's Irish pub since I now had an obscenely large trust fund and a limitless credit card with his name on it. I was here anyway. Having a job was normal for me, and I found peace in the routine. Doctoring my coffee with plenty of cream and sugar, I took sips from it as I polished glasses, adjusted the strings on my little black apron, and finished my other little tasks.

"Morning, Casey!"

"Morning," I smiled, trying not to grimace at the sour coffee.

After adding another splash of cream to my cup, and greeted the handful of elderly customers who came by every day for a hearty Irish breakfast. Chairs squeaked along the floor as they shuffled into their seats, signaling me that their usual will be just fine. No need for menus.

"Thanks, love."

Consistency. That's what made the Chancer where I wanted to be. It was a safe place to hide. All I had to worry about was if the shakers got filled and the expensive liquor bottles got dusted. With everything in good working order, I had nothing to worry about. The Chancer beat a lot of the places I'd worked in before, but lazy employees weren't something that my father tolerated. Laziness certainly wasn't something he allowed in me or my brother, Killian.

Killian, being the only boy, was allowed to go anywhere and do anything he wished. While I was grateful for everything my father provided, I was kept under close watch. Everywhere I went. Everything I did. Everyone I dated. Though he didn't interfere, his thugs kept him informed. If something upset him, he didn't hesitate to let me know. It was why I'd kept my job at Muse a secret from him. Avoiding the judgment of his goons, most of whom were my cousins, was just a bonus. From the day he found out about his teenage daughter to now, he'd told me he only wanted to protect me. That protective nature was exacerbated after I was victimized by a human trafficking ring and barely escaped with my life.

I blinked, dragging in a breath as the door to the bar opened. Plastering a pleasant look on my face, I continued my task of cutting fruit for cocktails and greeted the customer without looking up from the knife.

"Welcome to the Chancer. Seat yourself anywhere, and I'll be with you in a moment."

A motorcycle helmet appeared on the bar in my peripheral vision, making my stomach flip. Without looking up, I knew exactly who had entered the bar. The helmet was a big black thing that hid his features perfectly. His golden-brown hair was longer than I'd last seen it. Shaggy and messy in an intentional way, like he'd actually had it cut by a professional. Maybe he'd tried to do something with it before he'd put his helmet on. His stubble looked slightly overgrown. Just long enough to suggest he hadn't shaved the day before. Thick brown brows lowered as his caramel brown eyes fixed on me.

Clayton fucking Wrigley.

"Hey," he rasped.

Nope. Absolutely not. Not today. Seeing him here had become a regular thing, especially since he was one of my father's favorite contractors. That didn't mean I had to be nice to him. Especially when I was already feeling so raw. The urge to duck into the kitchen to get away from that spiced rum voice was strong. My lips pressed together in a thin line. I threw back my shoulders and put my hands on my hips.

"Good morning," he tried again, that half-cocked smile I used to daydream about catching the sunlight.

He rubbed the back of his neck with his free hand and glanced at the door. Caramel eyes flickered to more of a bronze color in a flash of sunlight as they looked toward my father's great hall. His throat bobbed above the banded collar of his leather racing jacket, grazing the faded black collar of whatever vintage t-shirt he'd thrown on today. Here for a meeting. Of course. Every time we saw each other, he just acted as if nothing had happened.

Pretended that he hadn't humiliated me.

He'd taken me for a ride along the coast on his motorcycle before we came back to his place. When we started making out, I wanted to take things further, and he rejected me. Made it seem like it was for my own good. Like it wasn't just a pathetic excuse to not get involved with a mess like me.

"Is he here?"

Unable to look at him for another second, I shifted my focus back to the task of cutting fruit garnishes for drinks. I gave a brisk shake of my head.

"Nope," I started, popping my lips on the word.

The door swung open, light rushing in behind him, and the man in question walked through the door. Dressed in his usual three-piece suit and a crisp white shirt, he strode in like he owned the place. My father was the head of the Arawn family, the largest Irish mafia presence in the country. Possibly the world.

People say that money talks and wealth whispers. My father's wealth whispered in so many ways. This suit was one of dozens. The Breguet Type 20 watch from 1954 that flashed in the sunlight as he rubbed at his jaw was another. It was the kind of money that made people do what he wanted. People like the mercenary hacker who was still watching me too closely.

His thumb and forefinger straightened his salt-and-pepper mustache before smiling at me.

"Mornin', my darling girl."

TWO

CLAYTON

There are a few things you need to know if you're going to do business with the mafia families of Los Angeles. The first thing is that trust is a commodity. It's in short supply, and no matter who you're doing business with, you'd better be worthy of it. Trust, that is. If someone thinks they can trust you, they'll do business with you again, and they'll pay you well to keep their secrets. Really fucking well. The second thing you need to know is that it's best to get used to swimming with sharks. People in this world move with purpose, and they don't hesitate to show you their teeth. I'd seen a hell of a lot of sharp teeth in my time. Not one set compared to this man. No, if they were great whites, then Ronan Arawn was a fucking megalodon.

Ronan trusted me. At least, I *think* he trusted me. He gave me *I trust you* jobs. Jobs protecting his money. His men. His arms business. Stuff that mattered to him. I reminded myself of that detail as I tapped my fingers on the arm of my chair.

In the middle of fall in Southern California, a lit fireplace is excessive. It popped and crackled as I waited to kiss the ring of the man whose daughter I'd helped to rescue. The daughter I could feel staring daggers at me through the door. The chair at the end of the long wooden table was reserved for the conquering king. A throne for the King of the Underworld. Tendrils of smoke curled around his hand, almost a mockery of the tattooed whorls of ink that were mirrored there. The back room of the Chancer was uncomfortably warm. Ronan lifted his cigar to his lips and took a drag. The tip flared at his inhale, its embers reflecting light into the man's dark brown eyes.

One last thing you need to know? You didn't start conversations with the head of the Irish mafia. You waited for permission to speak.

"I've not seen you around here in quite some time," he began. Not a summons to speak. Not yet. "My son tells me you've been of some assistance to him in Belfast. Then he had some trouble tracking you down."

Those eyes fixed on me as he let me digest the unspoken question in his statement. Almost walnut brown in the midmorning sunlight. Different from the liquid chocolate and hazelnut color of his daughter's. Shifting in my seat, I tried to loosen the fleeting tension that thinking about her caused. It was a useless effort when she was only a few yards away. On the other side of that door, standing behind the bar, hating me. It was impossible to ignore the feeling. Forcing a casual smile to my face, I answered with a shrug.

"You know how it is, Ronan. People want what I have to offer, and I'm a busy man."

A non-answer, but it was part of my service. Privacy. It's expensive, and I excel at providing it. Something from which he, the importer and exporter of many nefarious products, including automatic weapons for his associates in Ireland, had benefited. As if remembering that fact, he nodded to himself. The hand tattooed with the signature smoking skull set down the cigar in a heavy ceramic ashtray and reached for his cup of tea. When you grow up adapting to new environments all the time, you quickly learn to read a room. A shift in mood could decide everything. I could feel the tension rippling out from Ronan. It was a stone dropped into a lake, and I was on shore, miles away. Small and subtle tells. The tightening of his mouth before he spoke. The flex of his hand as he reached for his cup of tea.

Anger.

That had been the emotion I'd best learned to detect. Detecting it meant defending myself from it. Because it was the one that usually cost me.

"How's the family?" I asked, leaning back in my seat instead of picking up the cup in front of me.

Taking a long pull from the delicate cup, the blue floral trim disappearing beneath his mustache, Ronan watched two of his men enter the room before setting it down again. The twins, Sean and Rory. He sighed through his nose, dipping his chin at them. I did a mental inventory of the weapons I'd stored on myself. A pistol in the waist of my pants. The knife in my boot. Trust. They'd gotten to know me. Stopped patting me down. I avoided looking at the back door that was now being guarded, instead focusing on the man at the head of the table. A pained expression flickered across his dark brows as he ran a hand through salt and pepper hair.

"This isn't a fucking social visit, Wrigley. It's about my daughter."

Cold washed over me. Casey was alright. I'd just seen her. Still, the urge to jump out of my seat to set eyes on her again to confirm her well-being was strong enough that I curled my hands around the arms of my chair to hold myself in place. The wood creaked under my grip as I considered that maybe she'd finally asked her father to end my life. This man was the king of the Arawn family, and his princess wanted nothing to do with me. Not that I deserved death for what happened between us. Killing me in the middle of the pub on a Tuesday morning felt unlikely, but if anyone could make me disappear, it was this family. Not to mention that I'd made it easier on them by operating on a silent stack, no leaks, no logs. Nothing to let the world know I was still here.

"Ilia Kremnik has been released from prison."

The Russian Reaper. Head of the Bratva. Ilia Kremnik, a leviathan and the only man with the means to destroy Ronan Arawn. Recent weeks had seen an uptick in violent crime on this side of town. Shipments stolen. Important people found dead. People in Ronan's circle. His eyes slid to me again.

"He's got it out for me, which means he's got it out for my family. You understand how men like him work."

I nodded. I certainly fucking did.

"I'll take a look at your security. See if I can make any improvements."

Ronan grunted at my offer, folding his hands over his chest as he reclined in his seat. Flames licked around his silhouette, framing him in their glow. I felt a bead of sweat roll down my spine. The Irish king simply sighed, used to the fire at his back.

"My home is a fucking fortress, Wrigley," he said, jerking his chin toward the men behind me. "Loyal men follow me day and night. Men who would die for me. I've ordered Killian not to let Ainsley out of his sight. He takes her to school and back home. He's her goddamn shadow. That's what I need. Someone I can count on."

Oh, fuck.

"I'm flattered, Ronan, but I didn't think I was your type," I deflected. "Besides, we should keep things professional. For the kids."

Ronan shifted in his seat, glancing at the door. For someone who grinned at his targets, he didn't do a lot of laughing in my company. That didn't mean I wasn't going to try. And try. And try again. Another retort bubbled up from the traumatized recesses of my subconscious in order to avoid what I knew he was about to say. Except the next words out of his mouth beat me to the punch.

"Casey. Shadow her. Guard her. I want eyes on her every hour. I'll not have any harm come to her again, do you hear me?"

My mind raced with the last time Casey let me near her. Candles and soft music. Getting lost in the sumptuous lips and curves that haunted the skin of my palms. A standing order to stay away. Doing all that wasn't exactly staying away. Lingering around her was likely the last place she wanted me to be.

"Does Casey know about this?"

Out popped the question, but I already knew the answer. His precious daughter wouldn't have given me the time of day if she'd known why I was here. I would have been thrown out on my ass. Ronan gave me a flat look before sipping from his tea again. The smoking skull tattoo on the back of his hand gaped at me as it lifted the delicate cup to his salt and pepper moustache.

"She's not in charge here, boyo. I am," he blustered, though I heard the statement for the half-truth it was. "You've got a home. Take her to it. Keep her there. I know you've got other business, so she'll be safe under your roof while you attend to that business. Won't she?"

I nodded, grabbing at the tea in front of me that had gone cold with my neglect. It was more of a threat than a question. Still, it was true. No one could get into my place. Between the biometric locks, voice commands, and encrypted passcodes, it would be impossible to break in. That and the fact that my loft took up the top two floors of a building that wasn't technically residential to begin with. The tea was black, cold, and bitter, a mirror to the yawning pit in my gut opening at the prospect of retreading old ground with the girl behind the bar. That history had to be foreign to this man, I realized, knowing there was no way he'd ask something like this of me were it otherwise. I opened my mouth to protest, but it didn't matter. Ronan had made up his mind.

"I assume you know where I live."

A manor on a sprawling estate in the middle of the hills of Hollywood, overlooking the reservoir. Practically a castle. Yeah, I knew where the guy lived. However, it had absolutely nothing to do with the man sitting across the table and everything to do with the redhead who hated me. A normal person would ask the girl they were interested in, okay, more than interested, about her life. Where she grew up. All that. Thanks to some proprietary technology and light stalking, I didn't have to ask. I already knew it all.

"Sure. End of the rainbow. Just a reminder, I don't accept pots of gold."

Ronan let out a snort. I slugged back the rest of my tea, internally celebrating my minuscule victory, trying not to think about all of the things I'd learned about this man's daughter in the last two years. Things I found out with some casual internet sleuthing. Things like the fact that Casey Arawn was born to her mother, Rose Collins, in Los Angeles almost twenty-five years ago. Her mother was only twenty at the time. She gave her daughter her last name and moved them both to an apartment in Monterey. Worked as a mechanic and housekeeper to support them until she tumbled into finance. No child support from Ronan. He wasn't even listed on Casey's birth certificate until a corrective court order was filed when she was sixteen, along with a name change.

After making some pretty good grades and graduating from high school, Casey moved down to the Los Angeles area to attend an art school's photography program. A program she dropped out of only a year later.

There was no doubt in my mind that Casey, with that deep red hair and those gorgeous doe eyes, could have a successful career in front of the camera if she wanted one. With no reason for her departure listed, guessing what happened to make her leave often occupied my mind. The pictures on her social media page suggested she had a natural gift for composition. There was a carefully honed aesthetic to every shot, which still managed to have an effortless quality somehow.

Thanking myself for not being stupid enough to use any of her photos as a lock screen, I glanced at my phone to check the time. Not because I had anywhere to be, but because I needed something to do with my hands. Something to make the winding anxiety work its way out of my fingers as I agreed to fetch Casey from the manor in an hour. One hour to figure out how to manage this anxiety. To manage her anger toward me. One hour to figure out exactly how to unfuck this entirely fucked situation. I stood from the table, confident I had my marching orders, when Ronan spoke again.

"One more thing, Wrigley," he rumbled. His near-black gaze shifted beneath his black brows. "She's not to be touched. Not by anyone. Do we understand each other?"

THREE

Casey

Clayton hung from his hands on the top of the door frame, thumbs tapping and biceps flexing as he leaned in to watch me pack my things. Having any man in my bedroom would be uncomfortable. This guy was looking at all my little crystals, the stack of romance novels, the dirty clothes flowing out of my hamper. The smell of my incense was too overwhelming. Too hot. I took the grey sweater I'd been wearing all morning off and tossed it on the bed beside my bag. The tank top underneath still felt like a wool blanket. The door frame creaked behind me. Too much. This was too much.

"Stop doing that," I snapped.

After their meeting in my father's hall, the door swung open into the Chancer in time for the lunch crowd to pack the space. The music had gone from soft morning melodies to more aggressive Irish rock. It was because of the louder music that I thought I hadn't heard my father correctly when he told me to go home and pack. Clayton had followed him out of the room only to bypass me entirely, heading straight for the front door. I'd thought I got lucky and could avoid any further encounter with the man, only to find him waiting on the front steps of my father's large stone manor. Waiting for me.

"Doing what?"

"Either come in or get out, but don't just hang in the door like that. It's unnerving."

Pale caramel eyes scanned the room, then me. Clayton shoved a hand through his hair as he entered, nudging the door behind him with his free hand.

"Leave it open," I spat, then added. "Please."

At my command, he pulled the door open again. Leaning against the wall beside it, he crossed his arms over his well-muscled chest. The faded black Guinness tee shirt he wore stretched with the movement, causing me to wonder if he'd worn it because he knew he'd be seeing my father. I turned back to my bag, cursing myself for noticing him at all. It'd been a long time since I let myself look directly at him. I'd felt what was under that shirt. Knew the topography of lean muscle that shaped him. Knew the tattoos that covered his arms up to the shoulders. The face made of bone, wreathed in tentacles, and the words beneath it.

Memento Mori.

Of course, my father would employ a man like that. Clayton crawled to my father and asked for work. I wasn't sure why. Men threw themselves at my father's feet. I guess I shouldn't have been surprised that Clayton would follow suit. I'd just thought he was different.

But disappointment was a beat that set the rhythm of my life.

"I didn't realize you still live here," he said.

I turned to look at him again and saw him pick up a small rose quartz heart from the top of my white French dresser. Everything in this room looked like it had come from Versailles, a detail my father oversaw. Gilded details on painted white wood. Pale blue linens on the large wooden bed. There was even a small antique crystal chandelier hanging over it. Though it wasn't my taste at all, I appreciated it. My father wanted me to feel cared for. Spoiled in some way, probably to make up for the sixteen years he didn't know I existed. This room sat at the top of one of the stone towers of the manor. I didn't have the heart to tell him that it made me feel locked away. I pivoted, opening a drawer to grab underwear. One, two, three too few. Shit. With a huff, I stomped over to the hamper.

"It was supposed to be a temporary situation. For my safety," I grunted, yanking things out of the hamper and tossing them to the floor. "I decided not to go back to my apartment. It wasn't a good spot for me anymore."

He grunted in agreement. We both knew why. I shuddered at the memory and continued my search.

Fine. This was fine, I thought as I dug through the dirty clothes to find more underwear. If I were going to be staying with him, then he was going to get the real me. Not the cleaned-up, cute, edited version I saved for boyfriends. The version of me he got two years ago. The version of me that had put on a matching bra and panties set for him. No. He didn't deserve that version of me. If I were being honest with myself, I wasn't sure that version of me even existed anymore.

"Bring the whole basket. I have a washer and dryer at my place," Clayton offered, not doing a thing to avoid eyeing the colorful scraps of lace I'd pulled free.

"How long am I supposed to be your captive?"

"Until it's safe." Before I could respond properly, Clayton moved. His large form bent over in front of me, scooping and stuffing the clothes that had poured out as I searched for what I needed back into the wicker laundry basket. Then he picked the whole thing up with a grunt and brought it to the door. "Just pack up whatever else you need. I'll wait downstairs."

Without another look in my direction, his clopping motorcycle boots receded down the hardwood hallway toward the spiral staircase. I didn't let myself dwell on how empty the room felt without him. He was six-foot-three and long-limbed in every direction. Any room would feel empty without a tree like Clayton Wrigley taking up space.

A grateful puff of air burst from me. It was bad enough that he was now in possession of my dirty underwear. He didn't need to see my ten-step skincare routine or anything involved in making my body hairless and odorless. Coupled with the luxury luggage, another guilt gift from my father, and the look of my bedroom, he was probably wondering if I'd finally become some kind of spoiled bitch.

I found it unlikely that Clayton had any idea what it took to make sure your skin was soft and dewy. Stomping back into the bathroom, I looked for my makeup bags and products. Sorting through the cabinet, I hoped he had a second bedroom in that loft of his. It was definitely big enough for one.

"There's no way I'm sharing a bed with him," I scoffed at myself in the mirror.

My reflection didn't say anything, obviously. I'd gotten in the habit of talking to myself in the mirror. I know, I know. It wasn't the most mentally stable thing I could do. It started with affirmations. Then I added little asides. Random thoughts while I put on makeup. Things I would have told my friends before I isolated myself from them. Until I was imagining both sides of the conversation with people and arguing with myself.

"Knock, knock." I poked my head out of the bathroom to see my father standing in the doorway. Being in his late forties, he always looked young, but worry made his eyes look older by a decade. "May I come in?"

"I can't believe you're doing this to me," I huffed as I shoved bottles into my bag, each word punctuated with the motion. My father gave an aggravated sigh as I strode back to my duffel, stuffing the bag of toiletries and monogrammed makeup bags inside.

"I had to, darling girl. You'll be safe with him."

How my father could be so confident about a computer-obsessed mercenary, I didn't understand. Clayton Wrigley was a gun for hire, a hacker, and the kind of man who took the easy way out. His loyalty was for sale. The kind of man who would rather give up than try.

"You're not sending Ainsley away."

The salt and pepper stubble covering my father's jaw flickered as the muscles there tightened.

"Ainsley is only ten," he lectured. "She has your brother. She has all of my men to make sure she's safe at school. You are a grown woman. You have twenty-four years of life experience."

I picked up my sweater and pulled it back over my head.

"So," I huffed as I stuffed my feet into my boots. "I'm being punished then? Or what? Because I don't get it."

"This isn't punishment, love. This is temporary."

He fully entered the room, pulling me into a hug as my garbled protest died in the soft material of his dark suit. I was still getting used to it. The affection. Being close to my father. For so many years, my mother kept me from him. To protect me. The irony of that never escaped me. That she didn't know what happened to me more than two years ago, and I couldn't tell her. I could barely let myself think about it. But my father knew everything, down to the darkest details. He'd even gone after the Caccia family because he assumed they'd found out about me and done something nefarious because of the rivalry between them. It was only because of Lilith Caccia that I was standing here now. Between my father and Lilith, the organization responsible for my abduction and assault collapsed.

People still talked about the fire at the Allerton mansion. It had claimed the lives of several very wealthy, very powerful people. Everyone called it an unfortunate tragedy. A dinner party full of people claimed by a fire, all of them too drunk or high to escape alive. They assumed the blaze started in the kitchen by accident. Except it wasn't accidental at all. It was my father's specialty. The reason the smoking skull became our family's unofficial sigil. Fire was his way.

"Burn out the rot and grow from the ashes, darling girl."

"You. Your brother. Your sister. You're the only things in this world that matter to me," he said weakly before clearing his throat. "Ilia Kremnik knows that. He'll be wanting to take you away. Killian can take care of himself. He's got Ainsley to watch over as well. This is the only way I can keep all of you safe. Mr. Wrigley is the best security money can buy. I know he won't let any harm come to you."

His arms tightened around me. Just for a second. Then he let me go. The dark eyes I'd inherited from him were fixed on my face. Looking me over. Letting me see the truth he'd laid bare. My father was a man whom many feared. But he couldn't protect me.

FOUR

Clayton

Deep red waves bobbed as Casey's boots hit the front steps. Those same boots that stomped out of my place were going to walk her back in. The heels were high enough that I briefly worried about her twisting an ankle on the cobblestone driveway. My eyes traced up the butterscotch leather, skimmed the jeans, and traced over the soft grey sweater that hung off her hourglass frame in a way that left little to the imagination. Rocking on her heels, a strange sort of energy emanated from her. Unease. I forced myself to move past the shame that bubbled in my gut at the sight of it.

"Ready?" I huffed out of my mouth as I moved to take her bag.

Her hands released the leather handles as I grabbed them, careful to avoid touching me. The sting of that was too sharp to avoid. Moving to load it into the back of her car, I took a breath to compose myself. A small electric Mercedes SUV that was given to her by her father. In the short period when Casey was still talking to me, she lamented about the gifts her father showered her with upon her return home. The Louis Vuitton bag she apparently tossed around like an Army surplus duffle was another of those things, I imagined. The cargo hold was half full with the hamper I'd already loaded inside. I'd been waiting for her out here, thinking better of sitting inside the car with all of her things. Things that smelled like her. My place. She was going to be living in my home until we got this shit sorted with Kremnik. Having promised to help Ronan track the Russian mafioso down, I would at least have something to occupy my time while Casey occupied my personal space. Sure. No problem.

"Clayton?"

"What?"

"I said I'm ready. Can we go?"

Her bag was still in my hand, the other propped on the tailgate above my head. Idiot. It's so fucking awkward. *Forced lab partners in science class* kind of awkward. The gilded initials monogrammed into the matching leather pieces glinted at me as I shut the tailgate.

C.E.A.

"What does the E stand for?"

I sat in the driver's seat, grunting a curse as my knee hit the steering wheel. The car hummed quietly as I turned it on to adjust the seat, ignoring the amber and incense scent of the woman seated beside me. Casey dropped her purse beside her feet and turned on the stereo. Her phone must have connected to the stereo already because an audiobook started up with the voice of a male narrator. Before he could get a full sentence out, it was quickly changed to Ariana Grande.

"The E in your initials. What does it stand for?"

She pushed a red lock out of her face. Deep brown eyes rolled before they fixed on me with irritated disgust. Honestly, it was an improvement from her not looking at me at all, which was usually the case. Adjusting herself in the passenger seat, she clicked her seatbelt into place before deigning to answer my question. A question I happened to already know the answer to, but she didn't need to know that.

"I'll never tell."

"Fine, I'll just guess until I get it right," I said as I set us into motion. "Eloise."

A shake of the head. We weren't far from my place. Only a twenty-minute ride on surface streets. Faster on the bike, which I took back up to my garage. Still, I felt the need to fill the time. Close. We hadn't been in confines as close as these in ages. She wouldn't let me get within five feet of her over the last two years. The last time I'd been this close to her was in the very apartment we were heading to now. I threw out another phony guess.

"Evanescence."

That guess got a snort. Casey stared out the window, watching the enormous houses become smaller ones as we drove down the hill and into the city. Her fingers tapped rapidly against the wooden panel of the door, completely at odds with the beat of the music on the radio. After a few minutes, I threw out another guess.

"Epsilon."

Her eyes cut to me as red gates and lanterns started to appear around us. I noted the tightening of Casey's shoulders. I wondered if I should feel flattered or worried that she remembered where I lived. After growing up bouncing around the suburbs of Chicago, Little Tokyo seemed like the furthest I could get from that existence. I pulled the car into the garage below my building, parking among the bank employees.

Most of the building was office space being taken up by the administrative operations of a global bank. A bank that happened to pay for my cybersecurity expertise and allowed me to purchase part of the building to suit my own needs. They even let me purchase one of the two elevators that led upstairs. Since the large freight elevator was the only one that reached the top floors, it belonged to me. It was perfect for moving my bikes into my sixth-floor garage, coming and going unnoticed by the other occupants, and for moving the clothes of the redhead who boarded the elevator car beside me.

"Ebenezer."

"Nope."

Three thousand square feet felt like a shoe box with Casey E. Arawn inside it. She was in my home. Again. Casey's purse thumped onto the entry table. The entry table that I bought when I was trying to impress her. Topped with lemongrass candles and a little rock garden. For her. Her eyes moved over the sand-colored sectional sofa and large stone coffee table. Skated over the grand arched windows crafted with exposed brick and the credenza that sat in front of the big white wall that separated this large open space from the rooms on the other side.

"Where's my room?"

I ignored the question and picked up her bags, carrying them to the bedroom. The only bedroom. Well, the only room with a bed in it. Despite having the entire floor, almost all of it was being used for one thing or another. Being here by myself meant I needed only one room for sleep. She followed me, boots clicking on the polished concrete floors as we walked past my office. The clicking sound stopped behind me as Casey leaned into the doorway of the second bedroom of the loft.

"What's in there?" Her question echoed into the room as she poked her head in to look around.

Another question I ignored. Not because I didn't want to tell her, but because I wanted to get this part over with. The part where she realizes there is only one bedroom.

Once we reached the end of the hall, I gestured to the open door and what awaited beyond it. I changed the sheets. The duvet cover. Stacked the bed with extra pillows. Even as I stood there, I fought the urge to light the candles on the dresser below the window to make it smell nicer. More like the herbal oils she liked to use. Less like me. Still, it was clean. That's all that she could ask, right?

"Wait."

Here we go.

"There's only one bedroom?"

Placing her luggage on the bench at the end of the bed, I turned and folded my arms. Waiting for her to say exactly what I knew she would say. I'd known it was coming when Casey's doe eyes widened like she'd been caught in headlights. Her skin went as pale as the grey sweater she had on as she surveyed the California King bed. The only bed.

"Oh, no. Absolutely not. I'm not sleeping with you."

The fact that she thought so little of me shouldn't have stung as much as it did. I sighed through my nose. She hadn't exactly been kind to me in all this time, but I couldn't imagine where this low opinion of me had come from. As I unfolded my arms, I took careful steps toward her.

"No, you're not," I monotoned. Her feet moved backward, away from me. It wasn't a surprise. She'd panicked in her room. At my nearness, but also at being alone with someone in a small space. It wasn't hard to pick up on that, especially with the heat rash that had spread across her chest. I could see the same reaction happening now. With a response like that, I sure as hell wasn't going to pull some bullshit on her. "I'm not sleeping in here with you. You're sleeping in here alone."

"I am?"

I nodded. Her shoulders slumped from where they'd been hoisted around her ears as she released a breath. She'd been ready to fight. Or run. I could see the unspoken words in her eyes. The ones she'd never admit to me.

Crisis averted.

Chewing on the corner of her lip, she avoided eye contact as her hand drifted over the duvet. A pale green color. Soft. I'd made sure of that. Back when I thought I had a chance, I'd done everything to make this place

Casey-friendly. I'd been living in a hell of my own creation for just as long. Deep red eyebrows lifted slightly in appreciation.

"Wait. Where will you sleep?"

It was a half-hearted question, easy to hear in the pause before the word 'you'. The tone of her voice was soft, like she cared, but was trying to stifle the urge. She tugged on a loose thread at the end of her sleeve. Stuffed her hands into the pockets of her jeans. Looked down at her shoes. Everywhere but at me. Embarrassed at herself for a reasonable reaction.

"I'll be on the sofa."

"Oh."

The soft syllable made her lips pout. The plump pink lips that I'd kissed. Licked. Sucked. On that sofa.

"Go ahead and get unpacked. I've got things to do."

It was two years ago. But even as I left her in my bedroom, even as I sat down on that same damned sofa, I could still feel the sensations that tightened my skin before she pushed me away.

"I can't believe this."

The memory was fresh, appearing in my mind as I shut my eyes. I rubbed them hard. Still, it didn't drive out the image of her face as she yelled at me. Or the memory of her pulling her dress back on with shaking fingers. I could still feel the sting of her hand on my face as I picked up her keys and headed back to the garage. Only someone with my expertise or many, many explosives could find their way into my little fortress without my presence. I knew she was safe without me there.

It helped that I could also keep an eye on her through my extensive interior surveillance system. Something I probably should have told her about, I mused as I pulled my phone free to observe the stream. Of course, if I mentioned the cameras, she probably would have bolted for the door, and we couldn't have that. I needed to keep her safe, which meant keeping her here. Her father asked me to keep an eye on her at all times. So that's exactly what I was going to do. It's not like I was just going to watch her for fun.

Casey was still in the bedroom, looking around as if expecting something to leap out and bite her. The elevator jolted to a halt at its floor, prompting me to close the app where I could watch the little bird in her cage.

I could have said no. Could have referred Ronan to someone else. Could have asked West or even Lilith to intervene and take her in. God knows they had enough room at that sprawling compound of theirs. It was only a few miles away. But here I was. Right in the middle of Casey's fucking business, with no one to blame but myself.

FIVE

CASEY

With not much else to do and no desire to talk to my keeper, I stood up and unpacked my bags. The dresser clacked as I rolled a drawer open, cringing as I remembered I was not alone here. This was Clayton's room. But there wasn't a thing in here that would indicate that he lived here. No personal photos. Nothing. Expecting to find socks or underwear, I was instead met with an empty drawer.

"He cleared out a drawer for me?" I muttered in surprise.

I pulled the next one free. Empty. Then the next. Empty. Three of the six drawers were completely empty. Deciding how to organize my clothes took up a decent amount of time. By the time I was done, I was fishing around in the bottom of my duffel for anything I might have missed. The deep leather bag had a few things I hadn't thought about in ages. Eyelash glue. Moisturizing socks. My hand paused when it met with a bit of fur. I set the little white paw on the dresser. The rabbit's foot Clayton had given me the day we met. The day I was rescued and realized I wasn't going to die in that trailer.

My knees felt weak under the weight of those memories. The backseat of West's Bronco as it peeled down the highway. Showering with the hottest water I could tolerate after weeks of nothing but wipes and feeling the scum of everything wash off me, swirling down the drain. Lilith shared snacks in a motel room in the middle of the desert, staying up with me until I fell asleep. The dreams that plagued me then. The same dreams have been following me every day since.

Despite the utter irritation at having to be here in the first place, I had to admit there was something about the minimalist design of everything that was sort of comforting. I decided this was especially true for the bed as I flopped down on it. A truly enormous bed for someone who lived alone, even if he was a relatively tall man. The modern upholstered frame made the queen-sized bed I'd been sleeping in feel childish by comparison. Or maybe it was the feather-soft duvet and luxuriously smooth sheets.

I wasn't sure when I drifted off. The large window that had let in the golden sunlight of late afternoon was now filled with city lights and the night sky. Squinting to adjust my sight, I looked around for my phone. It was here. It was right here on the nightstand. My laptop was also conspicuously missing. Shuffling toward the end of the bed, I saw my boots on the plush rug that covered the floor. I hadn't taken them off. But there they were. Sitting beside the bench. He took my boots off. He must have. As I thought about it, I realized exactly what had happened to my phone. My socked feet slid slightly on the polished concrete floor as I raced down the hall and into the open living area.

"Where's my phone?" I barked.

Clayton, the thief, was in the kitchen facing away from me. His light brown hair was darker. Damp like he'd showered. A loose white T-shirt and grey sweatpants had replaced the street clothes he'd worn to meet my father. To take me here. His attention was fixed on the brown bag in front of him.

As he pulled cardboard cartons out of the bag, he spoke but didn't look at me.

"I took it," he answered flatly, muscular shoulders shifting with a shrug as he opened a carton to look at the contents. Then he removed something flat wrapped in foil from the bottom of the bag.

"I know you took it," I seethed. "Where is it?"

"It's staying in my office until I can tighten up your settings. Until then, you can use my phone if you need to call someone. Your laptop will be returned to you as soon as the security software is finished installing."

His tone was casual, as if he were already bored with this conversation. Or he'd been expecting it. The probability of the latter made my fingers curl into fists at my side. Forcing myself to speak through clenched teeth, I said, "You took it without even asking me."

"I don't need to ask, Casey. I'm supposed to protect you. That includes taking your phone when I need to," Clayton stated as he turned on his heel, pulling out a pair of plates from the cabinet beside the stove. The large stoneware plates were beige, just like almost everything else in his kitchen. I was almost too busy looking at the plates to notice the glasses perched on the end of his nose. Gold, thin square frames that, if I was being honest, only complemented his angular face shape and strong features. Had I ever seen him in glasses? "I ordered dinner. I know it's early, but you slept through lunch, and I figured you'd be hungry."

I wanted to keep arguing. Really. But heady spices and garlic scented the air, firmly tugging at my very empty stomach. I hadn't even had time to eat my breakfast at the bar before my father took me home. A plate appeared on the counter in front of me. A heaping portion of seasoned rice and what looked like some sort of deep orange chicken curry, along with a piece of garlic naan tucked in beside it, was looking up at me. My hands curled around the plate, but I was stopped from taking it off the counter by the hand that still held its rim.

"Fork?"

Clayton held up the little steel utensil in question, grinning at me as damp hair fell over his forehead. I snatched it away from him and suppressed the urge to stab him with it. Choosing to avoid sitting in one of the leather seats at the counter with him, I strolled over to the sofa, hoping to set myself as far away as possible. Rich spices and chilis soothed the raw edges in me, warming from the inside long enough for me to note that I was sitting on the sofa.

The sofa.

He placed a glass of water on the coffee table in front of me and took a seat on the other side. It may as well have been on the other side of the room, for as large as the sectional was, but it didn't stop me from scooting a bit further away until I was tucked into the sofa's plush corner. My thoughts pelted me one by one as I avoided looking at him.

Maybe he isn't thinking about it. He probably isn't. God only knows how many girls he'd brought here since he'd decided he didn't want me.

The last time I was here was a mistake. Or at least that's what it felt like in the end. I wanted to sleep with him. The day he'd helped pull me out of that hole in Joshua Tree, he'd fooled me into believing I could be vulnerable with him. It would be foolish to say I felt an immediate attraction because I wasn't capable of being attracted to anything, but I'd felt something. With him, that night, when he gave me that damned rabbit's foot. It was the first time in weeks I'd felt something other than fear, sadness, or anger.

Then, a few months later, I thought things were going well between us the night he'd brought me back to this apartment. He'd touched me all night in small ways. A hand on my thigh as we soared down the highway on one of his motorcycles. A quick wipe of my lip to remove a little extra chocolate as he laughed, sucking the finger he'd used into his mouth. An arm around my shoulder to keep me warm as we watched the sun go down. It had all added up to an inevitable conclusion. I wanted him. Sure, there was fear. It would have been stupid not to be afraid. I hadn't been with anyone since that box in the desert, and I was afraid of how it would make me feel. Or how I would perform. Then he embarrassed me.

Rejected me right here on this goddamn sofa.

He made me believe he wanted me and then shut everything down, acting like he was doing me some goddamn favor. By the time my ass hit the seat in my Uber, it was clear to me that he'd decided not to get involved with someone as fucked up as me.

"Everything okay?"

No.

Clayton blinked but didn't say anything else. Just quietly ate his meal, scooping up bits of curry into his naan and tucking it into his mouth. I followed suit, chewing as I focused on the glasses. Those little glasses on the end of his slope-straight nose. Focused on whether or not they would break if I punched him right between the eyes.

SIX

CLAYTON

*O*ff *to a great start, idiot.*

Wine-red hair was up in a messy bun, tendrils falling out of it in loose curls around her freckled cheeks. Curled up on my sofa with her shoes off, eating one of the chicken dishes from the Indian place down the street. As I took in the redhead sitting across the sofa from me, the sip of water I took tasted like regret. This could have been every night for us if I hadn't colossally fucked it up. All this time later, I still couldn't figure out how anything I could have done would have been any better than what happened, but I knew there had to be an answer. Not that it would matter.

Brown eyes narrowed at me. It was easy to see that she was angry about the phone, but the truth was that her anger towards me was an ever-burning flame.

"Stay the fuck away from me, Clayton Wrigley."

I tried. Hell, I went to the other side of the planet for a little while just to get away. Ireland wasn't far enough. Egypt hadn't been far enough. Antarctica probably wouldn't be either, but I thought about giving it a try as I focused on ignoring the way she stared while she ate. Hangry Casey, I could deal with, but this was a step beyond that. The words *I hate you were* practically shooting out of her eyes, laser-beaming into the side of my face.

For a moment, I thought about trussing her up and driving her back to the Hollywood Hills. Surely she'd rather live under house arrest in that pretty little tower. If two years of our one-sided relationship had taught me anything, it was that Casey was a champion at holding a grudge. Living under one roof sure as hell wasn't going to help things. The last roommate I had hated me, though I wasn't sure if that had more to do with my complete inability to organize my shit or pay bills on time.

Silently congratulating myself for having those things figured out now, I jolted at the clink that sounded from across the sofa. Casey stood up suddenly, striding purposefully toward the kitchen with her plate and glass in hand. The dishwasher was flung open, and dishes were put away after a quick rinse. Her sock-covered feet slipped a little as she hastily walked away.

"Good night," I shouted toward the slamming bedroom door.

I tried reading a book. Tried cleaning up the kitchen. Tried playing a game on my phone. None of it worked to distract me from the thoughts I had about the girl down the hall. The girl in my bed. Having her here was bad for my concentration. Before I even bothered trying to rest, I went to my office. All of my screens lit up, my laptop docked in the center. My first task was to deal with Casey's phone. Simple enough. She'd set the lock to open with her face, but she also had a passcode. Easy.

"11:11! Make a wish!"

Wishing on numbers. Reading her horoscope. Carrying little rocks with her for luck or protection. I never understood superstitions until I met Casey. I thought people were dealt their cards in life and that was it. You got what you got. With the USB-C plugged into her phone, I sighed and got to work. Her screen was mirrored on one monitor to my left as the ghost program for disguising IP addresses ran its code on the screen in front of me. From there, I implemented signal encryption for any of her apps that used location tracking. Done.

As I unplugged her phone from my computer, I looked at the home screen. Ainsley. She had a picture of herself and her adopted little sister in front of a bounce house together on her phone. Both of them were in pale blue feathered angel wings with glitter on their cheeks and ice cream cones dripping down their hands. A birthday party for the girl, if I had to guess. Obviously, I wasn't invited.

The two of them looked like sisters. Not physically. The small blonde girl with crystal blue eyes would never resemble the brown-eyed woman with striking red hair. But it was in Casey's smile. In Ainsley's relaxed shoulders. Their matching joy. Something gnawed at my insides at that open expression. A look I'd only gotten a glimpse of in real life.

Her social media was set to private. Easy enough for me to work around on my computer, less so on my phone. With the option to streamline watching her through the app, I took the opportunity to follow her from a ghost account I'd created and approve my follow request on her device. It was easy enough to delete any record of the interaction. This app. It was all pictures and clips. Some I'd seen already. Saved them onto my backup drive, having downloaded them when I would occasionally hack into her profile from this office. Rarely. Only like once a week.

Now that I could look through her photos from the app, it was even easier to get lost in her feed. It was somewhat less active after she'd been abducted and subsequently rescued. The pictures from her life before showed two sides of a complex creature. Crystals and meditation. Peaceful sunrise hiking photos. Serenity embodied by a girl who was naturally beautiful. Golden skin and freckles. A freckle on the tip of her lip. On the other side was a siren. Red lips. Red hair. Black mesh and pink neon lights. Two sides of one unbelievable coin. Both of them devastating. Both of them dominated my fantasies.

HeartShapedLens.

That was her handle. Some nights, I went to bed thinking about the girl on that stage. The one whose deep red lips were curled into a coquettish smile as she lifted her hips off the gleaming surface beneath her, dragging sharply manicured nails up the flat planes of her stomach. Others, I spent wondering what it would be like to wake up next to her, freckles scattered over her button nose as her hair shone like molten ore in morning sunlight, buxom and bare.

"Fuck me," I muttered under my breath.

I put the device face down on my desk. That was enough. Instead, I decided to refocus my attention on the problem. Ilia Kremnik. I didn't know much about the man. Only that he'd spent the last twenty years in prison for being in the wrong place at the wrong time during a drug bust in his shipyard in Long Beach. For someone with offshore accounts as impressive as his, it was hard to believe he couldn't beat the drug trafficking charges levied against him. Seven figures was in an account in Barbados when he entered the federal correctional facility in Victorville. Upon his recent release, that money had increased to almost nine figures. In or out of prison, Ilia Kremnik's business never stopped booming. Account numbers went up. Way up.

Kremnik's strange eyes stared back at me as I looked over the multi-million dollar drug portfolio I'd put together. One blue eye. One milky white. The white eye was likely due to whatever had put a scar through his alabaster skin. Skin that matched his hair, eyelashes, and eyebrows. The portfolio wasn't very diverse, seeming to deal in only two products. Most notably, gamma-hydroxybutyric acid and heroin. The latter was no surprise to me.

Arrest records detailed a staggering amount of the product packed into several storage containers imported from unknown suppliers stationed overseas. The former seemed to be a more recent development, highlighted by records of known associates busted for possession with intent to distribute.

GHB.

Lilith Caccia had been dosed with it when she was abducted two years ago. She'd detailed helping Juliet Ambrose, her right-hand woman, through a near-overdose after an Eros party she'd attended with the now deceased Benjamin Camden. Camden had facilitated the trafficking of women using the now-defunct Eros dating app to find targets. Targets like Casey. Only an extra gram would have taken her from me before I'd even met her. She'd told me that much. Someone dosed her drink, then she woke up in a trailer she couldn't escape from. I didn't need details to understand what happened. To know what they took from her. The thought made dinner rise in my stomach, forcing my jaw to squeeze until my molars slipped and clicked together. The sensation snapped me back into my darkened office, noticing the LED lights behind my computers had shifted to glow in a low red.

Bank statements. Transfers. Arrest records. A dizzying amount of information was right at my fingertips, none of it useful yet. Ronan hadn't told me why Kremnik was after him. But the fact that he was after the family implied personal reasons. Not business. With business being the only thing I had to go off of for now, I wasn't left with many options. My mouse hovered over the little brown and white furball icon. Two clicks and the system was ready. Dragging and dropping the necessary starting points to deploy the malware, I reviewed the code, ran the crawl, and then moved on to another task.

Being a mercenary was like what I imagined being a sex worker must be like. You don't always like the people you're doing particular jobs for, but money is money. Sometimes the person paying you is the biggest creep on the planet. Busying myself with another task paid for by one such person kept me at my desk. A very high-powered individual with a lot of influence wanted me to scrub all evidence of their illicit affair from the internet. Messaging history. Location history. Photos stored in the cloud. Everything.

The problem with people who pay you to do their dirty work is that they never realize you're perfectly capable of screwing them over completely and disappearing without a trace. Why? Because they got my information from a friend of a friend. That information is just an email. A nondescript email to a nonexistent NPO that goes through countless levels of encryption before it even gets to me. They don't get a name. Only my signature, a smiley face. And a geotagged location with a time and place to drop off payment.

Cash only.

They would have no record of our transaction. Unfortunately for today's piece of human garbage, nestled alongside my desire to pay bills was my desire to help people who were being harassed by the scumbags of the world. It didn't escape my notice that the person being targeted by my patron had very recently gone missing. That voice in my head that sounded a whole lot like a snarky cartoon rabbit asked me if I was going to actually do something about this or if I was just going to let the opportunity pass me by.

I couldn't resist. The convenience of this timing, coupled with memories of a certain redhead, put a bad taste in my mouth as I set Gizmo into motion on another crawl. This specific set of tasks was accomplished by me, but not before I made sure the family of the person in question had everything they needed to get a conviction against the asshole with the deep pockets.

"And that, dear children, is why you should never trust a stranger. Especially someone you met on the internet," I muttered as I stood up from the desk and walked away, scratching my stomach with a stretch and a yawn.

Destroying someone like that hypocritical assclown before dawn was one of the best ways to end the day. Emerging from the office, I paused, eyeing the bedroom door. Considering the woman inside. The bedroom door was open. I remembered the way she panicked at the closed door in her bedroom. I'd assumed she didn't want me shut in with her, not that she had a problem with closed doors in general. I returned to the office to grab what I needed and headed into the room.

Light filtered in through the drawn shade. I scanned the room. Bag unpacked and put away somewhere. Probably the closet. Blankets strewn about the bed. A red-haired woman in the center of it, surrounded by pillows. She'd put on a cream-colored pajama set made of soft ribbed cotton. If you could call the small top and tiny shorts pajamas. Her body was tangled in the sheets and blankets, one leg peeking out from underneath.

She shifted, rolling over with a sigh. I'd been in standoffs with the most dangerous people in the world, and here I was holding my breath, worried a five-foot-five redhead was going to wake up and set eyes on me standing at her bedside.

"Go back to bed, Ains," Casey sighed softly, nuzzling into another pillow.

I needed to get the hell out of here before I did something stupid.

Dragging a hand over my face, I turned and left. The sofa would have to do. The sofa where I blew my shot with her. It was here that I'd almost had everything I wanted. I just couldn't ignore the conflict in her eyes. My gut hollered at me that she wasn't ready. That we were moving too fast. It was my gut that dampened the need the rest of my body felt. It threw on the brakes as I went from needing her to needing to hurt the men who'd wounded her in the space of a second. As I pulled a throw blanket over myself and beat my pillow into submission, I decided that if this was punishment, the punishment fit the crime.

SEVEN

CASEY

It took me a moment to remember where I was. Brick walls. Large windows covered in large rolling shades. Modern furniture. None of that tipped me off as quickly as the smell. That *him* smell. Citrus and sage. So distinctly Clayton that my blood simmered, anticipating his nearness. I took a breath. It was still quiet. Still dark. Still very early in the morning. I told myself that was why I didn't move. That was why I'd just rolled over and tried to go back to sleep.

Only, I didn't sleep.

The sheets were a mess of tangled fabric around me. By the time the clock clicked over to six in the morning, I'd been awake for two hours already. Normally, I would have gotten up. I would have started getting ready for my day. If I were at home, that's what I would have done. But if I'd been at home, I wouldn't have gone to bed so early in the first place. Going to bed at eight o'clock had been such a crazy, childish way to avoid a conversation. Avoid a conversation and avoid him. It was exactly the same thing I was doing now.

All it did was imprison me in his bedroom. Surrounded by his things. His scent. Him. Him. Him. I'd spent all night in it and decided that sleeping on the sofa would be more comfortable than this.

Except I couldn't sleep on the sofa. The sofa. The fucking sofa. The sofa in this apartment, the apartment that belonged to the man who humiliated me by rejecting me. The cherry on top of the entire situation was, of course, that he was also taking money from my father. My big, scary father, who decided that I would be better off here. With him. Safer.

With Clayton.

Someone once said we were only as strong as our weakest moments. Alright, it was probably something I read in a yoga magazine at the nail salon. That felt like yoga magazine material. Maybe it was that Oprah magazine. Whatever. Staring up at the ceiling, I wanted to be better than the grudge I was holding against Clayton Wrigley. He had been doing his best to see to my needs. I didn't like the way he went about it, but that didn't mean I needed to behave like a pain in the ass. He was putting himself out to protect me.

I mean, he did sleep on the sofa.

It was for what was most likely a big fat paycheck from my father. Regardless of that annoying probability, when my feet hit the floor this morning, I decided not to let him rile me. When I was in high school in Monterey Bay, I had trouble with the other girls. I wasn't rich like the other girls. I wasn't developed like them. I wasn't as popular with the boys as they were. Then all of those things changed over the course of one summer. Did I punish them for it? No. *Be the bigger person*, my mother had told me. *Be cordial. Be nice.*

"You don't have the heart for cruelty."

She'd been right. Even when I was furious with someone, I couldn't yell at them. Even when my best friend Aly stole my boyfriend in my senior year, I couldn't. I had every right to be angry. I knew that. It simmered under my skin every time I was in a room with him, but Clayton Wrigley was not going to steal my fucking sunshine.

I didn't let myself think about the fact that he'd come in here while I was sleeping. It was obvious when my phone and laptop were sitting on the nightstand, waiting for me once again. I also didn't want to think about what he'd spent so long doing to it with that expensive hacker stuff he was always doing for my father.

Picking up my phone, I opened my music streaming app and got on with the business of being me. Snuck across the hall with all of my things and took a shower. Put my hair up in a towel and sat on the floor for a few minutes of morning meditation while I burned some incense. Took an extra-long time doing the most elaborate version of a nude makeup look I could manage. Anything to avoid going out into the living room. A very small part of me wondered what the hell I would be doing with all of my time if I wasn't going to be able to work. Which, as my father had informed me as I walked out the door yesterday, I would not be doing for the foreseeable future.

I wasn't allowed to do anything I normally did or see anyone I normally saw. Excluding my support group, which was basically anonymous, so it wasn't exactly social, I was allowed only one friendly exception. That exception was probably because she was just as deadly as my brother.

You could text her, I thought.

I thought about it as I blow-dried my hair. If anyone could understand the current situation, it would be her. It wasn't as if I could tell any of the other girls at Muse about my situation. *Hey ladies, remember how two years ago I vanished for a little while? I was kidnapped and held in a trafficking facility in the Mojave Desert for almost two months until Lilith Caccia found me. Thanks to that, she and my father are now allies. Did I mention he's in the mafia, too?* I couldn't imagine how that would go over.

Besides, Lili was probably busy anyway. She was the boss of a major crime family and a mom now, so she was almost always busy. Still, I could shoot her a text. That would be harmless. I mean, hey, the worst she could do was ignore me.

> Hey, Lili. It's been a while. Let's get together soon.

And just as I expected, I got no response by the time I was finished with my blowout. My hair came down to my waist, so she'd had almost an hour to look at it. Nothing. Not even a read receipt. But an alert flashed on my phone. A calendar reminder. At least I was dressed and cleaned up, because I only had half an hour to get to the community center.

My vintage campus boots clopped on the concrete floor as I strode into the living room to find Clayton standing there, motorcycle helmet tucked under his arm. Tugging on little black leather gloves, he didn't look up from them as he spoke.

"We have an appointment, right?"

He was dressed. Black jeans. Black hoodie. White sneakers. The only thing that was askew was his hair, which looked like he'd been running his fingers through it.

"You looked at my calendar?" I blinked.

"I added your calendar to my calendar. I'm supposed to be everywhere you are, Casey."

I didn't know why I was surprised. Hours had gone by without my phone. He shrugged, taking me in with that caramel-colored gaze. Those eyes fixed on the pale green floral skirt I'd paired with the cropped dark green cardigan I had on over my T-shirt. Between my hair and makeup, I felt like I looked good. Those feelings dissipated the second I saw him wince.

Be nice, I told myself.

"Go put on some pants. It's cold out, and we're not taking your car."

I blinked again. Pants. Car. I tried to summon logic because it was clearly absent from this conversation.

"Why? Why do I need pants, Clayton?"

Be nice. Be nice. Be nice.

"Because we're taking my bike. And your car is currently being torn apart."

"What?" I sputtered.

He said it so casually, like I should have known or guessed that would be the case. Other questions flooded my mind. Questions about who was stripping my car or would ever get my car back at all. My hands fisted at my sides as I tried not to scream at him. Every charitable thought I was forcing myself to have about him as I got ready this morning went right out of a pretty arched window. Clayton strolled toward me in taunting steps.

"It's a really nice car, Casey. Super modern features. All those little features mean it has all kinds of traceable systems in it. A computer. Sensors and shit. Until we get rid of those things, you can't drive it. So, if you're going anywhere, you're going on the back of my motorcycle," he said, a gloved hand patting the large black helmet he was holding as he grinned down at me. "I don't have a spare, so you can wear mine until we get you one. Or your car is done. Whichever comes first."

EIGHT

Casey

Another morning and another meeting spent not sharing. Despite my inability to open my mouth, something about these meetings made me feel better. I would never wish what happened to any of us on anyone. I don't even like hearing the stories from the other women. But just being in the room with them made me feel less alone. Like what happened wasn't my fault. And maybe the world was just full of god-awful people looking to take advantage of others.

Today was not one of those days.

Usually, I sat here listening to everyone else's issues. The struggles with telling the person they were dating about what had happened to them. The struggle to date at all. Dealing with intimacy issues. Or sharing what had happened to them if they needed to work through it. I'd always felt guilty about just sitting here like a statue. Today I felt even worse because I wasn't even listening. I was thinking about *him*. The ride over here had been brief, but I experienced every second of it. Riding on the back of Clayton's motorcycle had been an experience I wasn't ready to repeat. He told me what to do. Where to put my hands when he hits the brakes. How to wrap my arms around him.

Nope.

All I could think about was the fact that my legs were squeezing around him. My arms were around his waist. His body was so warm. It was more intimate than I was ready to be with anyone. Especially with him. Except my body didn't seem to know that. It had been so long since I'd been with someone in that way. I hadn't wanted it. Not since that night in his apartment. The night he'd decided he didn't want me. I hadn't even bothered trying to date anyone. Sure, I'd hopped on the apps. For like five seconds. Messaging with the kind of men that were out there was enough to make me jump right off and choose my own company for the foreseeable future. Being alone felt like less of a risk than dating a crypto bro in their mid-thirties who was still figuring out their relationship goals.

In the last two years, I'd been almost entirely celibate. Those men. The ones who... It was like they had destroyed me so thoroughly that even the thought of pleasure barely occurred to me.

I remembered that part of myself this morning. I wanted to experience pleasure with him. Before. There was no mistaking that. I'd felt echoes of that desire in my fingers as they clung to his hoodie. The heat from his legs pressed against mine. The rumble of the bike. The motorcycle made us too close.

The vibrating Triumph Bonneville T120 and the warm man between my thighs. I felt that. My hands tingled with it. And when I came into this room filled with people, that feeling I'd been trying to ignore transformed into something completely different. It kept me company through every story. All the way through the ride back to the loft. It was enough to send me down the hall, slamming the bedroom door closed behind me. Another feeling I'd come to know well and hadn't been able to face.

Anger.

For someone who once told me he didn't see me as a princess, he had no problem with keeping me locked in a tower. Locked away alone. Clayton shouted through the door, instructing me not to go anywhere. That he would be back. I would have been annoyed at that if I hadn't already been vibrating with rage. Rage and need. After I was sure I heard the front door close, I undressed down to my little cotton thong, putting my clothes in the hamper beside the dresser and pulling out a yoga set. If he asked, I could say that I was getting ready for a workout. It was a perfectly reasonable explanation. Not that I needed one. I was an adult. Adults did this sort of thing.

The bedding was soft under my palms and knees as I crawled toward the headboard, pulling the covers up around me as I sat against it in order to protect myself from whatever cameras he had going in here. I wasn't stupid enough to think that Clayton wouldn't have every inch of his apartment under some sort of surveillance. Especially after he'd bragged about it being so secure.

A shaky breath loosed from me. It was only me. Just me and my thoughts. Safe. Secure. Far away from anyone or anything that could actually do me harm. Some part of me wished I'd finally purchased myself a vibrator or any other type of device to make things easier on myself, even if another voice was whispering that I wasn't ready to know what that would feel like yet.

My hands set the tone, skimming over my belly. Down to my thighs. I let my eyes fall closed. It was easier to guide my thoughts this way. This was simple. A human reaction. Totally normal and totally safe. By myself. I let myself imagine that I was leaning against the chest of a lover. Warm in his bed. A lover's hands were moving over my skin. Taking in the topography of me. Goosebumps lifted in the wake of that touch. He would be gentle as he kissed the space between my shoulder and neck. Graze my fluttering pulse with his teeth. Capable of devouring me, but restraining himself. To ease me into him.

Into this.

A hand would dip between my thighs. Stroking the soft inner skin of each leg with long tattooed fingers before coming back to the center of me. Brushing over the sensitive apex with a feather-light touch before moving away again. Teasing me. Working me with a wry smile until I begged for more. His scent enveloped me. Heating me down to the core, he skimmed with a callused palm. Whispering in his dark rasp that I should be patient. That he never stopped wanting me. The admission would come as he made contact with my core, easing the tips of those capable fingers inside. Then up, around where I was swollen, aching for him. Repeating that motion with increasing speed and pressure until his attention was focused on that damned spot. Working me until my legs were shaking.

"That's it," he'd praise. "Come for me."

"Hold her legs, damnit."

My hand shot away from me as my knees slammed shut. It was all I needed. A moment. A flash of memory. The profound discomfort. The wound that felt like it would never close. A sob burst from me on the heels of my throat-ravaging scream.

I tried to catch my breath. Tried to ignore the voice in my head as I got up and dressed. The voice that insisted that this was an exercise in futility. I dressed and took myself to the kitchen to pour myself a glass of water with trembling hands. Drank it down and chased it with another, hoping to extinguish the feeling burning in my center as tears rolled over my hot cheeks. Because I wasn't just broken. I was deeply and profoundly fucked up.

NINE

CLAYTON

Children shouted as they punched the air in sync, balancing their small feet on black protective mats. The instructor, a woman who looked like she could easily take me in a fight, watched me out of the corner of her eye. Tattoos marked her dark skin; some I couldn't quite make out, but there was one on her shoulder that was clear in the midmorning light: USMC.

I chuckled to myself.

It was just like West Hale to hire another veteran to work at his gym. I wouldn't be surprised if all of the people who worked here had served in one way or another. He'd told me that working for the Caccias had changed his life. This place had been a gift for him. Brought him out of that post-service haze I'd found myself in before teaching myself about programming. I had no doubt that it wasn't just the purpose that brought him peace, but the woman he'd met in this establishment. The one he now called his wife.

"Hey," a friendly greeting rumbled from across the gym.

West, my former Lieutenant Commander, stood in the open door of his office. Tying his shoulder-length hair into a knot on the back of his head, he wore only a pair of gym shorts and no shoes. Obviously, the giant was getting ready to begin a workout. My eyes skated over the Kraken tattoo that matched my own.

"Hey," I said, returning his greeting. "Can we talk?"

I jerked my chin toward his office, hoping he understood that I needed privacy.

After our rocky start, I thought things were getting better. My inner idiot screamed at me for making her change out of the skirt that showed off those muscular legs that were somehow both delicate and strong from all that yoga. Probably the dancing, too. That voice was still shouting at me as I thought about the way the feel of her arms around my waist lingered. She'd gone from barking at me and silently hating me to occasional seething looks in my direction. Progress. That is, until I got here.

I'd been checking the cameras when feet slapped across the floor. Casey approached a patch of sunlit space, rolling her yoga mat out with a flop. The light bounced off her skin in a faint glow, the two of them existing in luminous harmony. The sun drank her in, gilding her as she moved through her salutation. Breath wooshed out in measured puffs, almost a chant. There she was in a little mauve shorts and bra workout set, hair bundled into a loose bun. It didn't take long for me to decide that yoga in the living room was my new personal hell.

That skin, because there was so much of it in yet another outfit designed to make me chew the furniture, was gleaming with sweat. The sports bra was darkened with it. Her matching shorts were practically painted onto the heart-shaped ass as it elevated with another deep stretch. A sigh that sounded more like a moan puffed out of her with the motion.

Downward-facing kill me.

I needed help. I needed West. It was six years before he'd gotten together with his woman. Six years of training her right here in this gym without acting on how he felt about her. His mouth quirked to one side as he looked at his watch.

"Yeah," he said, still looking at the timepiece. "I've got some time. Come on in."

The office hadn't much changed since the last time I'd been here. White paint, just like the rest of the place. A small leather sofa. Bookshelf laden with his ratty old paperbacks. The desk seemed to be carefully organized. His computer, which I'd set up for him, was in screensaver mode. It flashed photos he'd most likely uploaded.

There we were, holding up our targets in my shooting range. Another photo of our unit in the middle of a faraway desert. I felt a twinge of sadness at seeing a few long-gone faces. Then, he and Lilith Caccia Hale were standing under an archway. He's holding her face in both hands, looking down at her like she was the only person in the world. For him, she was.

West reclined on the top of his desk, thick arms folded over his chest, looking down his nose at me like a father ready to scold a child.

"Alright, chill out with the look. You may be a father now, but you're not *my* father," I started.

"Do you want to explain what this is about, or do I already know?"

I cleared my throat.

"I assume Lili told you what's going on with Ronan and Ilia Kremnik."

His scarred eyebrow shot up. The scar that had been caused by a poorly timed joke by yours truly and some unruly bar patrons down near Pendleton. Memories of the ER visit to remove the fragments of the beer bottle from his face were still fresh in my mind.

"The Russian mob boss? She told me he got out of prison and that Ronan asked her for backup."

I nodded.

"Ronan asked for your help, too?"

I nodded again.

"You're going to have to start saying some words, Wrigley."

"He asked me to provide security for Casey. To be a bodyguard, basically. He thought it would be best for her to hide somewhere Kremnik couldn't find in any of the Arawn records, so I've got her hiding out at my place until we get the all-clear."

"She's staying with you?"

I nodded. For a long while, I thought he wouldn't say anything. Sounds of the class happening filtered through the closed door. Then West, the bastard, burst out laughing. Loud, full-chested laughs. Tear-inducing laughs. My expression flattened as I waited.

"Oh, fuck," he sniffed and giggled. "I'm sorry."

"I'm glad my life is so amusing to you, you dick."

He lifted his hands, using one to wipe away a tear before holding his palms out in a mock apology.

"No, I just," he sniffed again, wiping another tear from his eye. "I've been there, man. I've been there. Really. Now I have a wife and kid to show for it."

I rolled my eyes. Yeah, I'd been a side-character in his own little drama. Alright, maybe it wasn't little.

"You're forgetting a key detail."

He shrugged.

"She hates me."

West rolled his eyes, bracing his hands on the desk. He coughed, probably covering another laugh because I could see his teeth flash at the sound. He took a breath, then schooled his face into a more serious expression.

"Why do you think she hates you?"

"Because I, well, we were," I paused. This is why I'd come. But telling him this, even though he was the closest thing I had to family, felt like a violation. "Alright, so we were getting close to being intimate, and some stuff happened. It was a few years ago. A couple of months after we met. And now she hates me."

A wail cracked through the air, easily heard from beyond the closed door. West rolled his eyes, but a stifled grin appeared on his lips at the sound.

Standing from his perch on the desk, he walked the short distance to the door and opened it. The squalling sound blasted into the room.

"There's my girl," he said over his shoulder to me.

I leaned forward to see Lilith walking in while carrying a car seat, the source of the sound was nestled within. Only a few months old and louder than a cat being shoved into a garbage disposal. That sound was already frying my nerves. If the desire to never reproduce had been waning in any capacity, it was renewed by the sensation of my shoulders shooting up to my ears. No, thank you to that. Babies were fine. Cute, even. I just never wanted any part of the whole parenting thing. The plan quickly became to say hello to Lili, then get the hell out of here. I glanced at West.

With a broad smile, he approached his little family, kissing his wife on the forehead before leaning down to pick up the screaming bundle. His daughter almost disappeared into his sizable hold, but she quieted quickly. West peered down at the baby, who'd taken one of his fingers in her tiny hands and beamed. The guy couldn't be happier.

I strode out of the office and over to them. With the baby temporarily occupied, now was as good a time as any to make my escape. Lili caught my eye. Dressed in expensive-looking black gym clothes, she looked a whole lot better than the last time I'd seen her. West had told me the little one was going through something called sleep regression, so I'd brought them takeout. She'd cried from gratitude and sheer exhaustion. Sounded like a nightmare and another big mark in the no thank you column.

"Hey," she said awkwardly. "Come to train?"

"I was just dropping by," I said, shaking my head.

Now at West's side, I took a look at the little one. Less like a ball of pink flesh, she actually started to resemble a human. Brown hair like her father, olive skin, and gold eyes like her mother. Kai Hale. Named for the sister we buried two years ago. I wondered if someday her mother would tell her how I'd met her. Or how she'd fallen in love with her father. It was a bloody story, but still a good one. At least when they told it. They exchanged a look as the kid started crying again.

"He's got girl problems," West said in a high-pitched voice as he pretended to address the little girl in his arms. Lilith scoffed, a knowing smirk crossing her lips as she adjusted her black ponytail. "Be nice, Trouble."

"I'm always nice," she winked. West arched that scarred brow at her, rubbing their crying daughter's back with patient circles. Lilith rolled her eyes and sighed. "Fine. I'll be nice. What's the problem?"

I leaned in to whisper my explanation of my current situation in order to keep the information away from curious ears. There were a few details I left out. That I hadn't been able to date anyone else. That I hadn't slept with anyone else. That letting myself hope for another shot with her was as poisonous as anything out of Lilith's lethal apothecary. You know, the parts that made me look like even more of an idiot. When I was finished, I stood back and looked at the world's shortest mafia boss. Raven black brows pinched together as she frowned, wariness entering her gold-rimmed eyes. Impatience forced me to prompt her for an answer.

"So, what do you think I should do?"

"She's been through a lot, Clay," she grimaced.

"I know," I growled through clenched teeth.

"But just because she's been through all that doesn't mean she doesn't want," Lilith paused and made a lewd gesture with her hand. "I know she's shut you out; she won't shut you out forever. She just needs time."

West elbowed her, eyeing the dozen six-year-olds who were training only a few yards away. A parent caught his gaze, and he mouthed a silent apology. I chuckled, remembering all of the filth that used to come out of this guy's mouth when we were in the service together. Now he was censoring his wife's gestures for touchy parents.

"I'm not trying to get her to sleep with me. I just want us to be better. I want to fix it."

"Nothing is going to change between you two until she stops being mad at you," West said, returning his attention to the conversation at hand and subtly walking us toward the black locker-lined corner of the gym. "My advice? Act like it doesn't bother you. Be a rock and let her crash into you."

Lili snorted, placing her things inside one of the lockers. Her words were muffled as she tugged her sweatshirt up over her head to reveal the black workout top to match the leggings she had on.

"Or you could just speed up the process and be the cocky pain in the ass I know you can be."

"How would that help anything?"

"It'll force you two to stop dancing around each other and have a fight," she shrugged, stepping out of her shoes to shove them into the locker behind her other things. "There's too much unspoken shit between the two of you right now. Once you guys have it out, you can start to move on."

Move on. As if it were that simple to say goodbye to the hope I'd let burn in me for over six hundred days. I knew I should move on. I tried it already. I'd done everything in my power to make it possible for myself to leave her alone. Not because I wanted to, but because she told me to. If letting her go was the right thing for her, then I'd do it. Even if I had to fall on my own sword. The idea coated my tongue with acid.

I looked at West, who gave a small shrug. Their tiny daughter held another one of his fingers. As if she were finished with my little problem, Lilith picked up the car seat and carried it toward the office, leaving me alone with her husband once again. He watched her over his shoulder as he spoke.

"Or that. To be honest, that's probably the better plan."

"Why?"

"Because you're naturally annoying. It might happen that way even if you're not trying." My middle finger gave him the gesture that statement deserved. West winced and glanced in the direction of the parents again. After his wife took their baby from him to place in his now darkened office, he sighed. "If you want things to get better, you're going to have to wade through the shit. That's all there is to it."

I pulled my phone from my pocket, checking on the problem in question. Sprawled across my bed, face lit up by the blue screen as she scrolled through her phone. Huffing a sigh, I closed the app and pocketed the device again. I wanted her to feel safe in my space. I couldn't pick a fight with her. But I'd take whatever she wanted to throw at me. With a half-assed salute, I headed toward the door.

"Copy that, Commander Hale. Waders on. Nose plugged."

TEN

Casey

Scrolling through social media on my phone had become my only pastime, which was not good for my mental state. It's probably not good for anyone's mental state, actually. Even if I kept seeing advertisements for therapy apps and interesting book recommendations. In fact, I wasn't far off from caving and downloading one of those apps just to have someone to talk to. Scrolling was what I had resorted to after spending the night trying and failing to bring myself some release. I needed it to take my mind off the way being pressed up against Clayton made me feel. It wasn't fair that he could still affect me in such a way and leave me with no relief.

Even though there was no way he knew he'd had this effect on me, I resolved to get revenge. Clayton's sidelong glances at me as I ate stoked an idea. Not a great idea, but it was better than nothing. After finishing another almost silent dinner of takeout, I went to bed with my plan dancing in my head as I drifted off to sleep.

He'd been working at the kitchen counter when I entered. Positioning myself within his eyeline, I went through an entire yoga routine in my smallest outfit. Every opportunity to let out a noise or display myself in front of him was taken advantage of with zeal. Was it childish? Absolutely. It was with no small amount of satisfaction that I noted that Clayton had stopped typing about ten minutes in. A stolen glance in his direction confirmed he'd stopped whatever it was he'd been doing to watch. I strode down the hall to take a shower, enjoying how much I'd affected him. By the time I came out, he was gone. The only evidence of his departure was the terse text message he'd sent me. It didn't escape my notice that he'd unblocked his phone number when he'd had my phone, something I'd done from the second my Uber pulled away that night.

> Stay put. I'll be back.

That was almost three hours ago. I closed the app, unable to look at the messages he'd sent while I'd blocked him, all of them there in the one-sided chain. Dozens of them. Their contents nagged at me as I showered and changed. Pillows surrounded me in a makeshift cocoon, helping me to feel less lonely on the massive bed inside the massive apartment. A soft, sage-colored throw blanket kept me warm, completing the soothing retreat. Everything in the immediate vicinity was designed to bring me comfort. Even the butter-soft green leggings and cream-colored sweatshirt I'd thrown on. That didn't mean I was comfortable. No, instead I was shifting around. Making infinitesimal adjustments to the position of my body every few minutes.

It was impossible that I'd made him so miserable that he couldn't stand to be around me for another second. I'd barely spoken to him in the last two days. Before that, I'd made it clear I wanted nothing to do with him. Whenever he had business with my father, I made it my business not to be around. The last two years, I'd thrown him countless jabs and dirty looks. He had to be used to it by now, right?

Right.

So why was I so worried that two days of uninterrupted time with me pushed him over the edge, and he was at my father's pub at this very moment, begging him to take me back?

I jolted up from the bed when I heard the sequence of beeps from the alarm, followed by the deactivation message. My feet padded on the polished concrete floor toward the living room in time to see Clayton shutting the door behind him.

"Where did you go?"

He set a small white bag on the countertop and shrugged off his black leather motorcycle jacket. A sigh through his nose was the only indication that he'd heard me. My feet carried me closer until I could smell what lingered inside the bag. Cinnamon, maple, and the unmistakable scent of fried bread. Donuts. Clayton entered the kitchen, throwing open the refrigerator door to pull a carafe of orange juice out of it. It was set on the counter beneath the cabinet he opened to grab a glass. It was filled. It was consumed, downed in a few gulps, and finished with a satisfied grunt. He filled it again, then wiped his mouth with the hem of his grey t-shirt, giving me a glimpse of his sculpted abs. Clayton then pulled a small plate from the cabinet behind him and grabbed the bag, fishing out a maple bar and plopping it onto the plate. All of it without so much as a look in my direction.

"So, where were you?" I asked again.

Finally, he paused, arching a dark brow at me.

"Why, did you miss me?"

"No," I scoffed.

A shallow nod accompanied a roll of his eyes. He'd expected that response. I folded my arms over my chest, huffing an impatient breath. Picking up the donut from his plate, he opened his mouth around it and took a large bite. A bite that left bits of maple glaze around the corners. His tongue lazily licked the remnants away. A flicker of something entered his gaze as he took another bite, watching me as he chewed. The process went on. Bite. Chew. Lick. I was watching him clean his fingers with his tongue when he tossed a question in my direction.

"Did you need something?" A half-cocked grin wide enough to show one of his dimples accompanied the question. He was provoking me. There was no other explanation. Long, sinuous fingers curled around the little white bag. Clayton held the opening to his face, giving it a deep sniff before removing the other donut from inside and placing it on the now-empty plate. Ceramic scraped stone as two fingers pushed the donut in my direction. "Go ahead."

An apple fritter. Big, deep brown, and shining with glaze. Hesitant to reach for the fritter, I extended my hand toward the plate as I waited for him to pull it away. Clayton just watched from beneath dark brows, smile growing as I picked up the plate. He was definitely baiting me.

"Come on. I need to show you something," he commanded, standing upright again and rounding the counter. His fingers circled my wrist, tugging me and the fritter down the hall. "I should have done this before I left."

"I've seen your office," I said, my mouth half-full of the cinnamon-drenched fritter I was half finished with eating as we entered the room. Tangy, sweet, and so delicious. The donut was almost enough to make me forget how irritated I'd been.

Clearly, it had been intended to be the other bedroom in this loft; the room we now stood in had been turned into a workspace by the man beside me. It didn't have a window, but it could have been the same size and shape as the room I'd been sleeping in. In fact, the only real difference was that instead of an entrance to a closet like the one in his bedroom, there was a wall-to-wall bookshelf. Well, that and the desk that had several monitors of various sizes on some sort of intricate mounting system and an LED light bisecting the wall for ambience. It was pulsing pink now. In front of it sat a chair that looked more like it was meant for racing a Formula 1 car than working at a desk.

"Your computers are very impressive," I deadpanned, popping the rest of the donut into my mouth. "Is that all?"

"Pay attention," he ordered. "I'm only showing you this once."

He approached the bookshelf, looking around for something. The shelves in front of us were lined with binders. Dozens and dozens of black binders. Each of them had a printed black label with a date in white lettering. His hand skimmed the binders, fingers tracing over the dates. It would have been impossible for me to spot it if I hadn't seen him pull it free. Almost free. The spine of the binder separated from the object to reveal a keypad. Clayton quickly punched in a code.

A deep electronic tone sounded before it was replaced by the sound of metal sliding against metal. I jerked. One section of the bookshelf slid away from the wall. A wall that wasn't a wall, but a small room.

"Is this a panic room?"

Clayton nodded, lifting a hand to invite me to walk in and look around. Stuffing his hands into the pockets of his jeans, he leaned against his desk and watched me take it in. Not much inside. A small supply of shelf-stable food. Metal containers that I assumed had water inside of them since they were sitting on the shelf below the food. A small sofa with some pillows. A phone mounted to the wall, connected to a landline. I turned, looking back to the man looming in the office. He opened his mouth to say something else when an alert pinged from his computer. He'd put on those little square glasses when I wasn't looking, the lenses now obscuring his caramel irises in the glare of the soft white light coming from inside the panic room. Leaving the doorway open for me to exit, he shoved the elaborate office chair aside to type while standing.

"If, for some reason, you're alone and anything happens, I want you to wait for me in there. I made the code your birthday so you won't forget it."

I stepped over the track for the sliding door. My father hadn't explained why I was here beyond a rival on the loose and a pressing need to keep me safe, but the truth is, I'd been treated like a porcelain doll ever since I was sprung from that trailer, and I was sick of it. I didn't need that kind of treatment from anyone, which was why the next words came out of my mouth with a little more bite.

"I'm not some damsel in distress who needs to be locked away. You don't need to ride in on your noble steed to my rescue."

His head dropped, hanging in front of him as he heaved a sigh. Shoulders slumped as he pinched the bridge of his nose with his thumb and forefinger. Whatever energy he'd come in here with evaporated. For a minute, I thought we were done talking. I crossed the office, stopping in my tracks when he spoke, his voice a low rasp.

"Fuck, Casey. Are you really still this angry at me?"

A syllable came out of my mouth. Not a word. Not entirely, anyway. Clayton shoved away from his desk, anger coloring the features that had been arrogant only moments ago. Only a few short strides had him towering over me. Between his tall frame and long reach, I would have already felt small. With that look on his face, the one filled with undiluted ire, I felt even smaller as he caged me in against the wall with one long arm.

"You rejected me," I reminded him, my voice snagging on whatever emotion this was. Leftover embarrassment, probably.

"I wasn't the one who walked out that door, in case you forgot," Clayton seethed through clenched teeth, a muscle in his jaw flickering with the motion. I could see the tension ripple down the column of his throat.

"Because you humiliated me!"

"Fine. Blame me for what happened between us. But I'm done pretending. You're the one who gave up. You want to keep hiding from everything, and I understand that, but you built that wall between us, not me."

I'd never heard him speak this way. His tone, even when it was tired or bored, was always filled with a sense of play. This man was tired of me. Done. I wanted to argue. To say something, anything, to prove him wrong. Words turned to ash on my tongue. Caramel eyes searched my gaze for a response. As if seeing it trapped inside me, Clayton let out a bitter laugh and shoved away from the wall. Unable to bear his resentment for another second, my attention dropped to my bare feet. I tried not to notice the larger set walking away from me.

"Casey," Clayton huffed as he paused in the doorway. The irritation was still there. Still simmering under the surface of his voice. "Don't go anywhere."

"Couldn't if I wanted to," I snapped at my toes, regret immediately flooding me at the knee-jerk response.

I hated myself like this. This unhealed version of me. Footsteps departed, their sound fading down the hall until I heard the large steel front door slam shut. He left. Again.

A few hours later, I was lying in bed when I heard the alarm beep. Heard the door close. Heard all of it from the other side of the closed bedroom door. Closed because the suffocating feeling was better than looking at him. Because I needed a barrier between the two of us. A barrier and a warning so I could wipe away any evidence of the tears I'd shed under the covers. I didn't want him to see. Not when there was the smallest, quietest voice inside me whispering truths to me. He'd embarrassed me, but I'd also embarrassed myself. I'd walked out on him. I'd shut him out.

He was right. I hadn't just built that wall between us. I'd hand-selected every brick.

ELEVEN

Clayton

The sound of metal clanging on metal sent me jolting upward. My eyes adjusted as I turned, sitting on the sofa. I looked around for the source of the sound. The kitchen. The woman standing in those excruciatingly sheer pajamas, hair piled atop her head in a bun with several curling red strands glowing like molten glass around her perfect face in the morning sunlight.

"Sorry," she winced, hissing through clenched teeth. "I swear I was trying to be quiet."

Her brown eyes looked softer than yesterday. Warm in a way that made me rub a hand over my chest. I'd take that. Between the tousled hair and mouthwatering amount of skin on display, I resolved to remain seated on the sofa until I could convince my body that absolutely nothing was about to happen. This wasn't a daydream. I couldn't walk over there and pick up where we'd left off two years ago, though every instinct screamed at me to do so. Bracing myself with one hand on the back of the sofa, I winced as it creaked under my grip. Casey's gaze snagged on my hand. She picked up a bowl and started whisking, beating the hell out of whatever was inside.

Say something, I begged myself.

"Are you hungry?" Her question was a squeak. A lifeline. A simple question requiring a simple answer.

Say yes, idiot.

"There's coffee," she quietly offered, trying again.

I picked my phone up off the coffee table and checked the time through bleary vision. Almost seven in the morning. Good god, she's a morning person. I squeezed my eyes shut and shoved my phone into the pocket of my faded grey sweatpants. Morning people. Years in the service, waking before dawn couldn't make me a morning person. A few weeks with Casey probably wouldn't either, but that didn't mean I wouldn't try. With a growl, I cleared my throat before attempting to speak.

"Coffee would be great."

There. A normal response. Ceramic clinked on the stone counter as Casey plunked a mug down. She filled it with coffee from the pour-over carafe and pushed it toward me as I approached the counter. I picked it up and took a sip, watching her over the rim. She moved through my kitchen like she knew it. Like she'd always known it. I took another sip of coffee, trying to convince myself that the warm feeling building in my belly was the beverage and nothing else.

"How long have you been up?"

Casey paused and gave me a queer look, one hand holding the whisk over a skillet on the stove. She was making pancakes. Resuming her task, she dropped batter onto the skillet. The wet blob sizzled as it hit the heated surface.

"I've been awake for a while."

Another pancake blob hit the pan. She continued speaking, though she kept her eyes on the task in front of her.

"I wanted to do something nice for you."

Another blob. Another sizzle.

"Oh, why is that?"

Just because she was making me breakfast didn't mean I had to go easy on her. West's advice floated through my mind as she propped a hip onto the cabinet beside her, watching the pancakes bubble on the stove. Wade through the shit. A deep breath rushed in and out of her, preparing for whatever she was about to say.

"I, uh, haven't been very kind to you. Despite what's happened between us, I just... That's not who I am. And," she paused, picking up a spatula to turn the pancakes over in the pan. When she was through, she stared at them for a long moment before looking over a freckled shoulder at me. Chewing one side of her lip, the admission came out a little muffled. "You were right. I was the one who ended things. You didn't deserve all that."

"I deserved some of it," I smirked.

"Yeah, maybe a little," she said, a small laugh bubbling from her.

I contemplated asking her why she would change her mind now, but it was possible that Lilith was right. Confronting Casey with the truth was enough to break the silence between us and create a little tentative peace. Thank fuck for that because I wasn't sure I could take any more of this weird tension between us. A bottle of syrup appeared in front of me with a small smile. I smiled back at her. Pancake mix. Syrup. These were things I'd bought to make for her. To give her some sense of comfort while she was here. Not for this.

You should apologize. You need to apologize.

"Casey," I started as she set a plate of pancakes in front of me.

"Don't. We don't need to talk about it," Casey interrupted, sensing the shift in my tone as she topped her coffee cup off with cream, then poured more pancake batter in the skillet as its sizzle continued to fill the room. "We didn't work. Case closed."

We didn't work. As if that was the end of it. I tucked into the food on my plate, enjoying the butter and maple syrup on my tongue. It didn't wash away the bitterness of what I'd felt at those words. *Case closed.* This girl was in my kitchen, looking like that while making me breakfast, telling me we would never work as a couple, while giving me a glimpse at my daydreams realized. It was the cruel irony of the universe I'd gotten used to. That *black fly in your chardonnay* Alanis Morrisette brand of ironic that followed me everywhere. There was only one problem.

My goddamn heart.

Giving up on her wasn't an option. *Case closed?* Not an option. Casey picked up the spatula and flipped pancakes. Avoiding my gaze, she picked up her coffee mug and stared down into the depths of it.

"I thought we could start over. Be friends."

Friends. I heard it for the lie it was. She couldn't see the way I drank in the sight of her in my kitchen. Dressed in that barely-there pajama set that left very little to the imagination. Leaning over and taking a bite of pancake into her mouth, she gave me another one of those restrained smiles as her eyes flicked over my bare chest. I let my incredulous expression explain exactly what I thought of the word "friends" and noticed the way her freckles became lost in the flush of her cheeks. Friends? Not when she looked at me like that. Friends? No fucking way.

"Yeah. Friends."

TWELVE

Casey

Bright morning light filtered in through the window, making the floor beside the bed the perfect place to do my makeup before group. After agreeing to be friends, it only took about a week for Clayton and me to fall into a little routine. Get up. Make coffee. Get ready for group or whatever the day holds. If I didn't have meetings with the support group, I pretty much barricaded myself in the bedroom, and he went about his business. With or without me.

Today was no different. While I put on my makeup, I sat here and swiped through my social feed. It was better than getting lost in his texts, something that tempted me every time I picked up my phone. It was also a little window into the outside world. A way to check in on my friends. As I dressed myself, I got an alert that Sophie, another dancer from Muse, had tagged me in a post. I navigated to my profile to look at what she'd posted. A throwback from my first year at the club. Back when I was still learning. Twisting around on the pole at the instruction of my fellow dancers. Clapping and cheering rose from the background of the pink neon-illuminated stage. From behind the camera, Isabelle cried out.

"Yes! You've got this!"

In my little mauve yoga set, I had finally mastered the butterfly. I looked happy. Carefree. A weight pressed in on me at the lack of that feeling. Even having a core group of friends felt like a distant thing now. After liking the post and posting a few little hearts, I let out a deep breath. My nail clicked on the protective screen cover as I tapped it to close the video, coming back to my profile. My private profile. I'd never wanted the guys in my life and the guys in the audience to interact on my account, so I kept things tight. Seven hundred seventy-seven followers. No more. Except I had more now. One more. I tapped the number to see the list of names. The newest sat right at the top. A user with no profile picture. Nothing was posted to their account either.

Username: MotoDisco312.

There was absolutely no doubt in my mind about who belonged to that name. I sat down on the bed, looking over my shoulder toward the closed door. I would have noticed if he'd requested— the obvious answer popped into my head, causing my expression to flatten. He'd had my phone. He unblocked his phone number. He could have easily requested and approved himself to follow me, too. That presumptuous bastard.

Did he really think I wouldn't notice?

A small thrill shot through me at the opportunity that now presented itself. If he thinks I don't know, then I'll act like I don't know. I lifted my phone, opening the camera app to photograph myself. I opened my jeans and pulled them down. Lowered the camera to the space just above my hipbone. The tiny strap of lace that cut across the area was the perfect distance from my navel and the freckle just below it. I angled the lens out to capture the thumbnail-sized heart outline tattooed on my hip. A tease. I maneuvered my fingers to slide the fuchsia fabric between them. A hint at something suggestive. The memory of that powerful version of me danced beneath my skin. The version who could make men go stupid for her with a well-placed smile.

Do it, she whispered.

I righted my clothes and stood from the bed. He was in his office. I could hear the tap-tap-tapping of his fingers on the keyboard. Striding down the hallway, I posted the photo. It would appear and disappear in a day. Just long enough for me to see if he was following me as my father's hired dog. Or because he wanted to watch.

By the time I entered the support group, I had checked the views on my photo a dozen times. Nothing. The usual suspects, but no MotoDisco312. When we were done, I took the opportunity to slide my phone from my purse and check again. Unfortunately, I'd gotten to the door at the same time as Lisa. Our leader shoved her sleeves up her lean black arms and huffed her thank you to me for helping out with the chairs. Opening the door, I said goodbye to her as I kicked myself for the missed opportunity to look at the screen. I heaved a sigh and shoved the phone into my pocket.

A cold whip of air blew hair into my eyes, obscuring my view of the man waiting for me in the parking lot. The chill spiked every hair on my body, forcing me to wonder just how long these modifications to my car were going to take. We were almost two weeks into this odd arrangement, and things were starting to feel normal. Meeting my bi-weekly support group was just part of our routine. Coming out of this building was so uninteresting to me that I was too busy moving the hair out of my eyes and watching the steps below me to notice the figure approaching me from the right of the building's exit. Clayton, who'd been perched atop his bike, straightened as he reached beneath his motorcycle jacket for the gun I knew was holstered at his ribs.

"Hey!"

I twisted to follow his line of sight, seeing too late that the person approaching me was not an attacker but my ex-boyfriend. Tyler, the wannabe grunge rock frontman of a band that barely had a negligible amount of followers, had a deceptively friendly smile on his face. In the heeled leather boots I had on, we were almost the same height. I'd managed to stop at the beginning of the asphalt while he stood at the bottom step. Incredibly vain and self-conscious about his height, of course. I stifled the urge to roll my eyes and smiled at him instead.

"Casey, baby, where have you been?"

A snort of a laugh sounded from behind me. I glanced over my shoulder. Clayton had crossed his arms over his chest, one hand within easy reach of the pistol I knew was inches away from his fingertips. Not convinced this man wasn't an attacker. I forced the smile to remain on my face as I gave him a noncommittal answer.

"Here and there. What are you doing here?"

"We're playing a secret show at their auditorium tonight."

Secret show. There were so few people who knew who his band was to begin with that I didn't see the point. But his ego was always going to be the death of that band. I let my eyes skim over his beaten-up jeans, the leather motorcycle boots for a bike he didn't ride, and the graphic tee with the logo of a band I knew he didn't listen to. His porcelain veneer smile was completely at odds with the carefully curated hipster appearance. A blonde curl bounced free from his meticulously tousled hair as he jerked his chin toward the man behind me.

"Is that my replacement?"

My lips formed the denial, only to be interrupted by a large, warm hand squeezing my shoulder.

"You ready to go?"

Clayton smiled that dangerous grin as I glanced at him. His teeth were just slightly imperfect and somehow more pleasant to look at than Tyler's. Probably had something to do with the dimples. The shirt he had on had some sort of vintage motor oil advertisement on it. Standing between them, it was impossible not to compare the two. The small, petty voice in my head began plotting how to end this interaction in the most spiteful way possible.

As if sensing the direction of my thoughts, Clayton's hand fell from my shoulder to my waist, clutching me through the cropped pink cardigan I'd thrown on this morning. Tugging me against the hard plane of his body, his head dipped to my ear where he spoke in that low voice that made the hairs on the back of my neck stand on end.

"Who's this?"

"Clay, this is Tyler. He's the lead singer of Paper Radio. Tyler, this is Clay, he's my uh-"

"Boyfriend," Clayton finished with a wink in my direction, holding out a large tattooed hand to shake the one Tyler didn't offer. It hung there for a moment before falling to the other side of my waist, leaving my body buzzing with the touch. I felt the reassuring squeeze there as he placed a kiss on my neck. If Tyler hadn't scoffed, the way my skin pricked at Clayton's mouth on my skin would have distracted me entirely.

"You guys seem pretty serious."

The statement came out with as much venom as Tyler could manage against someone who could probably beat him into the ground. For the briefest moment, I debated letting my *boyfriend* shoot him. My objection was still forming on my tongue when Clayton interjected again.

"Well, she just moved in with me. So yeah, it's serious. Good luck with the secret show."

Clayton made air quotes around the last two words, then patted my ass through the vintage jeans I had on, turning me away from Tyler before I had a chance to say goodbye. Instead, he grabbed my hand and tugged me toward his motorcycle as he muttered through clenched teeth.

"That was the ex-boyfriend you told me about, right? The jealous one." His voice was low enough that I could barely hear it. With Tyler walking toward his little black BMW, I knew he couldn't hear a word. I nodded. In our earliest interactions, I'd told him about my last relationship. How I'd broken up with Tyler because of how possessive he'd gotten and started using the Eros app on Isabelle's advice. "Not a nice guy, if I remember correctly."

For a man who met me at Muse, it was incredible how quickly Tyler had judged me for my job. He wanted the ability to brag about dating a stripper without actually living the reality of it. Between the things I wore and the hours I kept, it felt like he always had some kind of complaint. It wasn't until West had to carry him out of the club by the scruff of his neck for starting a fight with a customer that I'd finally had enough.

"He didn't like having a stripper for a girlfriend," I muttered. Throwing one leg over the Triumph's chestnut leather seat, I plopped my butt down with a thud. Clayton laughed as he handed me his jacket, shaking his head in disbelief. That citrus and sage scent filled my nose as I pulled the leather over my arms. "What?"

My question was muffled as I pulled the helmet he offered over my head. Two long thumbs flicked up the visor to look me in the eye.

"Sometimes I think I'm a world-class idiot. Then I hear a story like that," he smirked. "A girl like you deserves a champion. Not some flaccid douchebag."

Clayton settled onto the bike and turned on the motor. Its rumbling purr filled the chill early autumn air as my eyes skated over the parking lot. Tyler was still here, watching us through his windshield. I knew Clayton had spotted him, too, because he revved the bike's engine once. Loudly. Knowing I had a few more seconds before we actually got moving, I checked the views on my photo again before I took the opportunity to wrap my arms around him. To complete the illusion, of course. One more person than the last time I'd checked. Smiling to myself, I tucked the device away and relaxed against Clayton's muscular back. MotoDisco312 had viewed the picture.

THIRTEEN

Casey

> Watching Pretty Woman. Julia Roberts has the same hair color as you.

> I saw you at the Chancer today. You pretended not to see me. You looked beautiful. You always look beautiful.

Wrapped up in my towel from my shower, I was still damp as I sat on the bed. Clayton had sent me a text stating that he was fetching lunch for us from the taco place down the street. Instead of sending a response, I found myself scrolling up. There were so many messages. So, so many. It seemed like any time Clayton thought about me over the last two years, he sent me a message. The front door slammed shut, the sound causing me to yip and throw the phone to the bed. Sure, it was my phone. Sure, they were my messages. It just felt like I was invading his privacy by looking at them.

Should I just delete them? Did he assume I had already?

"Casey! They gave me extra guac! Hurry before it oxidizes. Should be any second now."

"Just a minute!"

I threw on a fuzzy cream lounge set and hustled into the living room. Clayton had made himself comfortable on the sofa for lunch. He was already crunching into a couple of chips that were drowning in guacamole. Plopping into the corner, which had become my usual spot, I pulled the takeout container of tacos into my lap. After picking up my first carne asada taco, I tucked my pinky under the end to hold everything in place. Clayton noticed the motion and chuckled.

"Wait a second. That's actually brilliant."

"Maya taught me to do that," I laughed. "One of the girls at the club. She said it keeps all the good stuff from falling out."

Clayton picked up a fish taco from the container in his lap, lifting his pinky to the end with a flourish before taking a bite. Cabbage and salsa remained within the tortilla in his hand. A victorious and surprised snort huffed from his full mouth. I lifted my brows at him in an *I told you so* motion and took a bite of my own taco. Through his monstrous bite, Clayton began speaking.

"Can I ask you something?" I shrugged, taking another bite of the taco in my hand. Comfortable. Each of us was clad in lounge clothes and slouched next to each other on the ridiculously large sectional. It was so comfortable. It was a feeling I hadn't felt with many people. Probably just my mother and Ainsley. Before I could contemplate how strange it was that we'd gotten so comfortable so quickly, Clayton cleared his throat, setting his food down again before continuing. "Why'd you quit that photography program?"

The urge to ask him how he knew about my dropping out of college or even which program I was attending fizzled under the realization that he'd probably learned a lot about me. Whether it was because he felt the need to as my assigned bodyguard or he was just curious, I didn't know. Ignoring the instinct to lob questions at him, I swallowed the bite I'd taken and washed it down with the soda he'd set out for me on the coffee table.

"I barely had enough money to go through the program. My mom encouraged me to save, and she invested what I got through work in high school. Made enough to pay for my tuition. It was this expensive private school, and I could barely afford to buy my camera. One day, while I was at my part-time job at the campus bookstore, someone broke into my car and stole all of my stuff. My laptop. My camera. Lenses. Thousands of dollars' worth of stuff in my camera bag, sitting in the trunk of my car. Oh, and they fucked up the car pretty badly, too. Everything I had was just gone. I didn't have the insurance to cover the equipment, just the car. So I got another job. At Muse."

Clayton settled back against the cushions of his sofa, angling his head. Golden brown hair fell over his forehead with the motion. I glanced at the soft waves and took another bite of food. As I chewed, he asked, "That's when you started dancing?"

"No, actually, I was a waitress at Muse first. Then a dancer," I explained. Thoughts of Isabelle flashed through my mind. Teaching me to move. Cheering me on. Telling me how to keep the audience's attention not just with my body but with my eyes, to play with the men who paid for me. I swallowed around the lump forming in my throat. "Anyway, to make a long story even longer, I meant to go back. I just never got around to it. Then everything happened, and I don't know. It didn't seem that important anymore."

The room went quiet as we both continued eating, but the thoughts that plagued me were loud enough that I didn't notice. He wouldn't understand the rest. There was no way for me to know how to explain the other things. The truth of why, even with my now unlimited resources, I hadn't picked up a camera again. That I was too much of a coward to even enter the camera shop near the Chancer, even though I intentionally parked down the street so I could look at their selection through the window as I walked by. None of that could fix the fact that the spark that fueled my creativity seemed to die the moment I woke up in that trailer.

Clayton set down his empty container of food and strode to the kitchen. I reached over to grab a handful of chips, dipping one in the cup of guacamole. Creamy avocado, citrus, and garlic filled my mouth. Small metal clinks tapped onto the counter before footsteps approached. A brown beer bottle with a gold label was thrust into my face. Glancing up at the man holding the Mexican beer out for me to take, there was an expression on his face I couldn't quite nail down. He must have noted my confusion because he wiggled the beer a little and sighed.

"You need a beer. I need a beer. Beers need to be had. Then we're going to watch something funny and forget about reality for a little while."

FOURTEEN

CLAYTON

Casey set down her empty beer bottle onto the table and loosed a satisfied sigh. The messy knot of red on her head was loosening tendrils around her face. Leaning back into the throw pillows on the sofa, she tucked her legs up next to me. Perfectly pink pedicured toes spread and relaxed as she stretched.

"Alright, Wrigley," she yawned. "How are we supposed to watch anything when you don't have a television?"

"You think I just hold up here dicking around on my computer?"

"You don't have a TV and I," she trailed off as she looked around, searching the living area. Her eyes scanned the shelves below the window, causing her to pause and shake her head like she was shaking a thought out of her mind. Blinking again, she yawned and shifted in the cushions of the sofa.

"What?" I prompted, unconcerned about whatever thought she'd abandoned.

"Oh," she sighed. "It's nothing. I just realized I forgot to pack books."

"You can read anything I've got," I offered, gesturing toward the low bookshelf in front of one of the windows. It wasn't a very diverse collection, but I did have some books.

"I can't read those," she giggled, playfully nudging me with a foot.

"What does that mean? They're still books. You open them. Read the words. Poof. Book."

"They're nonfiction," Casey grimaced, tugging on a loose strand of hair up into the messy knot on her head. Her eyes darted up to the arm I had draped over the back of the sofa and the bottle that swished in my fidgeting hand.

This version of her, pink cheeks and freshly scrubbed skin, was becoming an addictive sight. I wondered what she looked like on the stage at Muse, ignoring the pang of regret I felt knowing I would never see her dance. That utterly unevolved voice in my head imagined her there. Before her world shrank down to a trailer in the middle of the desert. Sitting up a little straighter, I cleared my throat and gave my best impression of being offended.

"And?"

"It totally defeats the purpose of reading for me," she said with a shrug, stealing the bottle from my hand to take a swig of beer.

The shoulder of her fuzzy white top slid down to reveal a small swath of golden, freckled skin and a lacy bra strap. Her eyes flicked to mine. Shit. I was staring. Not good. I pretended to be a condescending asshole.

"The purpose of reading is to learn."

"Not for me," Casey snorted, shifting to lounge more comfortably on the sofa as I silently reminded myself that this was something friends did. Friends talked about books. Friends watched movies together. Friends did not think about each other naked. Friends did not wonder what kind of bra came with a lacy purple strap.

"So, it's what... Escapism?"

"No. Yes. Sort of."

I arched a brow, silently requesting that she elaborate on her vague and not at all confusing statement. Reading for fun wasn't my thing. Nope. I read because I had to. Because I needed to glean some information from something important. It was never easy. Always difficult to keep my attention, so no, I did not read for entertainment. Not unless you count audiobooks. Besides, that was what movies were for.

"*Of course I get stuck with a kid who can't fuckin' read.*"

A quick pull from my bottle wasn't enough to wash Halloway's memory away. Instead, I focused on the redhead sitting across from me. Her face lit up as she threw her hands in the air, preparing to make a grand statement I couldn't wait to hear. Why was she so fucking cute?

"Life is so short. So ridiculously short. We get only a few decades on this planet, and then we're done. Dust. Reading is my way of living as many lifetimes as I can during that time. I can rule a kingdom, die and be reborn, or fall in love, all in a few hundred pages. Books aren't just words. They're experiences. Portals to other worlds."

I puffed a laugh. What in the hell was I supposed to say to that?

"Speaking of other worlds," I said, reaching for the remote on the coffee table. "Let's do this."

The projector mounted to the ceiling whirred to life, grabbing Casey's attention. A blue square illuminated on the white wall in front of us, which was then replaced with a menu of streaming options. She laughed, toes curling a little in what I wanted to believe was excitement. It was easy to get lost in the fantasy of it. A casual night in, lounging on the sofa together. I flipped through the streaming options, wondering what to put on when I heard a contented sigh loose from beside me.

"That feels good."

Her foot. I was rubbing her foot. I hadn't realized I'd grabbed it. Not only had I grabbed it, but I'd apparently started to squeeze it. A deeper hum of pleasure met my ears as I started rubbing her arch with my thumb. Casey's lips parted on a breathy sigh. I pretended not to notice as I selected an action comedy from the 80s for us to watch. Attempting to remain casual, I tossed the remote onto the table with a clatter. Taking both her feet into my lap, I started rubbing her foot in earnest as the movie began.

"I should tell you to stop, but I don't want to," she smiled, sucking in a breath as I hit a tight spot. "Oh, harder."

A soft whine preceded a shift of her legs. The foot I wasn't massaging grazed my thigh, close enough to where things were coming to attention. Repositioning my hips to avoid certain fucking disaster, I dug into the ball of her foot. Another moan.

"Keep going."

Kill me. Take me to the roof and shoot me. Shove me over the ledge. Patting her ankle, I moved her foot away from me and took the other into my hands. The sooner I finished this study in self-sabotage, the sooner I could stop imagining very specific scenarios involving this woman's feet and the part of me that was now rock fucking hard. It had taken too much time to stop thinking about that photo she'd posted. Stop imagining taking those panties down with my teeth. Licking that heart tattooed on her hip. Alright, fine, I was still trying not to think about it. Her little noises weren't helping.

Not. One. Bit.

Two hours and several internal recitations of code fundamentals later, Casey was quietly snoring through the climax of the film. I shifted her legs off of me, standing from the sofa with a stretch. I'd seen this movie dozens of times. The bad guy kidnaps the girl. The girl gets rescued and ravished by the hero. Happily ever after. Blah, blah, blah. The room went dark when I turned off the screen. A little huff into the pillows brought my attention back to the redhead. It was late. Deciding two beers meant she was out for the night, I scooped her into my arms to carry her to bed.

Stay the fuck away from me, Clayton Wrigley.

There hadn't been anyone else since that night. I tried. Joined the apps. Deleted the apps. Met people in bars. Did all the normal things people do to meet other people. Every date went the same way. I asked the questions and pretended to listen to their answers as I tried to force the image of a perfect smile and brown doe eyes from my mind.

Every date ended the same way. A friendly hug. No text. No call. Not because I had a bad time. They were nice enough. All of them. Pretty, too. I just didn't want to waste anyone's time. Not when some small part of me knew I was a lost cause. Each one of them would have come in second to the girl I gently placed in my bed. This girl was impossible to compete with. No one should have to be a consolation prize. I was an asshole, but I wasn't that much of an asshole. Drowning in Casey was all I wanted to do. A good sailor knew better than to chase a siren. But here I was, looking up from the bottom of the ocean.

It was why I couldn't sleep on the sofa that was now steeped in her scent. It was also why I went into the office and sat down at my desk. Grateful she was sound asleep in the next room, I opened the folder of photos I'd saved from her social media. Looked at the photos again and again. Scrolled all the way back to a shot that had become a favorite. Red light. Red hair. Red lips. Black leather bustier. Head tilted back as if she was experiencing the height of desire. My hand ran over my stiffening length. The girl in the picture took her exquisite, leather-covered breasts in her meticulously manicured hands and squeezed. Pearl white teeth sank into that full lower lip, the one I'd never forgotten the taste of, as the siren got to her knees before me. Tearing my pants down, her tongue was a hot brand searing up my thigh.

"Is this what you want, Clay?"

"Yes," I groaned.

My fingers skimmed along my shaft, imagining her tongue tracing the vein underneath. My cock jerked at the image. It was always like this. Two years without anyone else's touch. Two years of needing it. Needing her. Circling my hand around the base of myself, the closest approximation to the lips I'd tasted, I gave myself a firm stroke upward. My hips began pistoning up from my chair as I stifled another groan. This was all I could do. Imagine her. Because I couldn't cross that line. Wouldn't let myself. All I had was the

Casey in my mind. In my mind, her mouth was everything. Warm. Wet. Most importantly, *mine*.

I lifted my shirt, letting the tensing muscles of my stomach take the release that suddenly flooded from me. Looking to the door I'd forgotten to close, I quieted my breathing and listened. Still nothing. Still in bed. Not kneeling between my legs. Not smirking like a cat at the way she'd made me moan. Sound asleep. Tissues. I needed tissues. Pinching the sheets between my fingers, I tugged several out of the box on my desk and cleaned myself up.

This shit needs to stop, I told myself. *You're a grown man. Not a love-sick teenager.*

I tossed the tissues into the trash at my feet, resolving to take the can out to the chute first thing in the morning. With a deep breath in, I returned my focus to the screen. The siren was still there. Still tempting. I closed the window, reminding myself that the girl in the picture and the girl in my bed were one and the same. Flawed. Human. Most importantly, not mine.

Not at all.

That would never change so long as she felt embarrassed by me. *Humiliated*. That was the word. Though she'd offered her olive branch, I'd not extended one of my own. All of the time that passed between that night and now, all of the apologies I should have said in person felt like they were cued up. Waiting to come out. So, I decided I'd start with a peace offering. My mind drifted back to our conversation on the sofa and my utterly unacceptable book collection, because when the girl who haunts your dreams tells you something, you remember every damn word. The computer whirred to life after I jiggled the mouse. I waited. Lost in thought. Blue light filled the room as the screen flicked on. I opened the browser to the last website I'd been looking at.

"Portals to other worlds."

With a few clicks, it was done.

FIFTEEN

Casey

> St. Patrick's Day in an Irish Pub where the gorgeous bartender hates your guts. Is there anything better?

On days I didn't have a meeting, I didn't quite know what to do with myself without work. I took my time in the shower. Washed and conditioned my hair. Shaved everywhere. Exfoliated. Mentally calculated how many days my car had been in the shop since I arrived at this place. After I scrolled through a few more of Clayton's old messages, I dried off and left the room smelling like three different products. I went back to the bedroom and discovered a small flat box waiting on the bed. An e-reader. A tiny pink sticky note sat attached to its center with three small words scribbled onto it.

Other worlds await.

A surprised breath puffed out of me. I couldn't believe he did this. It would have been easy to dismiss what I'd said last night. I did love to read, and doing it on my laptop just wasn't cutting it. It was strange to feel so understood by someone I'd harbored so much anger toward for the last two years. Like a cat being understood by a dog. It wasn't the oddest thing in the world, but these were two creatures who seemed destined to misunderstand each other. Yet, here he was. Wagging his tail at me. It was impossible to be angry with him. Deciding to dive into the gift, I put on my comfiest lounge set and tucked myself under the throw blanket to download every single book I'd been dying to read.

Who knew how long I was going to wind up being here, right?

The young assassin was about to start training with the captain of the guard for the king's competition when there was a knock at the door. Clayton poked his head in, glasses perched on the tip of his nose. His brows rose high with amusement when he saw the little nest of pillows I'd created for myself in the bed.

"I'm making some lunch. Macaroni and cheese. Do you want some?" He asked as his brows pumped suggestively.

"Obviously," I huffed, scooting off the bed.

The e-reader hit the pillows with a plop as I tossed it down. In those grey sweatpants and an oversized tee shirt, he looked more relaxed today. More normal. Except his shoulders tensed and his steps slowed the closer to the living room we got. He was hesitating. I realized why when I spotted more boxes on the coffee table in the living room.

"There are a few more things here for you," he rumbled, almost too low for me to hear.

On the large coffee table, the pile of boxes sat, neatly arranged the way a parent might arrange presents under a tree for Christmas morning. Each thing proudly displayed. Small on top of large. I bit back my smile, taking in every object and marveling at the thought that went into each one. Some essential oils and a diffuser for them. A pair of noise-cancelling headphones.

Another fluffy throw blanket and matching fuzzy socks. I leaned forward and picked up a bottle of eucalyptus oil, twisted it open, and greedily inhaled the crisp herbal scent.

"Why did you do all this?"

"Listen," Clayton sighed. "I know how disorienting it can be to leave your home. I just wanted you to be comfortable here."

He scrubbed a hand through his light brown hair, rubbing hard at his scalp, and looked down at his feet. Not looking at me. Turning on his bare feet, he plodded toward the kitchen. I wondered how many times he had come home only to leave again. He'd been in the military for almost a decade. Now he was what, a mercenary? A hacker? I still didn't quite understand his job, though calling what he did a 'job' also felt like an understatement.

Following him to the kitchen, I perched on the countertop to watch him. He filled a pot with water and broke out a box of white cheddar macaroni. I stifled the urge to tell him it was my favorite. Long tattooed arms flexed as he carried the water to the stove. Veins trailed up beneath the tattoos. Why were veins on a man so incredibly hot? Especially the way they crawled up his forearms, swooping through the patchwork tattoos like vines climbing a marble statue.

Get ahold of yourself, girl, I winced. *This is just pent-up sexual energy. That's all.* Clayton angled his head at me. Those slutty little glasses were doing something to me, too. Had he said something? Or, no. Shit. *Shit.* Shit! Did I say any of that out loud?

"What?" I spluttered.

"I said I need to talk to you about something. I mean, I have something I need to say."

Any lingering feelings of interest extinguished with a cold splash of anticipation. *I knew.* I knew exactly what he wanted to talk about. I wasn't interested in having that conversation. Not at all. I would have told him as much if he hadn't beaten me to the punch.

"I'm sorry," he said, focusing his attention and those gold glasses on me. "I'm sorry about what happened. Between you and me. I would never want to embarrass you." The room started spinning. Worried I was about to tip over, my hands reflexively curled around the edge of the counter. No, I did not want to have this conversation. Clayton continued, the box of noodles clattering and splashing into the boiling water. "I just wasn't sure how to move forward with you. To do what was best for you."

"Clayton," I hesitated, my skin tightening with the urge to change the subject. Reliving that night after we were barely regaining our footing felt like a really bad idea. "It's fine. Really."

"Let me finish," he urged, running his hands through his hair again. A few swift steps and he was right in front of me. Eye to eye. His hands bracketed my own. "I wanted to stop because I was scared. If we went too far before you were ready, I was afraid of how you'd look at me. But you were right, too. It wasn't up for me to decide."

The air went taut between us. Clayton waited for my response. For the acceptance of his apology. I could taste the words on my tongue. That I understood now. That deep down, I knew I hadn't been ready to be with anyone in that way. After two years of trying and failing even on my own, I knew it would have been a mistake to sleep with him. But he was an easy target. Someone I could throw all my anger at without having to worry about being wrong.

I'd been sitting on that for a couple of weeks now, I guess. I was just right enough to get away with my bad behavior. My lips parted with unspoken words when a hiss snapped us from the conversation.

"Shit," Clayton muttered, rushing to turn the heat down as water boiled over in the pot.

Without his eyes on me, summoning the right words felt easier. Maybe it made me a coward, but it was the only way I could say what I wanted to. Even if my admissions were just bite-sized portions of the truth.

"You were right, too," I offered. "It wasn't fair for me to take my anger out on you. You were just in the wrong place at the wrong time."

"Just a casualty, huh?"

He stirred the pot, adding the other ingredients without looking up at me. A casualty. A bystander. Someone who took shit from me for two years, even though he probably didn't deserve it. An infinitesimal part of my ego refused to take the thread of this conversation that far, but I glanced at the stack of goods on the coffee table. Thought about how welcome he'd been trying to make me in his home from the start. For all the anger I still had, it was hard to lob any more at him.

"Yeah, kind of."

Things went quiet in the kitchen. Clayton scooped noodles into two bowls and retreated to the refrigerator to grab the pitcher of water from inside. He poured two glasses, handing me one and returning the pitcher to its home. I sipped, watching him. Strange. It was so strange to feel so at ease with him here when the conversation felt unfinished. Too many little things to explain. Things I needed to work on. Things that made me wonder if I'd ever be able to let my guard down with anyone again.

That worry fed into the rising tide of anguish inside me. The part that still felt everything. The part that wanted to undo it all so I could go back to feeling normal. The part of me that worried I'd always feel the residue of what had happened. A heavy sigh pushed out of me as I attempted to loosen that feeling from my gut. Clayton looked over the top of his glasses at me as he ate from his bowl, leaning against the counter across from me. The slightest smirk lifted at the corners of his lips.

"What," I deadpanned, stuffing more noodles into my mouth.

"Eat up. We're going on a field trip."

My hands squeezed together where they were joined at his waist as he zipped through traffic. He hadn't told me where we were going, so I let my mind wander. The bike. It was like desensitization therapy in a way. It helped me get used to the feeling of someone's body pressed up against mine. As he pulled into a parking lot in the middle of some industrial office area, I wondered if I would ever get used to the fact that it was him I was pressed up against.

Clayton killed the engine and pivoted in his seat. He reached out and flipped up the visor of my helmet, his helmet, and smiled at me. When I gave him an expectant look, a *you haven't explained what we're doing* look, he held out his gloved hand.

"One last surprise."

It seemed like an unimpressive old building. A single-story painted stone structure with a small sign over the entry that said Smash Lab in big bold black letters. My feet came to a stop behind Clayton, who was halfway through the open door. He gave my hand a small tug and pulled me inside.

Old televisions. Vases and delicate wine glasses. Long tubes of lighting. Fax machines. A printer. Even an old computer or two. I scanned the room, pulling up the zipper of my coveralls as best I could with the thick gloves covering my fingers. Clayton walked into the room behind me, pulling the thick leather gloves the employee had given us over his hands. They'd made it very clear. We could do whatever we wanted in here, so long as we were wearing our protective gear. I'd even tucked my braided hair into the covering to keep it safe. Covered from head to toe, it was difficult not to feel like a welder or something.

"So, I just smash? Like the Hulk?"

A short nod was my answer. My fingers curled around the crowbar. The whole point of this room was to get angry. To let out every bad feeling you have as you destroyed useless property. Smash it to smithereens. I understood the appeal, really. Except I hated that feeling. That anger. When I felt angry, I remembered all of it. It rushed at my thoughts and coated them in oil until

I was drowning in it. Once it was there, it was so hard to wash away. Flexing my grip on the iron, I took a breath.

Angry. Just get angry.

"Holding in anger is a lot like holding in a fart. It's coming out one way or another. Better to choose your moment."

"You have a lot of experience with this?"

"More experience every day. Go on," Clayton said behind his protective face covering. "Let it out."

When I hesitated, he picked up the baseball bat he'd chosen and gave it a showy little flip like he was a professional stepping up to the plate. He positioned himself in front of a green glass vase perched on an old table, hoisting the bat up.

"Stepping up to bat for the Chicago Cubs, it's Clayton Wrigley!" Green glass exploded as the bat connected with the vase in a loud crack. Its pieces tinkled down to the stone floor. I jolted, a laugh of disbelief rupturing from me. Clayton turned on his feet, grinning from ear to ear. "Come on, beautiful. Give it a shot."

He picked up one of the lighting tubes scattered around the room, extending it to me. Alright. Easy. I could smash a lightbulb.

Before I knew it, we were laughing. Both of us were laughing as we went hard at an old printer. Beating it as it clattered apart. When that was destroyed, Clayton turned away to go after an old box television set. I pivoted, looking around for something to let loose on.

Red.

The doll stared up at me. Big eyes with long lashes. Red curls. Porcelain. She was so breakable. So defenseless. What was she even doing here? How did she end up in a place like this? She deserved to be broken. Iron crushed through pale white skin, collapsing under the weight of my strike. Again and again. More and more. Eyes became dust. Hair clung to the bar's curved end. Loud clanging filled my ears, barely able to cut through the sound of my screams. The ground. I knew I'd hit the ground, but I couldn't stop. Didn't want to stop.

I hurled the crowbar into the wall with a throat-ravaging scream, splintering the protective plywood that covered it. Breathe. I needed to breathe. I commanded myself to breathe, stacking my hands on top of my head as I rushed in one breath after another.

"Whoa, hey, hey, hey." Clayton took my hands in one of his, the pair of them fluttering behind his long fingers like birds in a cage. His free hand lifted my face covering off my head, the rush of air doing nothing to calm me. Only cold where wet streamed down my face. "You're alright," he soothed. "You did so good, Casey."

Where before I'd been gulping down air, I stopped and focused. Box breathing. I could do that. Inhale for four seconds. Hold for four seconds. Exhale for four seconds. Again. Again. Again, until I could feel the tips of my fingers. Clayton's head angled to one side, taking off his face shield to observe me. We sat there, watching each other in the room we had torn apart. My breathing evened out. My hands stopped shaking.

"It's not your fault."

I wasn't sure why he said it. It was so soft. I wasn't sure why I said what rolled off my tongue before I could stop it.

"Sometimes I think I died in that desert."

I'd said it so quietly, I wouldn't have thought he heard me if his face hadn't gone slack. A sigh that sounded a lot like my name rushed through his lips. The large hand holding mine gave them a squeeze. A dark brow arched in question. I knew. Without another word passing between us, I knew what he was asking. A small dip of the chin was all the permission he needed. Clayton scooted closer, long arms circling around me. I let my head fall to his shoulder, feeling the dampness of my cheek stick to the column of his neck.

"Clay?" I sniffled. He let out a low hum in response. "I'm really glad that you're my friend."

SIXTEEN

CASEY

> Sometimes I wish I had torn them apart. Especially when I think about that look on your face.

The rage room was a good idea. A great idea, really. Except it felt like I had opened a door to all the things I didn't want to feel. Uncomfortable. Scratching me from the inside. The rest of the night had been quiet. Clayton made dinner. Chicken soup. We watched another movie. *Set It Up*, my choice this time. I went to bed with my e-reader and tried to take my mind off things, eventually getting tired enough to fall asleep in the middle of the final duel between the assassin and the dark warrior.

Expressing that anger, even just for an hour, helped me to see myself a little more clearly. Swinging, breaking, screaming. It brought down part of the wall. Bit by bit. When I woke up this morning, I made a decision. Riding over to the community center on the back of Clayton's bike only solidified it.

Nothing was going to get better if I didn't try.

Moving forward with Clayton felt like a step in the right direction. His friendship was strangely comforting. We'd fallen into it so effortlessly that it was easy to forget that things between us had ever been rotten. The fact that he was lending me his support was an unexpected benefit. If we stopped letting what happened define our relationship, then maybe I could stop letting what happened define me.

Getting started was an entirely different problem. I'd walked into the room with all of the confidence I'd mustered on the back of Clayton's bike, bristling with purpose. As soon as I started speaking, the bravado dried up faster than I could get the damned words out.

"Uh, anyway," I tried.

The coffee machine spluttered. They were all just staring at me, patiently waiting for me to continue. I didn't know how to talk about what happened without inviting people into the parts of my life I had to keep hidden. The family. The violence. It was all attached with little threads, a giant tapestry of pain and brutality. Blood and politics. Why did my soft green turtleneck, which I normally loved, feel like it was trying to strangle me now?

"A couple of years ago," I started again. "I was abducted. There was this party. I thought I had too much to drink, but I guess someone drugged me. When I woke up, I was somewhere else."

The yellowed linoleum stared back at me as I tried to summon the next bit. The part that drove me from sleep. Because the first jolt of it, my new reality, had been the part I thought of most. My dress was pushed up to my waist. The top tugged down. I was sore. Sore in a way that informed me of what had happened while I was unconscious. It was still happening when I'd come to. Rough hands held my arms down as I tried to jolt upright, two men working together to make sure they'd both had their fun.

The men hired to guard the trailer in the desert were not kind. They were plain, in their way, but their cruelty made them ugly. The first instances had been rough, but they'd used protection. I remembered hearing one of them imply that I would give them an STI. Or that the last thing they needed was to spoil one of us. It was a small mercy. The girls who fought them off didn't last long. They were taken away. Or they were drugged into unconsciousness. Or worse.

So I didn't fight. Let them do what they want. I noticed that they kept me around longer, surely because I'd attempted to accommodate them. Because whatever came next, that container I'd seen through a crack in the window, it couldn't have been better than that dust-covered nightmare.

"There were two of them. They both," I croaked, my throat aching from the stone that seemed to lodge itself inside.

Someone stifled a sniff. I looked up from the floor to see that a few of the faces had gone distant, likely reliving their own history. I was guilty of the same thing when a few spoke of their past. The things that brought them here. When my gaze fell on Lisa, I saw her already watching me. Her fine boned face was plain, calm, and open as she waited a few beats for me to continue. At the small shake of my head, she nodded.

"Thank you, Casey," was all that she said, and moved the meeting forward.

Clayton was waiting for me on his Triumph Bonneville, one shoe propped up on the foot peg. Still looking at his phone, I took the opportunity to drink him in. Worn-in jeans. Lace-up black boots. A white t-shirt with a faded black cat logo that I couldn't make out. One tattooed arm resting on his handlebars to complete the image of a casual rebel, scruffy stubble and all.

It was the kind of sight that made me wish I still had my camera. Caramel eyes peered at me through strands of hair as they blew in the cool morning breeze. His eyebrows raised a little, noting that I must have been standing in front of the building for a minute if there were so few people departing now.

"Hey," he smiled warily. "Ready to go?"

I nodded and clomped down the cement steps in my little heeled boots. I'd done that. Put that hesitation there. We'd turned the page or a new leaf or however that saying goes, but that didn't mean things were always easy between us. There was still this odd tension sometimes. It was there when

Clayton stood from his bike, taking his jacket off where it had been draped over the chestnut leather seat to hold it open for me. Bunching the sleeves of my sweater around my wrists, I twisted to push my arms inside. That citrus and sage scent enveloped me as the arms and shoulders were set into place. I zipped the front and turned toward him, not realizing how close we'd been standing. He let out a sound halfway between a grunt and a chuckle, picking up the helmet to place on my head.

"Two things," Clayton announced, his voice gaining the more playful quality I'd come to know. "First, we need to get breakfast because I caught a whiff of something maple or bacon a minute ago and now I'm starving."

"Uh-huh," I smirked, pulling my hair out of the jacket and securing the clip of the helmet under my chin. "And the second thing?"

"We need to get you your own helmet. This one is too big for you and kind of makes you look like one of those Funko dolls."

A laugh burst from me. Clayton's smile was as bright as the sun peaking over the hills while he patted the leather seat and threw one leg over the bike. The ignition roared in the now mostly empty parking lot. Muscles flickered up his arms as he moved into position, shifting his legs so the bike was upright. My jeans were pale and soft compared to Clayton's as my legs bracketed his. Threading my arms around his waist, I leaned into his warmth and closed my eyes with the promise of breakfast and the rumble of the motorcycle driving away the lingering shadows in my mind.

Almost.

Screaming. I must have been screaming because my throat was raw as I tried to get words over dry lips. A sheen of sweat coated my body, but I was trembling as I looked around the darkened bedroom. A bedroom. Not a trailer. Too fast. My heart was beating too fast. Pressing its raging rhythm against my ribcage, making my chest feel too small. Far too small.

"I'm right here. I'm here."

A warm hand smoothed my hair away from my face, bringing me out of the dark hole I'd been in only moments ago. I took in his features, gradually coming back into my body with each one. Caramel eyes. A sharp jaw. Tattooed arms. Light brown hair falling into his eyes.

"Casey?" Clayton's voice was husky with sleep. "Are you awake?"

"Yeah."

Nodding shallowly, I pulled my legs up as I came to sit and wrapped my arms around myself. Clayton was perched on the edge of the bed, sitting up a little straighter to give me space. Another shiver wracked my body.

"Does that happen a lot?"

The question was careful. Not judgmental, just considerate. As though he was not trying to offer advice, just trying to understand. I shrugged.

"Not so much anymore. Just when I," I paused, trying to find a way to explain without explaining. If giving the barest details of what had happened triggered this, then I wanted to stay away from the subject, at least until morning. I glanced at the clock on the nightstand. A little before two. Based on the black boxer briefs and the disheveled hair, I'd say he'd run in here from the sofa. "I shared in group today, and I guess it brought up some stuff."

Clayton stood up and braced his hands on his hips, looking around the room as if it would offer him a solution for how to deal with me. Deciding I'd shared enough, I tried to steady my breathing with the same method that helped to calm me in the rage room. I took a breath in through my nose and counted to four. Held it for four. While I was holding my breath, Clayton walked out of the room. I continued with an exhale for four more counts. By the time I was holding my breath again, he'd returned with a glass of water and set it on the nightstand. My exhale seemed to be the dismissal he was looking for because he turned to go back to the living room.

"Stay," I rasped. "Please."

For a moment, I thought he wouldn't do it. That he would tell me to go back to sleep and leave. He just stood there. Even though it was dark, I could feel him watching me. Then he motioned for me to scoot over. I did. He reached for one of the pillows I'd cocooned myself with and righted it before reclining in the soft sheets, propping one arm beneath his head. I adjusted a pillow and lay on my side, looking at the man lying beside me, limned in the glow of the streetlight filtering in through the sheer window shades.

"I'm sorry I woke you," I whispered, as if there was someone else in this loft I might wake.

"Don't apologize, Casey," he said with a tired sigh. "Not for this."

Unsure of why I did it, I reached for the hand resting on the bed between us and took it in my own. Long fingers twined with mine. Neither of us said anything else. We just lay there in the dark, the warmth of his skin giving me something else to think about. Trying on motorcycle helmets. The sparkly pink one Clayton bought me because he said it made my head look like a disco ball. Blueberry pancakes drowning in butter and rich maple syrup in a cafe down the street from the loft. Comfortable silences like the one that was happening now. With him.

SEVENTEEN

CLAYTON

One word. A sob. Over and over.

"*Stop.*"

If I could kill them again, I would. By now, I'd killed them a hundred times over in my mind. The way she was tangled in the sheets from twisting and fighting invisible attackers. Her screams were reverberating in my mind. The fear in her eyes as she woke. The way her breathing hitched. I wasn't sure I could take that look on her face. That look that was filled with fear and embarrassment, like her natural reaction to one of the worst things that could happen to a person was somehow her fault.

It was a feeling I knew well. It wasn't until she fell asleep again that my pulse normalized. *Stop.* That word. I'd said that word. Begged that word. The other boys, the ones in the home who picked on me because they'd determined I was the lowest on the food chain, mocked me with it. The last person to shelter me. Halloway. He hadn't cared either. *Stop.*

It didn't save me. It hadn't saved her.

There was nothing else to think about as I lay in bed beside her, the sound of my heart still pounding in my ears after jolting awake to the sound of her muffled cries in the middle of the night. I'd grabbed a gun and sprinted into the bedroom only to find that there was no one there. No one but her and the demons chasing her from sleep. She wasn't even awake. Once I realized she'd been having a night terror, I put the safety back on and set the weapon aside.

Knowing that waking someone during a night terror was a bad idea, thanks to all of the fucked-up situations I'd been around, all I could do was wait. Her plea alternated between screams and garbled sobs of protest. I wasn't sure I'd even taken a breath until her eyes opened to look at me. As I poured boiling water over the coffee grounds, I considered what she'd said. She'd shared in her group. I knew that sharing experiences like that, the kind that leave a mark on you, was sometimes as difficult as living the experience for the first time. They could be a tripwire for things like nightmares. My hand flexed around a trapped bit of memory.

"Get up! Be a man and fight back."

Yeah, the things that get stuck inside us have a way of screwing you up forever. Even with years and years of therapy. I should know.

"How long have you been awake?"

Casey emerged from the bedroom, padding toward the kitchen with an oversized grey hoodie thrown over herself. My hoodie. Deep red hair bobbed in a messy bun as long, shapely legs made their way toward me. Friends, I reminded myself. We were friends. Last night was just one friend consoling another friend. Holding the hand of that friend. Hoping that my friend got back to sleep without any nightmares, while the other friend lay awake imagining killing the men who hurt his friend with his bare hands. In a platonic way. Friends did that.

Friends definitely did not wonder what it would have felt like to roll over and spoon.

"Not long," I coughed. "Coffee?"

The mass of red hair bobbed with her enthusiastic nod. Shrugging up her shoulders, she sat on the stool with a yawn. I continued pouring over the grinds, eying her from under my brows. Attempting to remain friendly, I pushed my glasses up with a knuckle as I asked, "How did you sleep?"

Breath whooshed out of her pursed lips. Tiny bubbles fizzled and popped in the coffee grounds, filling the silence between us. We fell asleep holding hands. I could still feel the soft skin of her hand under my thumb. It had still been there when I woke this morning. Long red waves splashed over soft white cotton. The freckles scattered over the bridge of her nose were somehow softer in the morning. Full pink lips parted on deep, even breaths.

"Good," Casey looked to the sofa, considering. I knew what she was going to say before she said it. "You don't have to sleep there if you don't want to."

I pulled the steel filter out of the pour-over carafe and threw out the coffee grounds, then grabbed a pair of mugs. She watched me expectantly. Cream and sugar in her coffee, I slid the steaming beverage toward her. Casey wrapped both hands around the stoneware cup and sighed.

"You're not going to make this easy on me, are you?" The apples of her cheeks went pink as she puffed out a breath of frustration. I sipped from my cup. Deflated, she huffed and sat back on the stool. Looking at the sofa again, she flinched. Fucking flinched. It was impossible not to kick myself for it. The memory we shared. We may have been okay, but we were not really okay, were we? I'd made her walk out that door. Made her second-guess herself when she had every right to walk all over every man in the city. "Fine. Never mind."

Thank freaking god.

Waking up next to her felt good. Too good. Noticing her hand still holding mine hours after she had taken it felt even better. I wasn't sure what to call it exactly. It wasn't serious. Kids hold hands. It had been an effort to leave her. It would have been more dangerous to stay. That didn't mean things were fixed between us, and I wasn't going to climb into bed with her now just to end up on the sofa again. I wouldn't have thought anything of it at all if it hadn't felt like a door opening.

EIGHTEEN

Casey

Two meetings a week meant that I had Friday through Monday to think about the small amount of progress I'd made. That's what Lisa called it. Progress. It felt like I couldn't escape that word. Waking up covered in sweat didn't feel like progress. Holding Clayton's hand all night. That could be something. As I showered this morning, I considered the small intimacy of it. His hand in mine. The way his thumb brushed my knuckles in small sweeps of quiet reassurance. I'd needed that soothing stroke to dull the edge of my anxiety. Without it, I wouldn't have slept as peacefully as I did. But that's all it was.

Reassurance.

Upon emerging from the bedroom, fully dressed and ready to meet the day, I realized I was alone. There was no clacking of a keyboard coming from his office. None coming from the living room either. Ignoring the fact that I'd noticed the absence of his energy before I'd confirmed it with the lack of noise, I returned to the kitchen and got a text that told me where Clayton had gone.

> Across the hall.

Rhythmic packing sounds slapped through the hallway. I knew he had the whole floor, but it hadn't occurred to me to look for another space. Sunlight poured into the hallway through the open door on the other side of the large elevator. The sounds I'd heard were now accompanied by sharp breaths and grunts. This was where he'd gone. Squinting, I slid through the gap in the doorway. The space was half-garage, half gym. It was here that I found Clayton, clad only in black compression shorts that stretched over his thickly muscled thighs. Sweat covered his body as he punched and kicked a beat-up brown leather punching bag that hung from a chain looped onto an exposed steel beam overhead. His movements were bladelike. Sharp. Precise. Deadly. Each strike caused the bag to swing as if attacking him, displaying his agility with every dodging movement.

Bright sunlight beamed in through the large arched windows that lined the gym side of the space. Light always seemed to find him. It bounced off his hair. Gleamed with his sweat. Clayton's body was lean and long. Tight muscle was packed onto every inch, suggesting that he'd continued whatever military training he'd received. This sort of training, I guess. I'd avoided actually looking at him when he wasn't fully dressed. Appreciating him seemed like a terrible idea. Tattoos covered the length of his arms all the way down to a few of his fingers, but most of his leanly muscled torso remained bare. I maintained my distance from him, keeping away from the rack of weights and bags that peppered his immediate vicinity.

The other side of the space was lined with large black tool chests, a rolling stool, and half a dozen old flags and posters with various motorcycle iconography on them. A black-framed picture of what looked like a rusted husk of a motorcycle in the middle of a junkyard hung on the wall to the left of me. The concrete floor was covered with black rubber, muffling my steps, clearly intended to protect it from whatever might drop or leak from the three motorcycles sitting there. There was the Triumph, his daily driver. There was also the Harley Davidson I'd already seen, a black bike that he'd told me he'd experimentally modified for stealthier operations. Honestly, it looked less like a Harley and more like a bike built for Batman.

Then there was the other bike, if you could call it that, with so much missing from its frame. It was clearly a different sort of vehicle. Sitting on a rack with no wheels, it looked old. Really old compared to the sleek black vision sitting next to it.

"Did you need something?"

My head jerked toward the windows. I hadn't noticed that he'd stopped. One wrapped hand was holding the punching bag as he huffed. Clayton sniffed through the drops of sweat that rolled down his face and matted his hair.

"No. I'm sorry. I didn't mean to bother you."

"What did I tell you about apologizing to me?" His question was puffed and breathless as his chest heaved with effort. Clayton smiled, wiping sweat away from his eyes with his forearm. He approached the weights lined up in front of the windows, tugging the towel he'd draped over them free to wipe at his face. The towel flopped into a black crate filled with other towels when he was through. Unwrapping his hands, Clayton stuffed his feet into a pair of black boots. Gesturing toward the bike sitting on the rack with a jerk of his chin, he said, "It's a 1975 Honda CB400F."

I folded my arms over the cropped white tee I wore, feeling more exposed as his gaze raked over the bare plane of my stomach peeking over the waist of my jeans. Shoes. I should be wearing shoes. Angling my head, I shifted my focus to the bike as he placed himself on the other side.

"A café racer," he continued, as if that somehow explained the state of it.

"What does that mean?"

Clayton pushed the tool cart aside to get closer to the bike. For a minute, he just stood there and considered it. Considered the bike. Consider how to answer me, maybe. Anxiety trickled through me as it occurred to me that I might have asked a stupid question. He placed his hands on his hips, something I noticed he did when he was making a decision. Clearing his throat, he turned his attention to me again.

"A café racer is a lightweight motorcycle built for speed and agility. It's made to be minimalist in design—something to race between coffee shops. They were popular in the 1960s as part of a whole counterculture movement."

It was a pretty bike. Or at least, it would be when he fixed it. Quilted russet leather covered the seat. Chrome parts shone in the midday sunlight, bright with care.

"Did you do all this?"

Clayton nodded.

"I got it off of a scrap lot for almost nothing, and the engine needed a complete overhaul. It'll be a while before I can get it running again."

A breath whooshed from me as I looked at the framed photo again. That rusted out husk. That bike. It had the same lines. Same hardware. It looked as if it had been through hell. I shook my head in disbelief. It must have taken ages to get it to this point.

"How long have you had it?"

"About two years."

His answer was quiet, an admission somehow. Silence settled between us, thickening the air. Two years of working for my father. Two years since we'd met. Two years since I'd told him to stay away from me. He'd been working on fixing this bike, and I'd barely begun working on myself. Ignoring the howling ache opening in my center at the thought of so much time passing, I examined the motorcycle.

Without knowing much about bikes, it was easy to see that things were missing. Parts reached out to other parts only to be met with vacant space. The waist-high tool chest had a red rag laid over the top of it, some smaller pieces I couldn't identify looked like they'd been recently cleaned. Rebuilding a motorcycle looked a lot like surgery. Putting something together like this took patience. A staggering amount of it. I wasn't sure I had enough to rebuild myself, let alone something as complex as this seemed to be. I ran a finger along the bike's bare handlebar.

"That's a long time to wait."

Clayton shrugged as he looked up at me through lowered brows, damp hair falling into his eyes before shifting his focus to the skeletal motorcycle between us. Air came to him more easily now, his chest rising and falling with a thoughtful breath.

"Someday she'll be whole again," he said, one hand coming to rest on the aqua and white striped fuel tank. "I can wait. Until then, I just have to wade through the shit."

NINETEEN

Clayton

I reloaded the clip. Reset the target. Then that target became every man who ever hurt her. Every man who touched her without her permission. Took that from her. I had known. Of course, I knew. But knowing that something happened to someone you cared about was entirely different from seeing its effects on them.

The large cement space was directly above my loft and garage at the top of the building. Several feet of concrete lined the opposite wall, making a sufficient enough bullet trap.

"I get the idea."

I'd almost forgotten she was here. Leaning up against the makeshift counter I'd created, Casey worked on piling her hair atop her head into one of those messy knots I was becoming deeply fond of. Resecuring the safety on the pistol, I set it down in front of me and pivoted toward her. The cropped sage green tee lifted with her movements, showing off her toned stomach and that little freckle below her navel. The whole thing was doing something unnerving to my insides.

After spending our Saturday morning making pancakes, blueberry seemed to be her favorite, then pretending not to watch her go through her yoga routine while I banged out half-decent code on my laptop, I'd suggested we come up here for target practice. The truth was that after spending the better part of yesterday beating the hell out of my punching bag, I still needed to blow off some steam.

I clapped a pair of protective ear coverings onto her and dropped a pair of protective glasses into her hand. The scent of maple syrup seemed to still cling to her this close, forcing me to wonder if there was any trace of it on her full lips. *No. That's the kind of thinking that gets you burned to death by her father.*

"Alright, you're going to hold it like this," I said, reaching out for the pistol.

"You don't need to show me how to fire a gun, Clay," she deadpanned. "Watch me."

As if I could ever not watch you.

My feet shuffled back, giving Casey the room she needed. She hoisted the gun and got into a decent weaver stance, angling her head as she squinted one eye shut. Red strands fell out of her bun with the movement. Cracks loud enough to penetrate the protective padding around our ears popped in quick succession. One, two, three. When she was finished, she rearmed the safety, then set the gun down on the bar top and turned on a heel. Her hands went to her hips, dragging the waist of her jeans down enough to offer a peek of the pale yellow lace she wore underneath.

"I think I'm good."

Giving her my best attempt at a cool glance, I walked to the crank and pulled her target toward the bar. Casey's hands went to her hair, removing the tie from the deep red strands. Her fingers combed through it as she shook it out, the mass tumbling down to her waist in a copper tidal wave. A whiff of amber and smoky incense rushed in my direction, forcing me to curse inwardly. As if the sight of her handling the gun wasn't enough to set my blood on fire.

"Yeah," I choked out. "Yeah, you're good."

She was. Really goddamned good. I lifted the target to examine more closely. All of her shots hit center mass. While the grouping wasn't exactly expert, she was no novice. I peered over the top of the sheet, locking eyes with her. She arched a brow, likely expecting some bullshit criticism about her handywork. Instead, I lay the sheet down on the bar and propped my hip against it.

"Alright, so you don't need any help from me to kill a man. Why don't you carry a weapon?"

"Who says I don't?"

I gave her the look that question deserved. I knew she didn't. Even if I hadn't gone looking through her things looking for any type of tracking device, I would have known that much from the gentle defensiveness in her voice. Her shoulders slumped a little as she released a defeated sigh.

"Fine," she huffed with a roll of her eyes. "I don't. But just because I know how to use one doesn't mean I want one. I don't want that kind of power at my disposal."

"Because you're afraid you'll use it?"

"Because I'm afraid it'll change me." Casey stuffed her hands into the pockets of her jeans, leaning against the bar beside me. Big brown eyes peered into mine as she went on. "Killian insisted I learn how to use one after I moved into my father's house. He actually gave one to me, but I didn't accept it. I couldn't. When he was teaching me, I could feel how much I wanted to hurt them. To hurt anyone who would do something like," Casey stopped, her voice catching on the last word. My chest ached at the tears that flooded her eyes, but I didn't reach out. Didn't try to comfort her. Simply waited for her to go on. In a blink, the tears were barely noticeable. "Every time I pulled that trigger, I could feel all of this rage surging in me. Rising to meet it. And

I know being angry is normal, or whatever, but I didn't want them to take something else away from me."

Casey sniffed, looking away to wipe at her eyes with the flick of her hand. Plastering a bright smile on her face, she looked at me.

"I don't know if that makes any sense at all."

If there was a man in this world who could stand to see this girl cry, it sure as hell wasn't me. Knowing the reason made it so much worse. Knowing I had been the reason at one time had been devastating. It still was. But that devastation was erased a little as my hand lifted to cup her jaw. She let out a soft laugh as I hoisted my t-shirt up to dry her tears. Big brown doe eyes stared up at me. Eyes that had looked at me with such hatred now looked to me for solace. Casey made up her mind about staying away from me. She'd looked to me for comfort from a nightmare. She looked to me for comfort from an ex-boyfriend. She looked to me for comfort now.

The heels of her boots ground into the concrete floor as she took one last step to bring her body flush with mine. It would have been easy to get lost in the feel of it. Her lush figure pressed up against me was something I craved. Except this wasn't about that. I knew that as I circled my arms around her, one firmly holding her waist as the other moved to cradle her head against my chest. Whether or not I'd ever get the chance to be with this woman again, I wanted to be the one to soothe her aching heart. To make the things that caused her pain seem like distant objects. I breathed her in as I sorted out what to say.

"More than you know," I assured. "Believe me."

Casey lifted her head to look me in the eye, teeth sinking into that lower lip as she smirked grimly at me. Yes, I knew exactly what she'd meant. Killing people changed you. It left a mark on your soul. It didn't matter if you were on the perceived side of right or if you were defending yourself from an attack. Arguments could be made for every death, and I'd heard plenty of them. That didn't erase seeing the light disappear from someone's eyes because of a bullet you put in them. It didn't erase the part of your brain that recoiled at the sight of it. Like a caged beast that consumes human flesh for the first time, there was no getting rid of that instinct once you got a taste.

"Alright. No shooting lesson today, then," I huffed as I gave her another squeeze and gave her back a friendly pat, clearing the lump from my throat. "Want to go for a ride?"

TWENTY

CLAYTON

The night she walked out on me started a lot like this one. Only tonight, we'd ridden out to the little seafood shack along the highway instead of that pizza counter. The one that overlooked the ocean. I was still thinking about the way the setting sun lit her hair. Wine and copper flowing down around her. It lit up her cheeks. Seated across from her at that table, all I wanted to do was brush the hair out of her eyes because it seemed like whisps of it were always falling into them. Except brushing the hair out of her eyes would be just the start. Her cheek would graze my palm. Eyelashes would brush my skin. She'd smile at me. And it would take everything in me not to kiss her.

Friends don't kiss.

The ocean crashed against the rocks alongside the highway. Booming and rushing waves filled the air as we soared down the highway. Back to my place. Back to reality. That reality had nothing to do with those kinds of thoughts. Casey's hold around me was tight, but less panicked than it had been when we'd started out. Every time we mounted my bike, it was like I could feel her start to trust me.

Little by little.

Casey ran into the bedroom and remerged bristling with excitement. She plopped onto the sofa with her e-reader, excitedly opening the case.

"I didn't realize my company was so uninteresting," I deadpanned.

"You don't understand. The lost queen has just returned to the conquered kingdom to free her friends. I have to know what happens next."

"There's no prince to do the rescuing?"

"She's rescuing the prince. But they're just friends."

Just friends. I let out a grunt of understanding and made some half-assed excuse about needing to work. The Kremnik files got picked through by Gizmo. A few monetary issues popped up. A distillery belonging to his son that was never claimed after the boy's death. Some ownership changes around a warehouse. I sent the details over to Killian, who promptly responded.

> We'll get eyes on it.

Everything felt normal until it was time to get ready for bed. Sofa. I was sleeping on the sofa. I entered the bedroom to grab my pillow and resume my vigil, the redhead lying on her belly with the e-reader propped up against the headboard. Casey's hand snapped out to grab my wrist.

"What are you doing?"

"Going back to the sofa," I grunted and used my free hand to grab the pillow. Casey rolled onto her side to look at me. "Go ahead and get back to your book."

"I started the next one already. Please don't go back to the sofa."

"We shouldn't sleep together, Casey."

"Why?"

Because I'm trying to hold onto some parts of myself, I thought. Sharing this loft with her was one thing. Sharing a bed with her was dangerously close to that fantasy that teased the edges of my thoughts. Spending time with her.

Curling up with her. Soothing her at the end of a hard day by feeding my fingers through her long, red hair. My hand flexed at my side as I released a sigh.

"Because we are just friends. Because your father would murder me, pretty brutally, if he found out I tried anything with you. Because you," I trailed off. *Because you look too fucking tempting in those flimsy little scraps of fabric you generously call pajamas.*

"We're both adults, Clayton. We can share a bed. It's a really big bed. Too big for just me," she smirked, blinking those big eyes at me. "Besides, I trust you."

I trust you.

A sigh of defeat huffed through my nose. The pillow bounced onto the bed as I tossed it back down. Casey made a little noise I chose to interpret as excitement when she shuffled over to make room for me. I climbed into bed beside her, hoping she'd keep her hands to herself. Praying that I could do the same.

One more night. I could make it one more night. Tomorrow she'll have her surprises. Someone else would take my place, and she would forget about me. Stop needing me. I couldn't help myself when she needed me.

"Clay," Casey sighed, rolling to face me. "What's it like to kill someone?"

"Why are you thinking about that?" I chuckled, propping my head up with my pillow. Casey shuffled toward me, resting her chin on her stacked hands.

"I don't know. My brother says it's like putting out a cigarette. Nothing. It doesn't seem like it bothers him. But he's not like you."

"No? What do I seem like?"

"Good," she yawned, letting her head come to rest on my bicep. "You care about people."

A slow blink. Then another. No. Oh no. She was starting to fall asleep. Those doe eyes got more glassy with every passing second, softening around the corners with a sleepy smile. I felt my mouth tug up at the corners. It was impossible to ignore her smiles. Even the sleepy ones.

"Goodnight, Casey."

"Goodnight."

Casey heaved a contented sigh and closed her eyes. I stretched, trying not to disturb her as I reached over to turn the light off. Once the room was dark, I could bear it a little more. Lying here beside her. She was just on my arm. That was all. In the dark, it could be anyone. Friends shared beds. Sure. It wasn't a big deal. The fact that the girl I'd been torturing myself over for the last two years was sleeping on my arm was not a big deal. It wasn't.

We were just friends.

In the dark, it was just us. Her. Me. Two people in one bed. It was fine. It was fine until a small hand came to rest on my chest. Fine. This was fine. She was my friend. My friend who I slept with. The friend who smelled incredible. Whose hand lifted and fell with every breath I took. Friends. Friends' hearts didn't race from this. I blew out a shaky breath. Friends.

Friends.

TWENTY-ONE

CASEY

Roses. Peonies. Pale pink. Magenta. Fuchsia. It was the scent that woke me first. Lush, floral air. The scent was heavy in a way that could only come from the real thing. Bouquets and arrangements were everywhere. Some were wrapped in brown paper with pink ribbons. Others were standing in boxes that were the same color as the flowers themselves. A small laugh of disbelief burst from me. As if he'd been waiting there, the bedroom door slowly swung open only a moment later. Clayton carefully moved through the room with a tray in his hands. A tray with a small white cake covered in frosting, sprinkles around the base, and a gold candle burning at its center. And a cup of coffee.

"Happy birthday."

"How did you know today is my birthday?" I chuckled and moved a bouquet of lavender roses out of the way, making room for him to sit down beside me. The small cake had very neat pink writing on the top. Writing that was definitely his. "Did you bake this?"

"Casey, how dare you? I'm a twenty-first-century man. Obviously, I baked your birthday cake."

Another laugh ruptured from me as I took in the simple words, enjoying the vanilla scented air. Happy Birthday. With a heart. He pushed the tray up so that the candle was closer to me, silently imploring me to blow it out. Shutting my eyes, I focused on one thing. The thing I'd wished for the second I'd been thrown into the shitbox in the desert. The thing I wished for when I walked out of this apartment two years ago.

Little tendrils of smoke rose from the extinguished candle as I opened my eyes to catch Clayton dipping his finger in the frosting. He grinned sheepishly and set the tray down in front of me. I picked up the fork that had been set on top of the carefully folded pink paper napkin.

"You didn't have to do all this, Clay," I said, motioning to the flowers around us with the fork in my hand. Stabbing downward, taking as much frosting as I could, I examined the cake before taking my first bite. Sprinkles on the outside. Sprinkles on the inside. And jam. How he knew what my favorite cake was, I had no idea. It wasn't like that information was available on the internet.

"Can't help it," he said as he pulled the little gold candle free from the top, licking the frosting-covered end before setting it down on the tray. "Birthdays are my thing. Prepare to be spoiled."

Before I could dodge it, a finger he'd dipped into the sugary frosting dabbed at my cheek. The look in those bronze eyes, full of mischief, told me that not only had he managed to surprise me to his satisfaction, but that he was not finished just yet. I took another bite of cake. Fluffy, buttery, and sweet. It was perfect. Attempting to clear my mouth of the frosting, I took a swig of coffee and shouted to wherever Clayton had gone.

"How did you know about the cake?"

"That's part three of your surprise."

His voice echoed from down the hall as I wiped the frosting away from my face with the napkin. A rustle sounded from outside the door. Anxious, I shoveled more cake into my mouth.

"Three?" I laughed. "Where's part two?"

Clayton appeared in the door again, this time bearing a big pink glittery bag with sprays of pink paper sticking out of it. The grin he wore as he set it down on the bed was nothing short of brilliant. I arched a brow at him.

"Go ahead," he smirked, waving his hands in front of me like a mother hen.

I stared at the bag, unable to move as guilt flooded me. Pushing back against the headboard, I sighed. A camera. A really nice camera. A really nice, really expensive camera. I pulled the box free from the paper.

"Holy shit, Clay," I breathed, opening the box. "You didn't have to do this. This is..."

"I thought you could use a new one. You told me that your camera was stolen and you couldn't afford to replace it."

I remembered our conversation. He'd asked me why I dropped out of photography school. It was why I'd started dancing. Then everything happened. It had been easy to hide behind the normal excuses. I didn't have time. I couldn't find a camera I liked. My phone worked just fine. But the truth. The truth set my hands shaking as they skated over the cool, smooth surface of the box. Something must have shown on my face because he rushed to sit beside me again, a pained look on his face.

"Do you like it? I can get you a different one. One with real film. I just thought digital might be better since you already had a laptop and everything."

Rambling. A small laugh cracked out of me. The look of surprise on his face only made it worse. Uncertainty dissipated into nothing as I threw my arms around his neck and pulled him in for a hug. His long arms wound around my waist with a relieved laugh into my neck. I pushed backward, my face split with a bright grin I could feel stretching to my ears, hoping to express my gratitude.

All the air went out of the room, as if neither of us realized how close we'd let ourselves become. Close enough to feel his breath on my lips. His thumb dusted over my ribs as caramel eyes dipped to my mouth. This pull we'd had toward each other, this feeling I resented for too long, brought my head toward his.

"Thank you," I murmured.

A loud chirrup sounded from his pocket, snapping us both back into reality. With a breathless little laugh, he shifted to pull his phone free from his pants. I watched him open his security app and check the cameras.

"Surprise number three has arrived," he grinned.

Maybe most twenty-five-year-old women wouldn't want a slumber party with their pre-teen sibling for their birthday, but I missed this kid, and Clayton knew that. He also knew that cake for breakfast was the perfect way to start the day. I was grateful for both surprises.

"Flip the record over!"

The camera snapped again as I took another picture of Ainsley, who would not stop giggling. If anyone was crazy for the man, it was my ten-year-old little sister. They were dancing around to Taylor Swift, both of them enthusiastically singing along to their shared favorite album. Clayton knew all the words, which didn't surprise me at all. They shook their bodies in time to the beat as they both ignored the sound of my clicking shutter.

"I was afraid of you, but I'm not anymore," she said through the puffs of air she was gulping down once the record stopped.

Clayton's eyes shifted to me, a puzzled look crossing his face. He'd met my sister before I did. On the other side of the world. He'd been there when they released the children from the container. He'd been the one to find the parents of each missing child. He'd been the one to discover that her mother had died and that the man who sired her was the one responsible for her abduction in the first place. I never found out what happened to that man beyond a vague but cryptic statement about justice being served by my father. I was still imagining that dark, awful container as I looked at the two of them. The man in front of me was likely wearing tactical gear. Gear I'd seen hanging in his closet. Knowing our brother, he'd probably been outfitted with all sorts of weapons when they arrived in Northern Ireland. My sister didn't need to know I'd met him under very similar circumstances.

"Oh, yeah?" He asked. "Why not?"

"Well, you're silly. If something can be silly, it's not scary anymore."

Something about that made my chest feel lighter. My little sister was so damned strong. I took another picture of her. My sister deserved happiness. She deserved freedom. Most of all, she deserved to see happy pictures from her childhood where she bounced around in a unicorn onesie with frosting all over her face. An idea struck her as I took another picture, making me grateful I was lucky enough to capture it.

"You should dye your hair a funny color!" Ainsley shouted at him. "Then you wouldn't be scary at all."

"Hey, whoa," I chimed in. "The record's off. No need to yell."

"Sorry," she muttered. "Can we watch movies now?"

The hunters were about to sing their big finale song when my sister passed out from too much cake and pizza. Our host scooped her up and carried her into his bedroom, depositing her in his bed like she was a tiny breakable thing. Grateful we'd changed into our pajamas after the first animated movie, the one about Rapunzel, I pulled up the blankets and tucked her in.

"Goodnight, kid," Clayton smiled, patting her little shoulder. My sister murmured something unintelligible, and Clayton headed out the door. I followed. Folding my arms over my hoodie-covered chest, I waited for him to say the same to me. He cast a look over my shoulder at the little girl sleeping in my bed. His bed. Clayton had braced one arm on the door frame, the tattoos on his bicep dancing with the flex of his muscles.

"That kid has a bright future ahead of her," he said in a deep, hushed tone that was doing something to my insides. "Interesting taste in movies. I'm going to have that soda song stuck in my head for the rest of the night."

"She's got a good head on her shoulders," I laughed.

Clayton's free hand lifted to my jaw in a brief glance over my skin before moving away again, as if he thought better of touching me. The action made me want to do something to challenge it. Something brazen.

"Did you get everything you wanted?"

I took one step toward him, closing the distance between us. Taking in the confusion that washed over his features, I whispered a reply as I slid my palms up over his t-shirt to rest on his sculpted chest.

"Almost," I purred. "There's just one more thing."

Clayton went rigid. Completely still as I moved my body into his. Bronze eyes watched me. Watched my hands fist in the black cotton shirt as his remained at his side. Watched my nose brush his. Watched the shaky breath pass my lips as I slanted my mouth under his. Still watching as I leaned into him. He'd spent the entire day making sure my birthday was perfect. Checking in on me. Making me laugh. Giving me not just things, so many flowers, but experiences. He made my little sister laugh. Made her feel safe. Made me feel seen. I'd never forget any of it.

"Casey," he huffed against me. Clayton's mouth was soft and still. It felt like I was learning to walk again. Like I was standing on wobbly legs in the middle of the forest, ready to fall at any moment. I wasn't sure if he was letting me set the pace or preparing to push me away. "Are you sure?"

I nodded and pressed my lips to his again, letting my lower lip glide between his narrow opening. Gentle and slow. A kiss for gratitude, sure, but also a kiss for me. A kiss that, after a moment, became a little more than something sweet as Clayton's hands settled on my hips. No desperate collision. Just a sip of what could be. I wasn't sure if it was the heat of his body pressed against mine or the way he hummed into my mouth for just a moment, but my chest began to ache.

"Good night," I said quietly, stepping backward into the room.

Clayton blinked, shaking his head like he was erasing an Etch A Sketch.

"Good night."

What I'd wished for, that thing I wanted, it was this. To feel like I could still be this girl. A girl who wanted. A girl with hope in her heart. And after cake. After flowers. After this soft, sweet kiss. After climbing into bed beside my little sister, I thought that girl might still be in there.

> Happy birthday.

I opened the text chain on my phone, scrolling back through the dozens of messages he'd sent. The message was a year old. He remembered last year. And the year before that. I wondered why he would do this. Let me see all of these messages. If it was some sort of manipulation. Some way to make me feel like he'd always thought about me. Always cared. Except it wasn't some grand plan. It was all there. Just like the flowers that still scented the bedroom with their perfume, it was right there for me to see. He cared. He thought about me all the time. He was still doing it.

I sighed, typing out a message and hitting send. My sister's light snoring rose from beside me as I tried not to think about it. Not the way his thinking about me made me feel, but the way I had tried not to think about him and failed. My phone chimed, showing he'd seen my text. A little heart appeared next to the message.

> Thank you.

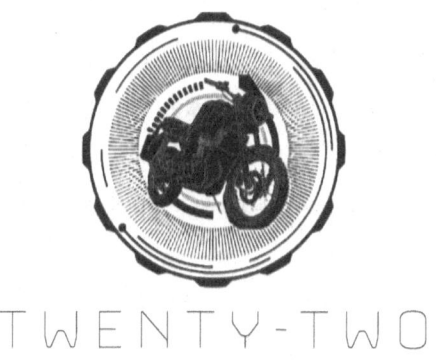

TWENTY-TWO

CLAYTON

Some reputations are created by rumors. Others by bad habits. My reputation was crafted with ill-timed, sarcastic remarks. The patriarch of the Arawn family had most definitely earned his reputation with a singular bad habit. A habit of setting fire to his problems and walking away. Staring at the photos taken at the scene of Alexi Kremnik's death, I knew that this was what Ronan meant when he stated that he'd taken everything from the Russian boss.

I'd seen a lot of fucked up things in this world, but this was one of the worst. A burned-out husk of an electric vehicle. The corpse of the man whose flesh melted off him. Sticky. Trapped. There wasn't much left of the man. Only melted clothes. Charred skin. Burned hair. Multiple organ failure and asphyxiation. Scratches on the inside of the vehicle from where he tried to claw his way out. Immolation. It forced me to speculate about what Kremnik might have done to warrant such retaliation. Fear bled into my mind, its frost crawled down my spine at the brutality of any planned retribution for Ronan's children. For Killian. Ainsley.

Casey.

My chair squeaked as I sat back and opened Gizmo again. Clicking through the list of acquired documents, I pulled up the notes from the scene on Alexi Kremnik. Battery failure caused the car to remain locked. That's what the diagnosis was. I knew Ronan had police on his payroll, but this was unbelievable. A lithium battery could catch fire. That was true. Except, if that was what happened, then the fire wouldn't have started in the cabin. It wasn't an accident.

It was a public execution.

With Ainsley carted back home in the safety of their brother's company, I prayed Casey would stay in the bedroom and busy herself with something. But since my luck has always been shit, I stepped into the living room to find Casey in the middle of her yoga routine. Warrior something in the patch of sunlight she favored. Pale green matching yoga set and long red hair twisted into two braids that ended in little buns. Before I could compare the look to a certain galactic princess, she turned in my direction. Brown eyes fixed on me with something akin to friendliness.

"Hi."

"Hi back," she grinned. "Thank you again for the great birthday."

"Sure. Any time."

With a laugh, she altered her position into something like a triangle. Yeah, I wasn't sure what I meant by that either. Shuffling into the kitchen, I wondered if she'd had anything else to eat after the donut hole she'd popped in her mouth before her sister left. The contents of the refrigerator were starting to look pretty sparse. There wasn't a damn thing left in this house. I opened the grocery app on my phone and started dialing in an order.

Her feet. She and Ainsley had painted their toenails while they watched animated princess movies on my sofa. Sparkly pink beacons. That's what they were. Unable to help myself, my eyes traced up the length of her legs.

Glowing with sweat. Stomach muscles flexing with her measured breaths. In and out. In. Change position. Out. I shook my head, trying to free my mind from the tempting thoughts. Friends didn't picture those kinds of things.

Right. Groceries. Focus.

Even if she *had* kissed me last night. It took the grisly sight of Alexi Kremnik's body to make me forget the feel of her lips on mine. For a few hours anyway. *No. Stuff it down, Wrigley. Friends, remember? Friends. Friends!* Casey stood up straight again, eyebrows bunched together, her eyes wide with concern. Horror washed over me. I hadn't said that out loud, had I?

Casey picked up the towel she'd set down beside her water bottle and dabbed the sweat off of herself. Her eyes narrowed at my feet. To my slippers.

"What are those?"

My eyes fell to my feet. Easier to look at them.

"They're slippers. Obviously."

"They're sharks."

Beady black eyes stared up at me.

We told you not to buy us. You wouldn't listen.

"It looks like they're swallowing your feet whole."

I shrugged.

"I'd lie and say they were a gift, but these were the result of mixing online shopping with late-night edibles. I have no regrets."

Casey rolled up her mat and tucked it under her arm, shaking her head in amusement.

"Does it hurt my image as a badass soldier for hire?"

She didn't answer. Only huffed a laugh as she picked up her phone. Walking past me, toward my shower, she smirked down at my feet. Tally one in the win column for the shark slippers. I wondered if she would have the same reaction to my Chewbacca onesie.

Sharks glided along the polished concrete floor as I made my way into the kitchen to poke around for a snack. *Say what you will about the damned things*, I thought, *but they were warm and comfortable.* I glanced at her disappearing feet and frowned at the sight of them. Bare. It was too damned cold to be walking around here barefoot, though her sweat indicated that wasn't the problem. Fuck, I needed to get some sleep. My thoughts were starting to run together. I opened the refrigerator and looked inside, careful to keep my gaze locked on the appliance.

"Hey, Clay?"

I pivoted, one had on the fridge. Casey propped herself against the wall in the hallway, peering over into the kitchen at me. One eye squinted, her mouth quirked to one side. Whatever she was about to say made her uncomfortable. Please don't say that kiss was a mistake. Please don't tell me to forget about it. I couldn't if I tried.

"Is it alright if we head to Muse in a bit? Lilith said she's free for lunch today, and I was hoping I could have a little free time out of my cage," she said, huffing a joyless laugh as she looked around the place.

"Of course," I agreed before better judgment could kick in. Any time we were out of this place, it was a risk. Not a huge risk, since no one knew where she was or had any way of tracking her. Still, she used to work there. They might know that. The thought of exposing her to any danger made my skin itch. Idly scratching at my forearm, I nodded. "Just, uh, let me connect with her security."

The Caccia organization was the only family in town that could truly rival the Arawns. That might have something to do with the fact that Ronan crushed the other option. The Caccias were classic mafia. Italians who bootlegged and gambled their way into power. The Arawns and Caccias had been at each other's throats for decades until the new leader, Lilith, rescued the redhead behind me. One desert. One trailer. One tracker provided by yours truly. She'd been the one to set out looking for Casey in the first place, though, I supposed I had as much to do with her rescue as Lilith did when all was said and done. It was why Ronan was so quick to accept my services. Because I had offered. For her.

TWENTY-THREE

CASEY

> I wish I knew how to fix this.

If the Barbie movie ended with the ladies of BarbieLand becoming a powerful mafia, you'd have the Caccia organization. There was the public face of Caccia Holdings, COO Juliet Ambrose, who even looked like a flesh-and-blood version of Barbie. She'd greeted us as we passed each other in the parking lot of Muse. Her high heels clicked over the asphalt as she walked toward the tattooed mafioso called Nico Ricci, who was holding the back door of a sleek black sedan open for her. The man ran an appreciative eye over her pink tweed skirt suit as she sat down, but he quickly looked away to watch us enter the club.

I'd only been working at Muse for about a year when everything happened. It was considered the nicest skin bar in the Southern California area. I'd just started to feel comfortable dancing for strangers with the help of Isabelle when everything happened. I was still thinking about the man who strangled her to death as we entered the club. Henry. Lilith had taken care of him, too.

In the middle of the day, the other dancers wouldn't be here for another couple of hours. I rubbed my hands over the yellow sleeves of my sweater, feeling the cold emptiness of the place I'd once thought of as a second home. Clayton had told me he'd wait for me downstairs.

"You deserve some time with your friend. Alone."

Lilith Caccia was frightening. To most people, anyway. A mafia boss with a deep catalogue of poisons she created, locked away in her hidden apothecary. In reality, she was my friend. Flawed, yes. But kind. Protective of the people who mattered to her. A perfect example of her thoughtful nature was that she'd ordered sandwiches from her family's deli in anticipation of my arrival. We'd hugged in greeting, popped open our sodas, and gotten to catching up as we chewed through lunch while sitting on the deep black velvet sofa in her office over the bar. I was still working on the last of my burrata and tomato sandwich when the truth of what I'd come here to do worked its way to the forefront of my mind again.

"I need your help with something."

Lilith took a sip from her soda and leaned back in her chair. Her face was expectant, waiting for me to continue. So I did. I told her everything. Everything that had happened between Clayton and me from the moment we met. Everything that happened afterward. It spilled out of me in long, rambling sentences. Some of the time, I wondered if I was even making any sense. I'd told myself that if there was anyone who would understand the circumstances leading up to my issue, it would be her. She'd witnessed enough of what happened to know it wasn't entirely my fault, at least.

Finally, when the last of my confession was laid out before her, I stopped. Her raven black eyebrows were practically burrowing into her hairline. For a while, neither of us spoke. When the silence in the office grew too heavy to bear, I cleared my throat.

"Say something."

"I'm sorry," she blinked. "You're telling me you haven't had an orgasm in over two years?"

"Say it a little louder, I don't think they heard you downstairs."

She looked over my shoulder, toward the door and the club beyond. Her hands went to her temples, the sleeves of her black cashmere turtleneck falling down her arms a little with the motion.

"Do you want to? Sorry, that's a stupid question. Of course you want to, otherwise you wouldn't have brought it up."

I nodded. Tugging my legs up under myself, I wiped my hands on my jeans and scooted closer to her to whisper conspiratorially.

"What do I do?"

Lilith picked up a little green pepper from the paper wrapping of her meatball sub and popped it into her mouth, chewing over what I'd asked as the pepper crunched between her teeth.

"I'm no psychologist, but I would guess you need someone you trust to help you get past your fear. Like an orgasm doula or something."

"Orgasm doula?" I laughed. "That's not a thing."

She balled up a napkin and threw it at me.

"You understand what I'm saying, though, right? Someone you trust to be by your side while you navigate the choppy waters," Lilith paused, a mischievous grin spreading over her lips in a slash of red.

"What?"

"Oh, nothing. I was just thinking this sounds like the perfect job for a certain sailor."

I straightened.

"Absolutely not."

"Come on," she whined, bouncing in her seat. "You trust him, don't you?"

"I do."

I did. I had already told him as much, but I wasn't sure. I believed it now. It wasn't just the messages, which were becoming addicting to read. It was the way he treated me. Every day, he made me feel a little safer. A little more sure of myself. Kissing him had been a leap. Just a spur-of-the-moment thing. Spur of the moment, in that I'd been thinking about it while I watched him compare himself to Rapunzel's boyfriend.

"You don't see it? I even have his haircut."

"Well," Lilith stood from the sofa, straightening her pants. "Think about it."

I made a noncommittal noise and picked up the wrapping from our sandwiches, crumpled them, and tossed the paper into the can beside her desk. Flattening her left hand in front of her, she examined the large opal and diamond ring on her finger. West Hale, her husband, had been Clayton's commander. His friend. I wouldn't have met one without the other. It was good to see that getting married and becoming a mother hadn't changed how blunt she'd always been. That belief was reaffirmed when she showed me to the door.

"Let me know what happens. Kai hasn't learned to talk shit yet. It's very boring."

Clayton was lounging at the bar, sipping a glass of water that the bartender poured for him. I didn't recognize the girl, but I watched the way she tossed her voluminous blonde hair and squeezed her arms into her sides to emphasize the cleavage on display in the sparkly pink bustier she had on. The bartender placed her hand on his arm, a smile shining bright as she laughed at whatever he'd said. Oily irritation coated me. Everything about her was sparkly. Even her laugh. I could hear the levity in it. It was something my laugh once had.

"You are so funny," she giggled.

Ugh.

Her eyes darted to me in time for her to see me roll mine. Clayton must have noticed her shifting gaze because he turned in his seat, one hand picking the bartender's off of his arm and tossing it away like he was flicking at a mosquito. His features shifted from his normal, affable appearance to something kinder.

"Ready to go?" Clayton asked, standing from the barstool.

"Actually," I started, smiling brilliantly at him. "I was hoping we could go by the grocery store on the way back to your place. I was thinking I could make you a nice dinner."

TWENTY-FOUR

CASEY

"It smells incredible in here," Clayton praised, shuffling out of the office in his grey sweatpants and the matching hoodie I kept stealing. Those little gold glasses glinted as he pumped his eyebrows. What was it about handsome men in little glasses?

I told myself I could do it. I could! I could just lay it all out on the table, as Lili suggested, and just move on. If he didn't want to help me, that was fine. He didn't owe me anything. The thoughts circulated through my mind, round and around as I chopped and diced. The loft was filled with the lemon and herb scent of the chicken I had in the oven. It was a butter-smothered recipe belonging to my mother, and it was what she made whenever she had bad news. *Bad news chicken.* It always softened the blow.

"If there's one thing I know how to do, it's roast a chicken," I said as I folded butter into the riced potatoes. "By the time I was twelve, I was cooking for myself because my mom always had to work."

"I don't know what's gotten into you today, but I love it if the result is a home-cooked meal like this," he said, dipping a finger into the bowl and sucking a blob of buttery potatoes into his mouth. The chest-deep groan he made was completely unfair and a reminder of why I was making him this dinner in the first place. Those brows flicked up again, taking in whatever was happening with my face. "You alright?"

Saved by the bleating timer on the microwave, I pivoted where I stood and sheathed my hands into skeleton hand oven mitts before removing the sizzling chicken from the oven. Butter, herbs, garlic, and lemon wafted from the roasting dish. The combined scents were almost enough to make me forget what I was about to ask him. Almost.

A glass of white wine appeared in front of me, held by masculine tattooed fingers. I took it as Clayton put his free hand on my waist, gently moving me aside.

"Let me carve it up. You've done enough."

Shoving his sleeves up his corded forearms, he grabbed what he needed and got to work. The wine was crisp and cool on my tongue. I took another larger-than-necessary gulp, earning an arched brow from Clayton. Shuffling aside, I removed a pair of plates from the cabinet and began serving up potatoes, piling the plates high because I never met a spud I didn't like. Especially when they were basically half butter, a fancy method I learned from my father's personal chef. Carefully carved chicken appeared on the plate beside them. Clayton jerked his chin toward the bar seating at the counter, where the bottle of wine was waiting.

"Go sit."

So I did. I parked myself at the counter, watching the bespectacled muscular mercenary finish plating our food. He'd already laid out napkins, actual cloth napkins, and flatware as I cooked. The plates scraped against the pale stone countertop in front of me. Clayton plopped down on the next stool and leaned over to sniff his food with an appreciative growl.

"Fuck, Casey. Don't judge me when I lick this plate," he said, stabbing some chicken onto his fork before dragging it through the soft potatoes as if they were a sauce.

I hummed in agreement and tucked into the meal, mentally rehearsing what I had to say to him over and over again as we ate in peaceful silence. At least he seemed peaceful. The only sounds happening on his end were the little yummy noises he made every so often. Meanwhile, my head felt like it was the loudest thing in the world. So much so that I kept checking from the corner of my eye to see if he could hear the thoughts screaming through my head. My chicken bones were bare, and my plate was free of the buttery potatoes when I reached over to the wine bottle to pour myself a hefty second glass. For courage. It was time to stop putting this off.

"I have to admit this meal was sort of a bribe."

"A bribe for what?" Clayton asked, mouth half-full with his last bite of chicken.

"I-uh," I warbled. "Listen, I should start off by saying that you're allowed to tell me you don't want to. I don't expect anything, and we barely sorted out our issues, so I don't want to ruin any kind of friendship we might be building here." His face was a mask of uncertainty. The way a deer looks uncertain when a truck is plowing toward it. Waiting for me to go on. To clarify. I was doing a godawful job of explaining myself. I went on, not doing much better. "I haven't been with anybody and I just," I paused glancing toward the sofa. Understanding washed over his features as he sat back on the stool. Conflict colored those caramel eyes. I couldn't take another rejection. Fear forced me to blurt, "I know it was me who said we should just be friends, and I still want that. To be your friend."

"Casey, what are you asking me?" His question was soft, completely free of judgment, a reassuring touch to my wrist accompanying it.

God, I was doing a horrible job of explaining myself. Why did it always feel like I knew exactly what I wanted to say before I said it, but when the time comes, it feels like my mind goes blank?

"I can't have an orgasm," I rushed out. Pulling my wrist away from his hand, I reached for my wine and took a gulp that felt like an icy rock shoving down my throat. "I used to be able to, but I lost it. Every time I get close, it's like I get scared of it, and I just can't. I know it doesn't make sense, but I don't know how to explain it better than that." His expression shifted from conflict to surprise. Eyebrows high. Lips parted. It was the eyes that made me speak again. That hint of sadness. Pity. That look made the chicken turn to stone in my stomach. "You don't have to do anything. Never mind. Just forget it. Forget I asked."

"Well, that's definitely not going to happen," he grunted, more to himself than to me. Removing his glasses, he placed them on the counter and began rubbing his eyes with his thumb and forefinger. A heavy sigh pushed out of him. "I don't know if this is such a good idea. You're right. We just sorted things out. Kind of. After, you know."

We both looked at the sofa.

Clayton reached out, taking the bottle of wine into his hand. I'd thought he was going to refill his glass when he moved to pour it into mine. I hadn't even noticed I'd drunk so much already. The empty bottle clanked on the stone countertop as he set it down. With a look toward the sofa, he blew out a breath. Long, tattooed fingers slipped around his glass and brought it to his mouth. A beleaguered sigh pushed out of him before he took a sip.

"Let me think about it."

TWENTY-FIVE

Clayton

R onan was going to skin me alive and serve me up for a Sunday roast.

She didn't know what she was asking me. She couldn't. Scrubbing my hand down my face for what felt like the fifth time in as many minutes, I sighed. I'd barricaded myself in the office for a while after dinner, placing the order I'd been thinking about since Muse and setting Gizmo up to crawl through Kremnik's financial documents to look for specific inconsistencies. Forensic accounting wasn't exactly my specialty, but I could figure out the basics. Who was he sending money to? Has he spent any unusually large amounts of money lately? You know, bad guy stuff. Only, instead of focusing on that, I was focused on the girl across the hall.

I glanced at my camera feed. There she was, curled up on my bed. Reading. She'd changed into her pajamas, but she looked uncomfortable. I knew the fucking feeling. Shifting in my seat didn't help. Nothing could help when the little angel and devil versions of me were hockey-fighting in my head.

The angel version of me was squawking in Ronan's voice. Telling me I'd better not lay a hand on that man's daughter. That he'd burn me alive just like he did the Kremnik boy. Not to mention dozens of other people who'd wronged him. Especially if I hurt her again. So, you know, there was that.

That little devil, though. He made some good points. Chief among them?

This wasn't just anybody asking me. It was Casey. Not just a pretty girl asking me for help with this, of all things. It was *the* girl. If she had asked me to run naked through a thunderstorm for her, I'd do it. Deciding to help her was a lot like deciding to buy a lottery ticket. The chances were pretty damned good that I was going to lose. Something good could come out of it, sure. But I needed to be smart. Tapping out the question on my phone, I hoped she'd see it as an effort toward a no-bullshit conversation and not a coward's way out. I could keep my hands to myself. Help her help herself. In order to do that, I needed to know more.

> You said you haven't been with anyone since me. Why?

I glanced at the camera feed again. Her head lifted from the book to the phone that illuminated at her side with my text. She picked up the device and read the message. Then did nothing. Unable to see her face at this angle, I waited while she just sat there, likely staring at her screen. For a moment, I thought she'd ignore me. Then a message came through.

> They all reminded me of someone in some way. All the guys I tried it out with were nice enough. But the problem with a rotating schedule of guards is that there wasn't any one person who...made things difficult for me. New people, coupled with that, I guess.

The ugliness of that confession made my mouth go sour. Picking up my water, I slugged back several gulps and asked a safer follow-up.

> You think it will be easier if you know the person pretty well?

> If I know I'm with someone who's safe, like someone I trust, then I hope it might be easier.

Someone I trust. No reason for that to make me all fluttery in the stomach. *Stop it, butterflies.* Wondering why she needed someone around when she could do it on her own, I changed the subject.

> What keeps you from finishing when it's just you?

An annoyed huff came from the other side of the hall. I looked over my shoulder toward the door, wondering if I might have worn out Casey's good graces when she answered.

> I don't know. It's like I get all the way up to that point and my body just rejects the idea. Like enjoying myself isn't an option. I don't know. It's a clusterfuck of overthinking. I can't explain it.

> So you have a hard time staying in the moment.

I stared down at my phone, anxiously waiting for her to respond, when my attention shifted to one of my monitors. To the little folder of Casey's photos. The siren. She'd seemed so sure of herself in those photos; it felt rotten to know that that certainty had gone. I typed out the question I was half-sure of the answer to and sent it off.

> Is there anything that you feel really confident about?

Her head tipped toward the ceiling as if she were searching for her answer. After deciding, she focused on her phone again and sent it off.

> Not lately. But I was confident onstage.

> Dancing at Muse?

> Yeah.

As if unable to keep from explaining herself, another text came in right behind it.

> Isabelle taught me. She treated me like a little sister. It was why I let her talk me into joining that stupid app. The truth is, I started dancing because she made it look like fun, but I kept dancing because I liked the way it made me feel. It was like, when I was up there…I had everyone in the palm of my hand.

> You liked being in control.

Casey readjusted herself, tossing her e-reader onto the nightstand and huddling into the pillows. Cradling the phone in her hand, I saw the screen light up her face and appreciated the better view of her from this angle. She was so goddamn beautiful.

> It was up to me what people saw or didn't see. Even in a scenario where I was one-on-one with someone, I took things as far as I was comfortable with, but no further.

A bitter laugh ruptured from her. Casey quickly wiped tears away from her eyes. Wretched wrath twisted in my gut at those tears. Only worsening with what she sent next.

> I just want it to belong to me again. You know?

> I understand. It's late. Let's talk more in the morning.

An exhausted sigh puffed from me as I stood from the desk. I'd wanted a second chance with her. This wasn't that. It couldn't be. An alert popped up on my phone, informing me that my delivery was dropped off in the atrium. Glancing at the screen again, I noted that the bedroom light had been turned off. A final message from Casey popped up on my phone as I walked to the front door.

> Sure. Good night.

Bleach. I hated the smell of it. It reminded me of hospitals, of stains that needed to be burned away, and Halloway's house. He made me scrub the floor with it. Toothbrush in one hand, Comet in the other.

"That grout better be spotless when I get back."

Light brown disappeared under foamy periwinkle goo as I smeared the concoction onto my strands, the contents of my delivery now spread out before me on the black bathroom counter at one in the morning. Sleep was not going to happen tonight, so I got started on my little makeover.

There was no way for me to know if doing what she'd asked would be good for her or bad. I wasn't a mental health professional, though I was pretty sure my therapist would tell me that what I was doing would likely end badly if I didn't set some healthy boundaries. That was something I'd have to think about, too.

But I'd told her I wanted to be friends. A friend would help. I just didn't know if a friend would do this. I also didn't know what exactly she was asking me to do. It wasn't until I was watching myself paint the color onto my freshly bleached hair that the idea came to me. A possibly disastrous idea, sure.

Just one friend helping another friend find their orgasm again. What could go wrong? Oh, just fucking everything.

TWENTY-SIX

Casey

> Icing me out? I'm from Chicago, sugar. I can handle the cold.

Pink hair. He had pink hair.

I'd emerged from the bedroom to find Clayton standing in the kitchen, cutting a bunch of produce. Cucumbers. Carrots. Kiwi. Strawberries. My gaze flicked back and forth between the new hair color and what looked like the contents of an entire farmer's market covering the counter. And, good lord, those glasses. The little gold glasses that made him look studious in a sexy professor sort of way.

"Good morning," he smirked, not bothering to look up from the very sharp knife sliding through a pink piece of fruit. Dragon fruit, I realized. "Did you sleep well?"

He already got dressed for the day, something he always managed to do without waking me. Though today it seemed he'd also done a bunch of other things I'd slept through. The pink strands were bright like the fruit on the cutting board in front of him. Almost exactly the same color, actually. The urge to capture the moment was strong. So much color. An aesthetically pleasing mess of produce on the counter. Even his faded olive green tee and pale denim fit in perfectly. I glanced at the clock. Just a few minutes after nine. He'd done all this, and I'd apparently slept through it. Ignoring his question, I asked one of my own.

"Are you planning to feed an army?"

His light brown stubble split into a grin, pink strands bobbing with the shake of his head.

"I, uh, I have ADHD," he laughed, using the knife to scoop the fruit into a glass container I hadn't noticed. When I didn't respond, he continued. "Most of the time, I'll eat whatever is easiest. If it's not right in front of me, I'll spend too much money on meal delivery. Hence, all the takeout. This way I can just grab things without thinking about it."

Clayton set the knife down and wiped his hands on a kitchen towel. Why couldn't I stop looking at his hands? Surveying the vast array of things in front of him, he chuckled.

"I guess I did go a little too far. This is what happens when I shop hungry. Thank goodness you're here, because half this stuff would go to waste because I overbought. I don't suppose you'd like some breakfast?"

Clayton Wrigley was flustered and rambling. Propping my hoodie-covered rear onto the stool in front of him, I gave him a sleepy smile. I lifted a finger in the direction of a little basket near his elbow.

"I'd love some of those blueberries."

"Is yogurt alright? You've got group in almost two hours."

I hopped off the stool and headed for the fridge, looking for the big fat container of Greek yogurt he'd started keeping around. Something just for me. I set the container on the counter beside me and started hunting around for other things to put in my bowl.

"Honey?"

"Yeah?"

"I was asking if you have honey," I laughed. He pointed to the top shelf of the pantry. The little bear-shaped bottle was looking down at me, unamused. My fingers circled around it. Facing away from him, I mustered the courage to ask the thing I'd been dying to ask since I set eyes on him. "Did you think about what I asked?"

Something clattered behind me. I turned around in time to see strawberries bouncing across the countertop. Clayton hastily picked them up and put them in a little ceramic berry basket I hadn't seen before.

"I d-did," he stammered. "Yeah. I did. Casey."

My name was a long sigh as he turned to face me. Oh god. He was going to tell me no. Well, at least I'd have something to talk about today. *I asked a friend to help me and he turned me down and now I feel like a complete idiot. Anyway, I'm going to stay broken forever.*

"It's alright. I shouldn't have asked."

"Whoa, hold on. I say yes, only for you to back out?"

"You said yes?" I blinked.

"You didn't hear me," he chuckled, grin wide enough to make those dimples pop. "I said yes, but you're going to have to trust me. We'll get started tonight."

"What are you going to do?"

"I told you. You have to trust me."

He picked up a kitchen towel, drying off his hands. I watched the way his expression shifted from one of amusement to one of mischief. That little flip sensation in my stomach was either a great sign or a terrible one. It took all the way through my support group to decide I didn't care which, because he said yes.

"You said you liked being watched. I thought you could," he trailed off, lifting a hand toward the full-length mirror that was now angled toward the bed.

"You think I can just play with myself in front of a mirror and everything will be alright?"

"No. I thought that maybe if you started with performing, it would help with your confidence."

"It doesn't work like that," I whined, bouncing on my feet.

He'd clearly moved the mirror into position while I was doing yoga. At the time, I'd thought he was pushing the furniture around. I hadn't realized he'd been doing this. When I came in to see what got moved, here he was. Of course, I'd tried this already. Granted, it was a mirror at my vanity facing my bed. How was I supposed to change my mindset when I was just doing this alone? Clayton put his hands on his hips, sighing as he looked around the room.

"I'll try it."

Goddamn my people-pleasing personality.

"You sure?" Clayton asked, moving those hands off his hips and into his pockets. I nodded.

"Let me just take a shower first."

By the time I'd finished cleaning myself up, he'd left the room. Apparently, I was on my own. I sat down in my towel on the corner of the bed, facing the mirror. This was crazy. But it shouldn't intimidate me. It *really* shouldn't. Staring into my reflection, I wondered if I would have had an orgasm with him two years ago. I could feel his length pressing into me. I'd enjoyed the friction of our bodies writhing together on his sofa. The dress I'd worn was no longer than the towel I had around myself. My hands wandered up my thighs, the center of me aching at the memory of his hips rolling between them and those hungry noises he made as he kissed me.

They paused at the hem the towel. I shouldn't have been thinking about Clayton like that. I knew that. Music filtered into the room. He put on music? My ear strained as I tried to pick out the tune. Teddy Swims, maybe.

I looked up from the mirror image of my face to find Clayton's dark reflection looming in the doorway. One arm braced on the frame. His other hand was rubbing at his jaw. Bronze eyes on me. We stared at each other through the mirror, both of us going still. I could stop now. Keep that line between us. The one that meant we were just friends. Case closed. Pretend that the attraction we'd felt for each other, the attraction I'd felt even when everything else around me was numb, had disappeared. Except that felt like a backwards step, somehow.

"Don't stop."

The hem of the towel slipped up my thighs as I parted them, everything bare before the mirror. Before him.

One hand snaked up to where I'd secured the soft cloth over my chest, tugging it free. If he wanted to watch, he could see it all. Despite everything, I'd never been very shy about my body. Only, it wasn't just anyone watching me. It was him. Heat began to pool low in my belly. I hesitated to touch myself where I really wanted to, instead moving to massage my breasts. Heavy and peaked with awareness, I let out a soft moan. A deep sigh sounded from behind me. My eyes flicked up to find his pinned to my hands. Small, subtle swirls had begun in my hips. This. I could do this.

Trailing one hand down over my stomach to find my gleaming sex, I stole a glance in Clayton's direction. He hadn't moved. The tips of my fingers only glanced over my clit. That slight touch sent sparks through me, tugging another moan from my lips. Just a tease. It was something I'd done regularly. A tease on stage. A tease in the champagne room.

A tease for him.

I let myself smile at him as our eyes connected. Eyes that took their time drinking me in. Tethered to each other through this energy that was flooding the room. It was tempting. Tempting to beckon him forward. To let him touch me. I thought about his hands on me as I slid my fingers toward my sex. His mouth on my neck, lavishing me with his lips and tongue as he took me in his large hands. Sinuous fingers wrapped around my neck, pulling me backward as his mouth slid over my shoulder. Watching him, I parted myself. Circled the swollen bit of flesh that yearned to be touched. Touched by him.

A low, desperate groan loosed from deep within him, finding my ears from across the room.

The mirror made watching him easy. He studied every movement of my hand as I let a finger slide inside. This was about me. It was just about me, but I wanted him to watch. I shifted my hips, still imagining that it wasn't my hand moving against me. I added a finger, tightening around myself as I pictured his digits thrusting into me, working inside until my body sparked with the promise of euphoria. My eyes fell closed, hoping to quiet the thoughts I was sure he could hear. Close. I was so close.

I'd thought I was doing so well. The signs had been there. Tension was building low in me as electricity shot through my system. The version of Clayton in my head was telling me I was going to be so lovely when I came for him. I was so near to the thing I'd been missing when stale coffee and bad aftershave flooded my memory. Pretend. Pretend to enjoy it. Pretend to want them so that they keep me there. Stay alive and let it happen. A rough hand smashed my head into the stinking pad below me as a belt unbuckled. My stomach tightened with the smell of it.

"No."

Shaking. My hands. My body. Everywhere. I was shaking as I caved in on myself, knees drawn up tight as breath sawed out of me. Recognizing the bedroom. His bedroom. Not a pad, but a bed. Clayton had come to kneel in front of me, the heat in his eyes replaced with concern.

"Hey, it's alright," he soothed. A tattooed hand reached out to grab the throw blanket from the end of the bed. Clayton wrapped the soft green fabric around me and began rubbing my shoulders. "I'm sorry. I'm so fucking sorry. This was a really bad idea."

"No," I said through a shaky breath. "It wasn't."

He continued rubbing my sides, thumbs brushing my ribs in a reassuring touch. Far from what I expected to feel when I could still feel the ghost of bruising gropes at my sides. My lip wobbled as I sucked in another breath. I kept telling myself all the things I always told myself when this happened. No tears. Nothing was wrong. I was fine. I was safe. No one could hurt me here. I must have said the last bit aloud because Clayton nodded.

"I don't know what I was thinking," he sighed.

"It was a good idea," I offered, adding more quietly. "I was close. You were right. I think I liked knowing you were watching."

His lips tugged up as he fought that half-cocked smirk, his dimple flickering into view. Tugging the blankets more closely to myself, I felt myself smile a little.

"Alright. That's something, at least."

"Clayton?" My voice was still brittle as I spoke, hesitating to ask for anything more. He raised his eyebrows, silently inviting me to continue. "Will you hold me?"

Something like relief washed over his features as his shoulders loosened. Instead of brushing me off or telling me I was silly for asking something like this of him, he simply slipped his arms around my waist and tugged me to the floor with him. Not that he would. Not when he'd already done this for me. It didn't matter that I was wrapped up in a blanket or that I was cradled in his lap. It didn't even matter that I was still shaking. He adjusted himself to hold my body tightly against his chest. We sat there in the fading light of his bedroom, listening to each other breathe. Completely still. Completely safe.

TWENTY-SEVEN

CLAYTON

Ronan Arawn was a scary motherfucker. He'd requested I bring his daughter to the bar for a Sunday roast with the family, claiming that it would be heavily guarded enough not to worry about exposure. Casey had hesitated but agreed. The ride over here had been long enough for me to forget where we were going and who we were going to see. I only thought about the feeling of her body pressed to mine. And the way she was looking at me last night before she'd crumbled under the weight of her thoughts.

Fuck, maybe he's going to kill me.

Ronan sat in his place at the end, fire blazing. Elegant porcelain dishes filled with enough potatoes, peas, and carved roast beef to choke an elephant were spread out on the table, and all I could picture was the girl seated across from me. It didn't matter that she was the daughter of the most frightening man I'd ever met. Hell, I wasn't sure I cared if he'd kill me upon finding out about our little deal. She needed my help, and I was going to do everything in my power to help her. When she asked me to hold her, I decided I'd been right about one thing.

I'd do anything for this girl.

The girl in the mirror had been so close to the one in my fantasies. Almost confident. Almost that siren. Little flickers of dismay had entered her eyes as her reflection looked at me. I'd dismissed them. Like a damn moron, I'd dismissed them because I was too occupied with the way she moved. The way she touched herself. The way I wanted to take over for her. Get on my knees for her and make her melt like chocolate on my tongue. Instead of taking care of her, I'd been focusing all of the willpower I had into keeping my feet planted exactly where they were. Until her panic plunged me into a glacial rage.

"Wrigley."

Everyone at the table had stopped speaking. All of them stared at me. Except for Casey. She was staring down at her now-empty plate, toying with a red tendril of hair that framed her face. I blinked.

"Sorry. My mind was somewhere else," I admitted.

"Clearly," Killian huffed, steak knife flipping in his grip. Stabbing the last bit of roast beef onto his fork, he grinned. "I asked if my sister was behaving herself over at that place of yours?"

Ronan was reclined in his seat, holding his pint of black beer. A crackling wall of flames framed the black-suited demon. He arched a salt and pepper brow in my direction, awaiting my reply. Casey cleared her throat, straightening in her seat.

"You're one to talk, K. I don't go around murdering people for our father."

"No, you just take your clothes off for strangers," the man beside me muttered.

A cousin of theirs. Big and bald with a thick ginger beard. I'd been introduced to him. Gone to Ireland with him and the rest of Killian's cronies. Clearly more brawn than brains. I had to be reminded of his name tonight, Donnelly, having completely forgotten he existed. He had my attention now.

"Careful, lad," Ronan snarled. "I'll not have you disrespecting my daughter."

"She disrespected you when she acted like a fucking tart," he snorted. Casey's brown eyes had glanced to me, filled with embarrassment at the man's barbs. She'd gone to extra trouble tonight. Done up her hair in a way that made her look even more like a goddess. Swept black liner over her eyes, only emphasizing the beautiful shape of them. All of it gorgeous but unnecessary. Now I understood why. Armor. For this. Her skin went so pink, I could see it beneath the sheer white sleeves of the top she had on. My hands fisted around my flatware. Molars ground together. This wasn't my house. I wasn't in charge. I couldn't overstep. Ronan slammed his pint down on the table, beer sloshing over the rim of the glass. The black liquid matched the eyes of the boss now silently warning his subordinate to shut the fuck up. "No better than a bloody whore."

"You think that because I was a stripper, I've fucked a lot of guys?" Casey barked a cold laugh, red waves bobbing as she shook her head in disbelief. "That was just dancing. It didn't mean anything." Though she hadn't been looking at anyone before, she was staring him down now. Brown eyes blazed. Her index finger jabbed into the table as she snarled at him. "I was good at what I did. I know because I used to go home with thousands of dollars in my hands every night. Money from guys like you who couldn't get a girl to look twice at them in the real world. Because I knew how to make men feel seen. Special, even. And I didn't have to let them fuck me to do it."

Angry Casey was spectacular. Her cousin scoffed.

The thick, dark wooden table had been perfect. Glossy with years of care and regular oiling. I'd admired it before. It was a perfect piece of craftsmanship. Until I'd plunged the knife from my boot into the meaty palm of the ginger-bearded man beside me. Plates clattered. Glasses clinked. Guns cocked. Casey's eyes flared wide, mouth popping open in surprise. Ronan cursed. The man screamed.

"Ye may not be a whore, Donnelly, but you make a good squealing pig," Killian snickered.

I turned in my seat, fist still clenched around the hilt of the knife. The bald man's blue eyes were bulging with rage as breath rushed through his clenched teeth. Plastering the easy smile I knew boiled the blood of men like him onto my face, I tapped the top of his hand with my index finger. Ronan gestured to the guards, who lowered their weapons at his silent command.

"Judgmental micro-dicked fucks like you should watch what you say in my presence, sweetheart. Especially when it comes to her," I smirked, bringing myself closer so only he could hear what came next. "Another word like that and I'll make you useless to women."

I gave a pointed glance at his crotch as I reclined in my seat again.

"More useless, I mean," I grimaced.

Killian snickered. The knife protruded from the back of his thick hand, leaking blood onto the floor from underneath.

"Clean Donnelly up before he ruins my floor," Ronan ordered, two of his men appearing at either side of the bearded bastard. One swiftly removed the blade, eliciting another scream from him. The fat bastard clutched his hand to his chest. "And quit your winging. You're lucky to still be breathing, ye cunt."

Casey watched me, her expression halfway between shock and something else. Ugly discomfort fizzed in my gut. I silently mouthed an apology in her direction, only for her eyes to drop to her lap. The loss of her attention felt like enough of a rebuke, more so than the one I should've worried about. I looked at her father. Ronan changed the subject, seeming to forgive the fact that I'd blatantly overstepped and not only injured one of his men but done it on his territory. I turned to find Killian wearing a knowing grin.

Dinner had ended after Ronan discussed his business. Something to do with an ATF investigation. Something I'd need to keep an eye on, though it didn't seem to bother me as much as it apparently bothered Killian. The stony expression he was wearing when we left was still eating at me as I drove us home on the bike. That and Casey's silence. I wanted to know how often people talked to her that way. Treated her like she was beneath them just because of how she'd earned a living.

Apologizing for small-mindedness felt like too much. Apologizing for my reaction felt like a step in the right direction, but it also seemed like something I should do while looking her in the eye. I had no idea what to say to make her feel better. Rolling to a stop at the next light, I decided a pat to her denim-covered knee would have to do. For now.

Checking my mirrors as we coasted through the intersection, I noticed we were being watched by two large figures sitting in the front seats of a grey sedan. A few cars back from us. After I made my turn, I watched my mirrors to see if they'd turn. They did. It could have been nothing. Could have been a coincidence. But I wasn't willing to bet her life on it. I turned right again. The sedan followed. Casey went tense behind me, likely noticing that we diverted from our route home.

"Is everything alright?"

Her voice was wary through the intercom. I turned right again. One moment passed. Then another. There they were. This time only one car behind us.

"No."

Going to the Chancer had been a bad idea, but at least we confirmed the bar was being watched. Evaluating my options as we headed down the street, I reminded myself of my only objective. Keep Casey safe. My name was a barked curse in the intercom as I opened up the bike. The little grey sedan sped up to catch us. Glancing at the reflection again, I clocked the pistol aimed toward us. At this distance, they'd already need to be good with that weapon. With the chase I was about to give them, they'd need to be fucking surgical with it.

Casey's breathing picked up, fingers tightening together at my waist. Her body was rigid with fear. It leaked into me, forcing the logical part of my mind to submit to seething animal instinct. Every raging thought was drowned out by the sound of my bike's engine roaring down the street toward a field of red taillights illuminated against a lavender sky. Traffic. Shots cracked from behind, bullets slamming into the rear of cars beside us. Muffled shrieks and screams surrounded us as I split the lane again, saved by a red light. We charged through the next intersection. Screeching tires and blaring horns informed me that our pursuers were plowing ahead through the traffic. Downtown buildings were enough to hide us from view, but I wouldn't be able to shake them long enough to get home unseen.

Cars were clustered on the bridge ahead, some half-merged into lanes. Casey's arms squeezed around my waist. Her chest heaved against my back in small, panicked bursts. We were in trouble, and she knew it. Options. Options. I needed options. Bridge. A crazy, possibly stupid option presented itself. I silenced the voice in my head screaming to find a better way. My tire squealed as I flipped us around, daring to face our attackers and darted through traffic. Aiming for the curb of the sidewalk, we careened toward my exit strategy.

"Hold on."

Sharp agony split across my shoulder. The familiar heat of a bullet hitting skin. A bullet meant for the woman clinging to me now. Clenching my teeth hard enough to feel my jaw click, I cranked the throttle. Casey's squeak rattled into my head through the intercom as her legs tightened around me. We jolted down the sidewalk and hurtled toward the park greenbelt. Screams were disappearing around us as we passed. Pedestrians jumped off the path as greenery blurred, melting into grey stone. The sounds of the street dropped away as we sped down through the dry concrete, filling me with temporary gratitude for the lack of water.

Close. We were so fucking close to where I wanted to be. My gut would have to direct us toward home. Toward safety. Another squeak popped through the intercom as I took us over the edge. Right into the concrete basin of the LA River.

TWENTY-EIGHT

Clayton

Casey was still trembling as she peeled her arms away from my waist, the garage mercifully absent of any other vehicles. Rolling my bike onto the elevator took more effort than usual with the stinging pain radiating from my shoulder. By the time we made it up to the loft, I could feel the shoulder of my shirt soaking through with blood. The fabric clung to my skin with what was likely a massive red stain, making me glad I had left my jacket on. It served to reinforce the thought I couldn't shake.

That bullet almost hit her.

If I hadn't been looking right at her, taking her in from head to toe again and again, I would have worried she'd been hit. My fists opened and closed, attempting to loosen the death hold I'd had on the grips. She was fine. She was fine and she was watching me, her face a mask of worry. A hiss filled the elevator as the bike slowly leaked air from its back tire. There was no way to know how I got us here in one piece at the speed I'd been going with a shot out tire. Metal doors slid open to the hall. Casey watched me wheel the bike down to my shop, waiting for me as I opened the door and positioned the bike for diagnostics I didn't have the energy to perform right now.

Another grunt huffed out of me as I closed up and walked past Casey toward the front door. Her feet hurried behind me, small steps compared to the long strides I was making once we got inside. The steel door slammed shut behind us. Pulling my phone from my pocket, I tapped open my security app. A few short commands had all of the locks sliding into place with satisfying metallic clicks.

"There's a med kit in the bathroom. Under the sink. Green box. Big red plus sign. Grab it for me."

My direction came out in a grunt as I headed into the bedroom, searching for a shirt to replace the ruined one I still wore. Shrugging off my jacket with a groan, I hung it on the hook mounted to my closet door. Rifling through the drawers for a fresh shirt took longer than expected. I hadn't accounted for how quickly she'd be able to find what I needed. A quiet gasp forced me to turn around, resulting in a wish that I'd pulled off the shirt before she'd seen the big red splotch covering my shoulder.

"Oh my god, Clayton."

"I'm alright," I insisted, hissing through my teeth at a bolt of pain my movement created. She winced. "It's just a graze."

I jerked my chin toward the bed, silently ordering her in that direction. She followed my footsteps, stripping the white blouse off of herself as I plopped down on the corner of it to reveal a little white tank top underneath. Casey set the first aid kit down beside my still booted feet and knelt between my legs. The metal hinges squeaked with the opening of the green box. Packages rustled about. She was searching for something.

"Iodine. Brown bottle. We have to clean it up. Then we can patch it," I offered.

Red hair bobbed around her face as she nodded, digging through the box and found the little bottle in question. I held out a hand for it, but she pushed it aside and sat up on her knees to examine the wound. Thoughtfully chewing at her deep pink lip, she opened the bottle and covered some gauze with the liquid. One hand went to my thigh, the other shaking as she pressed the gauze to my shoulder. I covered it with one of mine.

"I'm fine. I promise. I've had much worse," I soothed. "See the scar over my hip down on the right?"

Brown eyes skated down my torso to the star-shaped scar. At this distance, I could see little flecks of caramel in them. The little white tank top exposed freckles that seemed to stand out under her washed-out skin. I counted them as I went on.

"Stabbed there when I was on a mission in Fallujah. Big guy with a big knife. Cut me deep. Medics didn't clean the wound in time. I got a nasty infection. Super high fever. Hallucinations. Laid up for almost a week."

Casey bristled, her expression pinched with a wince as she met my gaze again, voice quiet as she interrupted.

"That's not making me feel better, Clay."

"These scars," I grunted, twisting to show her the scattered, raised skin flecked over my ribs. "They're from little bits of shrapnel. Explosion moving sensitive materials. Another mission. Took hours for them to pick all of it out of me."

Doe eyes blinked rapidly, glassy with emotion as Casey moved the bloody gauze away from my shoulder. I peeked at the wound, noting the lack of fresh blood coming to the surface. It still stung like a bitch, but it wouldn't kill me.

"See, it's not even bleeding anymore."

The declaration was meant to sound brave, but it came out with tenderness I'd been trying to stifle. It was easy to lie to myself. I could tell myself I didn't know why I reached out to wipe the tear rolling over her freckles. My hand remained there, cupping her jaw while my thumb made slow sweeps over the curve of her cheek. The skin was soft under my touch. Soft as the look she was giving me. Soft as the heart I once handled so clumsily.

"Don't cry," I said, the words hoarse with that resurfacing guilt. "It's nothing."

Paper crinkled between us, the wrapping of a bandage she'd pulled out of the med kit coming apart in her hands. Casey handed me the antiseptic package, already open and waiting to be applied to the wound. I withdrew my attention from her and smeared the clear gel over the gash. Two small, gentle hands applied the bandage a moment later. The warmth of her body flooded my bare chest as she leaned against me, her head just breath from mine as she examined the bandage.

That same lie pounded in my head as my hand circled her waist. The lie that claimed ignorance as I brushed her nose with mine. Our breath mixed while her bird-like hands fell to my chest. I took one in mine and centered it, feeling the hand that still felt cool compared to the liquid heat of my blood.

The declaration was right there. Close enough that I wondered if she could taste it on my breath. If the words weren't enough, she could feel it. My heartbeat slammed into her palm. Steadily drumming just for her. Worry entered her expression as I fought with myself. Fought the urge to kiss her, because I couldn't stop thinking about that birthday kiss and how I'd wanted it to be more. Or the way she looked at me in the mirror with her hand between her thighs. But most of all, I needed her. It was a beat that filled my mind and became an incessant command.

Tell her. Tell her. Tell her.

Casey tugged her lower lip in with her tongue and released it. Long lashes fluttered, lids growing heavy as she drew nearer to me. Fuck it.

I squeezed her hip, reminding myself that she was kneeling between my legs. Unable to resist the urge to feel her lush body pressed against me, I used my hold to pull her closer. There wasn't a chance I'd bleed out since all my blood was rushing south. Then my mouth slanted over hers. So close. So close to tasting her again, only for a sharp metallic ring to jolt us into the present. Her eyes shot open. Casey stood, freeing herself from my grasp, and approached the nightstand to pick up my phone. She held the device out to me.

"It's my father."

So. Fucking. Close.

Ignoring the sinking loss and sudden cold I felt at her distance, I swiped the screen and brought the phone to my ear. A rolling Irish accent filled with rage was already busy shouting directions to someone else.

"Ronan," I answered.

"Aye, boy. A couple of Kremnik's men tailed us from the bar. Bastards are negotiating their fate with St. Peter now. Were you followed?"

"Yes, sir. We lost them."

There was no need to add any details beyond that. I'd catalogued the license plates of the vehicles chasing us. If they were smart, the cars they'd used were stolen. That wouldn't stop me from searching anyway.

"Good lad. Where's my daughter?"

My eyes skated over the woman in front of me. No need to explain that I was seconds away from kissing her. Spilling my guts to her. All the things I told myself I wouldn't do. It was a moment I could tell I wouldn't get again. Not tonight. Not with the way she looked everywhere but at me.

"She's secure."

"Let me speak to her."

I knew it for what it was. The voice of a concerned father. Casey took the phone from my outstretched hand, pushing the hair away from her ear to better hear the call. Her greeting was casual, playing off the fear she'd still been trembling from only moments ago.

"Dad? Dad. Stop worrying. I'm fine."

From only a foot away, I could hear the cooing. The Irish mafia boss had gentle words for his eldest daughter. Her eyes skated over me before snagging on the freshly dressed wound. The corners of her lips turned down.

"No. Of course not," she spluttered in apparent surprise. "He was amazing. A regular knight in shining armor."

If I wasn't able to guess the direction of their conversation before, the next statement confirmed it. Casey's cheeks went from pink to red, teeth sinking into her lower lip. Brown eyes went wide as she quickly looked at me before turning away, covering her mouth as if that would keep me from hearing it.

"That is absolutely none of your business."

TWENTY-NINE

Casey

My father was the nosiest man alive. After asking me if Clayton had kept his hands to himself, he commanded me to do the same. As if he had any say in the matter. What he'd said in response to my declaration that it was none of his business was still bouncing off the walls in my head.

"I don't want you getting hurt again, love."

It wasn't his overprotectiveness that bothered me. In fact, that was sort of nice. I'd become accustomed to it in the last two years. In the moments I'd get annoyed with him, I had to remind myself that he almost lost a daughter. Still, that wasn't it. It was the implication that Clayton would ever do anything to hurt me that rankled.

I mean, the man had just taken a bullet for me.

Staring into his eyes. Breathing him in. We never spoke about the kiss in the days after my birthday. It didn't mean I stopped thinking about it. When I fell asleep in his arms after the mirror incident, it didn't feel odd. It didn't feel wrong. It felt completely comfortable, which was the strangest thing of all. Except he wasn't there when I woke. Asking him to help me with my problem was starting to feel like a mistake. He hadn't said a word about it since last night in front of the mirror. If tonight hadn't happened, I would have been convinced he didn't care. That he'd moved on from what happened between us, and this arrangement was just business.

It wasn't that he'd risked his life for me. Or the way wrath clouded his gaze as he searched me for injury. It wasn't even the way he talked me down from the ledge of worry with heart-wrenching kindness as I tended to his wounds. That was just who this man was. A giver. Someone who wanted others to feel at ease. A defender, too. All of that was a footnote compared to what I felt when he touched me. It was plainly obvious in the set of his jaw and the soft look in his golden gaze. And the near-miss kiss that had my pulse pounding everywhere. He was holding back. That realization forced me to look away.

"You should get some rest."

Clayton stood from the bed after removing his motorcycle boots, picking both up with one hand. I glanced at the clock on the nightstand. His form retreated from the room, halfway through the door, by the time I spoke up.

"Stay here. Sleep in your bed."

Pink hair fell into his eyes. Clayton looked over his bandaged shoulder at me, one hand propped on the door frame. Ignoring the little flip my stomach did at the look, I gestured toward the bed.

"Please," I pushed. "It's big enough for both of us. A California King is too big. I don't like being in here alone."

"Are you sure?" Clayton asked, displaying each little chord of powerful muscle. I watched the flex and expansion of his stomach as he puffed a resigned sigh.

"We've already slept together. In here, I mean. Don't make me keep begging you."

"Maybe I like to hear you beg."

The darkness in his voice pulled a breathless laugh from me. The kind that made his mouth pull into that half-open smile I'd been aching to see. The kind that made my stomach flutter. Clayton gave a nod of mock-defeat. His silent acquiescence was enough to set my fingers trembling again. Taking my pajamas in my hand, I muttered an excuse about getting ready for bed and left for the bathroom. Little pastel-colored bottles greeted me on the black stone countertop of the vanity. Grateful for the excuse of a lengthy skincare routine, I changed into my pajamas and set to work on the ten steps ahead.

"You can do this," I told myself in the brightly lit mirror. "It's one bed. This is not one of your romance novels. Nothing is going to happen. You're just going to sleep, and that's it."

I'd only been dancing for about a year when I stopped. When everything happened. It was incredible how used to being watched or touched by someone you could become. Desensitized to the nerves of being exposed to strangers. I had power on that stage, and I knew it. With all the eyes raking over me. All the attention was snared in my web. Even when I was stripped down to my skin, I felt a power like a layer of armor over me. It was the memory of that feeling that vexed me now. Brushing my teeth, staring at myself in the mirror, I wondered why I could do all of the scandalous things I'd done and find the prospect of sleeping next to Clayton still so nerve-racking.

So, I dawdled. I loitered. Alright, fine, I was deliberately stalling going back to that bedroom. I should have offered the bed and taken the couch. I could have used the excuse of being horrified by his behavior at dinner. The knife he thrust into my cousin's hand because the man insulted me. I'd heard it all before. Every time Donnelly visited the Chancer. Unfortunately for him, it was the first time he'd ever dared to utter such a thing in front of my father. Or Clayton. The casual smile my mercenary put on didn't fool me. While he was pretending to be unbothered by the man beside him, I saw the rage simmering in his eyes. It was why his violence hadn't shocked me. It was the way my body responded to him that was still taking me by surprise.

It took every step of my routine to get my pulse back to a normal pace. By the time I got back to the bedroom, the lights were off. Assuming he had already fallen asleep, I climbed into bed beside Clayton. The sheets were warmer than they had been, likely because of his furnace-like body temperature. It was a nice change. The bed was comfortable enough, but the loft was so drafty that it was tempting to cozy up next to anything that would keep me warm.

Instead, I remained on my side of the bed, hoping I would fall asleep and forget about the man lying in bed beside me.

Of course, because it was me that didn't happen. Nope. Next to Clayton, sleep had been a fleeting, slippery thing. I did everything possible to drift off. Changed my position. Flipped my pillow. Then I heard his sigh from the other side of the bed. He'd not been sleeping either. I couldn't have been bothering him with all of my moving around. The mattress was so large, we may as well have been sleeping on different continents. I rolled over, watching his chest rise and fall in even measure. Lying flat on his back, I knew he was awake from the faint glimmer of street light in his eyes. Staring at the ceiling. Just as I was staring at him.

"What are you thinking about?"

I wasn't sure what made me ask the question. It was barely a whisper between us. He let out another one of those agonized sighs, turning his head toward me. In this light, I could barely make out his face. Just the silhouette of his jaw and the straight line of his nose. It was only from the glinting dip of his eyelashes that I knew he'd looked me over. Then I felt his hand take mine. Fingers threaded together with a small squeeze. For a long while, I thought he wouldn't say anything. With the weight of his hand in mine, I felt that anxious animal in me curl up and close its eyes.

"I was thinking about what would have happened if things had ended differently."

He might have been talking about the chase. The fact that there had been men hunting us. Except that same flutter I felt climbing into bed was pulsing in me now. That flutter whispered all of the things I was still too broken to say out loud. My mouth made a humming sound, the only response I could muster. Let him think I was half-asleep. That I wasn't lying here wondering exactly what he meant. Wanting to tell him that, if I were really being honest with myself, I had been wishing things had ended differently for a long while now. Wishing that I hadn't let my fear put up a wall between us and light everything on fire. Instead, I squeezed his hand in return. A silent gesture I hoped conveyed everything that remained trapped behind my teeth and tongue.

Lisa's blue suede Birkenstocks stared back at me during my survivors' support group. The entire meeting, I told myself that this was the day I would open up and share my story. If the man sleeping beside me last night could look an imminent threat in the eye, I could do this. Echoes of my first disastrous attempt bounced off the walls of my mind, the noise so loud that I couldn't hear anyone else. Only the sounds of my own cowardice.

I'd been so disconnected from the discussion that I hadn't realized the meeting ended until the sound of chairs scraping the floor as they were being put away in the corner jolted me from my thoughts. Lisa crossed the circle, coming to a stop in front of me. Stuffing her hands into the pockets of her wide-leg jeans, she rocked on the heels of her mules. The greyer locks fell from her updo, framing the patient expression in her dark brown eyes. Well, mostly patient. There was wariness in her creased skin. Concerned for me, probably.

"You seem preoccupied today," Lisa inquired, looking at me through lowered brows. "Does it have anything to do with the man on the motorcycle who's been squiring you to our meetings? I've seen you leave together."

"Him?" The word burst out with a shrill laugh. I wasn't sure why. It was him. For the first time in a long time, I found myself constantly thinking about him. Not in a *his-face is so punchable* way. Now it was more like *please put your hands on me*. "He's just a friend who's helping me out for a little while."

Lisa arched a brow, probably at the uncertainty in my voice. God, it wasn't convincing me either. Friend sounded wrong. Tasted wrong. He wasn't a friend.

"And," I added, needing to move on from that thought. "He's been helpful. We talk about things. But there's this part of me that holds back because I'm worried about how much I might be dumping in his lap."

She chuckled, nodding knowingly. Shoving up the baggy sleeves of her rich, olive green sweater, Lisa moved a step closer as I stood to drag my chair back to its rightful place amongst the others.

"Having a friend is important. Having support is important, too. Our friends are wonderful providers of support, but your instinct is correct. We need space to work things out with someone objective. Someone whose opinion you won't worry about. That's why talk therapy is important. I know the goal here is to get the support you need from people who have had similar experiences, but I'd like for you to explore that option."

Lisa shrugged, as if our entire conversation was just a bit of gossip. We both made our way out of the room and down the hall. She waved goodbye to me as I paused in the atrium, looking for something on the bulletin board that had caught my eye. Another option. She was right. I needed another option. An outlet just for me.

A motorcycle engine fired up outside, muffled by the glass doors. Pushing up the cream sleeves of my sweater, I flipped up flyers pinned over other flyers. The bulletin board was full of them. I'd glanced at one a couple of weeks ago. It had said something about help. A text service. I'd almost given up when I saw the purple paper dangling toward the bottom of the near-desecrated cork.

SafeSpace is a text-based online therapy service with 24-hour care.

With a quick scan of the QR code, I downloaded the app. I was still setting up my account by the time I saddled up on the bike behind Clayton. He still had that odd energy around him. He'd been so brave yesterday. I could do this. Do the brave thing and make the effort to get stronger. I pulled my jacket over myself and plunked my phone into a pocket. It gave a muffled ping with a notification. Sliding it free, I saw the banner across my home screen.

You've been matched with a provider.

THIRTY

CLAYTON

Casey and I did a fairly good job of avoiding each other for almost two whole days. I busied myself with work, and she left food out for me like I was a stray dog. I worked into the night until I was sure she was asleep. By the next night, I'd opted to blow past, almost spilling my guts to her and stuff my feelings back into the piñata. It was better to pretend they didn't exist. She'd have to beat it out of me.

The problem was the request she'd made. The thing she'd asked me to do that I was doing just fine ignoring. Pretending I didn't want to help her. Pretending I hadn't looked into safe practices every chance I got. Things I could do to make her feel comfortable. The solution was still burned into my eyes. Staring at the article on my screen for the last ten minutes probably didn't help.

"I was thinking about your situation. The help you wanted from me."

Casey flung her phone to the nightstand. She'd been intently staring at the screen when I entered. A look of horror crossed her face as that intoxicating blush flooded the apples of her cheeks. I watched her eyes fill with reasons to turn me down after the abject failure of my mirror proposition.

In that mirror, she'd been an image of temptation. Putting on a show for me while trying to conquer the thing that lurked beneath her skin. A similar monster lurked in the shadows of my mind. A monster that liked to remind me about the worst things that had ever happened. A monster that reared its head whenever my mind was unguarded. On her own, she was left to defend against the toothy maw of that particular beast. Guilt gnawed at me because I'd promised to protect her and motivated me to fix it. Fix it now.

"Oh. That's not," she stammered. "We don't have to. I mean, you don't have to."

She must have only just come in from getting ready for bed, glowing and fresh from the little bottles of things she had lined up on my sink. Red hair piled on top of her head in a mess of sweeping waves and curls. Having changed into that cream-colored outfit she slept in, the light from my bedside lamps was doing nothing to prevent her from looking luminous and seductively angelic. Especially when her cheeks were so full of color. I approached the bed as I explained, Casey treading backward until she sat down on the bed.

"I have an idea. I want to try again. To help you. But, you need a safe word."

"A safe word? Like for bondage? Are you going to spank me or something?"

"Only if you beg," I laughed. She didn't. She was serious. I shook my head, putting my hands up in an absent gesture. "Okay, no jokes. No. A safe word gives you control. If you don't like what I'm doing, we can stop. But you might feel the need to tell me to stop when you don't mean it, so I need you to pick a word that tells me you do. Mean it, I mean."

I tried to be self-assured. Tried to sound as if I knew what I was talking about. I'd only barely finished researching the subject, and hell, if it wasn't both arousing and terrifying. The prospect of destroying her trust, something so fragile and breakable, and never seeing her again. A bullet would hurt less. Who was I to choose for her? She wanted control over her body. Control over how she felt. By giving her pleasure and the knowledge that she could stop what we were doing at any moment, I knew I could do that.

"Control," she repeated to herself. She shifted on the bed, hands gripping the mattress so hard that I wondered if she'd bolt if given the chance. Staring down at the comforter beneath her, she loosed a breath and started picking at her manicured fingernails.

"If you don't want to anymore, I get it. It was just an idea."

"No. I want to."

Casey shifted in place, brown eyes bright with something I couldn't identify as they finally fixed on me. A little smile tugged at her lips. Then she was scooting up toward the headboard as her eyes drifted down my bare torso to my sweatpants. Those bright doe eyes looked up at me expectantly. I could feel what she was thinking. I got to my knees on the floor beside her, relishing the feel of those eyes locked on me while also wishing they were filled with more interest than uncertainty. A shaky breath blew from her lips. Lips that, despite being so full and inviting, I would not let myself kiss again. Not for this.

"I can't," I started, the thought breaking free before I could stop it. "I mean, we're not going to have sex. What happens here should be about you. Everything we do should be about you."

And because if I am with you in that way, I don't think I could put myself back together if you shatter me again, I wanted to say. Grazing the length of her shin with my knuckles, relishing the way her soft skin met mine, I watched her face for any sign of discomfort.

"Before things go any further, I think we should get you used to being touched by me," I rasped, voice thick with intent I wasn't strong enough to disguise. "Because I am going to touch you, Casey. I'm going to make you feel the way you deserve to feel."

Flattening my hand, I let my palm glide over her. Goosebumps pricked like wildfire in the wake of my touch. Delicate hands balled into fists at her sides.

She moved, chest heaving with every breath, licking her lips. No. I would not kiss her. This almost-having-her feeling was dangerous enough.

"When do we start?"

It was a soft, nervous question. A question that made me want to take her in my arms just to soothe her. Comforting her was second nature to me now. In the interest of trying to manage myself, I took her chin between my thumb and forefinger and directed her gaze away from the other hand resting on her leg. Long dark lashes blinked as I looked into her eyes.

"Now."

THIRTY-ONE

CASEY

On my sixteenth birthday, my mother and I went to an amusement park together. The kind that was filled with rollercoasters with insane names and gigantic loops. Every time a rollercoaster clicked to the top of a gigantic plunge, I could feel my heart rattling inside me from the anticipation. That was the way I felt now. Rattle. Rattle. Rattle. The way my heart slammed through my chest, I was convinced Clayton could see it trying to break its way through my ribcage. Blood was rushing and pounding in my ears as my skin heated everywhere. Get used to touching, he'd said. Get used to being touched. Being touched by him. Unable to think past the feeling of his hands on me, I spluttered.

"What did you just say?"

The question was a breathless rasp between us. I must not have heard him properly. *Now.* Now? That cocky, lopsided grin he often wore had a softer edge as he looked at me through tendrils of pink hair.

"I said we will start now," he said, voice still husky as he continued. "But you need to choose a safe word."

"I still don't," I stammered, shaking my head. "I don't understand why I need a safe word."

Long tattooed fingers pushed through the strands of pink as his jaw flexed. Bronze eyes went searching around the room. It was the first time he'd looked away from me since he'd come in here. I'd delayed as much as possible, hoping he'd be lying in the dark again, only to find the room empty and him still in his office. We'd dodged each other all day, inevitably playing bedtime chicken. I'd thought, I really had, that he'd decided to give up on me when I crumbled under the pressure of touching myself in front of him. It was only now that I'd realized he'd been cooking up another approach. Ever the dutiful soldier, he'd seen his battle plan fail and decided to form another attack instead of retreating from the enemy at hand.

"I can make you feel good, Casey. Really good. You might be afraid of how good I can make it for you. You might tell me to stop. And that's fine. I want you to be in control of how far we go."

Clayton pushed off the floor and crawled up beside me on the bed. The bed I suddenly felt pinned to. He bent forward, bracing a hand on the headboard beside my head. In this light, his lean form was sculpted in gold and darkness. The stubble lining his jaw was almost wheat. Dark brows lowered as he took me in. I couldn't move. Not when he was this close to me.

He seemed to mark that. A breath passed between us. It felt like electricity was emanating from him. If I touched him, I'd be touching a live wire. Then he lowered his head until I could feel his breath warming the shell of my ear. Another surge of goosebumps blazed over my skin.

"You might say stop when you really want more," he graveled. " While I'm touching you, taking you to the edge, I want you to feel it all. I want to bring you to that place that scares you. Face it with you. But you're in control. Say the safe word, and we stop. Right then and there."

"If I want you to stop, we stop. But only if I say a safe word?" I asked, barely above a whisper, as I pushed up to kneel before him.

He nodded. Clayton's tongue swept across his lower lip. I watched his mouth, suddenly overcome with the need to feel it on me. Blinking that thought away, I forced down a breath. A breath that shuddered from me at the feel of a finger skimming the waistband below my navel. Need pooled low in my belly at that touch. Then he asked me again.

"A safe word, Casey. What do you say when you want to stop?"

It came out of my mouth without a second thought.

"Cinnamon."

Clayton grinned, repeating the word quietly to himself. That gaze remained on me as he moved away to tug open the nightstand. The nightstand I hadn't actually looked inside of. People's bedside drawers are their business. But as he dug around for something I couldn't see, I wished I'd snooped. The first thing looked like, well, a flower. Deep red, made of silicone, probably. A rose.

Then a big white thing. It had a long handle and a silicone bulb at the end. A back massager, maybe? Confusion must have been written all over my face because Clayton huffed a laugh at me and gestured to the object he'd just set down.

"It's a wand."

"A wand?"

He nodded, looking down at the device.

"Are you performing a magic trick?"

Clayton stood up, looking down at me with a thoughtful expression. His grip wrapped around the handle of the wand, a flare and flex of his fingers the only indication that he felt any nervousness as he let the object remain on the surface of the nightstand.

"I'll show you what I can do with this in a little while."

Rounding to the other side of the room, I wondered what sort of things he kept in the other nightstand when the bed dipped with his weight. Still half-dressed, he slid down beside me, bringing his body as close to mine as possible without touching.

"Face the wall."

"Wait, so I need a safe word for spooning?" I laughed as I rolled over, facing the wall leading to the bedroom door.

Clayton chuckled darkly, the bed bouncing as he scooted himself close enough for me to feel the heat of his body without touching me.

"Would you rather I fork you?"

I laughed again, not noticing the arm he threw over my waist. He was just going to touch me, I reminded myself. Just touching. Clayton's hand splayed over my stomach, a warm and welcome weight. One minute passed by. Two. By the third, I'd decided I could do this. My shoulders slumped with each passing breath, the nerves that were standing at attention settling again. That was when the stroking started. Tiny brushing motions with the knuckles of his curled fingers that were somehow soothing and stimulating simultaneously. Gradually increasing the length of his movement, callused fingers rasped over my skin.

Higher and lower.

Long, languid strokes over my belly. Need that simmered low in me turned to liquid between my thighs. I let myself sink into it. Into the way he played with me. His movements increased in length. More and more gradually until he reached the plump curve of my breasts, grazing the skin with just the edge of his knuckles. I let out a gasp at the jolt it left behind. Clayton huffed a sigh that sounded like it came through his nose. The hand that had just grazed me up top continued its rhythm, moving in a downward trajectory. The waistband of my shorts, which now felt far too small and too sheer for this, was suddenly his primary focus. Skimming along the material with his middle finger dipping in just beyond the tiny band of elastic. Shallow little teases that matched the depth of my breaths.

"Are you ready for more?"

Darkness had returned to his voice, the question a hot breath against the nape of my neck. I was grateful he couldn't see my face as I considered, noticing our bodies had moved until they were nearly pressed into each other. Close enough that I could feel his erection brushing the curve of my ass.

"More what?"

"I didn't get the toys out just to show them off, Casey."

A bouncy jostling motion announced a shift in his position. The man who'd just stirred me into a frenzy was now sitting beside me, one arm propped on a bent knee as the other held him upright. It was an odd thing to marvel at. The way someone moved. With Clayton, it was hard not to. A graceful jungle cat, casual and dangerous. He reached over me for something. It appeared in my line of sight only seconds later.

The wand.

THIRTY-TWO

Casey

It had escalated so quickly. No, that's not true. We'd arrived at this position after some negotiating. He agreed to keep his pants on. I took off my pajama shorts and left my panties on as I reclined on the bed. Then Clayton knelt down between my legs and started touching me again. Slowly. Fingers along the inside of my knee in another torturously gentle caress.

"Is this okay?" Clayton asked, his voice thick as the sweetest caramel.

I nodded, chewing my lip as he continued his ministrations. His grip shifted, this time moving his thumbs up my inner thighs. Still gentle. Still slow as he monitored my face for any tell. Any sign of distress.

"You're doing well," he crooned.

"This was never my problem."

With a cock of his head, he paused his movement. The expression wasn't irritated. Only curious. It was odd to feel so comfortable this way. With him.

"What, then?"

I chewed on my lip and wondered how to explain. I'd never told anyone this part. But how was I supposed to move past it if I couldn't talk about it? Especially with the person I'd asked to help me. Screw it.

"As soon as I get close, really toe-curlingly close, my body locks up. It's ashamed or something."

His eyebrows shot up.

"I mean," I continued, wanting to move past the discomfort. "It's like, when I'm about to orgasm, it feels overwhelming. I get hyper-aware of what's happening, and I don't want to be touched at all. But I really do want to be touched. I don't know if I'm explaining it right. I want to finish. It's just that I get there and something in me pulls the ripcord."

I covered my face with my hands.

"I'm sorry," I muttered into my palms. "Maybe I'm too fucked up for this."

The bed shifted. A soft woosh of air rushed from him as large hands squeezed my thighs. Something about that touch stabilized the wobbling something in my middle.

"Casey. Look at me." I cracked my hands open to peek at him. His caramel brown eyes were soft. In this light, his pink hair was almost shining like rose gold in some places. It looked so silky, I wanted to reach up and touch it as it fell into his eyes. It was always falling into his eyes. "Can I tell you a story?"

Nodding, I folded my hands on my stomach. He let out another breath, searching the room for whatever he was going to say next. Focusing on something in my middle, he began.

"When I was a kid, they used to take us out to this summer camp. For two weeks every year, out near Hudson. I looked forward to it all year. But one year, I almost drowned while I was swimming in the lake. The counselor had to drag me out and give me CPR." Clayton's hand squeezed my thigh again in an absent, thoughtful gesture. Dark brows furrowed as he laughed to himself, almost in disbelief. "I've been shot at more times than I can count, and that's the most scared I've ever been."

My hand covered his, unable to stop myself from comforting him. His attention returned to my face, one side of his mouth tilting up again.

"Do you know what I did the next summer?"

"Stayed the hell out of the lake?" I chuckled.

He shook his head, that smile growing on his face.

"Cannonball. Sprinted down the dock and jumped right in, screaming like a banshee. It's okay to be scared of things that hurt you, Casey. Just don't let it own you. We can wade in, or you can let me take you to the edge."

I looked at the toys he took out. The rose. The wand. I looked at the man kneeling between my legs.

"What do you want to do?"

"Cannonball," I said, jerking my chin toward the nightstand. Clayton picked up the wand and flipped it in his hand like a knight with his sword. It whirred to life with the flick of a switch.

"Cannonball," he parroted with a lupine grin.

The silicone head of the wand vibrated in a low, even hum. Clayton's gaze remained on mine as I tracked the toy. Little hairs on my body lifted as it drew nearer and nearer to my skin. Deliciously delicate zings teased where it grazed into contact with me. The inside of a knee. A swath of tender inner thigh. An amazingly agonizing retreading of territory he'd been touching only moments before. Only this time, it was winding me higher. My arousal forced tingling needles down into the tips of my fingers and toes. Each sweep of the device moved closer to my center, exacerbating my already sensitive flesh. A roll moved through my body. All of his touching, his teasing, now condensed into this feeling. This close-to-but-not-enough feeling.

My core began tightening, aching for something to fill it. Aching for the relief of release. I moaned at the feel of it. Kept my eyes on him. Him. The tight, powerful body of a warrior. Honed like a blade. Poised over me. There was only him. Only me. Safe in his bed. I could stop this if I wanted to. If I wanted to stop. Did I want to stop?

Absolutely not.

The nerves in my body fizzed and popped, the way your body knows to wake itself when part of it falls asleep. Swarming. Scorching me from the inside, flooding my skin with its heat. This wasn't a foot or an arm. It was everything. Everywhere. It stole my breath as he wound me higher and higher. My hips were rocking in answering movements. Caramel eyes watched me, fixed on my face with immutable interest. Then he focused the toy on the apex of my thighs. Another loud moan ripped from me with the small circles he made, firm and fast with the flick of his wrist. Corded golden muscle shadowed with tattoos flickered in the wake of that movement.

My back arched, body flexing and breaking under the need to feel the conclusion. The explosion. The thing. I couldn't think of the word. There was only this. Only the shimmering breaking that called out to me. Only more, more, more. Eyes squeezing shut, I let out another moan that turned into a sob of frustration. There was no safe word. No safe word needed when I couldn't even let myself tip over the edge. Ripcord pulled.

"No."

Hands pushing me down. Cramming me into the floor. Ripping. Tugging. Taking.

"Casey."

I would not let them take this from me. Not anymore. But that wasn't what came out of my mouth.

"Wait," I panted. "Please. I'm not..."

Blood rushed through my ears, drowning out the sound of the wand being clicked off and set down beside me on the bed. A breath caught in my throat as my eyes flew open. Here. I was here. I was with Clayton. I was safe.

Every inch of damp skin my panties touched felt like it was being rubbed with sandpaper. Fists clenching and opening. My body was still raging with the promise of a release not reached as I looked up at him. He'd said he would take me to the edge and no further. It had seemed like a good plan. For about five seconds. Until he went and made me feel like this.

"You did so good," he praised, still kneeling between my legs. "How do you feel?"

"Good," I said hoarsely.

More. I wanted more. Needed more.

Clayton's gaze raked over me. My skin flushed at the naked desire in it. Like he hadn't just been edging me to within an inch of my life. He stood from the bed, tossing the wand down beside me. Large hands pushed through his short pink waves. He laced his long fingers together where they met at the back of his head.

"We're not doing this if you can't be honest with me."

"What?" I sat up on my elbows to look at him.

"You're lying to me."

I flopped down and shut my eyes, blowing a frustrated groan up at the ceiling. My hands skimmed over myself. Over the tight, peaked flesh of my breasts. The planes of my stomach. The undulation of my hips resumed. The bed dipped. Warmth crowded over me. I wasn't alone. Soft puffs of air danced across my cheeks.

"Look at me, Casey."

My eyes fluttered open to find Clayton kneeling between my legs again, one patchwork inked arm bracing himself over me. The fingers of his free hand trailed my collarbone. Then my neck. My jaw. My lips. I shivered at the contact. At the need searing nerves, screaming for that touch to find its way to my sex.

"Please," I begged.

Beautiful. Bronzed skin and golden eyes. Ink drank up the light. He was beautiful like this. I moaned at the feeling of my hand connecting with my core. With flesh so sensitive, where he had focused his efforts. It wasn't enough. I needed more. Needed him.

"Please," I gasped.

"I'm not a mind-reader. Use your words. Tell me what you want."

The question was a low purr, almost lost to the sound of my heart thudding in my ears. His hand drifted down my neck to my chest. The warm weight steadied me. I met his gaze, and he smirked, a look of patient amusement crossing his face. He knew exactly what I wanted. So I told him.

"Make me come."

THIRTY-THREE

CLAYTON

It was a sight to behold, this fucking goddess of writhing ethereal splendor. Flush and pink against the cream fabric that was doing such a terrible job at hiding her from me. Red hair had come out of its bun, spilling around her in vines and splashes. Beautiful brown eyes blinked up at me. Blood thrummed in my ears. It was so loud, I almost didn't hear her speak.

"Make me come."

Of course, I knew what she was going to say. Not that it mattered much. The admission still stunned me. After everything she'd told me, I would have been fine with stopping. Well, not *fine*. I was going to need the world's most bone-chilling shower after this.

I glanced down at the pink flesh that had become exposed with the shift of her underwear. So wet and swollen. She adjusted her hips at my gaze, as though she could feel the weight of it. Without another word, I sat back on my heels between her legs.

Casey opened her mouth and closed it, thinking better of whatever it was she was about to say as my hand squeezed the wand hard enough to make it creak. Her eyes traced my arm, my face, down my body until they landed on what strained behind my pants. She licked her lips and looked up at me, moving her hand to touch herself again. Eyes on me.

No.

I'd said this was about her, and I'd meant it. Wanting her was second nature to me. I thought about it constantly. Every time I saw her behind the bar at the Chancer. Every time she tugged on one of her curls while she was concentrating. I could wait. I'd wait and wait and fucking wait some more until my bones turned to dust. Because I wanted her to be mine without uncertainty or fear. The uncertainty that now flashed behind her eyes as I turned the toy on again.

Deciding I couldn't look at those gorgeous doe eyes, I focused on the task before me. A dark freckle on her inner thigh became my focal point. Dragged the head of the vibrating toy over it with a feather-light touch. She whimpered and moved her hand away from herself. The oscillating wand skimmed here and there. Moving until she was mewling and squirming beneath me again. Begging for more direct contact.

"Clay, please."

Casey's hands moved from her sides to her exposed stomach. She tipped her head back, eyes falling shut with a sigh as she slid her palms up and down again. The tender caress of an imaginary lover.

Please be thinking about me.

I should have told her to open her eyes. Look at me. Instead, I watched her. Back arching. Hips thrusting. I let myself imagine what it would be like to be in this with her as I moved the toy to the top of her sex. To the bit of flesh that swelled beneath the soaking wet cotton. She had to be so sensitive now. Teeth sank into her lower lip as she bit back a whine. Head tossed back again. Wild curls spilled across my bed like fiery snakes coursing over dunes of sand.

Tremors started in her legs. Her tongue flicked out over her full lips as they parted. Panting. Moaning. She was close.

"Clay," she whimpered, peering at me through her lashes. "Please. Don't stop."

If I died tomorrow, I'd want to spend eternity hearing that. It made me weak. Made me lean forward again, balancing myself with one hand as the other worked that spot in tight circles. I brought my lips to her ear and spoke.

"I'm going to count down from ten, then you're going to finish for me. Are you ready?"

Casey's hands moved to her breasts, shifting under the creamy white top to squeeze and pull at herself. She gave a jerky nod in response. That ribbed cotton barely concealed a damn thing. My cock twitched at the sight of the feast below me. She was fucking breathtaking like this.

"Open your eyes now. Look at me."

Chocolate brown eyes were molten with desperation as they fixed on me.

"That's it. Keep them open. Here we go. Ten."

Casey's hips thrust upward in seeking movements as I applied more pressure to her. Lips parted, tempting and sumptuous as I reminded myself of the painfully hard truth. This was not about me. *Do not kiss her. Don't do it.*

"Nine."

Her breathing hastened as red splashed across her freckled chest. Helpless little noises squeaked from her. Her body crested and moved with the sensation I knew was taking hold. It was the same sensation that made her knuckles whiten around the blankets in her clenched fists.

"Eight."

A sharp breath inward. Her knees lifted, legs moving to wrap around me. *Fuck.* I hoped she couldn't feel my hips grind into the bed beneath hers.

"Seven."

This was going to kill me.

"Six."

Her hands left the blankets, bracketing the sides of my face, fingernails sifting through the short stubble I'd let get too wild in the last couple of days. Doe eyes went wide, making silent pleas as they locked on mine.

"Five."

My movements were tight. Consistent. I tried to stay on task. Keep doing exactly this. Keep doing exactly what was making her shake below me, around me. Even if all I could think about was how to make her feel like this with me inside her.

"Four."

"Clay. Please. St—I can't."

"Yes, you can. Three."

Her eyes wandered over my shoulder, brows furrowing together as her features went distant. Tension rippled through her muscles. The hands on my face started to slip away. That wouldn't do.

"No. On me, firebird. Eyes here. Are you ready?"

A blink had her back in the room. Casey nodded eagerly. I could feel the smile parting my lips as I spoke to her.

"Two."

I brought my mouth down. Let my lips graze hers. Not all the way. No. Kissing her now would shred me apart. If I let myself take that liberty, separating this from how I felt about her would go from difficult to impossible. I let my mouth brush hers again as I set her free.

"One."

Casey's face twisted on a silent scream that turned into a swear. The luxurious length of her neck bared before me as her head fell back. Her back arched, legs crushing my sides while her hips made wild thrusts. Because I was a weak man, I let the flat of my tongue glide up her throat and swore I could taste the pleasure on her skin as the orgasm ripped through her. A rush of euphoria forced my head to fall to her shoulder, barely able to keep my weight elevated. Blood pounded in my ears, so loud I thought I heard my name fall from her perfect lips.

Carefully, I unwrapped myself from her. Turned off the toy. Stepped away from the bed. Casey was still panting, eyes shut, when I left the room. The damp spot on my pants had me grateful for that. A look over my shoulder at the girl had a chorus of unhelpful thoughts clanging through my mind. The first was that I needed a cold shower. The second was that if experiences make you rich, then I was now wealthy beyond my wildest dreams.

THIRTY-FOUR

Casey

Ripples of gold and bronze. Dark, thick lashes around unblinking eyes. Brown brows raised in awe. The way he watched me come undone beneath him with parted lips. Watched me as if I were an exploding star. A burning building. A crashing tsunami. Something simultaneously beautiful and destructive. Something that you couldn't tear your eyes away from if you tried. Something inevitable.

"At least you finally broke the seal," I laughed to myself as I applied mascara to my lashes. "Progress."

It was impossible not to replay the night in my mind as I hurried to get ready for my next meeting. Having overslept after being in such a sex-addled stupor that I'd forgotten to set an alarm, I was already running late. Walking into those meetings late was always awkward. Not that I was even thinking about that. Nope. I was thinking about the hour-long session of overstimulation that led to possibly the strongest orgasm of my entire adult life.

Braiding back my hair, I couldn't help smiling at myself. He'd done that for me. Made me stay focused on him. Focused on his face and the numbers. The feeling he was creating in me. The things I wanted him to do to me. All of that and nothing else. Only a flicker of hesitation before bliss, warm and thorough, flooded everywhere. Relief followed close behind. I'd drifted off into satisfied sleep for the first time in years, only noticing his absence in the light of the early morning.

He made me see stars, and he freaking left. It would have been easy to feel used. Just like so many had used me. Only, it wasn't like that. No. He'd remained clothed. He focused on me. I wanted to kiss him. Not the other way around. All of it was for me. Still, he was kind of a prick for leaving. A freaking cuddle might have been nice. He didn't even come to bed.

Was he avoiding me?

I pulled my sweater over my head, needing something to keep me warm on the cool morning. The dress I'd thrown on was not enough. Not the wool tights and boots, either. In the house words of my favorite fictional family, winter was coming.

"We're going to be late if you want breakfast," Clayton said as I appeared in the living room. "But you should eat after."

The words trailed off. His eyes skated up from the floor, over my legs, and up my body until they connected with mine. His mouth opened like he was going to say something else, but then he quickly looked away. If I didn't want to address what happened, I guess he didn't either. We were both clearly thinking about it. How could he not be?

"I'm fine," I grunted as I walked past him and headed for the door. At my abrupt response, he followed me out.

A bell dinged as the elevator doors slid open. I stepped in and watched Clayton pull his phone from his jeans and take a place beside me and his motorcycle. Opening an app and clicking several options that changed from green to red at his touch. All I could think about was the way those hands made me feel. Confusing my observation for interest, he angled his phone to give me a better look at his screen. The options said simple things. Box A, B, all the way to Z. A glance at what had to be my puzzled expression prompted a half-assed explanation.

"Security."

I blinked. Ticking boxes for security? Shaking my head, implying I needed more information. At least we were talking to each other. Even if it was so uncomfortable, I wanted to scrape my skin off with my fingernails.

"I don't understand."

He stepped closer, the natural warmth of his body seeping into me through the dense knit of my sweater. The sweater I was starting to worry was a mistake with the rising heat beneath my skin. It was an effort not to smell him. Citrus and sage. I needed to find out what soap or cologne he used and stay the hell away from it because it did something to my brain that made my knees stop working. I backed away half a step. Clayton took a breath and explained.

"Each one of these is a sensor. They note everything in the place and hold it. Should anything move at all, I'll know about it. Some are also cameras."

My eyebrows pulled together. I shook my head.

"These are everywhere?"

"Yeah," he breathed as he stepped away from me to lean against the steel wall of the elevator. "Everywhere."

Cameras. He had cameras everywhere. I'd guessed as much, but to see the quantity right there in front of me was a little unsettling. Brown eyebrows flicked up, waiting for me to respond. Say something. Anything. I would have. Except that I got lost in shades of gold.

"I can't."

"Yes, you can."

Smooth and soft lips brushing mine. His tongue sliding up the length of my neck. My knees squeezed together at the memory. Dropping my focus to my boots, I watched him from the corner of my eye and hoped he didn't notice my cheeks flushing red.

The preparation for our ride, which was usually peppered with nonsense chitchat, was filled with only the sounds of clips being clipped and zippers being zipped in almost meditative silence. It wasn't enough to forget the way he'd made me scream only a few hours ago. I forced myself to stop thinking about it as we pulled out of the parking garage and into the world. Through the streets. Through the cold, misty morning of Los Angeles. Until the little hairs on the back of my neck went up at his hand covering my knee.

One little thing about yesterday was still plaguing me. A detail that pulled at my mind like a nail on a loose thread. The safe word. Clayton had urged me to use a safe word. Had edged me until I begged to come. He'd even bought toys in preparation. Was that what he was into? Was I into that? Was I comfortable with this approach? All of those questions were simmering in the back of my mind, but we were on such uncertain terrain that I was scared to ask a single one and step into a chasm I wasn't prepared for. Explaining this particular detail felt like it was beyond Lilith's ability to help. I needed an expert.

Halfway through the meeting, I decided to ask the only expert in the area I could think of. Someone objective. Someone kind. Someone who was about to leave, so I'd better get my ass out of my seat and summon the courage to ask, or I was going to have to wait until next time. My boots scuffed the linoleum as I rushed toward Lisa. Her eyebrows shot up at my rapid approach, expression turning expectant.

"Can I ask you something?" I huffed.

"Of course," she paused packing her bag to place her hands on the back of her chair. "That's what I'm here for."

With all of her focus on me, I lost the ability to speak. Before the question came out of my mouth, I decided to buy myself a little time to summon the courage to ask it and provide a little context. Context was good. Context would help, right?

"So, I'm staying with that friend of mine for a little while. A man."

"The motorcycle man."

"Yeah." I looked to my toes, suddenly feeling like eye contact with her was too much. Instead, I focused on a stray thread from the sleeve of my sweater. The angle of my head forced the words out in an odd mumble. "Well, he knows my history, and I asked him to help me with, uh, intimacy."

Peering up at her from my boots, I was surprised at what I didn't see. As always, not one lick of judgment. Just a friendly face.

"Wow. Good for you," she chirped, standing upright and clapping her hands together as her passive expression brightened with genuine excitement. "So, what was your question?" Her head toppled to one side when my brow furrowed in confusion. The grey locks piled on her head fell over with the movement. Gesturing toward me, she added, "You said you needed to ask me something."

"Right. Well," I stammered. "Before we got into anything physical, he said that I needed a safe word. I don't know very much about that stuff, and it seems sort of dominant, doesn't it? Like S & M."

She shook her head with a knowing smile on her face.

"Dominant, maybe. Sadomasochism? No. Those are completely separate things," Lisa breathed, placing her hands on her overall-covered hips. Her eyes shifted to the ceiling, searching for what she wanted to add. The addition trailed out of her mouth. "Were you comfortable with what happened?"

I nodded.

"If this is just about the safe word, I'd say he wants you to be…"

"In control, yeah. That's what he said."

Lisa nodded, bending forward to pick up her bag. Hoisting it onto her shoulder, she jerked her chin toward the door in a silent invitation to exit with her. I picked up my purse and slid it over my head, adjusting its position across my body while we walked. Her voice was low, considerate of the fact that maybe I didn't want everyone within earshot to hear my business. I could barely hear her over the sound of our shoes thudding on the floor.

"In a healthy dominant and submissive relationship, the submissive has a lot of control. Most of it, actually. You agree on boundaries beforehand. No matter what, if you're uncomfortable, you can just pull the emergency brake and end the scene. So, the real question is, does that work for you?"

I thought about last night. The fear. I'd felt it cresting. I could have used the safe word, but I didn't want to. Then I focused on the numbers. The anger I felt at having something I used to enjoy taken away from me. And him. His eyes. His mouth. The way his smile is just a little bit crooked. Then that fear went away, and there was nothing but the need to touch him.

"The safe word, part. Sure."

She gave a nod, then opened the door, glancing at the man in question. Clayton was perched on the seat of his motorcycle, as usual. His phone was in his hand, suggesting that he'd been occupying himself with something and looked up when he heard our feet hit the top step.

"Then I'd say that this is a good thing. Keep taking things slow. Keep the conversation going. Don't do anything you're not comfortable with," Lisa insisted, placing a hand on my shoulder. "Try not to judge the things that make you feel good."

THIRTY-FIVE

CASEY

> Sometimes I go to the bar just so you can spend the whole night not looking at me. Tonight was one of those nights.

"You're not into anything weird, are you?"

It flew out of my mouth with almost no thought. Alright, fine. I was thinking about it for hours. Chatting with Lisa had put me at ease, but sitting here in his living room had ratcheted up my anxiety. The turkey sandwich I'd eaten turned in my stomach at all the possibilities I imagined. Imagining him with other people had absolutely nothing to do with it. Nothing at all. Even if the idea of him using those skills on other women made me itch.

Clayton was still chewing his food, eyebrows popping up to his hairline with my sudden query. Long fingers curled around the neck of his water bottle, bringing the steel up to his lips for a swig before he answered my question.

"I'm not into anything weird. I *am* weird. There's a difference." He took another pull from the bottle, eyes on me. Reading into whatever my expression was doing, he put it down and shifted his position on the sofa to more fully face me. "Elaborate, please."

"The safe word thing," I said, shifting in my seat a little. He'd been working in the garage and hadn't changed since we'd been back. I had just finished going through a full sun salutation when he burst in with gigantic sandwiches. I was starting to get used to it, this almost-comfortable feeling. Except I was feeling pretty far from comfortable now."

"I think the word *weird* is a little problematic, but no. I wouldn't say there's much that is unusual about what I do," he shrugged. The corner of his mouth tipped up, bringing a dangerous edge to his voice as he looked over his glasses at me. "But I'm willing to try anything once. Except kissing. No kissing. Too personal."

"Did you just quote Pretty Woman?" A half-choked laugh puffed from me. With a sip from my water, I tried to look away, only to catch him winking at me. Quickly slapping my hand over my mouth, I held back another laugh. He bounced in his seat, proud of himself for pulling a laugh out of me. Unable to think of a single thing to say to that, I was relieved to hear the chime of his phone from his pocket. Less relieved when his face fell.

"It's your brother. I have to go. Stay—"

"Here. Yeah," I huffed. "I know."

Clayton pushed up from the sofa, a pitying frown drawing his features together. A sharp intake of breath indicated that he might have said something. Anything. Only, he didn't. He just took his food to the kitchen, threw it in the refrigerator, and walked out the front door after stuffing his feet into the boots he'd discarded beside it.

The little voice in my head that had been worrying all morning was drowned out by the more rational, centered version of me after a good yoga session. That version of me arrived at the conclusion that he was just giving me space. He was just a friend helping out another friend. That was fine. We weren't a couple. He didn't owe me anything beyond that. Even if I might have wanted more.

Time slithered by. Finishing the first book in the series I was reading didn't help. Giving myself a manicure didn't help. Taking the most elaborate shower known to womankind didn't help, but it did manage to wear me out. Washing, shaving, and moisturizing everything will do that to you. Skin raw from exfoliating, muscles tired from the acrobatics involved in scouring myself from head to toe, I shuffled back into the bedroom. Bed springs groaned as I flopped down on it to air dry. I checked the time on my phone. Another thing that had started out nibbling at my anxiety began to take bigger bites. With one long inhale through my nose and a drawn-out exhale, I started dialing. She'd be free now. It was about time I connected with the woman. The metallic ringing only sounded twice before she picked up.

"My girl! I haven't heard from you in weeks. Where have you been?"

My mother's voice shifted from cheerful to irritated in ten seconds. That had to be some kind of record for Rose Collins. I cleared my throat, forcing levity to my words.

"Oh, I've been busy with work."

"Work? I dropped by the bar, and you weren't there. They told me that you wouldn't be back for a while. You know how I hate it when you disappear on me, so don't lie to your mother."

I sighed. This. This was why I'd been avoiding calling. I loved my mother. She was a strong and capable woman. But she was also a world champion worrier. *I hate it when you disappear on me.* The only time I'd "disappeared" on her was when I was abducted and held captive by a trafficking organization. That hadn't been a choice. Unfortunately, because I was a total coward, she didn't know that. All she knew was the lie I'd told everyone else. I went on a retreat. My shoulders started creeping toward my ears as I searched my mind for a valid excuse that wouldn't give her heart palpitations. The first thing I could think of rushed out of me.

"I'm seeing someone. I've been staying with him. For a little while."

"And your father is alright with this?"

It was a flat question. I heard it for what it was. A criticism of Ronan. She hadn't been thrilled when he wedged himself back into my life. Even less so when I moved in with him. Not being able to explain why my father had become so protective of me didn't make it any easier.

"Yeah," I said, going for breezy. "I told him to deal with it. Besides, it's not that serious."

Technically not a lie. A cabinet closed. Rose made an incredulous little huff. Tapping that sounded a whole lot like her nails hitting the side of a glass filtered through the receiver. My mother always had a problem with sitting still. I let myself wonder what she was doing instead of worrying about her. The respite was short-lived.

"Honey, it's serious enough for you to shack up with him," she snorted. Ice clinked into a glass in the background. "You've never done that with any of the others. And there have been a lot."

She emphasized the last two words, as if that would help her point. I was grateful she couldn't see my face screw up at the thought. Alright, that was also not a lie. Living with any of my previous boyfriends was a concept adjacent to literal hell. Tyler's dismal illegal guest house on his parents' property flashed into my mind. The asshole might have judged me for my job, but at least I could afford my own place. I shrugged, rolling onto my back to stare at the ceiling.

"What can I say? I'm nice to look at," I chuckled.

"Yeah, you get that from me."

She wasn't wrong. I had her hair. Her smile. Her face. People always stopped her on the street to tell her how pretty she was, and I looked just like her. We were almost identical except for one thing. I had my father's eyes.

"If you won't tell me anything about him, at least let me meet the guy. See if he's good enough for you, honey."

If she were here, she'd tell me to stop tugging my hair. That's what I was doing as I reflected on her request. Well, not a request. Rose Collins didn't make requests. She made sugar-coated demands. It was how she always closed the deals she wanted. Being stuck in this loft for days on end was making me stir-crazy, and I did miss my mother. Clayton would just have to deal with it. I'd have to warn him that she probably wouldn't like him. She didn't like any of the guys I'd brought around. I'd also have to warn him off talking about how we met. The desert camp, too. And the fact that he was basically my bodyguard.

"Fine. I'll see when he's free and let you know," I agreed. My mother distractedly hummed her agreement. Needing to move on from the subject of Clayton, I feigned a bored sigh. "Anyway, that's not why I'm calling. I've been thinking about going back to school, and I wanted to hear your thoughts. It's not like I can't afford the tuition anymore."

A soft grunt and a pop sounded in the background. She was making herself a drink.

"You can learn photography on your own. You don't need to go to school to do it. It's an art form just like any other. You can learn by doing, if that's what you want to do. I learned my trade on my own."

"You taught yourself to trade stocks. It's not really the same thing."

"It is, though, honey. You've already shown yourself that you're capable of learning whatever you set your mind to. You learned to dance by doing it."

Shifting my weight on the bed, I tried for another position and wrapped myself up in the throw blanket the minute I remembered all the cameras.

"Do you ever wish I'd stayed in school and gotten a normal job? Or did the whole husband and family thing?"

I didn't know why I asked. Some internal residual guilt I picked up. A breath wooshed from me as I thought maybe my cousin's taunts had started to worm their way into my head.

"Oh, please," my mother scoffed. "Those things are a choice, just like everything else. Some people hide behind it because it's too hard to be a good person with stuff that matters. So they lord those things over other people. You know I don't care what you do so long as you're happy."

I could hear her dog's collar jingling as it pattered around in the background. My mother hated being alone. We were similar creatures in that way. The half-blind chihuahua, who was no larger than a grapefruit, was wildly adept at finding trouble. At least when he was conscious. My fingers twisted in my hair, idly braiding a lock from the back of my neck.

"I'm glad you're thinking about that sort of thing again."

"Why?" I wasn't sure why I'd asked.

"I don't know," she faltered. "You haven't really seemed like yourself. You used to run towards your life. Lately, it feels like you've been hiding in it."

The line went quiet as she waited for me to respond. Mothers notice these sorts of things. At least, the good ones do. Tension coiled in my gut at the truth. The reason I hid from things I used to run towards. Clayton had accused me of the same thing. Hiding. Unsure of what I was going to say, I hesitated, only to be saved by the incessant yapping of a chihuahua on the other end.

"Toast, come here. Toast, put that down. Toast!" Rose screamed, phone jostling. "I have to go, honey. Toast got into the pantry. There's cereal everywhere. Let me know what your guy says."

My guy. Why that made my stomach fluttery, I could only guess. Probably because I'd lied to her again. Without waiting for my response, my mother hung up. Talking Clayton into seeing her would be easy enough. He would coordinate things so that we were somewhere safe. Somewhere he could monitor with hacked access to all of the cameras in the area. Without me having to ask, he'd do that because he could. He'd bragged about that when I'd first met him.

"Don't worry. I'll keep an eye on you."

I put on my pajamas and downloaded the next book in the series on my e-reader. Uncertainty about Clayton's return would be too distracting. Knowing my brother, the command for help had come quickly because they were doing something extremely illegal or extremely dangerous. Probably both. Instead of letting myself worry while I waited, I could focus on the girl in my book and her problems. She'd been broken by the overwhelming circumstances of the previous volume. Now that she was on the other side of them, she could heal with the misunderstood lord, or she could let the weight of them crush her. With a heavy sigh, I flopped back into the pillows and opened to the first page.

THIRTY-SIX

CLAYTON

When I enlisted in the Navy, the recruiter told me it would take me to exotic locations. Places all over the world. For the most part, they were right. I'd been to Tokyo and Cairo. Australia. Colorful markets with bustling food stalls, sprawling deserts, and lush green jungles filled with exotic blooms. A dank, musty warehouse in the middle of a business district not far from Long Beach. Ah. Paradise. Large light fixtures dangled overhead, still dark after I'd deactivated their motion sensors. Rows and rows of shelving lined the space from the bare stone walls to the rolling cargo door.

Killian, Casey's half-brother, had called me here to deal with its complex security system. His father was only one of my clients, but he paid generously for my time. I was willing to throw in little extras like breaking and entering. Sean and Rory were mirror images of each other, moving like they'd spent their own time in the military. With their rolling accents and Irish tattoos covering all of the available space on their arms, I couldn't be sure they hadn't. Killian looked at the dark-haired brothers, making a silent hand signal to proceed forward without him. The black tactical gear they wore allowed the large men to disappear into the shadows. I disarmed the safety on my pistol and took a defensive stance at their leader's back. Not a footstep was heard. Not a breath. One brother sounded off from a distant corner where he was supposed to be planting an explosive.

"Clear."

The other echoed from the other side. Killian, who'd started counting the boxes of bottles in front of us, let out a curse. Unlike Casey, her half-brother had been raised in Northern Ireland by his mother and had a thick rolling accent like their father. The deep, lilting voice was a hoarse whisper in the dark as he instructed his men to move forward. A look at the black tactical watch on his wrist and a grunt confirmed what I'd suspected. He was pissed off.

"Their shipment is scheduled to go out tomorrow. The crate is short by half."

Ilia. We'd come here looking for Ilia, but this was part of his son's business. A little bit of information my system had turned up. In my research on the Soviet scion, the files Gizmo turned up painted the picture of a man who was nothing like his father. Alexi Kremnik went to a top-tier university up in the bay area. Studied business and minored in chemistry. It would seem like an odd choice of majors if you had no idea that this kid was raised by one powerhouse of a drug dealer. Except it didn't seem like that was going to be his game. Once the guy graduated from school, he worked normal jobs. Worked in sales at a biotech company until it was time for him to use some of that family money to his advantage and start a socially conscious vodka distillery.

In Long Beach.

It was an odd place to produce the stuff, but the company managed to distract people from that particular detail with all of their lore and social media presence. While no one stepped forward as the face of the company, it did a good job of creating a distinctive brand identity. Vodka that was created with the good of the planet in mind. Water waste was cut down to a minimum during production. Filtration of the product happened with a ten-step natural process that resulted in award-winning purity. People loved it. Celebrities were seen around town clutching bottles in photos at parties.

You'd never know it was all a front.

It was a massive success. Until the owner was found dead. At the time, it seemed like an unfortunate accident. Alexi Kremnik was trapped in his electric car when the vehicle went up in flames. No one was around to help him get free. Only that wasn't what really happened. The Arawns happened. Ronan happened and Kremnik's father knew it.

The GHB Kremnik was manufacturing was stored in barrels right next to all of that crystalline vodka. Only, instead of being decanted into the highly designed bottles that were flying off the shelves of liquor stores everywhere, it was going into the rows and rows of cobalt bottles that surrounded us now. This stuff wasn't going to be used for any sort of prescription. It was the worse-than-medical-grade variety that sent people to the hospital, if they were lucky enough to be conscious enough to seek treatment.

Killian had reasoned that if we'd eliminated the source of Kremnik's income, namely this warehouse filled with bottles and bottles of GHB, he'd be too busy trying to raise cash to worry about attacking the family. He also argued that it would smoke out the bastard. I didn't have it in me to argue with his self-proclaimed genius, but I knew that if I didn't assist them, I'd have to deal with much worse than a plan like this going awry.

Returning my attention to the shelf behind me, I picked up an empty cobalt bottle to examine it. I wondered if Casey had seen one like it before she'd been dosed. Or if she'd thought the person who'd done it to her was friendly. Maybe they'd been having a nice conversation. She might have even been flirting with the guy. My tactical glove made it impossible to feel the thing crack in my grip. Bottles clanked and clattered off the shelf. One or two shattered. Or three. My boot crunched over a fourth bottle when Killan's head whipped around towards me.

"What the fuck do you think you're doing?"

I shrugged, sweeping my hand through the rows of bottles. My boot crunched over blue glass as I moved toward Killian, the sound like half-frozen snow collapsing beneath my shoes.

"Redecorating."

Killian rolled his eyes and turned on his boot to walk away, stopping in his tracks as the lights flickered on overhead. Loud buzzing alerted us to the opening door. Rory hustled toward Killian, weapon drawn as they took cover. Sean took up a position behind a pallet of plastic-wrapped boxes. Dark eyes shifted to me as he hoisted his weapon and waited. I did neither of those things.

"Who the fuck are you?"

A man who was as short as he was wide barked at me after entering, the heavy steel door slamming shut behind him. Buzzed hair on all sides except for the top, where thin black strands were slicked to the surface of his head to create the illusion of hair. His clothes were flashy, the way all these guys' clothes were flashy. Gaudy with a hint of too much cologne.

"Oh, me? I'm just doing inventory," I smiled. "This is some fucked up shit you boys have here."

The small man smiled, one hand slipping behind himself to reach for the gun he undoubtedly had tucked in the waistband of his too-tight jeans. I tsked at him, aiming my gun with a quick flick of the wrist.

"It's good business," the small man quipped, growing only slightly less comfortable with my gun trained on him.

"People get hurt because of this business," I snarled, trying to push past the memory of a fear-soaked redhead running toward me.

The small man gave me a mocking frown.

"Boo hoo."

I blew the frown right off his face. Killian cursed, moving from his position to address me. The twins remained hidden, which was for the best because at that moment, the small man's entourage pushed through the door. A large, bald man as pale as the lights hanging over us and two shorter guys who looked like rounder versions of the first guy. All of them were dressed in black, which meant the first guy was probably the leader, and these guys were security. Not very good security, obviously. They didn't even notice Killian's movement to the next wrapped pallet. What they lacked in strategy, they attempted to make up for with artillery.

If he hadn't looked like a walking, talking dick, I'd say the oversized handgun he was carrying was compensating for something. His eyes fell to the floor, finding his companion sprawled in a blanket of blue glass and missing most of his nose. The bald man swore, correctly assuming I was the culprit who killed his buddy, and aimed the gun in my direction, only to find my aim already locked on him.

"Put the gun down," he barked, lowering his weapon a little. Realizing I had the drop on him meant he wasn't entirely an idiot. "You're coming with me."

"You're not really my type, sweetheart," I quipped to the taller Russian. "But don't worry. I'm sure these nuts would follow you anywhere."

The two short, round fellows looked at each other. Their leader snarled, lifting his gun.

"You little shit."

"Look at me when I'm talking to you, you little shit."

Seventeen. I was standing in a living room hundreds of miles from here. Not again. Never again. There and gone in an instant. The man who'd beat me to make himself feel stronger and the bald man were one and the same. One blink and Halloway was there. The next, he was gone.

"Stop! Please. Leave me alone!"

A body at my feet. Red blooming across the floor, trickling in tiny rivulets between the pieces of broken cobalt glass. I couldn't tell if I was looking at the mirror image of one man or two men running toward me. No, not me. The others. The other bodies on the floor. Killian's face was pale as it came back into focus, screaming something at me that I was too far gone to understand.

"Stop!"

"Stop!"

Everything was moving too slowly. Too slow. All I could do was feel. Feel my heartbeat coming down. Feel my breath begin to even out. Feel the pistol warm in my hand as I holstered it.

THIRTY-SEVEN

CASEY

> Every time I have more than three beers, I fall asleep thinking about you.

Six hours. It had been six hours since I last heard from him. I made dinner for myself. Sort of. Some people might say cinnamon and sugar on some buttered toast isn't dinner, but those people are categorically wrong. I nibbled at it, looking at my phone again and again. The bedtime wind-down yoga I used to do while working at Muse took far less time than I remembered. Without anything else to do but wait, I was sprawled across the bed, in the midst of a tension-addled scene between a faerie lord and his mate, when the telltale beeping of the alarm being disarmed preceded the metallic clacking of the front door unlocking. A heavy sigh followed the sound of the door shutting again.

"Clay?"

No answer. My feet hit the cold concrete floor, moving down the hall, toward the heavy thuds of boots. He was here. I knew it was him. Knew the sound of those footsteps. Followed them into the bathroom before I knew where I was going. I barely clocked the discarded clothes on the floor beside the big leather motorcycle boots. A long, powerful body stood before me. Completely naked in the large glass and onyx box that was steadily filling with steam.

It was like he didn't know I was here. In ghostlike movements, Clayton's tattooed hands were scrubbing his face in what looked to be sheer exhaustion. The clothes I'd ignored on the floor must have had blood on them because his skin was splotched with it, red splatters dotting his bronzed forearms and swaths of colorful ink bled as water hit them. It streamed down his face. Down his body. The pink hair that made him look playful darkened under the spray, turning it into the petals of a poisonous flower.

"Are you hurt?"

I wasn't sure where the question had come from. I could see that he wasn't hurt. Not except for the still-healing wound on his shoulder. His skin, despite the blood, had no other tears or cuts. No wounds to speak of aside from the raised bits of scar tissue. Scars from bullets. Scars from knives. Those I could identify thanks to my family history. But there were others. Others that hinted at a brutal past and the kind of cruelty I could only imagine.

"No."

The word came out like it was covered in rust. It didn't match the friendly tone I'd come to know. The one who liked to have fun with me. Try to get a rise out of me. This was a voice I'd heard once before. Hollow. The night we met. The night he gave me the rabbit's foot. It was that memory that informed the present. He'd shot people down that day. He'd killed people today.

"Good."

It was all I could manage to say, and I still kicked myself for such a weak response. Even though I was glad he wasn't hurt, it didn't feel appropriate to celebrate. Not when there was so much blood streaming onto the shower floor, running down the deep ridges of lean muscle as he fully stepped under the spray. Facing away from me, he braced his hands on the wall on either side of the shower knobs. Head hanging, back flexed with tension that didn't seem to ease. I watched the muscles expand and contract like wings with every tight breath. Realizing I may only be adding to his unease, I half-turned to leave.

"Don't," he rasped, still staring at the onyx floor below him. "Stay."

Stay. It was all he asked me to do. Stand there and keep him company. Only, I couldn't. I couldn't just stand there and watch the darkness that expanded with every passing breath consume him. Careful steps, the way you move toward a dangerous animal. That was how I approached him. A beast. A beast that had begun cleaning the blood of other men from his skin with a bar of soap that had gone from white to pink, scenting the air.

Sage and citrus.

I slipped through the opening between the wall and pane of glass that defined the shower's large space. He eyed me as I moved into the shower with him, still dressed for bed in my white tank and shorts. At first, I tried to just watch him from beside the glass panel as he rinsed the blood away. Clayton shoved the soap back into the notch on the wall. Running his hands through his hair, he squeezed his eyes shut and pushed out another breath. I took the opportunity to take him in again. Two years without seeing a man like this made me wonder if I was simply not used to it. If my hunger was distorting the way he looked, the same way food tastes better when you're starving. Hardened muscle everywhere, arms covered in ink, and lean from whatever training they must have taught him in the SEALs.

Bracing himself against the wall once again, Clayton released a shuddering sigh as if the act had taken everything out of him. It was that sound. That sound spoke to the wound in my center. Soothing himself. It made me move from my position against the glass. Toward him. It made me duck beneath one arm so that I was facing him, the water splashing off of his body onto mine. The thin material soaked through as we stared at each other, baring me to him so thoroughly that I no longer felt guilty for being clothed when I could see so much of him.

"Casey."

Clayton's voice was pained, his chest heaving as his eyes fixed on me from beneath his brows like a fallen angel. Muscles in his cheeks flickered as he clenched his jaw. My name had been a warning. I'd danced on stage in front of hundreds of men. They watched me writhe and move with the same superficial interest I'd seen from most of the ones I'd dated. That's what I thought it was to be wanted. To be desired.

I'd been wrong.

Their lust for me couldn't match this. It was a sorry shadow compared to the raw energy I felt radiating from him. Bronze eyes traced my lips. Skated over my throat. I swallowed hard at the need I saw in those eyes as they continued down, down over the now transparent white tank and shorts, until they hit my feet. He licked his lips, and I could almost sense what he was thinking. Thinking about tasting. Touching. They stayed there as one hand moved from the wall. Lower. Steam. There was too much steam in here.

"I'm not going to touch you."

Finally, his gaze dragged back up my body to snare on mine again. Cold pressed up against my back. The wall. My back had hit the wall. I drew in an uneven breath, forcing my hands to remain at my sides as I fought the urge to put them on him.

"Why?" I asked weakly.

That wry smirk tugged at the corner of his mouth. Barely a glimmer of it, not enough for one of those dimples, but it was there. The first sign I'd seen that the man I knew was still inside him. Under all that pain. Those dark clouds. All that bitter darkness I wanted to drive away.

"It's your turn to watch," he rasped, taking small steps to crowd into me. So close I could feel gusts of breath on my collarbone as he heaved them, in and out. "Watch, firebird, because you should know what you do to me."

A flick of his wrist snagged my attention, forcing it down to what strained between us. It flicked again as he gave one long pump over thick, pink flesh.

Oh.

He was perfect everywhere, but here he was flawless. I swallowed, biting my lip at the lewd movement of a clenched fist sliding over his shaft. Drawing hard pulls of himself, he groaned. The sound bounced off the walls, echoing into my bones. My fingers closed and opened at my sides, unsure about what to do next because he told me he wouldn't touch me. Did that mean I couldn't touch him?

God, I wanted to touch him.

I wanted it so much, it made my fingers quake. To take him in my hand and make him feel good. Wrap my lips around him. Make him groan for me. Clayton watched me watch him, his expression growing tight as the breaths dropping from his barely parted lips came in faster. The hand on the wall beside my head fisted, knuckles going white. That burning gaze dropped to my mouth, taking in the sweep of my tongue as I licked my lips. His hand paused, his hips moving into the tight ball to fuck his fist as more agonized sounds sawed out of him.

"Casey," he breathed.

Warmth built low in my belly. He'd seen me come. Unleashed me as he focused all of his attention on my pleasure. That had been just for me. This. It was about him. I could see the guilt in his eyes. Worried about what this was for me. The conflict about what we were doing here. I wanted that to go away, too. Wanted to tell him that I'd put myself here. I could walk out of this shower at any time. I wasn't some fragile thing that needed guarding. It was clear he still saw me that way. I could almost see the words he was holding back from me. The words he wanted to protect me from.

I want you.

If I had been a different woman, a braver woman, I would have told him the truth. I would have reached out and touched him. Or touched myself to ease the throbbing arousal between my legs. Instead, I stood there. A squeeze of my thighs confirmed that I wanted to be touched. Wanted to feel the thick length of him inside me. He marked the movement with a low curse, that flicker of a smirk returning to his features before his speed ramped up. Another deep groan lodged in his chest, brows drawing together as he shifted away from me, painting the black floor with his spend.

"Fuck," Clayton panted, his head hung there, water splashing over the strands of pink hair that dangled over his forehead. Perfectly sculpted shoulders heaved, lungs working to gulp down air after his release. An agonized laugh burst from his lips as one hand wiped water away from his face. The warm water washed over me as I tried and failed to get my feet moving, to get closer to him. To do something to close this distance between us. Instead, I watched as Clayton got out of the shower, toweled himself off, slinging the fabric around his hips when he was finished. He sighed as he shut the bathroom door behind himself, "It's never going away now".

THIRTY-EIGHT

CLAYTON

*W*hat the hell am I doing?

The thought beat in my head like a drum. After the night I'd had, every single moment was replaying simultaneously. Each memory was like a song raging from the loudest stereo. I couldn't think. Booming memories of bullets. Bodies hitting the floor. Blue and red mixed together on raw concrete. My mind didn't quiet until I saw her. After that, there was only one thought. Big brown eyes pinned to me. Pink cheeks. Thighs clenched together. A bitten lip at what she saw. The fact that what she saw didn't upset her. That look was unmistakable.

Desire for me.

Yanking a fried electrical cord from the carcass of the bike in front of me and tossing it into an open box, I told myself that it didn't matter if she stayed. Or watched until I spilled myself onto the floor. What I did wasn't right. It was an argument I'd been having with myself for hours since I walked out of that bathroom. Walked out, dressed myself, and came here. With my laptop sitting open on the low tool chest beside me, I was able to keep an eye on her through the cameras, but I needed distance. The 1975 Honda was supposed to clear my mind. Instead, I kept thinking about her. About that look on her face. About wanting to kiss those lips. About everything that made my skin feel like it was two sizes too small whenever I was around her.

Since firing up the feed on my laptop, she hadn't done much. There was only a camera pointed at the door of the bathroom, so I saw when she'd left and gone into the bedroom. The camera in the bedroom hadn't revealed much with the lights turned off. Enabling night vision right now felt like a violation of her privacy, and I could see well enough to know that she was alone in there. Eventually, the motion sensors from the bedroom went dark, releasing minimal alerts. Assuming she'd gone to sleep, I got back to work on the bike. Rewiring the starter relay wasn't going to magically do itself. The open box was beside my bare feet, next to the open computer. I was reaching down to pick the part up from its wrappings when I heard music.

Music?

Music filtered out of the little speakers on my laptop. Coming from the feed in the bedroom. I stopped, one hand clutching the new fuse, and watched for movement on the screen. Nothing from the bedroom. Still black. An alert came from the hallway as a feminine shadow moved through its faint light. The music moved with it, a glowing phone screen the only object on camera.

As soon as I realized the music was definitely coming from her phone, Casey appeared in the living room. The low light from the streetlamps outside illuminated her better, glinting off the curls of her still-damp hair. She had changed out of her soaked pajamas. Out of the pajamas and into—I swallowed as realization struck me. She'd put on *my* boxers. One of my shirts, too.

Casey looked around the room. Searching for something. When her gaze fell on the coffee table, she paused and leaned forward to pick up a small object. A flash of light turned into flame. The lighter. She bent forward again, lighting the three wicks of the big candle on the table. Her silhouette slid around the room until she lit every candle I owned. Golden light surrounded her. Picking up the phone she'd discarded on the chaise of the sofa, she typed something out. A text message popped up on the screen of my laptop a second later.

> I hope you're paying attention.

Without waiting for a response from me, she turned up the volume on the music and threw the phone on the sofa again. *Kill For Your Love* filled the room. A mischievous look crossed her features as she glanced over her shoulder at the camera mounted in the corner. The one she knew I was watching. A slow, seductive beat pumped out of the device as Labrinth's sultry voice started to sing. Casey swirled her hips, moving her legs with the motion. Widening her stance, she bent forward with a flick of her hair that moved in a flash of red and turned her eyes to the camera. I drew in a breath. Both hands went to the back of her legs in a tantalizing slide upward. Repeating the movement on each side, she flipped herself upright again and turned to face the camera. Manicured fingers skimmed below the hem of the shirt, lifting the material to tease with flashes of her yoga-toned stomach.

She was dancing. For me.

Another twirl and she was faced away from me again. Casey rotated her hips, hands moving over her ass to lift the oversized shirt a little and let it fall. Bending forward, in front of the camera, she planted her hands on the chaise and bent her knees. A slide forward had her torso flush with the top of the chaise, ass in the air, hands moving to the curve of it again. Sharp pain lanced into my hand. I'd gripped a small metal bracket too hard. Dropping the object, I returned my focus to the screen. In my brief moment of distraction, I hadn't seen her flip over.

Now lying fully on the chaise, her back flush with the cushion, her feet braced on the corners. Hips pushed up, Casey let her hands run over her stomach, skin bare from where the shirt had ridden up. In this light, I couldn't quite see what she was doing under the black cotton, but I knew. She was touching herself the way I had touched her. Her hands ran down again, connecting with the waistband of the boxers. Stretching and moving them, showing me she wore nothing underneath with little flashes of exposed skin, she released the material with a quiet snap. I was grateful she couldn't hear the small, helpless noise that came out of me at the sound.

This was the girl I'd never gotten to meet. The one who commanded a room with her body. The one who could bring men to their knees with a dangerous smile. A siren whose beauty could spark wars in her honor. The siren lifted the shirt again, this time revealing the generous mounds underneath. Curves that made my mouth go dry as I pictured tasting the pink, peaked flesh. An arch of her back and a swift movement of her arms had the shirt tossed aside. Her hands moved over the exposed expanse of her torso in appreciative sweeps and squeezes.

I hadn't noticed the song stop. It didn't seem as if she did, either. The rhythm still moved through her, like she could hear the beat of my heart and chose to keep dancing to it. A roll of her body. Another at the feel of her hands on herself. Hands that toyed with that waistband again. Skimming and sliding over the cotton like a snake sliding between her fingers. She threaded the material through, eyes locked on the camera as she let one hand plunge under. A moan followed.

"Keep watching," she breathed.

I was. There was no chance of stopping. Not as I saw and heard what happened next. The hand beneath her boxers, my boxers, was moving between her thighs. The other hand feathered over her stomach, pinching and kneading the breast she found. Her panting breaths picked up, interrupted only by the sound of her whimpers of pleasure. Sounds and sights that made my throat tighten. I thought I'd seen and heard enough to do me in forever when I heard her near her peak. Legs twined together, head tossed back, back arched. No. I hadn't realized how much more fucking difficult things could get for me until she cried out one word as she came. One damn word.

"Clay."

Cursing low, I balled my hands into fists and tried to take a steadying breath. Tried to focus on the important part. She'd finished. Finished on her own. That was good. Her first solo orgasm was a big deal. A *not about me* big deal. Even if her crying out my name made it feel like it was a little about me.

Had she been picturing me?

Stop it.

Casey lay there for a while. Collecting herself, maybe. A giggle cut through the dark. I couldn't help smiling at the sound of it. Picking up my laptop, I opened my text app and typed a response to her.

> I could never stop watching you, firebird.

I picked up my water bottle and slugged back, gulping the liquid down to cool me from the inside. It took half the damn bottle. This thing between us. It was a living, breathing entity. Chasing me down. Never letting me forget for one moment how I felt about her. Being in her atmosphere had made me forget everything bad. The light leaving the eyes of men I killed tonight had been replaced with her liquid fire. The squeeze of her thighs as she watched me fist myself. Knowing that watching me had that effect on her was what sent me over the edge. Crying out my name as she erupted? I'd be thinking about that until the day I died.

Letting her into my home was always going to be dangerous for both of us. I thought at worst, she'd hate me forever. This type of danger was a new tightrope for me.

Helping her was one thing, but toying with each other like this was risky. Unable to trust myself to sleep beside her, I lay down on the sofa hours later to try and find some semblance of sleep with that question, the same question I'd been asking myself all night, illuminated in my mind like it was plastered across a grand fucking marquee. What the hell am I doing? The answer whispered itself to me as I fell asleep. Falling. I was falling for her. Again.

God, who the hell was I trying to kid? My feelings for her were buried alive in a shallow grave.

THIRTY-NINE

CASEY

> That song with Ariana and The Weekend is playing in the bar. I remember when you joked it could be ours.

Clayton dropped me off at the loft after this morning's meeting. He hadn't spoken to me much. Only an innocuous question here and there. Then he left, explaining that he had to go take care of a security system at a home in the Hollywood Hills. He'd be back in an hour, he said.

Last night was a leap. A moment of wild abandon I'd never have allowed myself with another man. I'd gone to bed. Laid there. Stared at the ceiling, too full of energy. I was so wound up that I couldn't stop fidgeting under the covers. His breathless words replayed over and over again.

"You should know what you do to me."

The loft was too quiet for him to be working down the hall. I would have heard the clicks of his keyboard even with the bedroom door closed. He was still out. So I hopped in the shower. It was there that I was met with a vivid memory of his wrist flexing, the cords of muscle flickering up his forearm in the wake of his aggressive self-pleasure. The grip of his hand. The feral look in his eyes. Those beautiful, hungry caramel-colored eyes.

I stood there. Right where he stood. Right where we watched each other. Thinking about the fantasy I had last night. He would get on his knees, fingers hooking around the waist of my soaked pajama shorts. They would stick to my skin, creating resistance as he tried to pull them from me. His rich laugh would bounce off the shower walls. After the fabric was free from me, he would look up into my eyes. Through his dark gold brows, he'd watch me watch him. Soft kisses on my knees. My inner thighs. My hip. One long-fingered hand would circle around the back of one leg, bending it slowly to rest on his impressive shoulder. He would look at me, a silent question passing between us. I'd nod.

Yes.

Even in my fantasies, he protected me. Not just from the outside world, but from myself. I leaned back against the shower wall, flinching a little at the cold stone against my back. One hand parted my slick flesh, dusting over my clit. It had gone so sensitive at the thought of my mercenary. I touched where my fantasy licked. Rolled where he sucked. Moved my hips against where I'd grind into his face, gripping his hair, twirling it between my fingers. The same fantasy I'd brought myself to finish with on the sofa not so many hours ago.

"*Come on,*" he would huff against my skin. "*Finish on my tongue. I want to taste it.*"

The imagined command had my legs shaking, chest heaving as I moaned through my orgasm. Then I started laughing. It was the same reaction I'd had after Clayton left me in his bed, having wrung that delicious sensation from my body with his relentless efforts and spine-tingling countdown. It happened last night, too. It was as if the pressure of every denial my body dealt me was expressing itself with every stupid laugh. I couldn't pretend to understand the psychology of it. I could only finish cleaning myself.

"Unbelievable," I laughed.

When I emerged from the bathroom, I noticed Clayton had still not returned. Deciding that this was unacceptable, I unwrapped myself from the towel and lay across his bed. Strategically draping the fabric over myself, I took another selfie and posted it to the temporary feed on my profile. Practically a centerfold. Grateful that no one in my family had social media accounts, I went to close the app when a little red dot popped up next to the messages icon. I tossed down the device and rose to dress myself, opting to make MotoDisco312 wait for a response. My skin felt raw enough that one of his threadbare vintage t-shirts and a grey pair of my lounge shorts were almost too much to bear.

I shivered, picking up the phone to look at what he'd sent me when I saw the username. Not him. A girl. Some local food influencer who had been a mutual follow at the time. I'd commented on her page. I followed. She followed back.

How beautiful Ronan's princess is. You've even got his eyes.

I dropped the phone. From the comforter's soft surface, the screen stared up at me. Three bouncing dots. They were typing another message.

It doesn't matter where your daddy is hiding you away.

My hand snapped out to grab the phone, moving to block the user from my account. The button was just below my fingertip when the next message popped up. My eyes fixed on the thread, when I realized I hadn't checked this account. She wouldn't talk to me like this. We didn't know each other.

It wasn't her.

Opening the profile, I checked to see who she followed. No one. No one but me. This user had mimicked an account I'd seen just to gain access to me. Because it wasn't her. Some random influencer wouldn't know who I was. They sure as hell wouldn't know who my father was.

But Ilia Kremnik would. I had trouble imagining they were anywhere near as talented as the man I was staying with, but they'd found my social media account easily enough. I read the message.

I'll see you soon.

A gasp popped out of me, causing me to drop the phone again. My heart thundered in my ears, drowning out the sound of my bare feet slapping on the polished stone floor. Clayton had shown me what to do. He showed me. Scanning for what I needed, I loosed a frustrated huff. Rows and rows of binders with dates printed onto the spines in neat lettering. My hands fluttered over them, pulling each one a little as I cursed myself for not remembering this detail. So many of them. There were so, so many binders. Binders, binders, binders.

"Where is it!?"

I remembered the row, but not the number. Which binder had he pulled? Sinking resignation smoked like a bomb in my gut as my bleak fate became clear with every passing second. Until I was met with resistance. The binder slid free on the track, opening up with the keypad I'd seen before. Star symbols danced across the display. *Input access code.*

The code. The code!

Each number gave a small beep when it was punched on the keypad until a deeper tone sounded, confirming the correct code had been entered. Metal slid on metal as the door pushed open to the hidden space inside. Shoving the keypad back into place, I ran into the opening and tugged the door shut. For as heavy as it was, it slid shut with ease. Locks loudly clanged into place automatically.

Sweat. I was sweating. Was there air in here? It didn't look like there were any vents. If Clayton took too long to come back, I could die. He could roll the door open and find my corpse curled up on this little sofa. It was a soft, nice little sofa. A nice, cozy place to die. Better than the floor of a trailer in the middle of nowhere. My breaths came in shorter and shorter spurts, the space in my chest where air should be shrunk with each passing second.

Too small. Too small. Too small.

The first week I met with the survivors group, Lisa spoke to us about grounding to get through moments that felt out of our control. She'd said that situations that were stressful to us were inevitable. Managing our response to those situations was a skill we'd hone over time. I'd practiced. Practiced the phrase she'd taught us. I closed my eyes and inhaled, forcing more air into the tight space beneath my ribs.

"I'm safe. This feeling will pass."

Deep breath in. Burning resistance filled my lungs. I could do this. I could. Some stubborn part of me was extremely irritated that I was experiencing a panic attack within a day of finally finishing on my own. No. I would not be conquered by this.

"I'm safe."

Exhale. I was safe. I was in Clayton's panic room. Not a trailer. In Los Angeles. Not the desert. I was safe.

"This feeling will pass."

Over and over again. I wasn't sure at what point I'd closed my eyes, but they flew open when I felt large warm hands on my face.

"Breathe. Breathe, Casey," that deep rasp scraped over my nerves as he spoke. "You're safe. No one can get to you."

Clayton was kneeling before me, eyes soft with worry as he pulled me into his lap. Hard, lean muscle was warm as he enveloped my body with his, rocking gently as he made little shushing noises. One hand made long soothing strokes down my back as the other tucked my head into the crook of his neck.

"I've got you, firebird."

It wasn't until I became still that I realized I'd been shaking. He was still rocking me, petting me with a gentle touch. A steady stone hearth for the raging fire of fear within me, waiting for the flames to die down. More soothing noises came from his lips as I tipped my head up to look at him. Pink hair ruffled in little licks and flicks in every direction. That easy half-cocked smile brightened his features as caramel eyes met mine.

"You're here," I said, not recognizing the small broken voice that came out of me. Clayton's forehead dropped to mine.

"One knight in shining armor, no noble steed. You'll have to settle for a motorcycle."

A wet laugh burst from me. Of course, he remembered the snide remark I'd made about needing to be rescued. The hand that had been cupping the back of my head moved to support my jaw, a thumb brushing over the apple of my cheek to wipe away a tear. On top of losing myself in my mantra, I'd also been crying, because of course I was.

"You know," I sniffed. "The knight in shining armor usually kisses the princess after he rescues her."

He smirked, that dimple appearing in his golden cheek. The hand on my jaw firmed its grip, drawing my face toward his. Our noses brushed, and a fleeting look I couldn't identify passed through his eyes. They dipped to my mouth and drifted shut as he closed the last bit of distance. Warm and soft. Sweet and gentle. Slow. I could feel his lips part around mine. A low humming sound made my lips tingle, pulling a soft sound of surprise from me.

"I've got you," he said against me.

Opening for him was easy. Natural. The velvet slide of his tongue against mine was enough to make me forget the cobwebs of worry still clinging to my mind, only sharpening my focus on the heat pooling low in my belly. It was incredible the way my body reacted to him, like it knew exactly what lay in the promise of his touch. Clayton's thumb hooked my chin, drawing it down to deepen the kiss. That kiss walked a tight line between tenderness and dominance. My body pressed into his. The hand at my back fisted in my shirt. Thoughts of what those long, powerful fingers would feel like between my thighs pulled another whimper from my lips.

Another answering groan fell from him. My hand had lowered, meeting with the leather and steel of his belt. I wanted more. Wanted to feel what strained behind his fly. Desperate, my effort to free him was clumsy. The clattering jangle as the buckle collided with my fingers caused me to jerk back.

"What?"

Clayton's eyebrows shot up in surprise, wariness coloring those beautiful caramel irises. My lips half-formed around words and stunted sounds, attempting to answer. But my mind, my traitorous mind. It was already gone. Being crushed down on a dusty floor mat by a pair of men I'd never seen before.

"It's not fair. She didn't fight you."

I swallowed, forcing a smile to my face. Clayton's eyes filled with concern as they took in my expression. His eyebrows narrowed at whatever they beheld, hands releasing me.

"I'm sorry, Casey. I shouldn't have—"

"No, it's not you. It's fine. I'm sorry," I warbled. "Thank you."

Pushing up from the floor, I smoothed my hands over my clothes and brushed my hair out of my face. One deep breath followed another. I was fine. I was safe. And Clayton had just kissed me.

FORTY

CLAYTON

Every time I got into that black box to clean myself off, I was picturing her standing there. That psychotic moment in the shower. I couldn't stop thinking about it. Delectable doe eyes watching me as I took in her form. Freckles and furled flesh peaking at me from beneath her soaked clothes. My imagination was a devious bastard, gnawing at the bars of my self-control as it wove other pictures into my mind. It forced me to wonder how she would sound if I got on my knees and licked her where she so clearly needed relief. How she would feel in my arms if I hoisted her up and took her against the wall.

"*Clay.*"

That imagination of mine. It was a complete asshole. When Casey emerged from the bedroom this morning and strode into the living room in her little yoga set, I decided to search for electroshock therapy options. Those thoughts were better for my sanity than remembering the sight of her crouching on the sofa in the panic room, muttering nonsense to herself with her eyes shut much too tightly. Red hair was all tangled around her shoulders in half-damp curls. She'd been so pale. So washed out from fear that her freckles looked like blood splattered across the bridge of her nose. I checked on her again. Before I'd left her to come here, I'd tried to have a talk with her about what sent her into the room in the first place. She showed me the interaction on her social media account.

"You didn't know this person?"

"They were pretending to be someone else," she muttered. "All the pictures are the same and everything, except I'm the only account they follow. Plus, see the period between the first and second half of the name? That's not the way it is on her real account."

I scrolled through the short chain of messages. They were trying to provoke her. It was a sign of their impatience. Trying to flush her out of hiding by scaring the hell out of her. Probably to get her to do something irresponsible. A smart move, honestly. Something I would do if I were having a hard time tracking someone down. That conversation led to sifting through her social media page and validating every single follower with a thorough check. By the time I was done, I had mentally kicked my own ass up and down the street for not doing this in the first place. And for leaving her alone, a mistake that I'd already had to repeat thanks to her endlessly needy family.

Security system armed. Cameras on. Casey was safe. For now. For the fourth time in twenty minutes, I examined the feed. Casey hadn't moved from the corner of the sofa closest to the window. The last of the afternoon sunlight poured in, apparently nourishing both the houseplants and the woman. Her hair was tamed into a loose braid, and she still wore the T-shirt and shorts I'd found her in this morning. The thick knitted throw blanket from my bed was draped over her lap, where she cradled her e-reader. A cup of something steamed on the coffee table.

"She looks quite happy."

The dark, lilting voice gave me a start. Killian chuckled darkly as I minimized the window again. Installing his security system had been simple enough. Though with the ATF investigation he'd mentioned, I spent the first few hours of my visit here scanning the home for any sort of device that might be giving off a signal. I'd found and disabled three.

"Just checking in on her."

Aside from the provocation this morning, Kremnik and his Russian mafia associates had gone quiet. In my experience, quiet was almost always a bad thing. Killian grunted, seated next to me at the head of his large stone dining room table. The smoking skull tattoo looked more like a mask as he took a sip from a crystal tumbler. The rim of the dark glass flickered with light from the fire in the black stone fireplace only a few steps away. It was easy to see the resemblance between this man and his father. While Ronan was an intimidating man in his late forties, his son was terrifying at twenty-eight. Tousled dark brown hair fell into his matching eyes, giving me a glimpse of what his father must have looked like at this age. Minus the ink covering every inch of skin. The young man stretched, idly scratching the close-cropped beard covering his square jaw.

"Are we almost done here?" Killian asked, adjusting the cuff of his tight navy sweater.

The sweater was paired with deep charcoal slacks and black boots, making Killian look like he belonged in this space. A deep blue velvet sofa faced the fireplace behind me. His kitchen was crafted of dark walnut cabinets with black marble countertops and a matching backsplash. Even the exterior of the ultramodern home was made of black stone, making it look like a lump of charcoal dropped along the beaches of Marina Del Rey. It was completely at odds with his white stone cottage nestled in the lush green countryside outside of Belfast, which I'd seen not so long ago.

I shuddered as cold wind sliced through the space, coming off the beach and through the open floor-to-ceiling window that led out to a small stone terrace. I glanced at the progress bar on Killian's tablet. The download of my software was taking longer on a wireless connection, a fact I'd been cursing since I wanted to get the fuck out of here and back to his sister.

"Should be about another twenty minutes, then I can finish installation."

Killian let out a disgruntled huff and tossed back the rest of his whiskey. Sliding his phone out of his pocket, he looked at me through lowered brows as he tapped at the screen absently. The fireplace he'd turned on with a remote remained silent behind us, leaving room for the distant crash of ocean waves. I wondered if his father's crackling pyre bothered him as much as it did me. My eyes drifted to the minimized tab, anxious to check my cameras again.

I shouldn't have left her.

"Since it seems we have the time, I'd like to ask what the hell is going on between you and my sister?"

I let my eyes remain fixed on the computer. The answer to that question was dicey. I had no idea how to explain it to him. Not that I wanted to. At all. *Oh, nothing crazy. I'm caught in a weird bargain where I help your sister with sex and her PTSD, all while navigating my unresolved feelings for her. She wants us to be friends.* I heard him unstop the whiskey bottle and pour himself another drink, the liquid glug-glug-glugging into the smoky crystal glass. Heard him sigh through his nose before he continued.

"Come on, Wrigley. You put a knife through my cousin's hand for insulting her. It was all over your face. I'm not a damned fool."

Slowly, I met his gaze. It was incredible how simultaneously similar and dissimilar his eyes were to Casey's. They were technically the same shape and color, but completely different from one another. Her eyes were kind. Gentle. His eyes were the direct opposite. Unlike his father, Killian's wrath was cold. It crackled around his edges like ice crawling over a black lake. Cold eyes pinned to me, glaring up through dark brows as he waited for an explanation.

"She's my friend. I don't like people insulting my friends," I monotoned.

A half-truth. I didn't go around stabbing people for my friends. I also didn't make a habit of kissing my friends, something I'd done only a few hours ago, but here we were. Fuck, her lips were so soft. Killian smirked, taking a pull from his glass and letting his hand rest on the table with a clunk. His fingers tapped the crystal, the silver signet ring on his index finger clinking on the glass while he considered my answer.

"You're a shit liar, you know that?" He asked, righting himself in the seat so he could lean forward. "My father knows you were spending time together two years ago. He knows because I told him. I watch out for my sister. I know when something upsets her. She avoided you like the fucking plague for years, and now you're back to being thick as thieves. If all that wasn't enough, you look at her like she hung the fucking moon. You don't have any people, and your loyalty is for sale. So, I'll ask you again, and I want a straight goddamn answer. What the fuck is going on between you and my sister?"

Every window was open. Every single one, yet the air in the room felt thick between us. I'd earned the trust of this family. I knew that because they'd let me see behind the curtain. They'd put their safety in my hands. Yet, in this moment, I could feel the threat. The silent implication was that my life depended on my answer.

To me, she was the answer to a question I'd been asking myself for my entire life. The dream I hoped to find when I closed my eyes. The person I thought about every morning. To her, I was just a friend. Someone she trusted in her most vulnerable state. Someone she wanted. Those eyes that were so unlike her brother's flashed into my mind. Wide with fear as I took her into my lap. I could still feel the way she trembled as I wrapped her in my arms. Or the way she relaxed in my hold as I kissed her. I wasn't sure what I was to her. But I did know one thing.

It was none of his goddamn business.

The bottle of whiskey was crafted with thick glass. Heavy and stout. It was weighty as I took it in my grasp and unstopped it. Killian watched as I took a slug straight from the bottle. Sherry-aged liquid coursed down my throat, warming my belly. The heavy bottle clunked against the stone table when I set it down again and aimed my gaze at the Irishman beside me.

"Killian, I dealt with a lot of men like you when I was in the service. Highest on the food chain. King of the jungle. Each of them deadly in their own way. Feared by everyone around them. So, I want you to know that I know what it might cost me when I tell you to back the fuck off."

To the untrained eye, Killian's expression was blank, but I'd felt it. The shift in his mood. The corners of his eyes narrowed in tiny increments. His nostrils flared. It wasn't anger, but it was in the neighborhood. Irritation. I fought a flinch as Killian's arm shot up, tossing back the remainder of his whiskey. A satisfied grunt breached the air as he stood upright and slapped me on the shoulders with both hands. The heavy thud of his boots retreated from the room as I relaxed in my seat, realizing that I just passed whatever test Killian had just subjected me to. His muttered approval disappeared with him.

"Good man."

Four minutes remained on the progress bar. It wouldn't be long now. With the sun almost below the horizon, evening began to purple the sky over the blue water. I opened the tab at the bottom of my screen, punching in the code to access the cameras again. She was still there. While I wasn't looking, she'd gotten up to light a candle or two. The record player beneath the window was warbling out some peaceful folk song. A smile bloomed across my lips at the sight of it, the encounter with Killian washing away with the crashing waves outside. Ordering dinner for us before I packed up to leave, I decided that her brother had been right about one thing.

She did look happy.

FORTY-ONE

CASEY

"I'm proud of you."

Lisa put her hand on my shoulder, smiling at me as the others continued packing up. Her proclamation was low enough for only me to hear. I smiled back at her with a little shrug. Punctuating the moment with a small pat over my sweater-covered shoulder, she turned away to answer her ringing phone. In truth, I was proud of myself, too.

Today's meeting had been a step forward. Not a leap or a jump. Only a small step. I'd actually shared some things. I'd shared. It was becoming easier and easier to let myself be vulnerable with other people. It was still difficult to discuss what had happened. My role in it. So I didn't. Instead, I talked about the tiny advances I was making in my personal life. Being able to finish, finally, after not being able to for so long. The person who was making me feel feelings I hadn't been sure I could have anymore. People nodded. They understood. They knew how what happened could make you feel like you lost control. It wasn't just about control over your body, but control over how you react to other people, too. How it feels when someone uses you in that way, it feels like your body doesn't belong to you anymore.

With Clayton, it didn't feel that way. Not at all. There was fear, yes. Of course, there was. Things set me off. I talked about the false start in the apartment, leaving out the panic room for obvious reasons. The belt buckle. How I'd seen the pink hair and immediately known who I was with. I also knew that fear wasn't about him. Somehow, I knew I could find my way around that fear with him. Lisa had talked about how our journeys wouldn't happen in a straight line. That faith in myself felt like a step forward, too.

I had only one mountain left to summit.

That mountain had red hair and had twenty years on me. It had been all I thought about as I started a load of laundry. My mind raced with it even as I sat on the sofa, rereading the page I'd tried to read three times over. I was on my fourth attempt when the front door slammed shut. Clayton clopped inside in his motorcycle boots, shrugging his jacket off to hang on the hook beside the door. I closed up my e-reader and set it on the coffee table, throwing myself back into the cushions.

"Everything alright over there?"

I groaned at the ceiling.

"I think I'm going stir-crazy. Cabin fever. Whatever you call it."

I didn't feel like talking about my mom. Clayton grabbed a black hoodie from the hooks on the wall, removing the backwards cap he had on to tug it over himself as he approached the sofa. One swift movement had the throw blanket in his hand, the other outstretched to help me up from the pillows that were working on swallowing me whole.

"Come on," he smirked. "Let's get you some fresh air."

The rooftop wasn't much to look at. A bunch of what looked like asphalt surrounded by waist-high brick walls. That and the access door that leads up to it with its little single bulb illuminated over the frame. It was the kind of ordinary that made the view around it that much better by comparison. Pink skies and purple clouds. Buildings around us sparkled as each one lit up for the night. Twilight in the city. A cold whip of wind passed us by, making me wish I hadn't changed into a dress as its lilac skirt fluttered and exposed my skin to the chill night air. So much for wanting to feel pretty, I guess.

"Are we allowed up here?" I asked with a shiver.

Clayton shrugged, holding out the throw blanket from the sofa. I wrapped myself up in it, ignoring the way his hands rubbed at my shoulders, which warmed me everywhere. The heat from his body was close, but not close enough to warm me against the biting evening.

"Probably not, but I have more of an apologize later mentality about it. It's not like anyone else can get up here anyway," he noted. "Besides, I do the security for the whole building, so they'd just be reporting me to me."

We fell silent, watching the cars on the street creep by toward their destinations. I wondered who was going home from work or if they were on their way to meet their friends. That was something I missed. Sophie. Maya. They were my friends. I'd pushed them away after everything happened, not wanting to explain what happened to me. Or to Isabelle, though Lilith told me she'd explained to them about the man who killed her and what she'd done with him. A burned-out grave in the desert seemed like a fitting end for someone like that. Still, the pain from the distance was beginning to outweigh the anxiety. I wasn't sure how to start seeing them again. I couldn't just show up out of nowhere. As if sensing the direction of my thoughts, Clayton cleared his throat and angled his head toward me.

"How are the meetings going?"

"I shared a little today. Not much, but it's a start," I shrugged. "I've started therapy, too, so that's something."

"You have?"

The low light coming from the door made it difficult to see him, but I didn't miss the way his brows shot up in confusion, likely trying to figure out how I was going to therapy without him noticing. I laughed a little and explained.

"Yeah, it's through this app I heard about at the community center. It's totally anonymous. Honestly, that's what I like about it. I can just dump all my feelings on a total stranger, and they can tell me if I'm overreacting or if I'm being a stubborn idiot."

Clayton's face twisted in amusement.

"They've said that to you?"

I let out a joyless laugh, returning my attention to the city around us. Down below, a pair of drivers was shouting at each other in the crowded intersection. My ears strained to hear what was being said, unfortunately, too far out of range to make it out.

"Not in so many words, but yeah."

"About what?"

Heaving a sigh that just barely shifted the stone in my gut, I slid my gaze to him from the corner of my eye.

"About my mom. She and I have a good relationship, but I've been avoiding telling her about what really happened to me. Two years ago. She's the only one in my family who doesn't know."

Clayton was silent for a long time. Long enough for me to actually turn my head and look at him. Pink hair was moving in the breeze from the sides of his hat, but his face was still. The expression on it curious and careful as he asked me the question I knew was coming.

"Why?"

"I thought she'd be disappointed in me," I sniffed. "Like I'd failed at being self-sufficient."

Tension rose up from my toes, climbing my limbs for every second that he said nothing. He didn't know my mom. Before that happened, he didn't even know me. Explaining that someone might feel differently about me after learning about my assault to someone who only met me after the fact felt like trying to breathe underwater. It was only made worse by what he said next.

"It's not your fault, Casey."

"I know it's not my fault! I know that," I snapped. "Of course, I know that. I didn't ask to be kidnapped. I didn't ask for them to pump so many drugs into me that I couldn't fight them off when they started-" I choked on the sob. Fire lanced through my body as I swallowed through my rage-induced tears. Clayton moved toward me. To hold me, I knew. I didn't want to be touched. I couldn't bear the weight of it as the scalding words poured out of me. "Every time I say it out loud, it makes what happened to me real. My skin aches with it. I just want to burn it off me, and I can't, Clay. I can't ever burn that feeling away. If I think about it for too long, I can still feel it."

The cold air felt sharper up here. Being up, away from the protection of surrounding structures, was probably to blame. I let myself believe that was why I began shivering. Clayton slid toward me. I allowed him to brace his arms on the wall behind me as I turned to face him. Wind blew hair over my eyes, prompting him to lift one of those hands to push it away. The red strands caught in a trail of my tears.

"Hey," he crooned.

"I want to be who I was before. I was better before," I warbled. Crying. Again. I hated that about myself. That no matter what I felt, tears were the answer. I cried when I was happy, when I was angry, or when I was sad. I cried when a piece of art or music moved me. I was crying now because I was frustrated. It always made me feel weak, because I felt everything so deeply. "I want to go back to my life. Back to dating and having fun. I'm too young to feel like my life is over."

The hand that brushed my hair away moved to dry my skin. Cool against my hot cheek. It circled around to cup the back of my head, stroking the nape of my neck. Warm. He was always so warm. I rested my cheek against the soft cotton of his hoodie, enjoying the scent of him as I took one soothing breath. Then another. I could feel the moment he buried his nose in my hair, breathing me in.

"It's alright, firebird."

"Why do you call me that?" I sniffled.

Clayton kissed my forehead before looking down at me.

"Oh, I don't know," he winked, tugging on a loose lock of my hair. "It's better than 'Red,' isn't it? As far as who you were before, I don't know. I think you're pretty amazing now."

His warmth trickled into me with every passing second, pooling in my bones. The hand at the back of my neck seemed to tighten with urgency as Clayton's eyes dipped to my mouth. I rose on my toes, closing the distance between us until there was only a breath of air keeping us apart. Bronze eyes became like molten caramel as he watched me, a low curse falling from his lips in a hesitant growl.

"Can I kiss you?"

I'd said it. I'd asked him, and it was still a surprise to me. He breathed a little laugh, his lips cocking to one side in a smirk.

"I'll make a deal with you," he purred, moving the hand at my neck to frame my jaw with his thumb and forefinger. A shiver followed in the wake of such a possessive touch. "You can kiss me any time you want. As long as you agree to talk to your mom."

I gaped at him. Clayton raised an eyebrow in challenge, as if to silently say *These are my terms, take them or leave them*. To entice me into agreement, he leaned in, bringing me closer with the hold on my face. Our noses brushed, his mouth open on another one of those flirtatious smiles that taunted me. Teased me. It was unfair, this affect he had on my body. My chin dipped in the barest hint of a nod.

"Good."

My lips collided with his hard enough to make him grunt. It wasn't delicate or graceful. It could have even been embarrassing. But I wouldn't let myself be embarrassed anymore. Not in front of him. Instead, I took what I wanted, relishing the feeling of actually wanting something. Wanting him. The taste of those quiet whimpers was so addictive, I opened to take more of it. Kissing Clayton felt like breathing fresh air. His tongue flicked against mine in a taunting caress. My toes curled in my boots, and my answering moan prompted him to do it again.

"I keep thinking about that dance," he huffed into my mouth. "You're so beautiful."

It was a confession that tasted as sweet as it sounded. This. I could tell myself that this was what I wanted to feel again. That desire for someone. The need for their body to be tangled up in mine. Only, I'd be telling myself a lie. I'd never felt for anyone the things I was feeling now.

For him.

I let the blanket drop to the ground as my arms circled around his neck to deepen the kiss. An approving hum rumbled from deep within his chest. He was hard against my stomach, seeking relief as he pressed his erection into me. Another groan rumbled out of him as I reached between us, using the heel of my palm to grind down his length. Then he pulled away. His breath was ragged as that half-cocked grin lit up his features.

Clayton stared down at me and panted, "We need to stop. I need to." He bent over and picked up the blanket to wrap around my shoulders. When my brows drew together in confusion, he kissed the tip of my nose and added, "Just for now."

FORTY-TWO

CLAYTON

"I can't believe we're eating dinner at five. Your mom is only in her forties. Definitely not old enough for the early-bird special."

Casey let out a chuckle as she entered the Olive Tree, an oceanfront Italian restaurant on the Venice boardwalk. I followed behind her, just barely catching her give the hostess her mother's name over the music. Its downtempo electronic pulses were almost enough to drown out my thoughts. It was one thing to learn about the woman who birthed the one holding my hand; it was another to come face to face with her. As far as this woman knew, I was seeing her daughter. Of course, that little nugget hadn't been too hard to swallow.

Last night, she'd told me she wanted to go back to her real life. I wanted to tell her that if she thought I was going to agree to make her come and then send her on her way, she was crazy. We were going to figure this out together. Even if I was back on the couch until I could control myself. Kissing her on the roof had felt like it was leading somewhere I didn't know how to navigate. I could be her fake boyfriend until then. She hadn't bristled when

I said as much to Tyler. Tyler, whose death I'd been plotting. Something to do with stereos cranked loud enough to implode his brain while playing his own terrible music. Or a good old-fashioned baseball bat.

Casey's hand felt good in mine as she took it to tug me through the restaurant, toward the large glass wall facing the terrace. The dining room was almost empty, dotted with a few people grabbing drinks at the bar. Small potted olive trees flanked either side of the bar, the only color aside from the liquor bottles on the arched shelves behind the bar top in the very white space.

"My mom and I used to get brunch here a lot," she offered over one shoulder. "I've never been here for dinner."

"It's five o'clock," I reminded her. "Technically not dinner. Dinner is the ice cream I'll be picking up on the way home."

"I told you her workday starts at six. She goes to bed early."

Doe eyes that looked even more doe-like when she wore that eyeliner rolled at me as she smirked, sitting down on the bench side of the table facing where the boardwalk connected with a park. The hostess left us with menus we had neglected to look at as people passed by. Because we were nestled between two tower heaters, I knew it wasn't the autumn nip entering the evening air that sent a chill through the woman beside me.

Without thinking, I placed a hand on hers. There were no words of affirmation I could offer. Nothing to reassure her about the conversation she'd come here to have. Instead, we waited. I pulled out my phone to check the camera feed from the corner store as well as the bank across the street, both easy enough to hack before we'd left. By the time I thought of a single comforting thing to say, our guest was letting herself through the small gate separating the pedestrians from the diners on the patio.

"Casey, honey!"

The smooth as silk voice was deeper than I'd expected, filled with experience and confidence. When it came to the Collins women, mere mortal men didn't stand a chance. Casey was the spitting image of her mother, only twenty years younger. Though a bit shorter than her daughter, the woman was no less statuesque in a white button-down blouse and high-waist, wide-leg black slacks that were perfectly tailored to show off the narrow points of a pair of expensive black leather high heels that clicked toward us. Red lips parted in a sweet smile as Casey stood up to greet her mother.

"Hi, mama," she hummed.

Green eyes skimmed over me as I stood, soft at first. Once the woman was standing at our table, a sharp edge had entered them. She set her big red Hermès bag down on the chair beside her with a decisive plop. Pearl studs shone at her ears as she threaded her fingers through her shoulder-length auburn bob to tame an errant lock of hair. The warning I'd gotten on the way here entered my mind.

"My mother is a self-made woman. She doesn't like excuses, and she sees right through bullshit, so don't even try it."

Casey rounded the table to throw her arms around her mother, who welcomed her gladly. Shoulders loosening at her daughter's embrace. Her eyes closed for a moment, taking it in. Soft for her, but for no one else. A belief that was confirmed when she reaffixed her attention to me.

"And this is?"

"Mom, this is Clayton Wrigley. He's a friend."

Neither of us missed the way she hesitated on that last word. Friend. I shook Rose's hand before we sat down again, letting her grip outperform my own. No need to show any kind of dominance in this encounter since Ms. Collins struck me as the Doberman in Louboutins sort of woman.

"Good to meet you, Mr. Wrigley."

Though she put on a pleasant smile and sat down at the table, Rose scrutinized us. She watched the way I helped her daughter to reclaim her seat on the bench. She watched the way Casey leaned into me. The word her daughter used was in direct conflict with her behavior because I was sure her friends didn't hold hands under the glass table. Not because it was a lie. More like an oversimplification.

Once the waitress noticed our final person had arrived, she came and took our order. A pint of Guinness for me, an order Rose barely winced at. She got a spritz. Her daughter sipped from an espresso martini, a beverage that looked like the elegant twin to my beer.

In my research on Casey Arawn, who had once been Casey Collins, I learned a lot about the woman who'd birthed her. The daughter of a now deceased Morty Collins, a mechanic and widower, grew up around classic cars and eventually worked in her father's garage. That is, until she gave birth to Casey. After moving to Northern California, she held a number of different jobs right up until the last decade. Rose Collins, like her daughter, was a fighter. She brought the pit bull in heels energy to her career as a self-taught day trader. A little bit of harmless internet prodding had shown me that after digging herself out of debt, she'd created an impressive little portfolio and nest-egg for herself. Hence the Birkin.

"Wait," Casey said with a tentative smile. "Do you mind if I run over there? I don't want to miss this light."

Flipping the top flap open, her hand plunged into the leather backpack on the bench between us. Joy cracked like a firework in my chest as I realized she'd begun carrying around the camera I'd given her. Without waiting to hear a response from either her mother or me, Casey let herself out of the patio to move toward the beach.

"So," Rose said, pointedly sipping her spritz before placing it on the table between us. "Tell me about yourself, Mr. Wrigley."

"There's not much to know," I shrugged.

"Let's not start this relationship by lying to each other. Though I suppose I don't blame you for being tight-lipped. My daughter likely warned you about me since you two are apparently living together," she purred, raising a brow in silent question. I reclined, taking a sip from my beer. Ignoring my non-answer to the implied question, Rose continued. "Casey learned a long time ago that bringing her boyfriends around to meet me wasn't a very good idea."

"Because they were intimidated by her ball-busting mother?"

My question got a smirk out of her that didn't quite reach her eyes. The stubborn bastard in me resolved to keep trying.

"Because I don't buy the nice guy act, Mr. Wrigley. Just as I'm not buying yours."

"Alright," I sighed. There was no reason to lie to her, but I wasn't going to spill every detail. Especially if Casey had told this woman I was dating her daughter. "I grew up in the system, so I don't have any family to speak of. Then I joined the Navy. Now I do private security work."

"What kind?"

"Internet and personal."

"Both?"

"Both."

My gaze snagged on Casey, happily snapping photos of the distant boardwalk. Its lights brightened with irresistible effervescence against the pinks of the darkening sky. But it wasn't as beautiful as the smiling face framed by deep red waves spilling out of her loose braid. The sage green velvet top she had on looked almost blue in this light, dark compared to her pale green skirt and leather boots. Beautiful. She seemed to snap a few more pictures before moving toward a group of children watching a street performer. Her lens zeroed in on the expressions of the audience, innocent and captivated.

And I'm falling in love with your daughter, I almost said.

Her eyes shifted to where I was watching the gorgeous redhead I'd brought here. The sunset bounced off the large waist-length curls that were the same shade of red as her own, though in this light, it glowed like it was made of glass. Casey grinned as she lifted her camera to capture passersby, people caught in moments of play with one another. I marveled at the photographer. Rose's expression warmed as she watched, muttering quietly to me.

"I'm glad you're in security. My daughter has a soft heart. She's the kind of person people take advantage of."

An aggressive prick of irritation raged beneath my skin at her words. Casey was soft, yes. Kind, also yes. But the implication that her kindness somehow made her weak was not something I could tolerate. Her daughter's fear of being judged for the things she couldn't control made more sense, but that didn't mean her mother was right. Softness required strength. Kindness, especially after what she'd been through, required the kind of fortitude that outweighed some of the soldiers I'd stood shoulder to shoulder with. When we'd left the loft, I'd done nothing but think about how much I wanted this woman to like me. That probably wouldn't happen now. Nope.

"With all due respect, Ms. Collins, your daughter is a hell of a lot stronger than you know," I snapped, unable to stop myself. "Don't mistake her soft heart for weakness. It's hard as hell to be soft in this world."

A perfectly groomed red eyebrow shot up, waiting for me to elaborate. I said nothing, choosing to make my point with an unflinching gaze. Rose Collins had the same energy as one of my old commanding officers. The kind of person who was smart enough not to wound you, but instead gave you enough rope to hang yourself. I took a long pull from my pint and relaxed in my seat again.

She opened her mouth to say something, only to be met with the approaching footsteps of her daughter. Casey's eyes shifted between us, her face tightening as she feigned jovial nonchalance.

"Everything alright here?"

I looked at Rose. Not only was I prepared for this woman to badmouth me to Casey, but I was prepared to take the consequences. Casey had hated me unrepentantly for two years. Two years of taking shit from the woman who'd been carrying my heart around in her pocket. I could take whatever she had to dish out. Her opinion paled in comparison. Only, just like her daughter, Rose surprised me.

"Absolutely. Mr. Wrigley was about to tell me all about his time in the Navy."

FORTY-THREE

Casey

> A normal day together. That would be paradise.

"Thank you for dinner, Mr. Wrigley. Even though I said I was going to pay," my mom started, a little bite in her voice I recognized as fake disappointment.

"You can get the next one," Clayton waved her off, fishing the keys out of the pocket of his jeans as he whispered to me. "Still not dinner."

I still wasn't sure what was said while I was away from the table. During the few stolen glances in their direction, I was only able to see my mother's back and Clayton's reactions. The look on his face when I returned was firm. No nonsense. Rose Collins had clearly waved her white flag at their standoff when she acted like there was no problem between them, because she would certainly not have played nice the way she was pretending to if she'd had the upper hand.

Clayton regaled us with stories of basic training and what it was like to be on a ship while getting your wisdom teeth removed. Navigating back to his bunk after anesthesia apparently took long enough for a snack break, which was ill-advised with fresh oral surgery. Rose chuckled at the way he turned poker games on board into favors from fellow sailors. She had actually laughed at his jokes while the man at my side shot me subtle, victorious glances. I stifled smiles with bites of my meal.

"I had to park a few blocks over. Stay with your mom while I grab the car," Clayton said, squeezing my hand once before walking away. He didn't notice the appreciative glances from passing women entering the restaurant. Though he didn't need my answer, I nodded anyway. It was part of the plan. An opportunity for me to speak with her alone. Now that it was happening, I wasn't sure I could follow through.

"How far away did you park?" I asked, hearing a scoff halfway through my question.

"Oh, I didn't drive. The company gave us access to a car service as one of the benefits. I think it's to keep us from wasting time driving when we could be working, but I honestly stop thinking about that place the moment I walk out the door. Anyway, they should be around to pick me up in a few minutes. Come on, sit with me while I wait."

My mother gestured to the bench in front of the restaurant, the area around us getting a little more crowded as diners filled in to grab dinner at a more reasonable hour. I looked at my phone. God, it was only seven o'clock.

"So," she chirped. "That pink hair really works on him."

"Don't start."

"I'm serious. He's good for you. Protective, but sweet, too. Where did you find that one?"

Her neatly groomed eyebrows were lifted, waiting for me to answer the question. The question that was the perfect opening. It was right there. The ugly truth of it. Another thing for me to gloss over with my mother, to make sure she doesn't feel like she's not doing enough. To let her know I'm fine.

But what happened had nothing to do with it. It wasn't my fault. The last thought sounded an awful lot like Clayton's voice as it rang within my mind. Looking down at the hand he'd squeezed before he left, my mouth opened and my ears filled with the sound of my racing heart.

"Actually, he found me. Two years ago."

My mother's brows creased, amusement still lighting her features while she waited for me to go on.

"I lied to you before," I babbled. "When I went off the radar for a few months, it wasn't to go to study yoga at a health center. There was no retreat. I was at this singles mixer, and I was abducted. The men who took me, they hurt me. They..." Swallowing around the lump in my throat, it became easier to look at my hands folded over in my lap. Cool air cut through the wet streams on my cheeks. Sorting through details, I took a breath and pushed on. "They were trafficking girls. A lot of them. The men who took me kept us in an empty office trailer in the middle of the desert for weeks. Months, actually. Lili, my old boss, helped to get me out. Clayton was with her. He's the reason I'm here now."

When the courage to look my mother in the eye finally rose, I found tears spilling down her face. Silently, she mouthed the phrase *my baby* before speaking.

"You were there for months."

It wasn't a question. I nodded anyway. Bracing myself for questions I didn't want to answer or a lecture about keeping the truth from her, I waited. The sound of diners waiting for their tables filled the silence between us, laughter and chatter so at odds with the heavy feeling in my chest. My mother stared at me, not caring that there were now streaks through her makeup.

"I'm sorry," I offered, wiping at my eyes. "I know how crazy that sounds. I should have told you."

"Why didn't you?"

Not a judgmental question. Cautiously curious, maybe. This was the part I didn't want to explain, the reason I'd kept it from her. The admission lodged in my throat, barely squeezing past the emotion there.

"Because I was afraid that you'd think I was weak."

"Oh, honey."

Her arms were around me in an instant, small sobs shaking the two of us. The scene earned a few strange looks from bystanders, but I let it roll off me and returned her embrace. I didn't know how long we sat there, holding each other. Our embrace was interrupted by a strong hand on my arm. I didn't need to look up to know who was standing by my side.

"Ready?" Clayton asked gently.

Slowly, we unwrapped from each other. My mother's brown gaze fixed on Clayton, the tears she'd been crying gone in an instant. The brave face of Rose Collins was once again in place, steely armor applied everywhere. She stood from the bench, smoothing her hands down the sides of her black slacks. As I readied to stand beside her, she stepped in front of me and threw her arms around Clayton. A look of surprise washed over his features with a glance in my direction. The words were watery. Barely audible. If her face hadn't been angled toward me, I wouldn't have heard what she said to him.

"Thank you for saving my baby."

Clayton didn't respond. Only looked at me, something like pride shining in his eyes as he patted her back. A gleaming black Mercedes-Benz sedan pulled up at the curb, catching my mother's attention. She gave them a little wave and pulled away from the man in front of her. He extended a hand to me as I stood from the bench, giving my fingers a little squeeze.

"Alright, you two," my mother said, a steady step off the curb on her stilettos. The driver held her door open, waiting for her to get in. She paused with one hand braced on the vehicle. I hadn't realized Clayton was still holding my hand when he started tugging it toward my awaiting car, smiling while he opened my door for me. "Keep an eye on each other."

I waved at my mother as I sat down, wondering how she would feel if she knew the gregarious mercenary with pink hair was being paid to do just that. Clayton's answer was muffled as he closed my door. I saw his mouth form around the word, looking at me with a wink.

"Always."

FORTY-FOUR

Casey

I speared another bite of ice cream onto my spoon, the frozen chunk of chocolate chip cookie dough giving after a little resistance. Cool vanilla and brown sugar melted on my tongue. Beside me on the sofa, Clayton devoured spoonful after spoonful of chocolate peanut butter. Making good on his pledge to pick up ice cream on the way home from dinner, we'd walked down to the corner store for our pints and then headed upstairs.

"Wait."

He popped up from his seat, excitedly shoving his pint onto the coffee table, and scampered to one of the cabinets lining the wall of windows behind us. Clinking and shuffling prompted me to turn around, just to see what he was doing as he squatted in front of the cabinet and muttered quietly to himself. The cabinet closed, and Clayton rose to his feet again before taking long, proud strides back to the sofa with a mischievous smirk on his face. I didn't fail to notice that he kept one arm behind his back. He set his prize down on the table beside his pint.

Whiskey.

The top popped open, the brown liquor glugged to fill the vacant space he'd created in the center of his ice cream. A long arm reached out, offering me the bottle. When I didn't grab it right away, he wiggled it until I took it. I'd only done so to free his hand up to begin horsing the concoction down, which he did. Contentment washed over his features as he groaned deeply.

"Oh, fuck yeah."

I ignored what the sound did to me, along with the visions of our moment on the roof dancing through my head. The drive home had been too long. Being trapped in a vehicle with no fresh air made my preference for the motorcycle obvious, even if my car was available again. The disappointing distance between us had even washed the conversation with my mother from my thoughts.

"You're unhinged."

"I'm an innovator."

A little. Just to try. The whiskey dribbled into my pint, splashing over chunks of cookie dough as it swirled with little bits of melted vanilla. Clayton gave me an expectant look, raising his eyebrows while waiting for me to try it. I scooped the treat up and shoved the spoon into my mouth. Vanilla and whiskey danced with each other on my tongue, interrupted only by the brown sugar and chocolate. Before I swallowed, I dumped more whiskey into the pint.

"Atta girl."

Spoonfuls of the mixture chased each other into my mouth, and I savored every single ounce. At some point, I must have pulled the throw over myself because I felt warm all over. Clayton lazily lurched forward to chuck the empty pint on the table, throwing himself back into the warm embrace of the sofa after doing so.

"Can I ask you something?" He yawned, flopping his head over to face me while extending his arms along the cushions behind him.

"Sure," I hiccupped.

Clayton's laugh was a soft rumble in his chest. Long fingers curled around my pint, the mercenary tipping the container to examine its contents for himself. Empty. He removed the container from my hand and slid it into his empty one. The amusement on his face dissipated.

"When you were telling me about your problem, you said your body feels ashamed. What did that mean?"

I frowned. Dinner and ice cream twisted together in my stomach with a sickening jolt. His brows lowered. We both knew I meant something by that. It was the reason I didn't want to open my mouth in my group sessions. The reason I took so long to see someone and talk about everything that was going on with me. Clayton sat back, waiting patiently for me to answer. I chewed my lip, considering how I could explain such a thing. It was something I'd talked over with the online therapist. How to talk about it with the people in my life. They hadn't given me much. *Just be honest*, they'd said. Talking about what happened to me with my mother had gone better than I'd expected. Except that this road was darker. Too specific. My skin crawled at the memories that flooded me, forcing me to roll my neck.

"You don't have to tell me, I just," he paused.

"No, I do. I want to."

This man had been there for me when I screamed in the middle of the night. Took a bullet to protect me. Shielded me from harm, both real and imagined. He'd been there at my darkest moments. I put my hand in his and squeezed my eyes shut for a brief moment, collecting my thoughts because if there was anyone in this world I could tell about what happened, it had to be Clayton Wrigley.

"When I was out there in the desert, the people keeping me there brought lots of girls through. There were girls who fought back. They drugged. Sometimes too much. Sometimes those girls didn't make it out of the trailer. The ones who lived were taken away in containers. New girls came in and out every week. Except for me."

Clayton began rubbing his thumb over the back of my hand, silently urging me to go on. I bit back the nausea that rose in my throat. This. This was the part I could never explain.

"I realized they kept the girls they liked around a little longer, so I made them like me. Made them want to keep me around. Smiled at them, flirted with them. Let them," I grimaced, giving Clayton a sidelong glance to make sure he understood. His eyes were narrowed, a line between his brows as he took in what I was saying without revealing whatever it was he was thinking. I went on. "It's just that I never knew what happened to the others. I didn't want to know. Whatever it was, I didn't want it to happen to me. But I don't know. I feel like somehow my experience wasn't as bad because I allowed it to happen. And maybe my problem is that my body knows that."

Deciding that was as good an explanation as I could ever manage, I looked up from my lap. That furrowed brow remained. For a long while, we stayed like that. Silent. Every second of it felt like rot coating my skin. I had it better than the other girls. Clayton sat up, still holding my hand as he righted himself on the sofa and turned his body to fully face mine.

"That was smart."

"Smart? That's all you have to say?"

I blinked furiously and tried to ignore the way my voice broke. Tears trickled down my face, cutting through my heated skin. Shuffling a little closer to me, Clayton reached up to brush away a tear while he shook his head.

"It sounds like you were doing what you had to in order to survive," Clayton said, ignoring my derisive snort. "It doesn't mean they get a pass for violating you. They always had power over you. You couldn't have consented even if the words had literally crossed your lips."

"You sound like an afterschool special," I sniffled.

"It's true."

He breathed a laugh, casually wiping my tears away with the edge of his thumbs. The cradle of his palms held my face in place, making me unable to look away from the man for whom I was splitting my pain open. It sat between us, waiting for an autopsy. This truth, this thing that had been eating away at me, seemed to enjoy the light I gave it. Unable to stop myself, I went on.

"I thought they broke me forever. That no one would ever want me. Then that night happened. You looked at me like I was some ruined thing."

"That's not what I was thinking, Casey."

The response was low. Tired. Frustration knotted my muscles, working its way up from my toes to my twisting fingers. I was fine with moving on, but I wouldn't tolerate rewriting what happened.

"Yes, it is!" I barked, tugging myself out of his grip. Tears streamed from me, making the column of my neck slick. I violently wiped at them, cursing inwardly at myself for crying again. "You acted like you wanted me, and then you didn't. Because you remembered what happened to me and you felt sorry for me."

"No. No, that's not what happened. You looked like you wanted to stop. You might not have said it, but goddamn. I wasn't looking for the absence of a no, Casey. I was looking for an enthusiastic fucking yes."

Clayton rubbed his hands over his face, like he could scrub away the memory. I couldn't. I'd never forget the way he looked at me that night. Right here on this sofa. His desire for me turned to sympathy. I was just some broken doll he didn't want.

"I don't need your pity, Clayton."

"It's not pity," he huffed. I snorted. An agitated growl preceded his jolting movement, throwing his arms out wide. "You think I don't know how shitty pity feels?"

It was the first time he'd ever raised his voice at me. Clayton's face was twisted with anger, but there was also a sort of pain softening his eyes. He turned away from me, releasing a sharp breath. The cushions accepted him as he repositioned himself in them, eyes shut. He threaded his fingers together behind his head. Another heaving breath. Whatever he was about to say, I wasn't sure I wanted to hear. Not looking me in the eye was bad. The sound of his voice breaking was worse.

"I never had a fucking family."

FORTY-FIVE

CLAYTON

I learned a long time ago that letting people in was a mistake. Either someone would use those people against you. Or they were foxes in your hen house, and they were just waiting to sink their teeth into you. The people you could trust never stayed around for long. The men in my unit helped me to understand that some relationships could last. But this woman was the one who showed me that kindness was a flower that could grow in everyone's garden. Even if someone stomped all over it.

"Clay, I—" she paused.

Tears welled in Casey's eyes again, that soft heart drawing her features into a frown. She'd always been so soft. But right now, it turned the ice cream in my stomach sour. There it was...pity. She grew up with a mother, and I didn't. It was as simple as that. I had my shit. She had hers. God, after what she'd just told me, I didn't deserve an ounce of pity. I'd assumed what happened to her. Tried not to imagine it. But fuck. Now she was looking at me like my bullshit sob story mattered. Still, this was Casey. With anyone else,

I would gloss over the details like that. With her, it felt different. Important somehow. I took a sip directly from the bottle of whiskey and placed it back on the coffee table. Only one thought slammed through my bones.

Here goes nothing.

"The woman who gave birth to me wasn't a parent. Her name was Mary. She managed to keep me alive for a while, probably with the help of her friends, because she didn't have any living family. Then she died. Overdose, I found out later. If her new landlord hadn't done a wellness check and found her, I probably would be dead too."

It was one of the few memories I had of my mother. Her long fingers, fingers she gave to me, curled in distress. The base of her nails turning blue. Her lips turning blue. I couldn't remember her face. Couldn't remember the color of her eyes or the way she laughed either. There were no pancakes or cartoons. No decorating a Christmas tree. No birthdays. Just her. Dying in the middle of her stained carpet.

"I bounced around from foster home to foster home for years," I continued. "Some situations were nice, but short. Perfectly fine people willing to put a roof over my head and clothes on my back. I'd stay at group homes in between."

Casey shifted in her seat, tucking her legs under herself as she took the bottle from me. I went on as she took a mouthful of whiskey and set it down.

"The last foster house was the longest. It was also the worst. I almost finished high school there. It was like the longer I was there, the more my foster father resented me."

"After everything I've done for you, you should show me some fucking respect."

I choked on the last word as the scent of my foster father's aftershave flooded my memory. He'd get drunk and want to square up with me. Thought that he could prove his masculinity to himself by beating up on a teenager. For a long time, I fought as hard as I could. Then I realized I could win. Only I didn't. I let him win. Time and time again, I wound up on the floor. Lost some time here and there. It was part of my plan. The plan to let him think he could bully me. Let him think I was an easy target.

It wasn't right, what I did. But it was necessary. Steal a sleeping bag and a knife from the Army surplus. Steal a little money from Halloway, too. Enough for him to notice. Hide it away and wait for him to pick a fight. Then fuck him up until he was unconscious on his kitchen floor. Tension locked up my hands, forcing me to flex them as I brought them to my sides.

"I never did very well in school, so when I was old enough, I joined the Navy. That's where I met West. We went into the SEALS together. He was always one promotion ahead of me, but he's the closest thing I ever had to a brother."

Searching her face for any sign of that pity, I found her wiping the rest of her tears from her face. Not looking at me, though. No, she wouldn't want to do that now. I continued.

"What I'm saying is that what I went through isn't the same, Casey. I know that, but I also know that I had a lot of help to get ok with it. I did the work, and I faced shit. You weren't even talking about it. Not with anyone. I didn't want things to get worse because I couldn't control myself with you."

"That was my choice to make," her voice was soft. Not angry. Firm, but I could hear the tremor in it. Those tears were still there. Waiting to be shed. Tears for me. I didn't fucking want them.

"Yes, it was. But it was my choice, too. I didn't want it. Not like that." Unable to take another second of this conversation, I got to my feet and collected the empty ice cream cartons from the table. This day had been long. Really fucking long. Casey watched me, perched on the sofa with her legs tucked up beside her. That look. That sadness on her face. I couldn't take it for another second. Lips parted, eyes turning with the search for something to say. I just didn't have the energy to hear it.

FORTY-SIX

CLAYTON

Two fingers prodded my shoulder. I jolted as Casey jumped backward. Her lips mouthed an apology I couldn't hear over the music blasting into my headphones. The muted sounds of Arctic Monkeys filled the silence between us as I took her in. Long red hair braided over an exposed shoulder and bare-faced. Wearing that yellow sweater and fitted black leggings, she looked so comfortable. Relaxed, even. Casey lifted a plate and a steaming mug in my direction.

"I thought you might be hungry," she smiled, her voice tentative as she nodded toward her offering.

After our conversation, I'd closed myself off in the office, preferring to fall asleep in my chair doing coding grunt work to spending a second beside her in that bed. Or the sofa. That fucking sofa.

Eggs. Bacon. Crusty sourdough toasted with butter and jam. A steaming cup of coffee that looked like it was exactly the right shade of brown. My mouth watered at the sight as my stomach gave an embarrassingly loud growl. It pulled a small chuckle from the girl holding the plate. I couldn't help the grin that crossed my lips at the idea that she might be paying attention to how I liked my coffee. Even if she'd never admit it.

"You made me breakfast. I'm touched."

"Yeah, well," she shrugged, shoving the plate and mug onto my desk next to my cup of pens and pencils. "I wouldn't want my bodyguard to starve because he barricaded himself in his little office hole."

"Were you worried about me, firebird? How does that feel to admit?"

Casey rolled her eyes, smiling a little, and gestured toward the monitors.

"So, what are you doing in here?"

I pivoted my chair back toward my desk and picked up the fork from the plate to cut into the fried eggs. Yolk ran through salt and pepper toward the bacon. God, she even cooked the eggs just the way I liked them. Sliding the egg onto a slice of toast with my fork, I tried scooping the yolk on top of it. Yellow slid over the black diving swallow inked onto my hand. Casey watched me lick it off before plopping down in the oversized rust-colored beanbag chair in the corner. With her legs tucked under herself, she looked like she was being swallowed by a gigantic persimmon.

"Forensic accounting, sort of. I'm trying to figure out where Ilia Kremnik's money is going. Well, the money that's actually in his accounts," I said as I took a bite of toast. Crunching buttery crust filled my ears, drowning out the chorus of irritated thoughts that had been repeating in my mind all morning. A quick click minimized the browser on the screen in front of me. I picked the plate up off my desk, holding it in front of myself as I began eating in earnest. "Have you been..."

The question died on my tongue as I noted the way her gaze fixed on something behind me. Following her line of sight to the framed photo on my desk beside the cup of coffee. To her, it was probably just a bunch of teenagers standing in front of Wrigley Field, surrounded by people in Cubs jerseys. To me, it was one of the only times I felt normal. Went to one school for a whole term. Made friends. Real friends whose houses I crashed at when I skipped out on Halloway.

"Is your real name Wrigley?"

"No. And yes. I picked it. It's my name. It's who I am. But was it the name I was given at birth? No."

She shook her head.

"I don't understand."

"My mom gave me her last name when I was born. There was never any record of my father, and I didn't really know her either, so I picked my own."

"I'm sorry."

It was uncanny. I'd had friends. Shipmates. People I trusted to guard my back. People I would trust with my life. But the things I kept to myself, the things I made jokes to avoid talking about, had a way of falling out of my mouth around her. Brown eyes softened with patience, waiting for me to go on. Not an ounce of judgment in them.

"Anyway, I picked Wrigley because it was one of the only places I ever had any happy memories."

Casey angled her head to one side, her mouth twisting into a little bow as she considered.

"I like Wrigley," she smirked. "It's peppy."

"Peppy?" I echoed, lifting the coffee mug for a sip as I arched a brow.

"It's a word! Is the coffee alright?"

"Sure. It's *peppy*."

Casey rolled her eyes again and leaned on her elbow. I knew an uncomfortable question was coming when she started picking at her nails instead of looking at me.

"Did you ever look for your father? Later, I mean. You could do a DNA test or something."

I shook my head and set down the mug. That feeling. That *tell her everything until it hurts* feeling forced my lips to part around another truth I'd never shared before.

"It's just," I sighed, setting the dish down beside my mousepad with a soft thud. "It's not that I'm not curious. Everyone wants to know where they came from. The problem is that it's easier if I don't know. By not knowing the answer, the real answer, then he can be whatever I want him to be."

Casey chewed her lower lip, balling the soft chenille sleeves of her sweater into her hands as she stared down at them.

"I do understand, you know," she mumbled. "A little bit. I didn't know who my father was for a long time. My mother never talked about him, and it left me wondering. Now that I know, it feels better. Like that part of my mind could finally rest. Or focus on something else."

She stood from her seat, adjusting the waist of her leggings with a sigh. The dense red braid slipped over her shoulder as she leaned forward to brace her hands on the arms of my chair.

"This is your business. Do the DNA test or don't. I'm just saying that it might help you find some closure. That might be good for you."

A squeak popped from her lips, and I laughed. I couldn't help it. Her ass connected with my thigh, toppling her over with a violent jerk from the arm I hooked around her waist. Casey shook her head, shoulders shaking with the laugh she stifled behind closed lips. Those beautiful eyes fixed on me.

"You don't like talking about these things, do you?"

I frowned and took her jaw in the cradle of my thumb and forefinger, shaking her head to give my silent response. No, I didn't want to think about my father. I didn't want to think about the kind of man who'd sleep with someone like my mother. Some days, I thought I could remember her face. A vague picture of someone with the same nose as me. It was a painful passing thought. The fact that I couldn't picture my father at all felt like a blessing. Another giggle bubbled from Casey's perfect pink pout as her eyes teared with mirth.

My father was an age-old ache that may never go away. As if seeing that wound in my face, Casey brought those lips to mine and kissed me. Soft, sweet, and brief. So brief. My hand shifted from her chin to cup her jaw, greedily drinking in the feel of her mouth as she relaxed against me. Her scent filled my nose, the sweater tantalizing the tips of my fingers as my other hand trailed beneath its hem to graze over her stomach. She squirmed, another laugh following the movement. I grinned against her lips.

"I think I like being your friend, too."

She sighed and stood from my lap, waving me off with a smile.

"Eat your breakfast."

FORTY-SEVEN

Casey

> Please come back. I didn't mean to upset you. I'm sorry.

> Fuck, Casey. Please. Come back here.

> Text me when you get home.

> I'm coming over.

The front door slammed closed. I tucked my phone away, not bothering to see who it was. There was only one person with the keys to this place, and if that hadn't been enough, I'd learned the cadence of his steps the first week I'd been cooped up here. It was the same person who'd sent those texts two years ago. It was the first thing he'd sent after I blocked his number. I'd spent so long scrolling through his messages that I'd finally made it back that far. Curled up in his bed, I wondered if Clayton had been turned away at the gate of my father's estate that night. He could have decided it wasn't worth it to go after me. I hadn't seen him after I got home. Maintaining my focus on the grim contents of the refrigerator, I forced myself to start a conversation before he walked away and shut himself into the office. Again.

"Hey, Clay?"

Peeking over my shoulder, I caught a glimpse of him. His jeans and ragged, sleeveless shirt were covered in engine grease. Everywhere except those little glasses. Pink hair was a mess, like he'd been tugging on it. After dragging him out of the office, he mentioned that he needed to service his bike, and it would take most of the afternoon. Only, it actually took days. He definitely didn't like talking about himself. It wasn't like he was being cold toward me. Not at all. Every morning, he smiled and had polite conversations with me. Took me to my meetings and asked me how they were when I appeared again an hour later. Normal. Except, not. It was the superficial sort of conversation, which wasn't him. It wasn't us. That light that I'd come to expect was so dim, replaced with turning gears and unspoken words.

I wanted his sunshine back.

I'd been thinking a lot about what he'd said to me. About never having a family. The way he spoke about pity made my stomach hurt, but I understood. He didn't want me to look at him any differently. It made me look at my own childhood with kinder eyes. Growing up, I had only one parent looking out for me. We didn't have much, but my mother always made sure that we had enough. Enough to eat. Clothes to wear. A roof over our heads. She drove herself into the ground every single day just to make sure of that.

And somehow, after the twelve to sometimes eighteen-hour days, she always had time for me. Made me feel like I mattered to her. Let me climb into bed with her and watch old romantic comedies together. She never let me feel how little we had. Never asked my father for a dime, either. Just so I wouldn't be involved in any of the Arawn business and any of the danger that would subject me to. Clayton never had someone to look out for him like that. To make sure he had everything he needed because they loved him.

Because they wanted him to feel safe and cared for. Wanting that for him after he'd done everything to protect me was impossible to ignore.

"I was thinking I could make you dinner," I offered, hunting through the open refrigerator as if anything new would appear. "But we're pretty low on food, so any ideas you might have on the subject are welcome."

Footsteps approached, prompting me to turn around in time to see Clayton's back as he stood at the sink. Water. The lemony smell of soap. He was cleaning off. I shut the refrigerator and shuffled to the pantry, deciding immediately that we were going to be eating takeout tonight because we were actually completely out of food.

"I think tacos or sushi sound incredible," he offered, water slapping into the steel sink as he shook off his hands.

I turned to find him already looking at me.

"What about both?"

"Both is good," he smirked, though it wasn't wide enough for a dimple to make an appearance. Clayton looked away to slide his phone from his pocket. Strange energy radiated from him. Another distraction. Another excuse to push me away. "I'll order it."

Opening the fridge again, I pulled two beers free and popped their tops. Clayton glanced in my direction, but pretended to remain focused on his task. He'd watched every step I took when I first got here. Now that I knew something real about him, he couldn't take it. In a few short strides, I was beside him. The corner of his eye flickered with a glance, returning to his screen as he finalized our odd little feast. One hearty leap had my ass on the counter. I started tugging the hoodie I wore, his hoodie, down with odd little scoots to unsuccessfully put a barrier between the cold surface and my shorts. A pair of well-sculpted shoulders shook with suppressed laughter at my awkward movements.

"A crunchy dragon roll and a fish taco, please."

I got a grunt in response. Yeah, this not talking to me thing needed to end right now.

"Clayton," I hesitated, unsure of where I was going with the rest of this sentence. He leaned against the counter, making a couple more taps on his screen before dropping the device on the stone surface and folding his arms over his chest. The shadow of his defined triceps caught my attention, drawing my gaze to the tattoo of a dancing skeleton with a disco ball for a head. Perfect. "What is this tattoo about?"

He twisted his arm, peering over the curve of his bicep toward the little dancing creature. The definition of his triceps became even more severe with the new position. I was overcome with the insane urge to bite him there. A smooth chuckle tried to burst from the smirk on his face.

"Back when I was in the SEALs, we had handles. Mine was stupid, so I got this as a joke."

"Yours was what, exactly?"

One large hand went to the counter just an inch away from my leg, the owner of that arm flexing and relaxing his muscle so that the little skeleton was dancing. I giggled. You know, like a teenage girl with a crush. Clayton shook his head and rubbed absently at his arm, as if soothing a wound I couldn't see.

"Disco."

Another laugh escaped me. It was my turn to shake my head at myself as I covered my mouth. My stomach flipped the second he looked at me. There was a hint of it. That light. I wanted more.

"Please explain, I'm begging you," I smiled.

"Remember that stab wound I showed you? The infection I told you about?"

The thick scar tissue at his hip flashed into my mind. I nodded.

"When I was laid up in the field hospital, the rest of my unit came by when they could. Checked in on me. It took longer than usual for the infection to work its way out of my system because of a bunch of factors. It was the field nurse who said I would never die 'like Disco,' and the name just kind of stuck."

"Well, I'm glad you're still here."

"Are you?"

That half-cocked smile returned, bearing a wicked edge that matched his spine-tingling tone as Clayton directed his attention to me. His energy shifted, making the tips of my fingers tingle with anticipation.

"Yeah, you're protecting me. You're helping me with my problem. And you're good company. Even when you're covered in grease."

"I think we're making progress on that problem," he said, pushing off of the counter to face me. Clayton jerked his chin toward the sofa. "You were able to take care of yourself. No need for me."

I shook my head again. He closed the distance between us. Both his hands bracketed my hips on the counter. My fingers curled to grip the edge. An eyebrow arched as he brought his face closer to mine, close enough for me to see the stubble coating his jaw from spending all night in the garage. I knew what this was.

"No?"

God, his voice dropped an octave. Something about his nearness was causing my brain to short-circuit. Maybe it was that smell. That citrus and sage scent mixed with sweat.

"I still need you," I blurted. "I need to think about you. To finish."

Clayton's grin flashed as his head dipped. The sight of it made my insides explode into a frenzy of butterflies. His nose grazed up the column of my neck in a smooth, tantalizing motion. My legs wrapped around his waist on instinct. Hands rounded the curve of my ass, squeezing me hard enough to pull me toward the edge of the countertop. He was playing chicken with me.

"What am I doing when you think about me?"

"You're," I gasped, unable to think past the kisses he started planting on my collarbone. "Licking me."

He let out a knowing hum, one hand moving from my side to slip exactly where I'd pictured his attention. Another little flip feeling inside quickened my breath. We were doing this. This dancing around each other had to end.

I didn't know what we were. I just knew I wanted to feel him. All of him. My hands moved from the counter to his fly. Clayton's teeth sank into my neck, licking where he marked me before his low words heated my skin.

"I'll make you feel so fucking good."

If I said anything to that, I didn't know. I only knew the feel of his erection grinding into me. The grip on my ass migrated up under the hoodie I had on, calluses rasping over my bare skin. His hands ran over the planes of my stomach, the combination of rough and soft creating friction that made me want to squeeze my thighs together. I whimpered into his mouth, the sound dragging a rough groan from him as I sought more delicious friction against his hand. But he knew what I needed. It seemed like he always knew. Long digits slipped beneath the fabric of my shorts. The pads of his fingers traced my slit, that rasping voice was edged with wicked delight at what he found there.

"All this for me?"

Those fingers moved, up and around my clit, teasing my entrance for more lubricant. Again and again until I was a shaking mess. Another plunge downward had two fingers pushing into me. My body clenched around them. Then they were gone. Clayton locked eyes with me as he took those fingers into his mouth. I expected a smart remark. Another tease. But he said nothing. Only hummed with pleasure as he brought his mouth back to mine.

My tongue traced his lower lip, silently begging for more. I wanted more. Wanted him. My frantic fingers went to his belt, and the metal clacked together at my touch. Fingers that locked up with the rest of me. His belt. His goddamn belt. My shoulders hitched up toward my ears, the muscles tight enough to snap. Any lick of heat I'd felt was doused with a cold splash of discomfort.

"No. Cinnamon. Cinnamon, Clay," I yelped. My hands connected with his chest, ready to push him away, but he was already retreating. "I'm sorry."

Righting my clothes, I hopped off the counter. My arms wrapped around myself on instinct. Not to protect myself from him, I knew I didn't need that.

Only comfort. He didn't move beyond tucking his hands into his pockets. I looked at the floor, pink polished toes staring up at me as I tried to make sense of how I was feeling. All the desire I'd felt from him before had dimmed. Not gone, but hardly an ember compared to the blaze from moments ago.

"You don't need to apologize. There's nothing to be sorry about. Hey," he said, stepping forward again but careful not to touch me. "You did exactly what you were supposed to do. Understand?"

I nodded. A ping sounded from beside me. Clayton's phone. I couldn't understand how I would be alright with mutual self-pleasure one minute and unable to stand making out with someone the next. The inconsistency was bone-rattlingly frustrating.

"I'm sorry."

"I told you not to apologize. Come on, I have some stuff to take care of in the office."

Striding into the office, he flopped into his chair and woke up his computer. All of the screens fired up, illuminating the room. He opened an operating system I wasn't sure I understood. Numbers here. Boxes there. Lots of computer things I just didn't get. Similar to the security system he'd shown me, so it was clearly something he'd built, but beyond that, I had no idea what I was looking at. Surrendering to my ignorance, I fell into the bean bag chair and asked the obvious question.

"What is that?"

"This?" Clayton asked, pointing to the screen in question. I nodded. "Gizmo."

When I only blinked at him, he went on.

"Well, basically, it operates like a hydra. I give it an objective and some places to start. It gets information from those sources and then goes all over the web by breaking off into these additional spiders. But I hate spiders. So, you know. Gremlins. You know, like when you feed Gizmo after midnight, and all these other gremlins pop out."

"Clever," I laughed, not at all surprised by the naming choice.

"Anyway, it feeds all of that information into this thing over here," he said, pointing to a box with a bunch of tabs. "It sorts it into categories, and then I can parse through everything I need to know."

"I didn't know you were afraid of spiders."

"I'm not *afraid*. I just think we should all be on alert. They're sneaky."

I laughed and sank back into the chair, pulling out my phone to browse around on social media as Clayton got to work. It was incredible to me that he could make me feel normal after feeling completely wretched for stopping our encounter in the kitchen. Once it arrived, we ate our dinner in the office and fell into companionable silence. So quiet and comfortable that I jolted when I heard the chair squeak. I looked up from my screen to see him facing me.

"Tell me something about yourself. Something nobody knows."

He probably expected me to say something like I spend way too much time watching cute senior dog videos on social media or that I hate peas, both of which are true. Instead, I said this.

"I'm scared I'll always be seen as this victim. But after everything that's happened, I'm still like other girls. I want the same thing they all want. I want to be seen. I want to be loved. I want to be held at the end of the day and know that everything is going to be alright because I'm with my person."

Clayton's head went to one side, considering. Smooth and swift, he reached down to put his hand on my foot. The touch was gentle. Filled with a dangerous sort of tenderness I let myself ignore. At least for now.

"And you?" I pressed. "Tell me something no one knows."

"I hate peas."

FORTY-EIGHT

Clayton

In programming, you're meant to account for unexpected values. The user is unpredictable; therefore, you have to account for what is possible. *Unexpected* was part of my everyday, but this still made me itch beneath the surface. A black hole opened in my belly as I watched the box disappear. Steel clanged hard as I closed the outgoing mail locker. One sample of DNA, outbound. One question I'd held onto for my entire life, about to be answered.

In a weird way, it hadn't taken much for Casey to convince me to move forward with this path. We'd walked down to the little ramen spot down the street I'd told her about, talking about how knowing the answer to a question was better than leaving the unknown out there to surprise me and disrupt my peace. I was even a little proud of her when she'd made the argument about knowing your enemy left you better prepared to defend yourself while stuffing gyoza into her mouth. Now that the reality of incoming information was facing me, I wasn't sure she was right.

"My mama told me it's alright…"

Short shorts and a cropped T-shirt. Red hair twirling around with every dance step. I folded my arms over my chest and leaned against the wall, taking in the sight. Casey swirled her hips, mumbling the lyrics to the song playing on the record player as she cooked. I fought the urge to take her in my arms, not wanting to disturb the sight before me.

One dramatic turn toward the empty plate on the counter. Pancakes scooted out of the skillet with a spatula, followed by the skillet being returned to the range. Her final turn, hips moving as a finger dipped into the syrup on her plate, set her eyes on me and what had to be a stupid-looking smile on my face. They blinked in surprise as Casey pulled her finger from her pink lips.

"Hello there," I grinned.

"Good morning," she blushed.

I lifted my nose, making a show of sniffing the air even though I could see the fruits of her labor sizzling not far from me. Pancakes on the stove. Bacon, waiting to be eaten. Freshly brewed coffee steaming in the pour-over carafe. It had only been a couple of months since she'd unwillingly joined me here, and in that short time, she'd made it feel more like a home than it ever had before. Even after all of my decorating efforts and furniture purchases. It wasn't about things. It was about people. It was about her. A small pit opened in my stomach, warning me not to enjoy it too much.

"Smells good," I offered, earning a grateful little smile in return.

Casey's attention returned to the stove, affording me the opportunity to snoop. The camera I'd given her was plugged into her laptop on the counter. Photo editing software was open, and thumbnails of all the pictures sat there waiting for her keen eye. The file she must have been working on was a picture of me. Just me. Smiling, almost laughing, like I had a good reason to. The sun limned the lines of my face, making my jaw look strong and my eyes look bright. Even the pink hair looked good. I angled my head, trying to sort through when she would have taken this picture.

"Venice." I looked up to see Casey standing on the other side of the counter, watching me. Her head was tilted to one side, mimicking the curious angle of mine. She let out a soft laugh and set down the plate of pancakes she was holding, sliding the dish in front of the seat beside me. "When you were talking to my mom. I snapped a shot of you. A few actually."

She turned back to the range, flipping a pancake into the air and onto another plate. Grateful her back was turned from me, I gave myself a little pinch to make sure I could feel the pain. This was not a dream. This mouthwatering reality came with bacon and coffee. Not too shabby, Wrigley. Not at all.

"You know it's two o'clock in the afternoon," I noted, lifting a slice of bacon to my mouth. "Not exactly morning."

"You didn't come to bed."

"Yeah. I was working all night," I shrugged. "Having some insomnia issues, I guess."

Another pancake was flipped onto the plate. It wasn't exactly the truth. I'd spent the better part of my night working on doctoring tracking information for her father's smuggling business, but I finished up a little before two in the morning. The rest of my night was spent in my garage, working on my project bike because I couldn't keep my thoughts from crashing into each other long enough to relax and head to bed. It wasn't until well after nine this morning that I'd even set foot in this loft again.

"You're avoiding me."

"No, I'm not."

Casey gave me a flat look.

"I don't care why. I just want it to stop. The bed feels too big without you in it."

No reason for that statement to make me feel lightheaded.

We scooted around each other in the small space as I ducked into the kitchen to fish two coffee mugs out of the cabinet and doctored our beverages to bring to the barstools, where I sat down with a plop. Fluffy. Buttery. Blueberries, of course. Casey gave me a tentative smile as she turned the stove off and grabbed her plate to join me. My phone chirped at my side. I tugged it out of my pocket to see the message from Killian.

> The Russian has flown the coop. Father says we're good. I'll let you know if my boys find anything before we give an official all-clear.

That black pit in my gut opened to swallow what was left of my good mood. Our time was up. Fuck, I shouldn't have wasted so much of it avoiding her. I cleared my throat, picking up my coffee for a sip to wash away the dry mouth that text had created.

"Everything alright?"

Casey's brows were high, eyes bright with curiosity. I reached out and tucked a lock of hair behind her ear, relishing the way she nuzzled into my palm a little at the touch, like she just couldn't help herself. Only a few months to get here. It made me yearn for just a little more time.

"Yeah, I'm just tired. Your brother was updating me on the Kremnik situation. Sounds like you're going to be able to go home soon."

"Oh."

Casey's face fell as she returned her attention to the food in front of her. The rest of our little brunch was eaten in silence. Sipping the coffee did nothing to lift the exhaustion that was settling into my bones. She was leaving. I'd done all I could to mend the rift between us while trying not to rush her, but her brother had to go and douse the bridge in kerosene with that damn message. I yawned wide enough to make my throat ache, and set my fork down on my empty plate before I took the dishes and carelessly plunked them into the dishwasher. Casey took my hand, giving it a gentle tug.

"Come with me," she cooed.

"Where are we going?"

"To bed."

Shock must have shown on my face because she let out a little laugh as she yanked me down the hall and into the bedroom. Dread tightened my muscles as I realized I might be getting my shot with this girl only to be too exhausted to deliver. Releasing my hand, she moved around the room, drawing down the blackout shades.

"Take your shoes off," she commanded, crawling into the bed.

I must have been more tired than I realized because I would normally have taken them off by the front door. Letting the bed take my weight, I flopped down to sit on the corner and removed my boots. In one swift motion, I tugged my shirt over my head. The pants had to stay on. Golden, freckle-dusted legs were casually twined together in my view as I crawled toward the headboard and welcoming pillows. Casey propped herself up on one elbow, flicking her free hand toward the pillow she pulled up next to her.

"Come on. You get to be the little spoon."

A tired laugh ruptured from me as I pressed my face toward hers in the pillow she'd indicated and threw my arm over her waist. If this was all I got, I would take it as long as I got to hold her. Even if it was just for an afternoon. My eyes drifted closed as I enjoyed the fact that my bed smelled a lot like her now. Those fancy long nails trailed over my scalp as Casey stroked her fingers through my hair, sending a chill through my body that felt a lot like relief.

"Go to sleep," she whispered. "I'll be here."

It was the last thing I heard as my mind fell out of the room and into the unguarded thoughts of sleep. There's a reason they say you fall in love. It's because there's no control. You plummet into the void of it, unable to grasp at anything to brace yourself. If you're lucky, there's someone to catch you. To make it worth the plunge. When you fall alone, there's only pain. Pain and cold, hard reality rushing up to meet you. It felt a lot like sleeping in this bed alone.

FORTY-NINE

Casey

Darkness swallowed up the bedroom, only the dim glow of the street lamps below filtering in through the cracks surrounding the window coverings. We'd slept all day. Propping up on my elbows, I looked toward the sleeping man beside me. Strands of pink hair feathered across his forehead. Dark brows were still with tranquility. Full lips parted on soft, even breaths. Clayton's face looked so different in sleep. So relaxed compared to his waking form, like the tether of tension that informed his expressions snapped free. I pushed a strand of hair away from his face.

"What time is it?" Clayton asked, eyes still closed.

His voice was still dusky with sleep. That rasp, warm and deep, did something to me. I shifted my weight, positioning myself over him to reach where I'd plugged my phone in on the nightstand. Long fingers curled around my waist, safely holding me in place before I lost my balance. Squinting at the screen as it illuminated under my touch, I took in the time.

"It's just after nine."

A thoughtful grunt came from beneath me. Placing my phone back on the nightstand, I shifted back toward the bed, relishing the feel of him underneath me. That familiar pins and needles feeling rushed down to my toes. My body remembered the way he made me feel. Remembered what I wanted from him and that our time together was coming to an end. I threw a leg over his body, straddling his hips as I braced my hands on his chest. Clayton's eyes were open now, barely visible in this light as his hands pushed up my t-shirt, thumbs making idle circles on my belly as he watched me with wary interest.

"Casey," he breathed in warning.

Those sinuous hands skated upward, thumbs flicking over my breasts. My hips began to move. Submitting to the wisdom of my body, the part of myself that knew exactly what I wanted, I rolled and dipped until the friction wound into something delicious. A rough groan sounded from beneath me. Clayton's erection ground against my core. An answering moan spilled from me, my hands fisting in the cotton covering his muscled chest. His hands skimmed to my ass, kneading the flesh as he leveraged it to drag me against every thick inch of him. A bolt of pleasure seared me from within, pulling another moan from me, this one more helpless than before.

"Goddamn," he panted.

Control was slipping away as that thing I needed begged low in my belly. Too warm. I was getting too warm. The t-shirt felt like sandpaper against my skin. A decisive pull of the garment had it up and over my head in an instant. Clayton's eyes fixed on the simple black mesh bralette that covered my breasts, his hands moving to toy with the fabric. Soft, hesitant touches to the furled pink flesh. His tongue swept along his lower lip as he dragged it between his teeth, another low groan following the action. My hands came to rest on his thighs, propping myself up. The ends of my hair dusted my knuckles. My head tipped back on another moan. Arms coiled around my waist, warmth surrounding me. He'd sat up.

"I'm still dreaming, aren't I?" Clayton whispered against my chest, his grip returning to my ass. "So perfect. Fuck. I'm going to wake up alone on that fucking sofa."

The scratch of his stubble over my sternum warned me of the direction of his mouth, but I didn't care. Didn't care that he pushed the mesh aside to lave my breast with his tongue. My hips pushed downward. More, more, more. I wanted more. Wanted him.

"Clay," I sighed, that molten feeling burning through me like tissue paper. "I need to feel you. Please."

Another groan rattled out of him as his hips moved in tandem with mine, rocking me against him. He wanted this. His lips, his hands, his body screamed for it. The way his tongue flicked against my nipple through the mesh at my other breast screamed it, too. Animals. We were practically animals like this. Attempting to emphasize my point, I ground my hips down into him, the fabric of my shorts doing nothing to separate my soaking sex from what I really needed.

"What are you asking me, Casey?"

Fine. I was a big girl. I could say it. I'd said it to men before. Except now it didn't feel like just another step in a dance we'd been doing to get here. This felt more like a leap of faith. Looking down at him was like staring over a cliff, down into unknown waters. I didn't know what was on the other side. I only knew that I wanted to jump.

"Please," I said again, kissing the stone at the center of his throat. It bobbed under my lips, and I flicked my tongue over it. "Fuck me."

Large hands bracketed my hips to stop my movement over him. Dark brows drew together, shadowing his face as his jaw hardened. Cold washed over me as I realized what was happening. He was stopping this. No. Not again. He could not be doing this to me again!

"Wait."

"Don't do that. Don't you dare tell me I'm not ready," I spat.

"Goddamnit. Just listen to me for a second."

"No," I shot up from the bed and stormed for the door, his fingers grazing my waist as he reached for me. "If you don't want to have sex, that's your choice. But you don't get to take mine from me."

The words tasted so familiar on my tongue. I winced at their bitterness. Clayton stood. Long legs ate up the distance between us in mere seconds. Strong fingers grabbed my wrist, forcing me to face him.

"Fuck. We're not doing this again. Listen. Now."

A hand slapping the light switch on the wall, that stone in the golden column of his throat bobbing again as he stared me down. The once-dark bedroom now glowed faintly with the small light sitting on top of the dresser. In this light, I could see him clearly. A sharp jaw that was covered in dark stubble. Those arms made of lean chords of muscle covered in ink and winding veins felt too good wrapped around me only minutes ago. I'd lain awake for a while just to bathe in the feel of it. Of him. For two years, he'd been the target of my ire. The man I'd fooled myself into blaming for so much fear. Now he was all I wanted.

"I want to fuck you, Casey. Too damn much. I'm not sure I can control myself." His grip loosened on my wrist as his other hand moved to tip my chin up with two fingers. Warm caramel eyes met mine. "The last thing I want to do is scare you. Or hurt you. But this, I," Clayton sighed through his nose, dark brows pinched together as he fought to find the words. "I want you too badly to be gentle."

My hands were shaking. The tremors snaked up my arms, down into my legs.

"I don't need protection," I said, not recognizing the sound of my voice. "Not from you."

Clayton took another step toward me. My back pressed against the door frame. With shaking fingers, I reached out. They skimmed up the small veins and trail of hair on his stomach. Higher. Until they came to rest on the hard muscle of his chest. I let my touch fall again, nails trailing down to the waistband of his jeans. Goosebumps erupted over his bronzed skin. One large hand plunged into my hair. It wasn't just about need or desire, the way he touched me. I was fine silk he sifted through his fingers. The heat of his breath grazed the shell of my ear, the tug on my hair positioning it perfectly as his voice went heady with promise.

"Oh yes, you fucking do."

"I trust you," I gasped, arching against him.

"You shouldn't."

They were just words. I'd been with enough men to learn that actions spoke volumes. He never lied to me. Wanted me to be comfortable and safe. He would never hurt me. Despite his warnings, I knew that Clayton would protect me. Always.

"I have a safe word. If I need it, I'll use it." That knowing settled over me like a warm embrace. I pushed up onto my toes and brought my mouth to his. Our lips brushed as I whispered my command into the air we shared. "Just fuck me, Clayton Wrigley."

At my command, he lifted me into his arms, gently cupping my backside as he lavished my mouth with kisses so penetrating that I knew he'd been holding back before. My legs felt so good wrapped around him, enjoying the hard muscle against my thighs as I returned his kisses. These kisses were steeped in hunger. Drugging and claiming. The groans emanating from deep within his chest tasted even sweeter than they sounded.

"I'm all clear," he huffed into my mouth. "I've been tested, I mean."

"Me too," I answered, pushing away the thought of every test I'd taken and the reason for them. "I'm protected, too."

I felt myself being lowered to the bed. His bed. I'd been sleeping in this bed for weeks. Burying my face in his pillows. Wrapping myself up in his scent. Sleeping soundly because I felt safe. Not because I was being guarded by a mercenary. Because I was with him. My eyes opened to take him in. Pink hair. Caramel eyes. Golden-brown stubble that he'd definitely need to trim soon. Lips swollen from those deep, searching kisses.

"We can still use a condom. If you want."

I shook my head. No. I didn't want to. I wanted to feel all of him. What was about to happen between us wasn't a fleeting impulse. It wasn't a result of chemistry and frustration. It was inevitable. I knew that. That pink hair fell into his eyes as they crinkled around the corners as Clayton smiled down at me. Both dimples stood out in his five o'clock shadow. Pupils blown wide, glazed with lust as he took me in, the expression pure understanding as he nodded.

"Tell me something. Did you choose those pajamas just to torture me?"

His fingers skimmed the hem of my bra, thumbs grazing the underside of my breasts. I sucked in a breath at a zing of feeling. That night on the sofa, he hadn't been like this. He'd been careful, like he was testing the waters. Now I could feel what he was thinking.

Cannonball.

"They barely cover anything, just so you know."

"Poor baby," I mocked.

Clayton bared his teeth as he let out a breathless laugh. Beautiful. He was so heartbreakingly beautiful. He chuckled and lowered his lips to the swell of one breast, licking the thin mesh with the flat of his tongue until he sucked it into his mouth. Eyes dark as they pinned me to the spot. A helpless sound slipped from me.

"You might as well be walking around this place naked."

"That was the original plan," I purred. "I thought it might be overdoing your punishment."

Clayton's hips pushed forward into mine, grinding his thick length against my core again. I gasped. Sensitive. Ready for him. For so long, I couldn't feel this without feeling afraid. Without feeling the instinct to recoil. But I'd always known not to fear him. Not as he pushed the fabric covering my breast aside again to drag his teeth along the delicate curve beneath my nipple. Not even as he closed those teeth around the furled flesh, thrusting his still-clothed hips into me.

"Clay," I whined. "Please."

Another groan came from him before he sat up, looking appreciatively at the mess he'd made of the girl beneath him.

"We don't have to do this," he huffed. I reached to cover his mouth, shaking my head as he ducked away with another one of those dark laughs. "Don't get confused. I want this. Fuck, I really want this. I'm just saying we stop when you want to."

I pulled the mesh black bra over my head as long fingers hooked around my shorts and panties, tugging down with a swift yank. He was done waiting. We both were. My eyes traced the black ink up his arms. The kraken. The words. *Memento mori.*

Remember you will die.

It was a fact I could never forget. I remembered feeling like death was coming for me. Every second of every day felt like borrowed time. I remember feeling like maybe I died already and I was doomed to hell in a box in the middle of the desert. My skin tightened in a flash of memory. The feeling of a dusty, cold floor. I blinked it away, choosing to relax in Clayton's bed and enjoy the way he watched me. Caramel eyes greedily consumed me as he sat back on his heels, taking in my naked form. Long fingers circled my thighs as his palms skimmed over my sensitive skin. His gaze fell to the apex, the stroking movement grazing higher. An ebbing and surging sensation building in me with every sweep toward where I was completely drenched for him.

"I tried to forget about you. Really fucking hard. Nothing worked. Nothing could change my mind about needing you, firebird."

Clayton's confession was hot against my skin as he bent forward. Pink hair left feather-light touches on my stomach, following behind petal-soft kisses that trailed the arc of my hips. The small heart tattoo received a soft kiss after he traced the shape with his tongue. He nipped and licked a path downward, lowering himself until he lay sprawled between my legs on the bed. The grasp on my thighs renewed, holding me open for him. We shared a look. A silent conversation passing in the span of a moment. I nodded.

One long lick parted my flesh, a pitiful noise bursting from me at the sensation that followed. Clayton paused, arching a brow. My fingers twisted into his hair and tugged him forward. The grin that preceded the next lick was a sinful, toe-curling sight. Another and another. His efforts went from exploratory to worshiping, swirling, and firm. Caramel eyes marked every reaction drawn from me, taking the information and moving accordingly. Noting the way the swirl of his tongue made me tremble, he repeated the motion with swift brutality.

"Fuck," he sighed.

Tracing his tongue downward, I squirmed. His laugh was wicked against me. I felt his stubble brush me as he thrust his tongue into me, one hand moving to play with me. Release danced at the edges of my mind, causing my toes curl at every devious lick. The noises I was making must have sounded pathetic. Helpless. That's how I felt. Totally at his mercy. Especially when his tongue was replaced with two fingers, plunging inside to massage the inner spot that was dragging more of those helpless squeaks out of me. The other hand settled on my stomach, pressing down as he sucked my oversensitive bud between his lips. That new pressure, coupled with his humming approval and flicking tongue, sent the promise of release rocketing forward. Driving my heels down into the duvet, I tried and failed to steady my shaking legs. Fisting the sheets didn't help, either.

I kept expecting to feel afraid. To snap back to that trailer. To curl in on myself. But there was nothing. Only him.

"Clay," I moaned.

My vision fixed on the man staring up from between my legs, watching every little thing his attention did to me. A different worry slid between my bones. Worry that I wouldn't be enough for him. That I'd always be too broken to appreciate this. Too much work. The thought disappeared like fog in sunlight at the sight of another devious wink. A damned wink and a huffed command that preceded a dangerous increase in pressure.

"Scream for me."

Any lingering fear was submerged in the crash of utter bliss that roared over me, sweeping it away in its tide. The hand in his hair squeezing and pulling at him as I wailed through the orgasm, Clayton's soaked fingers and tongue still working as one. It was somehow everything I'd never felt and all of the things I never thought I would feel again. As he propped himself up to look at me, smiling and licking his lips, I realized what had replaced that fear. This. With him. It felt like life.

FIFTY

CLAYTON

I'd pictured exactly this too many fucking times. The sounds were so much better. The way her orgasm moved through her body was like a raging river. Her little nonsense syllables. All of it was enough and too much. I sucked my fingers into my mouth, savoring the way she tasted. Casey was still catching her breath as I stood from the bed and wondered if her need for me had come and gone with the orgasm I'd wrung from her. She'd thrown an arm over her flushed face, chest heaving as she tried to steady herself. The shifting mattress must have caught her attention because she sat up on her elbows to look at me.

"Where are you going?"

When I didn't answer, Casey shifted to her knees beside me at the end of the bed, wearing only the thin sheen of sweat that glistened on her perfect golden skin. I noted the freckles covering the peaks of her shoulders. Followed their scattered trail down to her nipples. Nothing could have broken my focus from her perfection, nothing but the way her hand gripped my shaft through the material of my jeans to give me a firm stroke. I bit down on a groan and looked into her hooded eyes. Batting those thick lashes at me, she smiled.

"We're not done yet, are we?"

A hoarse chuckle rumbled out of me. Dissatisfied with my non-verbal answer, she stroked me again, forcing a curse from me. Casey wore a fiendish grin, enjoying my torment and unknowingly adding to it with that smile. I brushed the hair out of her face, enjoying the silken slide of the strands tumbling over my fingers. The times I'd pictured this, exactly this, I'd never said no. Never once. I wasn't going to start now.

"No," I smirked. "We're not done."

Big doe eyes fixed on me, watching every move with the kind of desire I never thought I would see. They tracked my hands as I pushed off my jeans, along with the boxers underneath. Traced along with my grip as I pumped my length. I couldn't stop the thoughts that rushed through my head with every breath. She was here. Casey was in my bed. This was happening. I repeated the mantra I'd started internally chanting to myself from the second she walked through my door again.

Do not fuck this up.

Still sitting there like a goddess on an altar, I circled her throat with one hand and leaned forward to speak into her ear. The shiver that went through her body sent a jolt of pleasure down my spine in response. With a soft laugh, I nipped at her lobe before speaking in a low rasp.

"Want to go for a ride?"

Another shiver coursed through her, the loose curls of her hair grazing my face as she nodded. The knee I dropped between her legs with my hands moving to under her arms gave me enough leverage to twist and pull her over me, the momentum of my somewhat larger form dropping to the mattress, managing most of the work. A squeak of delight popped out of her. Another smile. Fuck, I loved that smile. Rich fire and copper waves bounced as I tugged her forward, golden thighs falling to either side of my hips. I swallowed, summoning all the confidence I could muster in the face of a sight like this.

"Clay," she faltered. "Are you sure?"

I took her in. Red hair rippling down to cover her breasts. That pink lower lip tucked between her teeth. Delicious brown eyes watching me with a mix of heat and wariness. Not fear. I smiled up at the sight and kneaded the muscled flesh of her hips. I lifted her slowly, hoping she'd understand my silent direction. She braced her palms on my shoulders as she tipped forward.

"Take what you want. You can have all of me, firebird."

That deep red curtain fell around me, her face a moon floating over mine. I gathered it and pushed it to one side, opening my mouth to tell her how breathtaking she looked like this, and lost the ability to think as I felt the slip of her sex coating my length. That mantra bubbled up from the dark recesses of my mind. *Do not fuck this up.* I let her take the lead. Massaged the curve of her perfect, round ass as I tried not to think about how wet she was, or this would be over too quickly. A sharp breath fell from pouting pink lips as her hips shifted, propping me at her entrance. Just barely inside.

We stared at each other for a long moment. The tipping point balanced on our quiet breaths. It was like we both knew there would be no going back. I looked to where we were barely connected and opened my mouth to say as much when she moved, sliding me in and in and in until she was fully stretched around me. She felt too good. Too damned good.

"Casey," I gritted, gripping her to keep her still.

"Yeah?"

"I don't think we can be friends anymore."

A breathy laugh preceded a push of her hips and another gasp. Ecstasy wrapped in fucking agony. That's what it was. Everything I wanted to touch and taste, sitting on top of me. Squeezing me. Instead, I lay here watching as the most mouth-watering vision I'd ever imagined began rocking her hips, strangling me into oblivion. An uncertain look washed over her features.

"What?"

"I've never been with someone as big as you."

"If you're trying to boost my ego, you're doing a great fucking job," I laughed, sitting up to put my arms around her the way we'd been in the dark. When the uncertain look didn't wash away, I kissed her deeply and said, "We can stop, if you want to. I don't want you to get hurt."

She shook her head, kissing me back as she circled her arms around my neck. I felt her start to move against me again. My hands dropped to guide her hips. Lavishing her mouth with another kiss, I tasted my name on her tongue as the deep friction between us made her shiver with pleasure.

"You feel," Casey swore as if that would finish her thought.

A flutter of delicate inner muscles did it for her. I was too far gone to appreciate her words, lost in the fact that this was happening. Aphrodite given form. A sculpture carved by masters, writhing on top of me. Riding me like she was made for it. I was inside her. She was moaning for me. There was no sky or sea. No north or south. Just her.

My head emptied. My focus narrowed to the taste of her collarbone. The flutter of her pulse under my tongue. The roll of her body against mine. Her fingers tangled in my hair as her head tipped back, brows furrowed. Each thrust had me trapped between wanting to go all night and worrying I was going to come at any moment. I was still hoping not to finish too soon when Casey frowned, staring down at our sweat-covered bodies.

"What's wrong?"

"I can't," she huffed, letting out a frustrated sigh. Casey groaned in disappointment, pouting at me as I cupped her chin. "Every time I get close, I'm just in my head, I think."

"Don't worry. I have an idea," I winked. Leaning back toward the nightstand, I slid the top drawer open to withdraw my assistant. After a few seconds of fumbling, the flower-shaped vibrator with its mouth-like opening buzzed to life in my hand. "Is this alright?"

Messy red hair fell into her face as she nodded, eying the red silicone in my hand.

"It doesn't, like, threaten your masculinity that I need extra help?"

"Fuck no," I laughed. "This little guy is for me as much as it is for you."

Her eyes remained on the toy as I lowered it between us. A surprised laugh was followed by a moan as I let the opening graze over the stiff peak of one breast. Casey bit into her lower lip, watching me move the toy to her other side. Winding her wrists around my neck again, she moved in my lap. I cupped her backside with my free hand, watching her expression when the toy hit exactly where I knew she needed it most. Brows furrowed and mouth popping into an 'oh' shape before her head tipped back on a whine.

"Oh my god. Clay."

I wanted to tell her how lovely she sounded like this. My name was music on her lips. Instead, I kept pace as I felt her near her peak. A muffled whimper told me she was biting her lip to stifle herself. Hands gripped my shoulders, nails digging in as she rode me. Body undulating, breath quick, lips parted with her eyes shut. The delicate muscles inside her squeezed in warning. She was so close.

"That's it. Casey, look at me."

She did. My hand firmed on her ass as I bent a leg and flipped us over, earning another one of those adorable squeaks from her. I couldn't help but admire the sight beneath me. Lower lip caught between her teeth, red hair pooled around her like a goddess in a Renaissance painting. I withdrew from her, moving the vibrator away from where it had so effectively brought her to the edge. A teasing slide through her as I used myself to continue massaging her clit made her shiver. Another. Again, until the crown pressed into her. Lifting her legs, I banded an arm around them and placed a kiss on her ankle as I slid home again, bringing the toy back to her swollen clit.

Brown eyes widened as she looked toward the nightstand. Away from me. I hadn't stopped working her. The decadently wet slide of her against me was enough to push me to the edge. It was soon joined by a merciless squeeze of muscles as Casey's hands scrambled in the sheets beside her.

"I want those eyes on me," I panted. "Now, firebird."

Dark lashes fluttered as she blinked up at me. Her skin was so flushed now. Eyebrows drawn together, she huffed strained breaths as she watched me. I could see the battle happening inside her. The war she thought she was waging alone. Tension leaked through her body, down the legs I was still holding. With as much ease as I could manage, I let them fall around me. Let myself cage her in with my body until the only thing between us was the toy I'd been using to pleasure her. My lips brushed hers as she looked into my eyes. Maybe someday it would go without saying. Someday, I could let her know with just a kiss. Today was not that day.

"It's just you and me here. Let go," I said, kissing her firmly before speaking against her lips. "I've got you."

She arched up to return my kiss, slow and sweet, the feel of her mouth on mine making my toes tingle. I was about to come. My strokes became deep and thorough, matching the increasing urgency of our tongues. Then her eyes shot wide open as she screamed into me. I felt the snap of her muscles as they bore down on me. Hard and fast, she wrapped her legs around me as she rocked her hips into mine. A low swear spilled from my lips with the brutal feel of her release. Blood rushed in my ears, muffling the sound of her moans as I emptied myself inside her.

Empty. Fantasy. Daydreams. Whatever you call the way I'd pictured this moment for two years, all of those ideas had been foolish. Black and white compared to the full spectrum of color this had been. The real thing. This was the real thing and it was so much fucking better than any of it. Casey relaxed beneath me, lips soft with something unspoken as she kissed me.

Legs tangled. Heaving breaths. It was all a beautiful mess. I braced an arm beside her head to take in the ocean of red hair and perfect face I couldn't get out of my mind. Tears were rolling down her flushed cheeks as she let out a broken laugh. Smiling up at me. A brilliant, heart-stopping smile as she kept laughing. Ease settled her shoulders, and light shone in her eyes. She was so fucking beautiful when she was happy. Absolutely breathtaking. It could have been relief flooding me. It could have been the tension leaking out of me from waiting for this. For her. Fuck, I would have waited forever. It could have been anything. I didn't know. Didn't have a damn thought left in me as I started laughing with her.

FIFTY-ONE

CASEY

Begin SafeSpace Session.

> It sounds like you turned a situation that frightened you into an enriching experience. That took a lot of courage.

> Honestly, I still can't believe it. It felt incredible. I didn't know I could feel like that, which is insane. We're not even dating each other. Just cooped up together for the time being.

> How would you describe your relationship with this man?

I peered down at the purple screen, my phone a weight in my hand. The therapist on my SafeSpace app had been available to text twenty-four hours a day, as promised in the advertisement. It had been a boon, really. Any time of day or night, whenever I had a thought I just couldn't push away, I sent it off for them to examine and went on with my day. After Clayton fell asleep, I snuck down the hall and perched on the bathroom counter to have a little session. The hem of Clayton's shirt twirled between my fingers as I wondered how to explain the dynamic between us before that. My thumbs hovered over the keyboard.

> Shaky. We dated. Well, we had one date, but then had a falling out a few years ago. He seems different now.

> Are you sure he's the one who's changed?

I placed my phone on the counter, screen down. Saying I'd changed felt wrong. It felt more like I was a sunflower starting to turn toward the sun. Two years ago, I'd been filled with anger. I was still angry. Except it felt like I'd been able to start processing that anger in a different way. None of it was fixed. Not at all. With a hop off the counter, I went to turn on the shower.

If I could start to enjoy things again, enjoy men, then maybe I could go through an entire day and not think about what happened to me. I could maybe even go back to having a real life. Having a future instead of treading water. The thought washed over me with the warm water. Another laugh bubbled out of me as I washed myself, noticing the pleasant soreness between my legs. Not only had I actually finished with him, but it was the most earth-rattling release I'd ever experienced. A laugh that was half-sob slipped from me. Not because it was Clayton. Not because of what we'd done.

Because I was still alive.

"I sincerely hope you're not laughing at me in there."

Steam fogged up the glass, but I knew he was there. I flailed for the knob, still looking in the direction of the door. The fluffy white towel was so soft as I wrapped it around myself. He was waiting in the hall, one hip propped on the doorframe. In another oversized tee, which somehow accentuated the muscled tone of his shoulders. The grey sweatpants he'd thrown on dipped low enough to show off the band of muscle lining his hips. Despite those devastating details, I was sure it was those little gold glasses that were making my knees go gooey. I lifted my nose, smelling something sweet in the air. Clayton raised his eyebrows, waiting for an answer to his question.

"I just," I blushed, biting back a smile. "I didn't know it could be like that."

He shrugged, folding his arms over his chest as if it was all in a day's work for him. Rolling my eyes, I shoved him, causing him to stumble backward.

"You're an idiot," I snipped as I made to move past him.

Quickly, he shifted into my path to block entry to the bedroom with one arm. I froze, trapped by the way he looked at me. Eyes dark. Mouth parted. The tips of his free fingers traced the towel's edge, dusting the tops of my thighs. Breath warmed my ear as he lowered his head enough to whisper in a tone that made the hairs on my neck prick.

"You've completely ruined every fantasy I've ever had. Nothing," he paused, noticing the way I shivered at his mouth grazing my skin. A smile curled his lips in my peripheral vision. "Not a single thought I've ever had about you, and I've spent so much time thinking about you, will ever compete with what I just experienced."

My toes curled on the polished concrete floor. The idea that our encounter had rattled him as much as it had rattled me was satisfying. Too satisfying. Pushing past the little kernel of something that warmed in my chest at that thought, I gave him a simpering smile.

"You've been thinking about me?"

"Every damn day," he declared. I arched a smug brow at him as I grinned. Obviously, I knew he'd been thinking about me. There were over a hundred messages to prove it. With a roll of his eyes, he laughed. "Yeah, yeah. Don't let it go to your head. Go put some clothes on; I've got food on the stove."

A kiss to my temple and a slap to my terrycloth-covered ass followed his direction. With a yelp, I shuffled into the bedroom and shut the door, enjoying the rich sound of his retreating laughter on the other side. Only five minutes passed as I tugged on a sage green lounge set and sifted my wet hair into a braid. Upon opening the door again, I was met with the sweet and smoky tones of a folksy singer coming from the record player. A raspy, deep voice was singing along from the kitchen. The voice grew louder the closer I came to their sources. A little off key, and somehow so pleasant to listen to. I leaned against one of the barstools and observed.

Clayton was pushing something around in a skillet with a wooden spoon, trailing off from the song when he swept a finger over the back of the spoon to gauge the thickness of his sauce. The source of the sweet smell, undoubtedly. I noted the large stockpot simmering with water and the package of linguini open on the counter beside it.

"Who taught you to cook?"

He didn't flinch. Not one bit. A little annoyed that I hadn't surprised him, I folded my arms over myself. Clayton only glanced over his shoulder, then dropped the pasta into the boiling water. Paper bags were folded neatly on the counter. A surge of pity rushed through me for whatever delivery driver was stuck hauling groceries in the middle of the night.

"I'm thirty-three years old, Casey. A grown man should know how to feed himself."

He shook his head like he was shaking a thought away, looking at the simmering skillet of sauce in front of him. Something creamy looking with sun dried tomatoes. Chili flakes went in. Then salt and black pepper. I scooted into the kitchen, deciding that whatever it was he was making would taste a hell of a lot better with a glass of white wine.

"Yeah, but you're good at it."

Clayton's hand went to his chest in faux shock. I chuckled and lifted a chilled bottle from the refrigerator. Shaking off my compliment, his brows drew together as he hummed thoughtfully to himself. From the more serious expression washing over his features, I wasn't sure I wanted to know the answer to my question. Maybe it was an ex-girlfriend. Or a lover. In all of this comfort that had grown between us, it was easy to forget that he'd had a life that didn't involve me. That there was a world outside of this loft. Especially after he'd just made me feel like I was the sun. And he was someone who…worshiped the sun. Then I wasn't thinking about the skills he gained in the kitchen. Anxiety tightened my gut as I waited for him to speak, internally begging him to put me out of my misery.

"I mostly know pastas. One of my foster parents was half Italian. She taught me more than that, but these recipes are easier for me to get through without screwing up."

Instant regret. Absolute instant regret from the tension seeping into the room. Clearly, talking about his past was not something he liked to do. He hadn't shared much about his upbringing, but it seemed like most of what he'd endured had been about survival. There wasn't any mention of anyone specific. Peering at me from the corner of his eye, Clayton gave me a small, sad smile that looked more like a grimace. I pulled a pair of glasses from the cabinet and set them down, the bases clinking on the stone. The domesticated mercenary hustled to the refrigerator and yanked what looked like a lump of cheese free, then resumed his position at the stove. Rolling his shoulders, he sighed.

"Diana McGill. She was an elementary school teacher who started fostering children after her husband died. He had been gone for two years when I was placed with her. I was fifteen. I'd bounced in and out of a few different homes, and by that point, I wasn't interested in getting to know anyone new. That didn't matter to her. That two-bedroom townhouse outside of Chicago wasn't enough space for me to avoid her, and she knew it."

As he explained, he grated the cheese into the skillet. I unscrewed the top from the bottle of wine and gave the opening a sniff. Grapefruit and pear. Filling one glass, then the other, I took the pair to the counter and hopped up to watch him work. Clayton dared a glance in my direction and snatched the second glass of wine. His long fingers curled around the stem. It was impossible not to watch as he lifted the glass to his mouth to take a sip. No, not a sip. A gulp. Then another.

"Days became weeks, then months. She put this old stereo in my room. At first, I wasn't sure why. Then she started to leave CDs of old audiobooks on my bed along with my folded laundry. David Copperfield. Tom Sawyer. The Hobbit. The last one was my favorite. I listened to it again and again. One day, the entire Lord of the Rings series was waiting for me. It was the first time anyone had ever," he paused, considering his next words as he pulled a pair of bowls from the cabinet overhead. "Ever noticed what I needed. There were other foster parents who did their best, but Ms. McGill. She saw me."

I watched him, sorting through the questions flooding my mind as I took a sip of wine. It was hard to know what to do or what to ask someone who'd experienced that sort of upbringing. My mother had always been there for me, the constant in my life. The only constant in his childhood was change. A selfish, awful voice in my head wondered if I'd even survive that kind of existence. The noise of my thoughts finally quieted enough to realize he hadn't said anything for a while. He just stood there, tearing basil. I settled for the obvious question.

"What happened?"

Clayton heaved a deep breath, one that seemed to come from his gut. After a pull from his glass, he looked down at the pot. Exchanging the normal wooden spoon with a spiky one, he pulled noodles from the water and dropped them into the skillet. Droplets of water fell off the ends and sputtered as they hit the burner's golden flame.

"We got into a routine. She'd give me the books. We talked about them at dinner, sitting at her little kitchen table. I learned about what it meant to take care of a home and myself. After a year, she told me she was trying to adopt me. So we could be a family. The day of my hearing, I was making breakfast for us when I heard a crash upstairs," Clayton said, the end of his sentence coming out in a rasp. "She wasn't moving. Wasn't breathing. I didn't know what to do, so I called an ambulance and stayed with her."

I didn't need to hear the rest. The only person to show him kindness as a child, and he'd lost her just as he'd almost found some stability. I hadn't had much growing up, but I'd had a mother who cared for me. She made sure I had everything I needed. She made sure I knew I mattered to her. To not know that. Or feel that. My hand rubbed at my chest, trying to soothe the ache building there. I couldn't imagine how someone could experience a life like that and still be so thoughtful.

Clayton dished the noodles into the bowl, grating more cheese over the top of them. That was followed by the basil he'd torn into little pieces. One bowl was dropped into my hands with a fork and a smile that didn't quite reach his eyes. An impressive hop had him sitting on the counter beside me. Had I not been thinking about what he'd just told me, I would have been astounded that he managed to do it with a glass of wine in one hand and a bowl of pasta in the other.

"I'm sorry," I said quietly.

It felt like the wrong thing. That word. *Sorry*. I hated hearing it from other people. People like the doctor who'd examined me after I'd gotten home after all that I'd been through. *Sorry*. Clayton took a bite from his bowl, the strangest expression cascading over his features. Something like uncertainty and assessment warred in his eyes. That pang of something awful tugged at my chest again. I twirled pasta onto my fork and stuffed it into my mouth, hoping it would prevent me from saying anything else. Creamy, sharp deliciousness exploded on my tongue, drawing an involuntary moan from me.

"This was her favorite dish," Clayton remarked. A smirk played across his lips as he looked up at me from beneath his brows, but the playful expression didn't reach his eyes. We sat there for a while, both of us stewing in unspoken words. He loosed a joyless laugh, causing me to jerk in my seat. Spearing more noodles onto his fork, he shook his head. "It's funny. The smell of burned toast still makes me nauseous."

FIFTY-TWO

CLAYTON

Marry Me Linguine. Dianne said that it had secured the proposal from Mr. McGill. I could still picture her little kitchen table and smell the garlic bread she made in her toaster oven to go with it. I stared down into the bowl, feet bouncing into the cabinets below me. We'd stayed on the counter, eating and talking.

Big brown eyes blinked at me, waiting for me to go on. She twined more noodles onto her fork, securing her bite with a piece of chicken. I took a breath, trying to decide what to say next. It was easy. Casey wanted to know me. Instead of looking at me with pity, she just slurped the end of a noodle into her mouth.

"You know, she's the one who gave me the rabbit's foot," I offered. "It belonged to her husband. He'd served in the military, and every time he got deployed, he'd bring it with him for good luck. That meant something to me. That she would give me something so precious to her."

"Is he why you joined the Navy?"

I nodded. I'd told her about enlisting so I'd have somewhere to go. She didn't need to hear about the two months I'd spent sleeping in my friends' closets or sheds, hopping from place to place when their parents caught on, just so I didn't have to go back to Halloway's house. Earning my GED with help from the local library had been the suggestion of one of the librarians who'd caught me sleeping in the playhouse in the children's section at the end of the day. Sharing so much with someone so quickly felt a lot like vomiting your guts up for hours on end. I wasn't sure how much energy I had left to get it out.

"I brought it with me, you know," she said after a long moment, her foot nudging mine. "The rabbit's foot. It meant a lot to me, too."

It was a precarious thing. This peace between us. I could say the wrong thing and royally screw it up. I knew that. From the way her eyebrows drew together, one side of her mouth tucking into a bite, she knew it too. I forced a laugh from myself and scooped up her empty bowl, hopping from the counter to deposit them in the dishwasher.

"Good to know it didn't wind up in the trash."

I wasn't sure why I'd said it. Her wince at the statement was enough to fill me with regret immediately. As predicted, the wrong thing came out of my mouth, and I didn't do a damn thing to stop it. Instead, I mumbled an excuse about having more work to do and left her there.

My eyes burned from staring at the screens for so long. For hours, I just worked. Checked in on the security feeds for various clients. Looked through Kremnik's files again for updates on his movements, with no new information to show for it. Got updates from my employees. Tried my best to stay quiet since she hadn't closed the door after she'd finished washing up. The headphones I'd put on felt glued to my ears as I peeled them off and glanced at the little clock at the bottom corner of my screen. Deciding to call it a night at well after one in the morning, I walked on careful footsteps to the bathroom.

With a glance into the bedroom, I noticed the light was still on. Casey was lying on her belly, texting, with a pillow tucked under her chin. Her feet bobbed an idle rhythm to whatever she was listening to on those headphones. She'd changed into that little pajama set. The one that made my skin feel ten sizes too tight over my bones. My hands went to the top of the frame, I just hung there, content to let her attention shift to me in its own time.

Don't push your luck. Just say goodnight and go crash on the sofa.

One minute went by. Then another. Until she looked over her shoulder. Blinked. Then propped herself up on one arm as she half rolled to face me. Red hair spilled over her shoulder with the movement. So many nights, I'd imagined the sight before me. Now that I was looking at it with my own eyes, I wasn't sure what to do with myself. Casey pulled the headphones off and smiled at me.

"Finally," she huffed. "Are you ready for bed?"

"Were you waiting up for me?"

She nodded. I had taken her here. Made her scream for me here. Yet, for some fucking reason, I still couldn't bring myself to get into bed without an invitation. Like I needed reassurance that she wanted me here. Pushing off the frame, I was gearing up to offer some explanation about sleeping on the sofa when Casey sat up and flipped the blankets over on my side. She smiled that brilliant smile and patted the empty space she'd created.

"Come on. I don't want to sleep alone."

The smell of her shampoo was still rich at the top of her head. I noticed that first. Second, that she'd slid her leg up over me so that her knee rested between my legs. Her hand nestled between my pecs, thumb moving back and forth over the patch of hair there. A deep sigh loosed from her followed by some satisfied little noise I wanted to hear again as soon as it hit my ears.

"I can hear your heart beating. It's strong."

Can you hear it saying your name?

A grunt popped out of me. Casey nuzzled into my chest with another sigh, giving me the opportunity to sniff her hair again. This casual intimacy was not good. No, that was a lie. It was so fucking good. Falling asleep with her in my arms was a dangerous indulgence. Not just because it was Ronan's daughter. The one I wasn't supposed to touch. But because it was all I'd wanted. Some part of me didn't want to get too comfortable. That part told me not to notice how perfectly we fit together. It reminded me of that peaceful time at McGill's house. Casey was all I'd imagined in the last two years. And I wouldn't let myself enjoy it because I knew it was all about to slip away.

FIFTY-THREE

Casey

> We've only known each other a little while, and you're the first person I want to talk to when I have something on my mind.

Everyone in the circle was looking at me, which was fine. Absolutely fine. I started talking, not knowing exactly what I was going to say. I just knew that I wanted to share. There were things I needed to process, not just with my therapist, but with other people who had been through what I'd been through. People who might be having a hard time being intimate with someone. People like me who thought that part of them might have too much scar tissue to feel again.

It was still scary. The way cliff diving can be scary. Or the final click of a rollercoaster before it drops you into an exhilarating plummet. It still felt that way in the small hours of the morning, when we'd reached for each other in the soft glow of dawn. My hands still shook as I'd climbed atop him. They stopped shaking when he sat up to hold me, kissing me deeply as I rode him. Watching the light catch in his eyes, looking at me with wonder as I writhed in his arms. He wore that lopsided sunshine grin as he flipped us over to straddle one of my legs, stroking me with every thrust.

Being with him felt like nothing else. Because the walls I put up between us tumbled down with every gesture. Every little thing he did to make sure I felt safe. They broke down with each talk we had about real things. I knew that I could never be in danger as long as he was around. Because it was *him*. Clayton leaned forward to take my jaw in his hand, turning my face so I looked at him while he moved inside me. His behavior had become cautious, the way people are cautious around a skittish animal, but his face screamed every word he was too afraid to say as we watched each other shatter.

Don't walk away from me again.

That look was still burned on my mind as I spoke. Searing me as I explained who I was and how long I'd been attending these bi-weekly meetings. I'd tried before. I'd paid the consequences before. But now I had someone to catch me. Someone who understood that sometimes healing means hurting, too. It's messy and unpredictable. And that's okay.

"I have this friend. Well, he's more than a friend now. For a long time, I kept my distance. I used a small fight as an excuse to stay away from him. But the truth is," I paused, releasing a shaky breath. I was fine. I was safe. They would understand. "The truth is that I was afraid to let him see how broken I really was."

Scanning the faces of the people around me, my eyes fell on Lisa. Her face was impassive. Kind, as always. Listening, as always. No judgement. Just presence. I went on.

"Some stuff happened at home, and I had to move in with him for a little while. Being around each other was difficult at first. Until it wasn't," I chuckled.

The faces went from impartial to confused. Hesitantly optimistic. I knew that expression because I'd worn it so many times. Over the last two months, I'd had that look on my face. The one that said *I hope this is going where I think it's going*. It was the look I wore before Clayton made me laugh. Because he did make me laugh. He made me smile. He did all of it because he wanted to. He climbed the tower I hid away in because he wanted to be my champion.

My knight in armored leather.

"We connected in a lot of ways. Then last night," I laughed. "We— I slept with him. He made me feel safe. I was able to finish, which I haven't been able to do since what happened to me happened. I mean, I have, but it was because I asked him to help me. I couldn't do it myself. No matter how many times I tried, and believe me, I tried a lot. I tried so many times. I thought they broke that part of me. But I'm not broken. I'm not."

My hands flew to my cheeks. Burning hot and wet with tears. That was okay, too. I wiped them away with a laugh and looked around, noticing one or two people wiping away tears of their own.

"I'm not saying he fixed me. God, that would be such a cliche, wouldn't it? But I dove in, and now it feels like I'm swimming."

A squeeze at my shoulder. Lisa. She grinned at me with something like pride shining in her eyes as we ambled down the front steps. I thought she might say something to me. About what I'd said. About the man waiting for me in the parking lot. Instead, she just looked at me. Looked at him. Then she gave my shoulder a pat.

"Everything alright?" Clayton asked, standing from the seat of his motorcycle. Black work pants. White T-shirt. Leather racer jacket. Pink hair finger-combed away from his face. I bit down on my smile and nodded. "Good. Let's go get some breakfast. I'm thinking pancakes."

"Blueberry pancakes?"

"Blueberry," he smirked, taking my hand in his to draw me closer. "Whatever you want. As long as you let me have a taste."

"You can have one right now," I purred.

Kissing was an incredibly underrated activity. One of the best things our species has ever created. Once upon a time, I would have seen it as a small thing. Something only teenagers got really excited about. Kissing Clayton disabused me of that sort of thinking. Kissing him was more than just kissing. It was his hand in my hair. The other at my waist. My fingers tangling in pink curls at the nape of his neck. His soft grunts into my mouth like I was his favorite food, and he was savoring every bit of me.

"Let's get you fed," he hummed against me, kissing the corner of my mouth. "But not too much."

I pulled away, moving my hands to his chest to keep him from leaning in again. At my narrowed gaze, a look of sheer mortification slapped over his features. Clayton rushed out an explanation, both hands going to my waist as if to stabilize himself.

"I'm not trying to tell you what to eat," he chuckled nervously. "You've got dim sum with your father this afternoon. Remember?"

Right. Ronan insisted on getting together with me since we were almost in the clear from this Kremnik situation. According to Clayton, there was evidence that he'd left the country. From the tone in my father's voice when he'd invited me, I wondered if he was reminded of the years my mother hid me away.

"In that case, let's go home."

"Yeah," Clayton smiled. "Let's go home."

FIFTY-FOUR

Casey

Two blocks away from the loft, there was a yum cha spot that served the most incredible steamed pork buns in the city. Apparently, this was something my father knew, because he insisted on meeting me there with my little sister. The two of them smiled at me from across the small table covered in a silky gold tablecloth and plates upon plates of various dim sum. Despite the fact that the Russian mob boss was seemingly out of our hair, several of my father's men dotted the room, watching us. Watching my father serve my little sister more tea, just as I watched them. The more I saw them together, the more I wondered how much regret my father lived with at missing my childhood.

It was nice to see her get the love and attention she deserved. A sore wound inside me was getting poked and prodded by it, reminding me of the days I went without a father. Days I spent alone while my mother worked. I'd been a teenager by the time I discovered who my father was. I could still picture him standing in front of our apartment as my mother and I got home from the grocery store. A tall, dark-haired man with stony features dressed in black. He'd only been in his mid-thirties then. Ronan's eyes locked on me, but Rose Collins rushed me inside, slamming our front door closed behind me. It didn't do anything to prevent me from being able to hear him screaming at her as they argued outside.

"She is *my* child, Rose."

"I didn't want her involved in your fucked up family, Ronan. She'd become another pawn to be used against you. You told me we couldn't be together because of it. Why would I think any differently of our daughter? She deserves better."

"She deserved a father!"

I'd peeked out the window to see them gesturing wildly at each other, but they'd stepped too far away for me to hear what was being said. My mother came inside and caught me sitting below the front window. Understanding colored her face, and she sat down beside me to explain. That man was my father. He was Ronan Arawn, the son of an Irish mafia boss who died when she and my father were together. She discovered she was pregnant as he took control of the family and decided it would be better if he didn't know about me. It had broken her heart to leave him. Based on the rage I'd seen, I knew it broke his too.

"Where's the man I'm paying to keep you safe?"

The tiny porcelain cup looked so ridiculous in my father's large hand, the smoking skull tattoo on the back eyeing me as it lifted to his mouth. In his slate grey three-piece suit, he looked more approachable than in his countless black ones. I was grateful for the lack of sartorial severity. Ainsley very politely excused herself to the ladies' room, the blue tulle dress that perfectly matched her eyes bouncing with every step. Paired with the soft green dress I'd thrown on after group, we all looked rather smart. My father and I watched the door she'd gone into, waiting for the little sign over the lock to go from red to green. It didn't matter that the door was now flanked by my father's guards. I sighed.

"He walked me here. Handed me over to your guys. He's waiting for a text from me to walk me back. I think he went into the little market next door," I said. Then Clayton's text messages from two years ago flashed into my mind. *Please come back. I'm coming over.* "Has Clayton ever tried to see me? At your house, I mean."

Ronan's salt and pepper brows furrowed.

"Aye. He was at the gates some time ago. Made a proper fool of himself when he went screaming at the guards."

A sinking feeling in my stomach dragged me down at that declaration. Pretending the thought of Clayton chasing me down didn't fill me with regret, I pulled a plate of dumplings toward myself. Locked away in my tower. I didn't even know he was there. My father set his cup down and scratched at his jaw. Narrowed eyes. Brows still drawn together. Mouth tight at the corners. His face always did that when he was working on what to say. I set my chopsticks down and frowned at him.

"What?"

"He's not tried anything, has he?"

This was one of those moments you take comfort in the fact that people were not usually clairvoyant. Because if he could read my mind, he'd know that it wasn't the mercenary who'd tried something with me. I'd asked him to cross that line so long ago that the line was now a distant memory. That first night flooded my thoughts. Clayton braced over me, wand in one hand as he counted down toward the first orgasm I'd had in two years. Sitting on the sofa with him, watching movies, and talking about our pasts felt like something, too. No, the bespectacled bodyguard hadn't tried anything with me. He'd succeeded. Still, I was more than confident that nothing would have happened if something hadn't changed between us. Something I couldn't quite name. Attempting to keep my face neutral, I lobbed a response at my father.

"If you don't trust him, why did you send me to stay at his place?"

I hoped my provocation would stop him from realizing I'd ducked his question. When he leaned forward, dropping his voice to avoid barking at me in public, I knew I had succeeded.

"I do trust him," he seethed. The bathroom door creaked open, my little sister happily bobbing over in our direction. He sat up straight in his chair again, watching her approach our table. I thanked whatever merciful deity was looking down on me for the ultimate distraction.

"Then what are we talking about here?" I rushed out in a harsh whisper.

"Can we get more custard tarts?" Ainsley chirped, seating herself beside our father, completely unaware of the conversation she'd interrupted.

The dark expression cleared from my father's face, greeting my little sister with a grin he reserved only for his girls. For a brief moment, I felt a pang of pity for my brother. I'd never seen Killian receive such a greeting. Only stern words and commands would do for his eldest. With the three of us here, his absence was a pointed one. Enough to wonder what sort of illicit task he was up to in the middle of the day. Duplicitous deeds didn't always wait for darkness.

"Of course, darling girl."

Ronan's hand raised to beckon the waiter toward our table again. Ainsley looked at me, and I smiled. She pushed a lock of blonde hair behind her ear and plucked up a pot sticker between two small fingers.

"I can't believe you're still hungry after all those pork buns," I laughed.

My sister shrugged, looking down at her stomach to give it a pat.

"I'm a growing girl."

Clayton was waiting at the front door when we exited the little restaurant. Standing there with a tote bag full of groceries, I hoped he'd planned a light dinner since I'd just eaten my weight in buns and rolls. Ainsley let out a squeal as she walked out with my father, delighted by the sight of Clayton's shaggy pink hair. The mercenary let out a laugh, followed by a grunt as she threw herself into him for a hug.

"You did it!"

"Yep," he huffed, removing my sister from his person under the watchful eye of our father. "I think pink really suits me."

"I agree," I smirked.

My father simply dipped his chin in greeting at Clayton, who returned the gesture with his head at an angle that matched the smirk on his face. A mask, I realized. A joker who protected him from the world. The urge to step between them was overwhelming. The desire to protect Clayton from my father felt strange. A new garment to replace that raincoat feeling I'd become so familiar with. It wasn't numbness that ruled my actions. It was something else entirely.

"We'd better get going," I rushed out. "Wouldn't want to be caught standing around out here like sitting ducks."

Clayton chuckled at my terrible excuse but nodded and slipped his free hand around my waist. Ainsley waved goodbye as we parted ways with my father and his men, a little blue flower surrounded by towering soldiers. I waved back, knowing I'd have another uninterrupted day with her soon.

"You two ready for your day at the park this weekend?" Clayton asked.

"Yup. We've got all the rides planned out and everything. Down to the last churro," I grinned. "I wish you could come with us."

"I know," Clayton sighed. "There's nothing I like more than massive crowds and the scent of stale popcorn, but your father has some product coming in that he needs me to deal with. Your brother promised that the twins would keep you company. I'll be waiting for you when you get home."

His fingers laced through mine, Clayton's natural heat leaking into my digits. The sensation stabilized some wobbling inner part of me. Strolling down the street, our little bit of sidewalk became like our own little world. He whistled a happy tune I didn't recognize. A bag of groceries in one hand. My hand in the other. It was an odd sort of comfortable. A *warm bed on a Sunday morning* sort of comfortable. When we came to a stop at a crosswalk, I stood up on my toes and kissed his cheek. I didn't even bother to check and see if anyone was still watching us.

FIFTY-FIVE

CLAYTON

Mary Morton. It was an ordinary name. Hundreds of women shared it. Women of all ages, all over the country. The woman who gave birth to me had that very same name. It was the name I repeated to myself over and over again as I picked up the notepad with my father's phone number on it.

Public records were a hell of a thing. You could find pretty much anyone's personal contact information with the right site access. The DNA service I'd used had access to other sample libraries, including one for ancestry. One that my father accessed, undoubtedly curious about where he'd come from. The irony of that was not lost on me. That information placed him right in my lap. Fifty percent match. Like a scab I couldn't stop picking, I dug deeper.

Jerry Buckley.

Armed with the name and location of the man who sired me, it didn't take long for Gizmo to track him down. Jerry was a sales manager at an automotive dealer outside of Naperville, Illinois. With that, I was able to get his home address, his email, and his phone number. Clicking over to the dealership's website, I got my first look at the man. The strange familiarity of his face was enough to curdle my lunch. Eyes were the same shape as mine, though his were blue. Same nose. Same dimples in his cheeks when he smiled. Any lingering doubt I'd had washed away. I sat back in my chair and stared at the screen. Jerry Buckley was my father.

"You found him?"

I hadn't heard her enter. Casey had walked in on cat-soft feet thanks to one of the pairs of fuzzy socks I'd gotten for her. Clad in a cropped cream-colored sweater that showed off the freckles on her toned stomach whenever it crested above the waistband of her leggings, she looked effortlessly comfortable. Her hand combed through her tresses as she sidled up next to me. They became covered by the sleeves of her sweater as she placed them on her hips. I nodded, returning my attention to the man on the screen.

"He's got your dimples," she noted, smiling a little. Brown eyes slid to the yellow sticky note on my desk, then noted the iron grip on my phone. They softened, turning as warm as the hand she placed on my shoulder. "Are you going to call him? You could just send an email."

I shook my head. No, I wouldn't send an email. Now that I had the information, it felt wrong not to use it, but my phone still felt like a brick in my hand. Tapping the screen, I opened the dial pad and started punching in numbers. Casey sucked in a breath.

"Do you want me to stay?"

"No," I stumbled. "No, I need to do this on my own."

Casey bit her lower lip, holding back a frown as she sighed through her nose. Looking around the space, she rocked on her heels. With a glance at the screen again, she bent down to kiss my cheek.

"I'm going to go start dinner."

Several seconds passed before I worked up the nerve to hit the call button, taking the opportunity to wipe my sweaty palms on my jeans. Worst-case scenarios played through my mind like film trailers, one after the other. One jab at the screen and it was done. The phone began ringing. I brought the device to my ear.

"You've got Jerry Buckley."

Words. I couldn't find words. I'd thought I'd ask for Jerry Buckley, but announcing himself threw me off. It was a small, ridiculous hurdle. Then I remembered the information I had. The name. The DNA test. Ammunition for a war of words I wasn't ready to march into. I debated hanging up.

"Hello?"

"Yeah, hi," I started. "I'm calling on behalf of Mary Morton."

If I hadn't heard the cough on the other end of the line, I would have thought we were disconnected. Footsteps slammed into a hard surface in the background. The sound of a door slamming closed soon followed. He cleared his throat.

"I'm sorry, I don't think I heard you. What did you say?"

Cold irritation trickled through my veins. He'd heard me. There was no way he hadn't heard me. It was only made worse by the fact that this guy sounded like me, only with a thick midwestern accent. I pushed down the instinct to hang up and pressed on.

"Mary Morton. I'm calling to settle her estate," I said. The lie came out so easily. "You had a relationship with her, didn't you?"

"No," he choked out.

My shoulders tightened. This was a waste of time. This guy was in denial about being involved with my mother. There was no way he knew about me. If he didn't have any affection for a woman he'd apparently fooled around with, I had my doubts about him taking the news of my existence very well.

"Wait," he said, voice muffled like he'd put his phone to his chest. It got clear as he continued, a heavy sigh pushing through the receiver. "I'm sorry. I do. I did. I knew Mary. She and I used to work together. I, we— had a relationship for about a year or so. Did you say her estate?"

"Yes," I hesitated. "Mary's dead. She died thirty years ago."

I'd expected some response. Some questions about why her estate was just being settled now if she'd died so long ago, because, hell, it wasn't exactly a great lie. It wasn't even a passable one. The phone went quiet for a long time. I pulled it away from my ear to see if maybe he'd decided to hang up on me. The call was still there.

"What happened to the boy?"

My stomach plummeted to my feet. Me. He knew. He knew about me. Unable to stop the bite in my tone or the nonsense question from rushing out of me.

"Who?"

"Ethan," Jerry cleared his throat again, the tone of his voice going from wary to indignant as he demanded, "Who is this?"

"This is her son."

It was all I would give. I hadn't used my birth name in decades. There was no Ethan Morton. Not since I turned eighteen and could legally change it. That boy. The one who'd been locked up with a dead woman for two days. The one whose only chance at a real mom died on a bedroom floor thirteen years later. I didn't know him anymore. Not really. But I could feel the dusty threads of carpet between my fingers as I thought about her, as if my body wanted me to remember that small bit of my past. Even if my mind had blocked so much from me.

"Why are you calling me?"

Fear dripped from his voice.

"You know that he— that I'm your son?"

The guy pushed out a graveled sigh. I heard it. That resigned irritation. Like he knew this call was coming someday, and he just had to get through it. To get through talking to me. I was a problem to be dealt with. Nothing more. When he went on, he didn't do a damn thing to disguise the irritation in his voice.

"Mary told me I knocked her up. Threatened to tell my wife if I didn't give her money. So I did. I thought she was going to take care of it. Then she had the baby and came after me for more. Thousands. For three years. I paid for that damned apartment until she got herself evicted. After a while, I didn't hear from her again. I never met the boy. Just saw a picture once."

Before I could think of a single thing to say, he cursed low and barked at me.

"Are you trying to get more money out of me?"

Sour rage turned to bitter ash in my mouth. The guy had gone from admitting he knew about me to saying he'd basically wished I'd never been born. It was the kind of emotional whiplash I wasn't sure I could come back from. The phone creaked in my hand as my grip squeezed around it. Some small part of me wished I hadn't sent Casey away. An angry throat cleared expectantly on the other end of the line. I forced out my response.

"No. No money," I seethed. I could probably buy and sell this guy's entire life twenty times over. Even if I were unhoused again, I'd never ask for a dime from him.

"So what do you want?"

The air I huffed through my nose felt like a dragon's breath. Rage. All I felt was fucking rage. This fucking guy.

"Nothing."

Ending the call, I slammed the phone down on the desk and shoved the heels of my hands into my eyes. Now I knew. A long moment passed. Then another. Closing the tabs on my monitors, I stopped on his social media profile. Friends wished him a happy birthday on his wall. Tagged him and his wife in photos from his party. It was like shrapnel lanced into my side. In the middle of the suburbs of Chicago, there was a man who was pretending to be happily married. Had children with a woman he deemed appropriate. A son he had given his name to and a daughter he seemed proud of. They even sort of looked like me. Two kids who lived a happy life without knowing who their father really was. A man who was capable of betraying his wife and turning his back on one of his children.

I used to imagine what kind of man my father was. He could have been a soldier who never came home from war. A good man who never knew about his child. Jerry Buckley knew. I would bet he knew Mary was an addict. Knew I'd end up in the system. And left me there. My father wasn't a good man. He was just a man who never cared about me. I dragged the file into the trash. Closed all of my tabs and deleted my search history, deciding to close the book on this story and find the one person I wanted to see.

"I'm guessing by that look on your face that it didn't go very well," Casey frowned.

"Some questions are better left unanswered."

He didn't want me. It was right there on the tip of my tongue. This. This was why I didn't want to go looking. The truth of it was worse than what I had imagined. I'd thought he didn't know. I'd thought at worst, I was the result of a one-night stand, and she'd decided to keep me. I hadn't anticipated that I'd been fodder for blackmail. That I'd been some thorn in an adulterer's side. Red hair bobbed as she angled her head, waiting for me to elaborate. She'd tied it into a ponytail. I shrugged, the gesture feeling unnatural with this new weight in my shoulders. Casey pivoted, turning the burner under the skillet off before striding across the kitchen toward me. She stopped abruptly in front of me, seeming to think better of whatever it was she was going to do.

"Can I hug you?"

I nodded. Casey stepped into me, threading her arms around my waist. The ponytail was almost high enough to brush my nose. I wrapped her up, enjoying the feel of her body pressing against me.

"It's his loss," she mumbled into my chest. She rested her chin on my sternum and blinked up at me. I loved looking at her like this. At this angle, I could see all the freckles dotting across her nose. Her eyes were soft as they stared up at me. The tender thing in my chest gave a painful thud when she said, "He'll never know the insanely clever, kind Clayton that I know."

"I do know my way around a dick joke."

"Stop it," she laughed, slapping me in the side. "You know what I mean. You're wonderful."

Some people think the color brown is unremarkable. Boring. Not worthy of note. Those people are wrong. Brown was the most beautiful thing I'd ever seen. Chocolate and caramel. Bright and warm. Brown made me feel better about the world. Brown made me forget the hollow ache my father had put in me, replacing it with one of pure adoration. Brown made me bend down and kiss her. Because maybe Jerry Buckley didn't want me. But I could see in those brown eyes that she did. She thought I was *wonderful*. That was the only thing that mattered.

FIFTY-SIX

CLAYTON

Living in the center of Los Angeles meant that it was easy to forget we were a beach city. Our sprawling metropolis went on in so many directions that you could drive for an hour and still be in the county. I'd driven us all the way out to Leo Carrillo, intent on a change of scenery. A hidden little spit of beach at the other end of Malibu was not originally what I'd intended when we set out, but I'd gotten lost in the feel of Casey's body warming mine and sped past my original destination of the pier just to feel it for a little longer.

If I'd been alone, I would have spiraled for weeks. Would have needled West until he caved and got a beer with me only to sit there talking about everything but what I needed to. But she'd been there to catch me. Listen to me. Stroked her fingers through my hair in that way that made me relax instantly. I fell asleep on the sofa watching The Princess Bride, unable to keep my eyes open past the pit of despair. It was a little bit of normalcy I knew I would miss. I wanted to do something for her, so I'd brought her here. Once I realized I'd blown past my original intention, I decided to come to this beach. It was the place I'd come to think about her.

I wasn't sure what to do about talking to my father yesterday. Not knowing who he was wasn't much different from him wanting nothing to do with me. Either way, I got the same thing out of it. Still, I'd spent a decent portion of the day looking into the lives of my half-siblings. Regardless of whether or not they knew I existed, I couldn't help the curiosity. My half-sister was working toward a doctoral degree in mathematics at Northwestern. My half-brother was getting ready to graduate from high school. He was an avid gamer and amateur programmer. They were smart. Earned good grades. Had lots of friends. It was kind of nice to see that I had something in common with one of them.

"You know, my mom used to take me to the tidepools up in Half Moon Bay," Casey said as she picked her way toward me over the rocks, supporting the camera with one hand even though it was strapped around her neck. The ocean hissed as it withdrew from the honeycomb of stone. "We'd walk there for hours. She used to give me a nickel for every starfish I found. One day I got a whole dollar. But my favorite thing was to go to Old Fisherman's Warf."

"Because of the restaurants?"

"No," she laughed, smile brighter than the setting sun. "Because of the otters."

I toed a rock into one of the small tidepools, barely able to hear the plop over the incoming wave. A few more shutter clicks. The camera was aimed at the pools at our feet. I almost asked her if she was counting starfish.

"You like the camera?"

"I love it," she grinned. Point. Click. "It's even better than the one I had before."

"Why were the otters your favorite?"

Casey lowered the camera, letting the device hang from its strap to free up her hands. Blush crept over her cheeks like the answer was embarrassing. God, now I wanted to know even more.

"Well, they're not always there. But sometimes in the bay, when they're all twisted up in the kelp to sleep, they hold their little paws," she said, linking her index fingers in front of herself to demonstrate. "So they don't drift away from each other. It's the best."

"Did you ever miss growing up without a father?"

Casey blinked, brows drawing together. Her eyes skimmed the ocean, watching the waves tumble toward us. The lilac sweater she wore was almost violet in this light as her shoulders lifted and fell with a deep breath.

"Not really. I mean, I love my dad, but my mom made sure I had enough. We had our own little world. Otters and all." She said as she lifted the device to her face, snapping a picture of something. I scanned the horizon. The sky was going orange where the sun met the sea. If I'd been alone, I would have thought it was beautiful. Scattered clouds colored pink from the waning light. Blue sky turning dark at the furthest reaches, little points of starlight illuminating the sky. On any other night, it would be gorgeous. Tonight, it was nothing because I was with her. The camera aimed in my direction again. "That pink hair looks fantastic in this light. It's practically a cloud."

I turned my attention back to my excited little photographer. Dark red brows were almost brown in this light, a line forming between them as she looked at her digital display screen. The disappearing light must have concluded her shots for the day because she packed the camera back into her little bag. Her sweater and jacket weren't enough to keep out the creeping chill, shuddering with her as she wrapped her arms around herself. I lifted an arm and tucked her into my side.

"You're cold."

"I am not," she shivered before muttering to herself. "I knew I should have worn pants."

"Fine," I laughed, pressing a quick kiss to her temple. Ushering her toward the bike, I insisted. "I'm cold. Let's go."

Her arms slid around me, legs tucked up against my sides. I cupped her joined hands, relishing the feel of them wrapped around me. I tried not to think about the fact Ronan's men were hunting Kremnik down, chasing sightings through Russia. That in only a few days, this part of our journey would be over and chose to focus on how far we'd come. The first time I'd taken her to group on this bike, I could feel how much she hated every second of it. She practically vibrated with it. As we sped down the highway and back to the city, night sky seeping over us, I decided I was glad. Glad I'd felt that anger from her. That hate. Because I could feel the difference in the way she held onto me now.

FIFTY-SEVEN

CASEY

> Another date. Another failure because she wasn't you. I give up.

Clayton rolled his bike onto the freight elevator, letting me follow him to avoid getting crowded. The doors slid closed behind me. Instead of turning to face the doors, I kept my eyes on the man standing beside his Triumph as I set my jacket and camera bag down. He'd shrugged off his own jacket and propped an arm over himself, against the wall. The black tee he had on was so faded that it almost looked charcoal in the dim light of the elevator. It was a stark contrast compared to the pale denim jeans. After so many washes, the material had little holes in it. I took the hem between my fingers, appreciating the soft cotton.

I was touching him. I'd crossed the elevator without realizing it. It had been an effort not to kiss him at the beach. He looked devastating in that light. He'd also spent the entire time asking me questions about myself.

Wanting to learn more about me. Things he couldn't learn from sitting at his computer. It felt like an actual date. I looked up into his face to find him already watching me, like he so often did. Arm still propped overhead, he smiled that half-cocked grin at me and said nothing.

"Thank you for taking me out."

He nodded, removing his arm from the wall. His hand lowered to my sweater. No, below my sweater to the waist of the skirt I had on. The heat of it was unexpected after riding down the highway in the cold, but his skin was always so deliciously warm. It was like settling into a hot bath. The fingers on my waist pressed into my skin as his other hand reached behind me. A loud buzz sounded as we jerked to a stop. I gasped, noting the lack of surprise on his face. He'd stopped us. Clayton crowded me into the wall, the hand at my waist giving me a squeeze. Thumb stroking over my stomach. Caramel eyes stole my breath as they searched mine.

"I know we don't have much time left together, so I'm going to do this before I lose the chance," he huffed before pressing a kiss to my lips that jerked me into the wall. Or it would have had his other hand not shot up to cup my head. The kiss wasn't polite or sweet. It was a deep drink from a rushing river after wandering through the desert. Clayton panted, resting his forehead against mine as he peered down into my eyes. The few breaths I got down were enough to let me process what he'd said. We don't have much time left together.

"What do you mean we don't have much time?" I blinked.

"This thing between us. Is it over when you leave?"

"What?"

"It's okay. I get it. You don't need a relationship right now."

"Incredible," I shook my head, taking his face in my hands. I didn't know what was next for us. If I'd learned one lesson from my brush with reality's cold brutality, it was that there was no predicting the future. My lips found his again, sucking and pulling from his mouth that had become surrounded by short stubble. A lick against his upper lip inspired a groan, the vibration of it tickling me enough to pull away. Our noses were still touching, his hand still cupped the back of my head. The sight of that dangerous smirk was more than enough to heat my whole body after being out in the cold. "It's the first time since I came here that you don't know what I need."

"Yeah? What's that?" he taunted.

"You, Clayton. I just need you."

My breathless declaration was all the permission he needed. The hand at the back of my head moved to my waist, flipping me around to face the wall. On instinct, my palms pressed against the steel siding. Clayton remained standing behind me, placing both hands on the wall, and grinding his hips against me as he took a deep inhale of my unbound hair. I arched into him, receiving a chest-deep groan in response. The sound reverberated into my shoulder, where his mouth blazed a trail toward the column of my neck.

Words lodged in my throat, trapped like a butterfly beneath his wandering tongue. Only a breathless moan escaped. A deep huff of a laugh told me he'd wanted that. My eyes fell shut, my desire to bask in this feeling stronger than the need to run away from it. Because it was him. Citrus and sage with just a hint of sea air. Laughter and blade-like violence he wielded to protect me. I didn't notice the hand he moved until it traced idle circles over my hip bone. Hips that pushed back into his to feel his erection.

That.

That was what I wanted. The way my core tightened, aching for more. Growing wet with every kiss to my skin that accompanied the roll of his body was a victory. If I had any sense in me at all, I'd thank him. Only I couldn't see straight. Couldn't think past the next second. Nerve endings fired like lightning striking trees everywhere he touched me. All I could think was *please keep touching me*, making my next statement shocking to both of us.

"I read all your messages," I breathed, noticing one of his hands had moved away from the wall. "Every last one."

"Yeah?" He huffed, belt jangling behind me. I peered over my shoulder to meet his eye, letting the wall take my weight as I shifted my panties down. In these boots, I could only get them to my knees. Clayton watched the motion with hungry approval, eyes lifting back to mine as he asked, "Do I seem crazy to you now?"

I nodded. That grin of his. It was devious enough to make my thighs rub together. He freed himself from his jeans, moving toward me again with the speed and grace of a wild animal. I felt the length of him brush through me, collecting the moisture he'd created. Clayton's mouth found mine, kissing me deeply as his hips rolled to repeat the motion.

"I like your crazy," I breathed. "I love it."

I love you.

It was right there on my tongue. I'd almost said it. Wondered if he could taste it. Almost let him hear what had been on my heart for weeks. Maybe longer. Instead, I moaned as his crown pushed past my entrance with a tight squeeze. He cursed low, muffling the word into my shoulder as he continued until his thick length was embedded to the hilt. My inner muscles clenched around him, as if just the feeling of his depth was enough to edge me toward bliss.

With my legs still so close together, the feel of it was beyond decadent. Clayton moved, drawing himself out and moving in again slowly. I met his efforts with my own, our heaving breaths offering up the only sound. The hand at my hip moved, reaching between my thighs to the sensitive flesh at their apex. I let out a helpless sound that earned a husky laugh into my ear.

"You didn't think I was going to forget how to take care of you, did you?"

He did not. He absolutely did not forget. No, he had me right where he wanted me. Circling my clit as he drove himself inside with increasingly powerful thrusts. Shimmering threads of release reached out, wrapping themselves around me, from the tips of my curling toes to the place where Clayton lavished the skin beneath my ear with his tongue.

"Clay," I gasped.

"Fuck. I love it when you say my name," he groaned, the word accompanied by a deep thrust. The feel of it dragged another helpless noise from me.

He repeated the motion, clearly noting my response to it. His hand kept moving. Stroking. Never changing pace, even as my thighs clenched together. Electricity tightened my body from the center out, forcing my fingers to curl against the wall. My eyes squeezed shut. "No, firebird. Look at me."

I did as he told me, eyes shooting open to look into his. Our noses brushed ever so slightly, that one small touch like a violent shove into euphoria. Clayton's lips crashed into mine, the hand beside my head slamming into the wall as I drank it all in. The release he'd brought me. The feel of him twitching inside me, groaning softly into my mouth as pleasure wrung him out. And the fact that I hadn't felt afraid of it.

Not for one damned second.

FIFTY-EIGHT

Clayton

Casey wiped her face, groaning with pleasure. Both hands braced behind her, she leaned back on the counter and smiled. I loved the sight of a sated woman. Her declaration in the elevator was still playing on a loop in my head. *I just need you.*

"God, that was so good," she cried out, voice husky.

"Well, I owed you after the elevator," I smirked, setting the crust of my last slice down in the pizza box. I picked up the box and hopped off the counter. "I'm going to adios this in the chute."

Her needy declaration, coupled with the look in her eye when I pushed inside her, felt too good to be true. That look said she wanted more than this with me. A future. It all felt like it was going to collapse with the sweep of a skull-covered hand. Some tiny, worried part of me settled when I saw her still sitting on the counter, legs swinging idly.

"Do you want to watch a movie?"

She shook her head, teeth sinking into her lower lip.

"Like you said, I'm supposed to head out of here soon. We should make the most of the time we've got left under one roof."

I braced my hands on the counter, caging her in. Her bare feet locked together at the ankles behind me. A laugh burst from me at her arched brow and her silent statement. If she was trapped, so was I. I pressed a kiss to her collarbone. To her neck. To the space beneath her ear. Blood rushed south at the sound of her breath picking up. Alright, so making the most of our time was going to mean wringing myself dry.

"I think I know exactly what you mean." A squeak popped from her as I hefted her from the counter, carrying her to our destination with only one thought in mind. Undo it. Undo that night. Undo the last two years. I didn't need to see where I was headed. I knew. As I kissed her. As I licked at the seam of her lips. Slid my tongue against her own, enjoying the way she moaned for me. Turning toward the sofa, I sat down, and my hands greedily roved up her body. I butted my forehead against hers, taking a swift inhale. "Casey, I need to say something to you."

There was no point in keeping it to myself. She was going home, and I was going back to being alone here. She could forget about it and decide to ignore me again. Go on living her life the way she was before. Without me. It wouldn't be the first time someone chose that route.

Fuck it.

My thumbs stroked over her cheeks. Her face felt so small in my hands. I couldn't keep it in. Everything. I would give this girl everything I had until there was nothing left but bones and dust. Our mouths collided with gentle ferocity, her hands meeting to lock behind my neck. A soft moan against my lips reaffirmed my courage. I could do this. Leave it all out there. Let her ruin me. Let her sever every last thread to the man I once knew. That was fucking worth it. She was worth it.

"I never stopped wanting you," I said between kisses as I cut myself open for her. "Give me a drop of your love and I'll fucking drown in it."

Casey's wrists tugged me into her, slowing to plant soft kisses on my mouth. The truth of what I wanted to say was there, right there. The words warmed her lips, barely more than a whisper, as I followed them with kisses of my own.

"You're mine," she whispered into me.

Yes, I fucking am.

She licked the words from my mouth, tongue stroking against mine with another one of those desperate moans that melted my bones, like she was the one who couldn't get enough of me. As if that was even possible. The hands that clasped at my neck slid down to my chest, pushing until I was pressed against the back of the sofa. She took my hands in hers and moved them over herself. They slid up her spread thighs, higher until they squeezed the ample mounds of her breasts. A pink lip tucked between her teeth as she writhed, hips moving in a hypnotizing rhythm.

This was the girl who'd confidently danced on stage. Fantasy and reality collided as I watched her move on top of me. The lilac sweater was taken off and thrown to the floor. Here was that siren. That creature that could bring men to their knees. I was helpless, trapped as her back bowed backward to display herself. The hands that massaged herself divided their efforts, one sliding behind her back to unhook the bright red bra she had on. The other slipping beneath the matching lace covering her core.

"Look at you doing so well," I growled, not recognizing the sound of my voice. "Show me, firebird. Show me what you like."

Even with the skirt concealing her movement, I could see the moment her fingers connected with that sensitive flesh. A shiver rolled through her, moving with her undulating hips. Agonizing anticipation tightened my skin because she was grinding over my length as she touched herself. I already ached for the chance to feel her squeezing me again. It was made so much worse as the bra came off, nipples pebbled as her lush breasts moved in a counter rhythm. Casey's eyes peered up at me, half-lidded and fiendishly satisfied as they took in my face. Quickly shifting her weight, she moved to remove the last scraps of fabric separating her from me. Unable to help myself, I looked at the newly bared flesh.

Somewhere, deep in my brain, there was a parade being thrown. Unicorns. Confetti. Marching band. All of it. Because the girl of my dreams was perched on my lap, looking at me like I meant something to her. Oh, and she was completely naked.

"Fuck, Casey. I'm going to grow a mustache just to watch you ride it."

A throaty, spine-tingling laugh. A laugh that showed me just how much she enjoyed the agony in my voice. I wasn't joking. Still, I wished I could see us. See the way we looked right now. A goddess perched on my lap, bare before me. Me, a lovestruck idiot who was still in his clothes for some fucking reason. Casey's hands came to rest on my shoulders, one idly sifting through the ends of my hair.

"Pink looks good on you," she smirked.

"It looks good on you, too," I breathed, glancing toward the pink parts of her I wanted to lavish with my tongue and teeth. My palms moved to take the mouthwatering swells in them. I hesitated. "Can I touch you here?"

"You can touch me anywhere."

"These are…" I groaned appreciatively as my thumbs drifted over the peaks of her breasts. A shiver moved her body in a torturous wave against me. Her head tossed back with a burst of laughter. "Oh, don't do that."

"Do what?"

"Laugh. The laugh. It kills me. With that smile? It's deadly. I'm a dead man."

Her lips curled around a feral grin as she let her hands meet behind my head, twisting the locks of hair between her fingers in a gentle tug. A hungry look took root in her eyes. My siren was looking for a willing sacrifice. I hoped she'd eat me alive.

"What was that you were saying before? Something about giving you a drop of love," she murmured, her voice a low rasp as she rolled her hips over my cock. Warm breath and lips grazed my neck. They trailed up the column of my throat, traversing the skin between my neck and earlobe. Her words were thick as honey as she purred into my ear before giving the lobe a tug with her teeth. "Drown in me, sailor."

Fuck.

Red hair flowed around me in thick waves. I slid my fingers through it, languishing in the silken glide over my knuckles. It didn't matter that she hadn't said anything back when I told her how I felt. None of it mattered. Not when she could look her fear in the eye and show it who was boss. This girl. I didn't give a damn if she ever told me she loved me, so long as she was in my arms. I looked to the ceiling, praying for an ounce of self-control.

"Yes, ma'am."

"Clay," she panted, planting a kiss over the bobbing stone in my throat. I hummed in response, unable to think past the way that kiss made my skin burn. "Take your fucking pants off."

My hands cupped her perfectly round ass and lifted her, setting her down on the sofa beside me. The sudden loss of her felt like a cold slap. A temporary discomfort. Brown eyes watched, liquid chocolate dripping down, down, down as I lifted off my shirt. Pausing at the belt I wore. Belt buckles. Careful not to let it make a sound, I slid the leather free of the hardware. She didn't flinch. Didn't falter as I approached her, pumping myself at the sight of her bare form perched on my sofa. In the very place where I'd fumbled the chance to be with her like a complete idiot. I hadn't expected to get another opportunity. It didn't stop me from wanting it.

Casey came to sit on the edge of the sofa in front of me, beckoning me forward with that look. The steps of my feet toward her were almost involuntary because of that look. My body screamed for her. Strained thuds in my chest pounded for her. That molten brown gaze flicked up over me, smile vulpine as she brought her lips to the blade of muscle over my hip. A groan cracked from my throat at the decadent touch, my eyes lifting to the ceiling again as I attempted to keep myself together.

Her hand wrapped around my shaft, pulling a more pathetic sound from me. A breath of laughter fanned across my stomach. Another kiss, this one closer to where she held me. The grip of her hand moved over my length in a long, agonizing stroke.

"Casey," I warned. "I'm not going to last long if you keep that up."

Her laugh was huffed over the delicate skin beneath my navel. Long, dark lashes fanned over her cheeks as she took me deep into her mouth, causing that familiar tingle at the base of my spine. Nope. I was not going to last long at all. There was no recovery time needed when it came to this woman. Especially when she wrapped that pouting mouth around me. One thought kept me from spilling down her throat.

Sifting my fingers into her thick red strands again, I gently tugged to get her to look at me. In a painfully slow motion, she let my cock go with a lewd pop and batted those pretty eyes in my direction. I shook my head at her and got to my knees on the thick shag of the cream-colored rug. Casey braced her hands on the sofa behind her, just as she'd done on the counter. I moved forward and took her jaw into my hand. We were almost eye to eye like this.

"I need to say one more thing," I huffed, kissing those perfect lips to find the courage to say what came next. She melted against me, meeting my movements with soft kisses of her own. I swallowed, pulling away to look into those mesmerizing doe eyes that looked at me with confusion. "I kept the truth from you, and it fucked things up, so here's me being honest. I'm in love with you, Casey."

A tremor rushed over her. I would have worried it was too much too soon had she not kissed me. That big, soft heart was mine to protect. One kiss melted into another, her tongue exploring my mouth in tempting teases as I mounted the sofa to settle in the cradle of her thighs. I paused, taking the opportunity to gaze down at perfection when Casey took one hand and guided me to her entrance, looking up at me just as she had that first night. Except now there were stars in her eyes as she nodded, urging me to undo that night. Undo everything wrong between us.

As I thrust forward to the sound of her gasp, the two of us watching as I disappeared inside her, I silently promised myself two things. First, that I was going to do everything in my power to keep that smile on that pretty face for the rest of her life. The second was that no one, not one fucking person, would ever get their hands on this girl again.

I braced an arm over her head, taking the back of the sofa in my hand to steady myself. A half-choked curse puffed out of her at the new depth. Some people didn't realize how difficult it was to pole dance. They didn't realize how much muscle it took. Casey had so much of it. I fucking loved that about her. Loved the way that muscular thigh felt under my grip, the other wrapping around me. The points of her nails scraped up my stomach. Over my chest. Trailed over scars I hadn't thought about in ages. Would I tell her those stories? The stories of Halloway. She looked at the raised skin, then back to my face.

"They're beautiful."

My elbows collapsed under the weight of those words. The weight of that unguarded appreciation. Nose to nose. She nudged hers against mine, still meeting me thrust for thrust. Our bodies moved with each other on a slow current, like we had all the time in the world. Lips parted on a sigh. I took them with my own. Tasted the sounds she made. Felt them with every flick of my tongue against hers. In the elevator, I'd been unable to control myself. She came to me. Touched me. It had been too much. But now. Now I wanted to show her how it could be. To be with each other without hiding from it. From our mistakes. From each other.

Holding her in my arms. I told myself once that it was all I wanted. I hadn't imagined this. Okay, fine, of course I imagined a version of this. But I couldn't have pictured what it would feel like to have my arms around her, buried inside Casey's tight heat while she looked up at me like I was the only thing that mattered in the whole damn world.

The unmistakable grip of her told me tipping over the edge was only a few moments away. She was nearing her peak, but I could see the conflict enter her face as she tried to look away. My right hand shot to her throat, lightly gripping to redirect her attention.

"Don't run from me," I panted. "You're doing so well. I don't want you anywhere else. It's just us here."

One strong shiver preceded her renewed sense of determination. That determination darkened her eyes, the only warning I got as her rhythm increased to match my pounding heart. Her breaths mirrored my own, frantic and thready. I wanted this to last forever. I wanted all of it. All of her. The bad. The good. The shattered remains of us that were molded into a perfect work of art.

"Yes, come on, Casey. You can do it."

Sweet little moans dropped from her parted lips. Lips that slammed into mine, pulling and sucking at me. Tasting and taking as she tipped, tipped, tipped over the edge. Wrenching down on me, thighs clenching, hips bucking. Casey's orgasm was a screaming riptide. Aggressive and unapologetic. She pulled me under with her. The hand I had around her throat maintained its hold, the other gripping the thick muscle that worked against my palm.

When she was through, when we were both through, we stilled. Breath sawed in and out of us.

"I'm so fucking proud of you."

Her smile was broad and open like the sun shining in the middle of a cloudless sky. A thousand miles away from the girl I met in that desert. The woman in my arms was stronger, even when she was shaking. Even as a tear rolled down her cheek. I wiped it away, anxious to touch her because touching her felt devotional. Casey breathed a heavy sigh.

"I've been thinking about that," she panted. "For two years."

FIFTY-NINE

CASEY

"Slow down!" Ainsley and her friend Zora sprinted ahead of us, making their way through the winding rope maze leading up to the haunted house attraction.

The bodyguards my brother sent with our little sister on this outing were doing a good job of remaining inconspicuous. While I was staying with Clayton, Ainsley was Killian's responsibility. That meant his most fearsome crew members, the twins, were doing their best to blend in at a theme park while two ten-year-old girls ran amok. Zora reached out for Ainsley's hand, pulling my sister to hurry her along. I let out a laugh.

Clayton squeezed my hand as I'd left him this morning, telling me to keep my phone handy.

"Don't leave their side," he instructed, kissing my knuckles before he let it go. I glanced at the men he was referring to in front, hoping they didn't see that. From the way my sister's mouth hung open, I knew that she had.

"Yes, Mr. Wrigley," I winked as I got into the SUV with Sean and Rory, scooting in beside Ainsley in the backseat. "I'll see you later. Tell my dad I said hello."

He snorted, shutting the door behind me.

I glanced over my shoulder to track where the twins had gone, only to see them working their way through the attraction line behind us. The sight of two gigantic, tattooed men dressed in black athletic clothing frowning amongst so many laughing children made me chuckle. As far as I was concerned, they were getting paid for a day of fun. Ainsley had been invited to spend the day with her friend from school, and instead of denying my little sister anything, my father asked me to go with her on the condition that his guards accompany us and Clayton track me with my phone. It was easy to explain their presence when I lied and said my father was an Irish diplomat. I checked the device as we entered the foyer of the haunted house ride.

No new messages.

Shrieks of fear, followed by delighted giggles, filled the dark air as we wound through spooky attics and a graveyard filled with animatronic poltergeists. Jesse, the mother of Zora and a tech millionaire who was not much older than me, gave me a sardonic smile. Despite being surrounded by ghoulish jump scares and singing statues, I couldn't stop thinking about Clayton. Last night had been a surprise. He'd laid himself bare for me. Confessed everything and topped it off by making love to me on the very sofa he'd destroyed me on two years earlier.

"I'm in love with you, Casey."

And I'd said nothing. He climbed up onto the sofa and worshipped me until we were both sweating and too boneless to move. Clayton picked me up and carried me into the shower. Washed me. Washed my hair. Made me laugh with a pink shampoo faux-hawk. Then we ate Chinese food in his bed. He didn't push me to declare myself for him. As I fell asleep in one of his soft band tees, one leg thrown over his, I thought maybe I could do it later.

Tonight. I'd even text messaged my online shrink about it on the way over to the Sparkle Salon.

Zora's mother and I leaned against a wall crowded with little ball gowns and glimmering plastic tiaras as we waited for the girls to get their fairy tale makeovers. Ronan Arawn, the scariest man in Los Angeles, had insisted on this detail. Jesse had begrudgingly obliged him.

"I am just so not a glitter girl," Jesse said as we watched our girls get another dose of sparkle applied to their cheeks at the princess salon. "But at least they know how to lay her edges."

Perfectly manicured nails tapped out a message on her phone with little clicks as they hit the screen. Every minute we were in the park, and her daughter wasn't looking, Jesse was checking in with her office to make sure things were running smoothly without her. It was a familiar sight. Moms worked hard in the wings so their children could have better lives. My mother tried not to let me see how hard she worked either. Jesse's eyes caught mine as she glanced up from her phone.

"You're being summoned," she laughed, nodding toward the set of girls in salon chairs.

"Casey!" Ainsley shouted, waving a hand in my direction.

"She needs to pick her accessories," an attendant at the boutique said as she approached me. "The normal package comes with one, but she was asking for a second one, which would be an upgrade to the premium package."

I glanced down at the menu the attendant shoved into my view. People think my father is a criminal, but wow. Jesse blew out a snort. The price difference was significant, but it wasn't a problem with Ronan Arawn's black card in my possession. I reached into my bag and slid it out of my wallet.

"Her and Zora," I said, gesturing to our two girls with a raised finger. "They both get the premium package."

"Wait, that's," Jesse interjected, attempting to stop me with a waving hand.

"You paid for literally everything today. Let me get this," I shrugged, handing the card over to the attendant to slide into her handheld terminal.

Ainsley looked to me for approval. With a thumbs up, I stuffed the last of the churro I'd been working on into my mouth with a satisfying crunch. As far as I was concerned, this kid could have whatever she wanted. Pink Converse kicked wildly with excitement as the attendant pulled a glimmering set of fairy wings off the wall. Dusting the cinnamon sugar off my fingers, I smiled back at her.

"Thank you," Jesse said quietly.

"Thank my dad," I laughed. "I need to, you know. I'll meet you guys outside."

Throwing my thumb over my shoulder, I gave a little wince to make it clear that I needed to get to the ladies' room. Understanding washed over Jesse's features as she nodded. Only sort of needing to go, I had really just needed to get away from the dizzying scent of nail polish and hairspray.

Sean and Rory were supposed to be waiting just outside. I debated texting Killian to tattle on them when I spotted the pair over by the sword jutting out of an anvil-shaped rock. They stared at the object, so clearly arguing amongst themselves over how to lift the object free. One moved to pull it. Then the other. Neither succeeded. They didn't spot me as I walked toward the bathroom, which was for the best since I was openly laughing at them. A fact I was sure neither would appreciate. Instead, I snapped a photo of the two of them fighting over the sword and sent it to Clayton.

> Wish you were here.

Women filed in and out of the bathroom in various states of dress. Some in high-end yoga clothes with themed animal ears on for a bit of whimsy, like Jesse. Others were in full fairy tale regalia. Honestly, it was probably smarter than what I'd put on because a sweater over my tank top had felt like a really bad idea when we got off the water ride. Grateful to be dry now, I stood in the short line, waiting for a stall to open up so I could attend to my needs. My phone vibrated, undoubtedly a response from Clayton, but a stall became available before I could slide it from my jeans.

I hadn't even latched the lock when the door burst open, a woman in a big blue ballgown storming through. Pale blue satin shoved through the gap as a mature blonde woman scooted into the tight space. My feet scrambled away, forcing me to fall backward onto the toilet behind me. My tailbone bruised on the hard surface.

"Excuse me," I snapped. "Someone's in here." The woman responded in a language I couldn't quite understand, her tone apologetic as she moved to show something to me on her phone. I waved a hand in front of her, trying to convey that I didn't need to know whatever it was she was saying. I just needed her out of the stall. "Sorry, what?"

She started speaking again, this time in English. Except her accent was so thick and she spoke so quickly, I still didn't quite catch what was being said. She'd crowded into me so much that by the time the needle she'd used flashed in my vision, I felt a prick at my neck. A shout lodged in my throat. Everything went dark around me as my mind cleared enough to hear the last word she'd said. Arawn.

SIXTY

CLAYTON

Ronan's warehouse was the stuff of nightmares. I thought that every time I was here, but the most recent shipment of explosives had the smattering of scars in my side aching with memory. Idly rubbing a hand over my ribs, choosing to remember Casey's delicate fingertips tracing over them instead as I sidled up next to Killian. The tall, dark Irishman was bent over a case of trigger equipment disguised as toys and gaming gear to be shipped overseas.

I'd laid my cards on the table for her, told her everything. But she'd seemed fine this morning. Last night, it had even seemed like she felt something for me. I looked at her text message again. *Wish you were here.* I wished I were there, too. I'd tracked her through the park. From the haunted house to the space ride on the other side of the park. They were zig-zagging all over until they stopped at a boutique, where they'd been for at least an hour.

"Ay, boy," Killian barked. "Everything alright there?"

"Yeah," I huffed, returning my attention to the screen in front of me. Weights and measures were applied to each box, their contents were balanced in order to avoid raising any suspicion. Every bit of artillery disguised as a toy weighing the same amount, bound for a Northern Ireland orphanage that didn't actually exist. "Almost done."

Ronan strolled in, smelling of cigar smoke and expensive cologne. Dressed in all black, his sharply tailored suit probably made my roughed-up jeans and Triumph shirt look like a potato sack by comparison. I was in the middle of thanking myself for not giving a shit about appearances when his phone began to ring. Salt and pepper brows drew together as he looked at his screen. A smirk tugged at the corner of his mouth, thumb accepting the call with a tap. He drew in a breath to speak, only to be interrupted by the other side. Someone rushed through what they had to say, too quickly for me to make it out.

"Slow down, darling girl. Say that again," Ronan soothed, eyes wide with panic as they shifted to me.

My gut went tight. Casey. A list of reasons she wouldn't have called me streamed through my mind, each of them quickly burned to nothing when her father twisted toward us with rage in his eyes. I looked at Killian, who seemed to stiffen at the sight of it.

"It's Ainsley," Ronan snarled quietly at Killian. "Casey is missing. Said she went to the ladies' and never came back. Her friend's mother saw them load her onto an ambulance when they came out of the salon. By the time they got out of the park to follow, the ambulance was gone."

"Are you telling me no one knows where she is?"

Killian. Probably on the phone with one of the twins. They were supposed to be watching her. They were supposed to keep an eye on her. Supposed to be trustworthy when I couldn't be there with her. I should have been there. Ronan put a hand over the receiver so his daughter couldn't hear what he said next.

"You failed me, Wrigley."

"Where the fuck were the twins!?" I raged.

Unwise to scream in the face of a man like Ronan, but I didn't care. Not for one damned second as I sat back down at my computer, pulling up the trace I had on her phone. Because I'd circumvented all of the apps she'd had on her device when she first got to my place, I'd had to upload my own software. The loading wheel whirred on the screen, costing me precious moments of patience. I'd failed her. I'd failed. My phone let out low, successive beeps. A video call. Fumbling movements caused me to almost drop the damned phone as Casey's name appeared on the screen.

Any relief I felt was temporary as I accepted the call only to be met with a different face. White hair. A white suit and shirt. One pale blue eye. A brutal scar slashed through a white eyebrow and a milky white eye. Both were weathered with age. His grin dripped with the feral delight of a wraithlike cat who'd caught the canary.

Ilia Kremnik.

"Well, if it isn't the famous boyfriend. Do you know you're her emergency contact? I assumed it'd be her father. Or her brother. Not the bodyguard," he trailed off, turning to look at something off camera. That grin returned with his attention. "It does make sense now that I think about it. You do know each other...intimately."

He pivoted the phone to show off his quarry. Deep copper red hair half obscured her beautiful face. Still dressed in the clothes she'd left in this morning. Face relaxed. Rage tangled every nerve as I realized my girl was on that table. Unconscious. I searched her for any sign of injury. Any harm he may have inflicted on her in the time he'd had her in his possession. No apparent bruises or wounds meant they might have used chemicals on her, which was a whole lot fucking worse.

"He's supposed to be in Russia," Killian snarled.

"A lookalike," the ghostly man simpered. "Clever, no?"

"She has nothing to do with this, Kremnik," her father barked. I hadn't realized he'd come to stand beside me or even how close he'd gotten, peering over my shoulder at the video feed on my screen.

"I'm afraid I have to disagree. You made her a part of this when you took my future from me. My boy. I'm merely balancing the scales, Ronan. You think of yourself as the guardian of hell. You don't know what hell is. Hell is losing a child. Hell is wondering about the state of decomposition happening to the little one you brought home. Now my baby is nothing but bones and decay. Soon you will understand."

"Let her go!"

Kremnik smiled as if Ronan's wrath was a dessert he planned to savor. His unearthly eyes shifted to me.

"This one," he said with a jerk of his chin in my direction. "I've seen the footage. He destroyed half a million dollars' worth of product, and he killed my nephews."

The order of my offenses hinted at this piece of shit's priorities. Kremnik approached the table where Casey still lay unconscious.

"I would think someone so good with computers would tell his woman not to scan strange codes. So trusting, this one. I have seen into her mind. Heard her darkest secrets," he crooned, running a hand over her prone form. The touch sent a fresh jolt of violence flashing through me. "Breaking her will be punishment for you both."

"Wait."

The word ripped from me in a growl.

"Oh, the clown has something to say, does he?"

"Harm one hair on her head, and you'll find out how fucking funny I can be."

Kremnik bent over the table, bringing the phone level with Casey's face and framing his own beside hers. A cruel grin stretched across his lips. The tip of his finger traced the bow of her mouth with grace, the ownership in that touch fueling the rage already burning through my entire body.

"You don't frighten me, boy. I have plans for the woman you love," he smirked. My eyes shifted to Ronan, who remained staring at the screen. "Just as I have plans for all of you," Kremnik crooned, standing to his full height. Casey's form grew small in the shot as footsteps clapped against metal in the background. I realized that he was not in a room, but a chamber of some kind. A heavy steel door closed behind him, locking mechanisms spinning and cranking until it was sealed. The ghostly pale man stood in front of a number of pressure meters, cranks, and knobs. His stark white hand reached up, turning the largest of them. "Fortunately, I know how to extinguish a fire."

Water. That was water we were hearing splash into the chamber. A tank.

"Ilia, you fucking bastard, wait!" Ronan roared, his voice growing distant as I raced for the door. For my bike.

Boots fell into rank behind me. Killian and his men mounted up around me, the Arawn heir shouting orders over their rumbling engines as they loaded weapons. Each gun on my person was inventoried with a quick once-over.

"I'm following your lead, Wrigley," Killian said as he climbed into a cargo van and slid the door shut.

There was no time. Not when I knew exactly where he'd taken her. Not when I knew I'd be lucky to get there before it was too late. I tore out of the parking lot, dodging cars and running lights as I pictured my siren looking up at me from her watery grave.

SIXTY-ONE

Casey

Throbbing pain. Familiar throbbing pain that flashed behind my closed eyes. This type of headache. This disorientation. Cold realization splashed in my gut. I'd felt this before. I wanted to move, but my limbs were too heavy with the sedative. That drug. This feeling. Nausea churned as I worked to rouse myself to consciousness. Somewhere, someone was speaking with a thick accent. It sounded far away from me. At first, I thought it was my father. The voice had the authority that could only belong to a man with power. My eyes peeled open to search for the source, only to be met with complete darkness.

"Hello?"

A hoarse voice I barely recognized as my own bounced strangely off the walls. Wherever I was, there was steel everywhere. Steel walls. Steel floor. Some kind of enclosure. The metal underneath me was cold. I jerked as my last memories crashed into me. Ainsley. The amusement park. The bathroom and the woman who attacked me. I tried to sit up, only for my arms and legs to meet with resistance. A loud clack of metal on metal echoed, dulled only by the sound of rushing water. Dread coated my gut like oil.

"Hello!"

My scream was met with smoky laughter. Severe clanging sounds accompanied the laughter coming from overhead.

"Good evening, my little doll."

That voice. It sounded different now. Not an Irish accent. No, the residue of my dreams must have been clinging to my mind because that accent was sharp and clear now. An accent born of Siberian winters and suffering. A fluorescent light fixture flickered on overhead, forcing me to squint at the silhouette looking down at me as it illuminated the large steel lined space. A catwalk stretched across the wide circular container. Slow, measured steps clanged against it. He moved out of direct light. White hair. White eyebrows. Perfectly tailored white clothes. Strange eyes. Teeth that flashed at me as he smirked with serpentine delight. The ghost of my father's past was here to punish me for his sins.

Ilia Kremnik.

"I hope you like your new container. Alexi, my son, built this place. A distillery for vodka in the middle of Long Beach. A little misguided, if you ask me, but the boy never listened to his father. Now it's a monument to all the ways in which we disagreed."

The tall Russian lowered himself onto a knee, scanning the area around me before returning his strange gaze to mine. That rushing water sound quieted. There was no longer empty space to fill. It was only churning and moving beneath me.

"I'm sorry about your son," I offered through clenched teeth to keep them from chattering. They weren't the right words. From the way his strange eyes darkened, I knew I shouldn't have mentioned him at all.

"He was a complicated boy. Just like you. You laid all of your secrets out for me to examine. Handed over every tiny detail you kept locked away in your heart like a jewel to be appraised. Quite a filthy thing you are, little doll. I would never tolerate such behavior if you were my daughter."

I blinked. Secrets. I'd never met him before. I'd certainly never spoken with him. At my apparently bewildered expression, his smile turned into a grin.

"That man should have told you to be careful downloading apps onto your phone with strange code, little doll. You can't trust everything you see."

Apps. The therapy app. That was how they found me. Acid rose in the back of my throat. Clayton had blocked every known tracker on my phone, only for me to replace it with some phony app. An app I'd poured every little insecurity into. Every thought. Everything I'd been too afraid to admit to Clayton. Things I'd been too afraid to admit to myself.

"Does he know?" Kremnik taunted, his awful grin melting into a mocking frown. "The funny man. Did you tell him the savory little truths you felt when you finally took him into your bed? Does he know that Ronan's little Irish doll burns for him?"

My hands fisted at the fact that I'd unknowingly told the man perched above me that I was falling hard and fast for Clayton. Now that confession would be washed away by the water coming to end me. The water. I could hear it moving and splashing only a couple of feet below me now. Maybe less. Kremnik waited for a reaction from me. When I gave him nothing beyond my unshed tears, he clicked his tongue, tutting at me like a disappointed schoolteacher.

"That's a shame. You should have told that man you cared for him. Confessed what was in that broken little heart of yours. Last words are so important."

Ilia Kremnik rose from his position, looking down on me with the eyes of a merciless god. I was chained to his stainless steel altar. Those eyes flicked to my wrists and my feet, making sure the cuffs he'd used were still in place. Their cold bite was the tactile reminder of my growing hopelessness. The man shook his head and crossed the catwalk, throwing one last barb in my direction.

"Time, little doll. It comes for us all. I'm afraid you've wasted yours."

The sound of ringing steel under heavy footsteps gave way to them scraping across the floor. A door squeaked on its hinge. Opening for him, probably. Swallowing back the bile teasing the back of my throat was an effort. Fear. Fear like this was familiar. It forced a cold shiver and a whimper from me. My skin ached everywhere, each tiny cell binding to me in anticipation of what was coming. Blazing white lights cut out overhead, followed by the slamming of that door.

"Somebody! Please!"

My voice rasped out of me, strangled by the tears lodged in my throat. Hopeless. I knew there wasn't any point in crying out. Alone. Surrounded by darkness and the approaching depths of my cold, watery end.

SIXTY-TWO

Casey

In the dark, there was only silence. Frozen silence. The table I'd been chained to was fully submerged now. Only my straining neck kept my nose and mouth above the icy water's edge. How it was so cold, I didn't know, but it was enough to steal what little breath I could manage. I could hear nothing. Nothing but my thoughts and my raging heartbeat as I worked to stay alive for a few minutes longer. Seconds. I tried to take deep breaths. As many as I could to buy myself a few more minutes of life. Because I was going to die.

Water enveloped me. Pressed down on me. Held me down as it planned to take everything from me. It could only have what I allowed. My lungs burned as I tried to hold out. Hold my breath. Just a little longer. I should have thought of my brother. My sister. Even my parents didn't cross my mind. It was only him. His face. His warmth. His laugh. I'd been given a second chance. A second chance at so many things, but the thing I valued most was the second chance I got with him.

A chance at life with him.

Forcing myself to remain calm, I focused on that one thing. The one thing that made me smile. The feel of wind ripping at my bare legs. A large, gloved hand covered mine for the briefest moment before moving back to the grip to hurdle us down the highway. A laugh. A smile. Pink hair because he wanted me to know I never needed to fear him. I knew. I knew I never needed to be afraid of him. Beautiful bronze eyes, warm with love for me. I'd seen the words in his eyes well before he'd ever let them cross his lips.

"I'm in love with you, Casey."

Pain lanced through my chest at the thought as cold needles pricked at my fingers and toes. Ilia Kremnik was right about one thing. I hoped Clayton could see it in the way I looked at him. I hoped my poker face had been shit, because I'd never get the chance to utter the three little words he needed to hear. The thing I felt every time I looked at him. Every time he held my hand or wiped away my tears. Breath slipped away from me now. My body felt far away. I wanted to reach out for it. For him. He deserved to hear them.

I should have told him.

I should have...

"Casey! Come on, baby, please wake up."

Light. So much light. Had I died? A pair of eyes the color of caramel peered down at me, filled with rage and worry. He was here. Questions swarmed through my mind, stinging me with unpleasant possibilities. The possibility that I'd drowned and now I was here with only the dream of Clayton to keep me company for eternity.

I squinted at the vision over me, trying to see past the bright lights. My chest. It hurt. Ached like someone had been pounding it like a drum. I winced. No, death wouldn't involve this much pain. A violent torrent of spasms began racking my body. Large hands turned me to my side. Water. So much water flooded from my mouth and nose as I gagged and gasped. It was almost too loud to hear the whispered prayers from the man sitting beside me.

Almost.

"Thank fuck," he choked out.

Wet. He was soaking wet. Pink hair was deep magenta as it clung to his forehead, water running down his cheeks in little rivulets. It dripped from his soaked strands onto my sodden chest. I sat up, throwing my arms around his neck.

"Clayton, I," I started.

Before I could get another word out, he swept me into his arms and heaved me off the table. I realized then that I was still here. Still in what seemed to be some kind of tank. Still in this place where Ilia Kremnik had left me to die. Boots rattled the panels of the steel floor as Killian approached the table.

"Jesus, Casey, you scared the shite out of us."

"Get her out of here," Clayton snapped at my brother, hauling me through a small maintenance door barely wide enough for his shoulders. My brother took me from Clayton's arms, hefting me into his own. I immediately missed the natural body heat of my mercenary.

"Where ye goin', Wrigley?"

"He's still here."

"Oi, wait!"

My brother's shout bounced off the stone walls as Clayton unclipped a sidearm and sprinted away from us. A large figure I hadn't noticed before followed him through the open door. I recognized his skull-printed gaiter and scarred eyebrow a moment later. West. Killian's shoulder bumped into my stomach, his long gait bringing us to a large steel door being held open by Mac. With the light pouring in from outside, I was better able to see my surroundings. Large stills. Steel tables. Containers of something that smelled nutty and sweet at the same time. A bit like grass.

Footsteps rushed up behind us, approaching from the direction Clayton and West had gone. Loud pops preceded cracking and snapping. Flickering light caught my attention from that same open doorway. My brother's right-hand man was shouting, urging him to speed up. The man behind us barked in warning.

"The bastard's lit the barrel room on fire. This fucker's going to blow!"

"Wait," I shrieked.

Clayton. He'd run into that burning room looking for Kremnik. West followed close behind. They couldn't be in there. No. Clayton was smart. He knew better. He'd gotten out of situations like that before as a SEAL. I watched the opening until we were out in daylight again, telling myself over and over that he would emerge soon. There was no alternative. No universe where he wouldn't meet me out here because I had to tell him that I loved him.

The alternative was...

Tympanic booms blasted from within the building, loud and bone-rattling as they seemed to approach us. Killian cursed, hurling me to the ground behind a parked van before covering me with his body. Fire surged, bursting through the windows in a violent roar. Glass snapped and chimed as it hit the ground around us.

My throat ached and my eyes burned. Killian's body still covered mine, but a greater weight settled on my tender chest. No. Fire licked down my throat, nearly drowning out the sound of someone screaming. One name, over and over.

"Clay!"

SIXTY-THREE

CLAYTON

One white eye. One gaping, bleeding hole. The shot I'd fired had burst through the back of his head to make a perfect exit wound through Ilia Kremnik's left eye after he ran out of his office, leading us on a chase through his dead son's distillery, only to be taken down as he was reaching for the handle of the exit. I turned him over with the toe of my combat boot. Everything white was slowly blooming with red. It wasn't enough. He could have taken her from me.

Floating just beneath the surface, my girl looked like she was frozen in time. Lost in the dark recesses of space, her hair bobbed around her. I jumped into the tank to uncuff her from the table she was bound to, shouting an order at Killian's men to drain the tank. Her blue lips. Shut eyes. Mentally returning to summer camp, I knew I was going to have to stop telling that story because now that was the most scared I've ever been. My whole life, I never had anyone to lose. Not like this. It made me a good soldier. Made me a good hired gun.

Once the water was low enough to set her down on the table, I started pounding on her chest as hard as I could, hoping I was wrong. Praying I wasn't too late.

Begging her to live.

The recoil of my pistol slammed into my clenched hand, vibrating down my extended arm as I emptied my clip into the dead Russian. Click. Click. Click. More red. A blank canvas sprouting poppies all over his torso. Someone's hand slapped onto my shoulder, shocking me back into rational thought. West panted, holstering his weapon at his side.

"He set some kind of explosive in the barrel room. There's no time to dismantle it. We've got to go."

Without waiting for a response, he shoved me toward the door, only steps away from us. I ripped it open, the two of us sprinting out as the explosion screamed from behind us.

"Hit the deck!" West roared, pushing me to the ground as he took cover beside me.

Asphalt below me. Fire roaring over me. West and I watched each other as we covered our ears and waited for the explosion to die out. The distillery crackled and popped in flames behind us.

A black van, one of Arawn's, appeared from down the street. West pushed his gaiter down, wiping away the blood from his lip with his forearm. The red smeared over the sweat-covered skin, the snarling wolf tattoo a mirror image of its bearer's face as he rose to his feet. Killian's right-hand man leaped from the driver's side door, striding toward us.

"Ronan wants Kremnik," Mac ordered. "Where is he?"

"He's inside," West huffed, hoisting me to my feet with a grunt. "Got a few holes in him."

Mac examined the burning building, likely questioning whether the orders from his boss were worth the effort. Fire licked out of the open doorway. The large Irishman winced.

"He's dead?"

"Yep," I declared. "You're more than welcome to scoop up the pieces of that Soviet shit. I hope you brought a shovel."

Choosing to ignore me, he drew his phone from his pocket and made a call. West decided that it was our dismissal because he walked away from the building, down the street. The white unmarked van he had rerouted here was parked almost half a mile away. Some part of me was grateful that the building had been nestled in the heart of Kremnik's businesses. No one around to hear the commotion. No one was around to call the fire department.

Or the police.

The vehicle came into view a couple of yards ahead. West moved to greet Killian, who'd been leaning against the back with crossed arms. Metal scraped metal as the van's door opened. Casey jumped from the opening, running toward me. A glimmer of memory hit hard enough to break me. The memory of a girl in a dress torn to bits, running through a desert. Running toward me. The face and clothes were different. The clothes were wet. Clinging to her curves. Her face was filled not with fear, but something like relief as tears spilled from her. My girl was a crier.

I holstered my weapon, my feet carrying me on swifter steps to close the distance between us. She was safe. She was safe. She was safe, and no one would ever take her from me again. Opening my arms to take hold of her, I was caught off guard by the small hands that shoved into my chest.

"Clayton fucking Wrigley, do you have any idea how scared I was? I thought you burned to death in that building. Don't you ever do that again!" Her shout was punctuated with another shove, undermined by the small pout in her perfect lips. I couldn't help but laugh. Even as she sniffled. "It's not funny."

"That is not my middle name, Casey Enya Arawn. I know. I know it's not funny," I said, enjoying the sight of her eyes widening at the use of her real middle name. Her hands fell to her sides with a wet slap. I took advantage of the position and wrapped myself around her, walking her out of the road with a few awkward steps. Her arms wound around my waist, unable to prevent herself from returning my embrace. I released a breath I hadn't realized I'd been holding. This. This was what I thought I'd lost. "I thought you were dead, firebird. I thought he took you from me."

"I thought I was too," she squeaked, pressing her head to my chest. "I think I was. I felt myself going away. But I wanted to stay. For you."

Casey shifted, her chin resting on my sternum as she looked up at me. Big brown doe eyes blinked their long black lashes. A soft smile crossed her lips as I cradled her head in my hand. Those eyes remained on me as she nuzzled into it and sighed. She spoke again. Words I thought I'd imagined. Just for a second. Her voice was quiet enough for only the two of us to hear what was said. At the sound of those words, I knew I was done risking my life for anyone but her. I gazed down at my siren, wiping a strand of deep red hair out of her face.

"Say it again," I grinned.

"I said I love you, Clayton Wrigley."

SIXTY-FOUR

Clayton

Music and laughter filled the Chancer, loud and insistent through every crack and seam. Through the shut door, I could hear her laugh better than anyone's. Sitting just on the other side in that booth belonging to her brother's friends, Casey was laughing. Laughing with friends she'd convinced to gather here after I nudged her into it. I'd wanted her by my side, but not for this conversation. Despite my current audience, I couldn't help but smile at the effervescent sound. The melodic notes of it. The freedom in it.

Two weeks had passed since I revived Casey in the bottom of a water tank, scared as hell that I'd lost her forever. As her eyes fluttered open to look at me, I knew I didn't want to waste any more time. Two years was too much. So, when Ronan called me in for a debrief at his bar, I decided I'd tell him that my work for him was finished. The other decision I'd made was still bouncing around in my skull as he poured me two fingers of whiskey into a snifter.

"This is the first of many drinks I owe you, my boy," Ronan said as he shoved the glass toward me. "It's also the first of my personal brand, so you'd better enjoy every drop."

I picked up the bottle, examining the label. Winding gold lettering explained that the liquor was cask-strength and sherry-aged. Black, of course. Everything he touched was hardened and burned to black coal. Except for the heart of the girl on the other side of the wall. That was still soft. For as long as I was around, it always would be.

"I wanted to thank you for taking care of my girl these last few months. She seems more like herself now, which means you kept her happy. But I believe we had a deal and you didn't keep your word."

Killian lifted a pint of dark beer, dipping his chin in my direction as he leaned against the mantle behind his father. I tipped my glass in his direction, still working over what to do or say in this particular situation. There were only three of us in here, sure, but I wasn't armed. Knowing these men, I was the only one. But I wouldn't step into this conversation looking for a fight.

"I really didn't," I smirked, sipping from my whiskey. "Couldn't stay away from her if I tried. Oh, and I'm in love with her."

I winked at Ronan, ignoring the way his knuckles went white as his grip around the glass tightened.

"She hated you."

I nodded, taking another sip while I gestured for him to go on with my other hand. Boots thumped over the hardwood floor as their owner approached the table. Killian's hands curled over the back of the empty chair he was going to claim. The little bulbous glass felt so delicate in my hand, the whiskey inside an almost red hue as it flickered with fire. I drank it down, letting the smoky flavor burn its way down my throat before I placed it on the table and leaned forward, looking the man who liked to burn people for fun straight in the eye.

"Now, after only a month or so together, you're in love."

The words were flat. Incredulous. I could have fallen for her that quickly. She crashed into me like a freight train. But falling in love with Casey felt like sinking into a bath. Unwinding with the passing of time until every part of me was eased into it. Sure, I could have probably explained it so that he understood. But I didn't.

"And she loves me," I winked. "Now, if you'll excuse me, I have to go see about a girl."

Killian's lips tipped up at the corner. His father looked less amused. I didn't care. He could burn me alive, too. It wouldn't undo anything.

"You heard the man. Pay him so they can have their happy ending."

"You think this one is good enough for your sister, boy?"

Killian shrugged, that serious expression pulling into a knowing grin.

"Not really up to me, is it?"

"You don't need to pay me," I said as my head started shaking in protest. "I didn't do it for you."

I didn't need to be paid for what I did. Didn't want to. Not when everything I wanted was on the other side of that door. Ronan huffed a joyless laugh as he refilled his glass.

"I told you I'd pay, and I have. It's already done, son."

The sound of roaring laughter and boisterous tavern music crashed over my ears as I opened the door into the main pub, stepping directly in front of the big tufted brown leather booth in the corner. Casey's head was thrown back as she let out a throaty chuckle, surrounded by the friends she'd asked to meet her here. Red lips were parted in a wide grin that made my insides weak. I looked at my watch, noting that the girls she was with would have to leave to make it to Muse soon. Brown eyes connected with me as I lowered my wrist to stuff my hand into the pocket of my jeans.

"Are you ready to go?" I asked, not wanting to rush her out if she was having a good time.

Casey wiped a tear away from her winged eye, shoulders still shaking with laughter as she nodded. After a few side hugs and cheek kisses, she was scooting out of the booth. Manicured hands slid over her oxblood bodysuit down over the tight high waist of her jeans. I held her jacket up to step into, aware of every set of eyes that watched us with knowing expressions. The kind of he's got it bad looks that women thought men didn't see. I saw. And they were absolutely right. I took a bullet for this woman. I'd take a dozen more, if I had to. Hell, I would crawl over broken glass for her. In a way, I had. Facing down the most frightening man in Los Angeles to tell him I intended to marry his daughter was probably more life-threatening than most missions I'd been on in the service.

Amber and rose, I'd learned the incense she burned was rose, flooded my senses as she turned around. Casey locked her wrists around my neck, prompting a low whistle from one of her friends at the table. Her smile brightened even the darkest corner of the bar.

"Did everything go okay in there?"

"Oh, yeah," I winked. "I got everything I wanted."

Red hair twisted between my fingers like vines I never wanted to free myself from. Aware of every set of eyes on us, I decided I didn't care as I nudged her nose with my own. Casey wasn't the first person to make me believe I was worth something. I did the work. I went to therapy and everything. My friends helped. West helped. But I felt like I was worth ten thousand pounds of solid gold when my girl smiled at me. Casey's big, beautiful eyes drifted shut the moment her mouth connected with mine. The hum she released lit a fire down my spine. She tasted like sugar and whiskey, pulling away to whisper against my lips.

"Let's go home."

SIXTY-FIVE

CASEY

Christmas in Los Angeles is completely underrated. Sure, there was never any snow, and people were usually too concerned about their dietary restrictions for cookie exchanges to be a thing. Barely a chill in the air. But the lights always made it look festive. Even if most of them were just from the skyline. From up here, we could see most of it. We could also see some trees in other people's apartments. We'd done our best to make the rooftop cheerful. Our big, comfy patio sofa and a gas firepit were surrounded by hedges covered in tiny sparkly lights. There was even a gang of blow-up characters from Christmas cartoons crowded next to the fancy outdoor kitchen Clayton had put in.

One month after being kidnapped and almost burned to death. One whole month, and it still didn't feel real. To say that thinking I'd lost Clayton forever had changed our relationship would be a lie. I'd fallen in love with him well before that. I could probably nail down the exact moment if I really thought about it. A cold wind thrashed through the air, forcing me to clutch the throw around my shoulders despite my oversized red mohair sweater. With a little wiggle, I hunkered down on the sofa and took a square of brownie off the little snowflake-shaped platter beside me.

"Are you warm enough?" Clayton hollered from the stairwell door, the heavy steel slamming closed behind him. In a forest green cardigan, white tee, and jeans that made him look like the romantic lead in a Hallmark movie, he approached with a wicker hamper wrapped in a big red bow. I eyed the container, giving the smirking mercenary an arched brow when our gazes met.

"That's part two of your gift."

My mind flashed to the beaten-up bike my brother had helped me track down. Clayton had looked so pleased with it earlier and stated that I would get my gifts at dessert. Dessert, he'd said, would be taking place on the roof. I watched him shuffle toward the mini fridge. With a quick squat, he removed a bottle from inside and took something in his other hand. Champagne and two flutes.

"Wow," I snorted. "This is starting to feel pretty cheesy."

Clayton chuckled, placing the glasses on the stone edge of the firepit as he popped the bottle. He filled one glass, handing it to me as he said, "I know. But, cheesy makes you smile."

Topping off his own glass, he plopped down onto the sofa beside me. He wasn't wrong about that. My cheeks were starting to hurt from smiling. One long green sleeve reached over me to grab a sugar cookie from the platter. The little snowman didn't see the decapitation coming. Clayton hummed happily as he chewed. I cleared my throat, demanding his attention.

"So, what's part one?"

Clayton leaned over, yanking an envelope out from behind one of the sofa's fluffy white cushions. Thick and red like the ribbon on the basket. I rolled my eyes. Waiting for me to open it, I slid a finger under the flap as the man beside me bristled with strange energy. The envelope held folded-up papers with something tucked away between them. Once I pulled them free to examine them, the object inside fell to my lap. A key. My eyes shot to Clayton's.

"I already basically live with you," I laughed. He gave me a flat look, jerking his chin toward the papers I still held in my hands. The first page didn't make sense. It was just a layout of the building. Or one floor of the building. A floorplan? I tilted my head to one side, trying to get a better understanding of what I was looking at. I flipped to the next page. Logo mockups. All of them with different designs and names.

Firebird Photography. Firebird Studios. Firebird Film. Firebird Shutterworks.

"I thought we could make you a studio. Give you the space you need to do whatever you want. Build a darkroom or whatever. It's going to be on the floor underneath us. If you want. The side that gets better light will obviously be the studio. At least, I think it should be."

He was rambling as he toyed with the black bow that was holding up half of my hair. In the few times I'd actually seen this abnormally unflappable man nervous, he always rambled.

"You're giving me a studio," I laughed. "Clay. I just bought you a rusty old motorcycle skeleton."

He took my chin between his thumb and forefinger, kissing my Christmas red lips with a hum before speaking softly against them.

"It's not a competition, beautiful. I love that crusty Yamaha," he smiled, placing a kiss on my nose. That was when the basket started to whine. Both our heads turned in its direction. Clayton's shoulders shook with silent laughter. "Besides, you have no shot at winning even if it was."

"Clay," I sighed through my smile. "What did you do?"

Jerking his chin toward the basket, he simply said, "Open it."

The bow fell apart as I pulled one silky red tail, lifting the lid to see what had started making all that noise. As if sensing its impending freedom, the whining got more frantic. The basket wiggled with a phantom tail. A little black nose poked through the crack, startling a laugh from me. A tri-colored head followed. The tiny beagle puppy whimpered more furiously as it struggled to get free, prompting me to work harder to get the basket open. Furiously fussing with the satin, I tossed the ribbon aside and hoisted the furry wriggling thing into my lap.

"He needed a home," Clayton shrugged, watching me wrestle with my new companion.

"Goodness," I giggled as it whimpered and surged for my face, licking me everywhere it could with wet little huffs. "You are a lot, little man. I can't believe you got me a puppy."

"Well," Clayton hedged. "I got *us* a puppy. Your second gift is on his collar."

My fingers secured the jangling tags. One circular silver tag with a name etched in big, elegant lettering. Disco. Chuckling a little, I didn't realize what I was holding until I flipped the other object over to examine it. A large rectangular emerald the size of my thumbnail, nestled in a gold Art Deco setting, glinted from the dog's little green collar. The gasp that popped from my lips startled the dog, forcing him to scuttle into Clayton's lap. He shook his head with a smirk, removing the ring to place it in my shaking hand.

"You walked away from me two years ago. Two years of being without you was too much," Clayton said, shuffling off the sofa while taking the dog under one arm and reaching for my hand with the other. "I thought the part of me that could love someone was broken. You proved me wrong, Casey. And when I thought you were...All I wanted to do was turn back the clock on how much time we wasted. Neither of us will be here forever, but I want to spend every second of the rest of my life with you."

Insane. A normal person would think it was insane to consider marrying someone I'd just barely started a relationship with. All of the worst case scenarios flooded my mind. We could split up. He could break my heart. I could break his. In every scenario, a little voice in my head told me how completely foolish I was being. Foolish to think that he would ever put any part of me in danger. This man had always protected me. Even from himself.

He protected every part of me. Especially my heart. Caramel eyes gazed up at me in question, uncertainty entering his expression.

"So, what do you say, firebird?"

When something bad happens to you, there's no one there to tell you how to get through it. No one walks in and tells you that you need to brace yourself for what's to come. You either get through it. Or you don't. Something really bad happened to me. No one told me how to handle the guilt I would feel for the choices I made. Because they *were* choices. But as someone said to me once, I was doing what I had to do in order to survive. Those choices. They were all I had to work with.

People will judge you. People will think you did the wrong thing. People will tell you that you could have gone down a different path. That doesn't matter. What matters is what you think of yourself. What matters is who you are. I didn't become who I was because I survived it.

I survived because of who I am.

I smiled at Clayton, reminding myself that the worst thing ever to happen to me had already happened. In a way, that's sort of freeing. I could let fear decide. Let it take control of my life as it had for so long. Or not. The ring glinted up at me from between my fingers, waiting for my answer. In the end, the choice was simple. It always had been. I nodded, grinning through wind-chilled tears at Clayton's smiling face as I gave him my answer.

"Cannonball."

Epilogue
Clayton

"Alright, buddy. This should keep you occupied for a little while. Mommy and Daddy have some business to attend to."

Disco looked up from the busy ball filled with treats. A you're good bro look seemed to cross his features. It was for the best. What I was about to do to my wife, no puppy should see. Strolling down the hall, I removed my shirt and grinned at how much my life had changed in a year. My business was thriving. Casey's photography studio was doing incredibly well. Word got out about her after she went public on social media, and she took off like a shooting star. We had vacations. Nights with friends. Adventures on the bike. But there were a few things in the world better than a night in with my wife.

Tonight was going to be better than anything.

Making a big deal out of birthdays was supposed to be my thing. Only now, I was being outperformed by my wife. My wife. My *wife*. I couldn't stop saying it. About six months after our engagement, we tied the knot at

Ronan's estate. The scariest father-in-law in the history of the world made sure he spared no expense. A gigantic white tent filled with lush white flowers and crystal stemware. So elegant. So luxurious. So completely at odds with the oversized pink castle-shaped bounce house my wife had insisted on.

We sang. We drank. We bounced.

I would never forget the smile stretching across her face while she and her sister hopped, scream-singing along to *Pink Pony Club* while I worked on my second slice of pink confetti cake. Pink. Everything was pink. Yes, even my hair. Did I expect her to pick a pale pink ballgown with yards of skirt? No. I knew she had spent the day with her friends and came home champagne drunk, laughing and telling me I wouldn't believe it when I saw it. I suspected then that it wouldn't have mattered what she picked. When our eyes locked as she appeared at the end of the aisle, grinning like sunshine at me on the arm of her father, the sight of her took my fucking breath away.

My woman. My bride. My wife.

A photo of us from that day was framed on our dresser. Her, sitting in the bounce house, wrapped in my arms. Me, kissing her bare shoulder and looking at the camera like I knew I was the luckiest man alive. I glanced at it after making sure the candles around us were still burning safely. It would be a while before they had my attention again. Especially with the vision on the creamy shag rug in front of me.

Mrs. Casey Wrigley was waiting for me on her knees.

After spying the photo of her in that leather bustier on my phone, the one I couldn't resist looking at time and time again, she promised she'd let me see her in it one day. That day was here. Of course, at the time, I had no idea that it was going to be paired with a little black mesh thong and little else. Hair fell over her shoulders, obscuring the swells of her breasts in a crimson waterfall. A flicker of candlelight caught on her ring as she placed her hands on her thighs, eyes on her lap. I reached down, tilting her chin up with my thumb and forefinger. Long dark lashes blinked up at me. Shadowy dark makeup surrounding liquid chocolate eyes.

"What's your safe word, firebird?" I coaxed, running my thumb over her wine-red lips. So fucking soft. I pushed the digit into her mouth. She took it willingly, eyes locked on me. My siren. A flick of her tongue sent fire coursing through my blood. She was beautiful like this. Beautiful and so fucking mine. My thumb popped free, my wife smiling wickedly as she answered.

"Cinnamon."

Growing up in the system isn't the same for everyone. Sometimes people get lucky and end up finding the family they always needed. That wasn't my story. For a lot of people, a withdrawn kid with an atypical learning style was really hard to relate to. Matching with a permanent situation never happened for me.

Casey didn't make all that disappear. Nothing did. It was like she was the star on the horizon, and I was steering forward through the storm. Every decision I'd made in the last two years had been because of her. There was always some part of me that was convinced I didn't belong anywhere.

But I belonged here. With her.

Tonight, I would make her scream. Make her shake and writhe for me. Take her to the edge of her sanity. Her perfectly pink nails scratched up over the material of my jeans, the only clothing I'd decided to wear for this occasion. The polished tips clicked against the buttons of my fly, sparking little jolts in me at every touch. It was enough to feel what was happening. Especially when I couldn't take my eyes off that face. That face that looked up at me like I was everything. The face that had looked at me with so much anger on that elevator, a moment that felt so far away now. That face that still looked pleasantly surprised when I sprang free from the fly of my jeans. Big doe eyes stared up at me, full of trouble as she took me in her hand and licked the vein on my stomach that traced a short and sensitive path down to my length.

"Fuck, Casey."

Walking this path, the one of discovery and desire, it was a curious thing. We were always learning. Testing some barrier. Finding some boundary.

Tonight was no different. She'd given me oral pleasure before. Only a handful of times, but we had to figure out what worked for her and what didn't. She preferred me standing. Preferred a room with an open door. Even if she knew I would never hurt her, that door stayed open. For her.

Anything for my girl.

Sifting my fingers through the ocean of coppery red hair, I groaned at the feel of her warm mouth closing around me. There had been so many times I'd dreamed of this. A hundred nights. Nights alone at my desk. Nights alone in this room. Nights I spent thinking I'd never have another chance with this woman. Hot and wet, her cheeks sucked in and fluttered around me. A deep moan rattled my shaft as I used my hold on her hair to work myself inside. Her palms were braced on my thighs, ready to pinch me if it was too much. But she loved this. This control she had over me. I knew it as I continued fucking her mouth, enjoying the sounds of pleasure escaping from her. I knew it from the way she looked up at me through her lashes. I knew it as I spilled down her throat.

It was only the beginning.

Gesturing toward the bed, I tucked myself back into my jeans, enjoying the sight of where her lipstick marked me. Casey got to her feet and crawled onto the mattress, lifting her ass in the air to give me a show. She was always showing off for me. Moving for her audience of one. I let out an appreciative growl at the sight of all that golden, freckled skin. The restraints were simple enough. Each of them available at every corner. Butter-soft skin slid against mine as I secured each one. Wrist. Wrist. Ankle. Ankle. Until she was spread wide for me.

So much trust. Trust I'd spend the rest of my life earning. She licked her lips, watching me with anticipatory delight as I crawled to kneel between her thighs. Those eyes remained interested, locked on the little switchblade I pulled from my pocket. A metallic click broke through the air. The edge of the small blade must have been cool against her hot skin, gradually warming as I brought it to her hip. Black mesh separated at my will. One side. Then the other. If I were concerned about this being too much for her, I would have been assured by the sight bare and gleaming before me.

"Are you ready? Use your words."

Taking her to the edge was my favorite thing to do. Give her the stars as they burst in her vision when she finally came. Afterwards, when everything was quiet, I would wrap myself around her. Snuggle with our dog and watch the movies that make her smile. Do everything I could to protect her.

Love. It felt like the smallest descriptor of what I felt. I burned for her. If she set me on fire, I'd want my embers to keep her warm. She was my beautiful bird of flame. Never broken. Always mine. Risen from the ashes to spread her wings. And no one would ever hurt her again.

"Yes, Mr. Wrigley."

Those big, beautiful eyes watched me as I reached for the nightstand. A small array of toys neatly displayed in their velvet box. Toys I'd bought for her. Some new ones she'd chosen for herself. My hand moved over each item, selecting her experience the way a sommelier chooses a bottle of wine. Gripping the handle of her favorite device, I pulled it free from the box and clicked it on. Yeah, we were barely getting started.

"Good girl."

THE END.

www.ingramcontent.com/pod-product-compliance
Lightning Source LLC
LaVergne TN
LVHW031609060526
838201LV00065B/4781